ALL IN A HARD DAY'S WORK . . .

Marty jerked a small drawer open in the tall desk and got a small white-handled automatic out of it. He held it out to the blonde. She went to him and took it gingerly, not liking it.

"Sit down next to the shamus," he rasped. "Hold the gun on him. If he gets funny, feed him a few."

The blonde sat down on the davenport about three feet from me, on the side away from the door. She lined the gun on my leg. I didn't like the jerky look in her green eyes.

"FOR ANYONE INTERESTED IN CHANDLER— AND WHAT CRIME FICTION READER ISN'T— THIS IS A NECESSARY, EVEN INEVITABLE BOOK."
—*The New York Times*

By Raymond Chandler
Published by Ballantine Books:

RAYMOND CHANDLER

KILLER IN THE RAIN

With an Introduction by

Philip Durham

BALLANTINE BOOKS • NEW YORK

"Killer in the Rain," "The Man Who Liked Dogs," "The Curtain," and "Try the Girl" were first published in the magazine *Black Mask*. Copyright 1934, 1936 by Pro-Distributors Publishing Company. "Mandarin's Jade," "Bay City Blues," and "The Lady in the Lake" originally appeared in *Dime Detective Magazine*. Copyright 1937, 1938 by Popular Publications. "No Crime in the Mountains" fiirst appeared in *Detective Story Magazine*. Copyright 1941 by Street and Smith.

ISBN 0-345-28858-0

This edition published by arrangement with Houghton Mifflin Company

Printed in Canada

First Ballantine Books Edition: July 1972
Sixth Printing: December 1983

First Canadian Printing: June 1977

Cover art by Whistlin' Dixie

CONTENTS

CONTENTS

INTRODUCTION

DURING his lifetime Raymond Chandler published twenty-three short stories. Yet of this relatively small output only fifteen are generally known to the reading public. For a quarter of a century the remaining eight have lain buried in the crumbling pages of old pulp magazines.[1] And these eight stories are among his finest.

For one who became, with Dashiell Hammett, a leading writer of "the poetry of violence," it is odd indeed that Chandler should have published his first story at the age of forty-five. When this first story, "Blackmailers Don't Shoot," appeared in December 1933, Chandler was only one of the many good writers of the old *Black Mask* school. But when he died in 1959 he had been translated and published in eighteen countries and his work was sought throughout the world by those who recognized a good story and appreciated artistry in detective fiction.

Born in Chicago in 1888, Raymond Chandler went, as a small boy, to England with his mother. There he grew up and received his education, excelling in the classics at Dul-

---

[1] Two stories, "Marlowe Takes on the Syndicate" and "A Couple of Writers," were published posthumously. And three of the present eight, although they were never collected by the author, appeared elsewhere: "No Crime in the Mountains" in *Great American Detective Stories,* Anthony Boucher, ed. (1945); "The Man Who Liked Dogs" in *The Hard-Boiled Omnibus,* Joseph T. Shaw, ed. (1946); and "Bay City Blues" in *Verdict* (1953). Chandler maintained that these three stories were reprinted by mistake and without his conscious permission.

wich College. Shortly after reaching his majority he returned to the United States, from where he went on to Canada to join the Gordon Highlanders. After serving in England and France in 1917-18, he returned again to America to begin a business career in Los Angeles. By the early 1930's he had become an executive in five oil companies, and had it not been for the great depression, it is probable that he would be unknown today—buried in forgotten records as a writer of oil reports. For not until the depression caused the oil business to collapse did Chandler abruptly become a writer of fiction.

In 1950 Chandler published his "official" collection of short stories under the title *The Simple Art of Murder*, but that volume does not include any of the eight stories of this collection. Although all eight had been published, the author excluded them because they had been "cannibalized."

When Raymond Chandler published *The Big Sleep*, his first of seven novels, in 1939, he did what multitudes of writers had done before him: he reused some of his earlier material. Unlike most writers, however, reusing previously published stories left him with an uneasy feeling. Once a story was used in a novel it became—to use his word—"cannibalized." Therefore he could justify this writing method only by leaving such stories buried, virtually unknown in the pages of the rapidly disappearing pulp magazines. The stories in this volume, then, were not collected during the author's lifetime. Since his death, however, there have been very many requests that they should be reprinted and there no longer seems any good reason why, provided their origin is clearly explained, they should be denied to the many thousands of Chandler's readers. Apart from the pleasure Chandler's audience will derive from the stories themselves, it is further hoped that his readers will realize that only a skilled craftsman could turn eight separately conceived short stories into three excellent novels.

A substantial part of Chandler's first novel, *The Big Sleep* (1939), was made from "Killer in the Rain" (*Black Mask*, January 1935) and "The Curtain" (*Black Mask*, September 1936); the second novel, *Farewell, My Lovely* (1940), made extensive use of "The Man Who Liked Dogs" (*Black Mask*, March 1936), "Try the Girl" (*Black Mask*, January 1937), and "Mandarin's Jade" (*Dime Detective Magazine,* November 1937); and the fourth novel, *The Lady in the Lake* (1943), relied on "Bay City Blues" (*Dime Detective Magazine,* November 1937), "The Lady in the Lake" (*Dime Detective Magazine,* January 1939), and "No Crime in the Mountains" (*Detective Story Magazine,* September 1941).[1]

Turning short stories into cohesive novels tested the extent of Chandler's skill. It meant combining and enlarging plots, maintaining a thematic consistency, blowing up scenes, and adapting, fusing, and adding characters.

To illustrate Chandler's method of combining and enlarging plots, one can see in *The Big Sleep,* for example, how the author drew from "The Curtain" for Chapters 1-3, 20, 27-32 and from "Killer in the Rain" for Chapters 4, 6-10, 12-16. With the exception of small bits borrowed from "Mandarin's Jade" and "Finger Man," Chapters 5, 11, 17-19, 21-26 were added. Ten chapters were drawn from "The Curtain," eleven were taken from "Killer in the Rain," and eleven were almost all new material. The twenty-one borrowed chapters, however, were expanded considerably beyond their original state in the short stories.

In "The Curtain" Dade Winslow Trevillyan killed Dudley O'Mara, his stepfather, but to shield the family Dade's mother had O'Mara's body disposed of, leaving the impression that the missing man had pulled down the curtain. In "Killer in the Rain" young Dade's counterpart is Carmen Dravec; both are psychopathic. In *The Big Sleep* young Dade Trevillyan and Carmen Dravec are fused into Carmen Sternwood, the twenty-year-old girl who had "little sharp predatory teeth, as white as fresh orange pith and as shiny as porcelain." Carmen Sternwood, the thumb-sucking psychopath, committed the murder which had been performed in "The Curtain" by Dade Trevillyan. The central portion of the novel, largely added, linked the two short stories together, but throughout the novel the plots of the two stories were neatly woven into a unified whole.

At times Chandler lifted whole passages, changing only a

---

[1] *Farewell, My Lovely* also used a small part from "Trouble Is My Business"; *The High Window* drew a small portion from "The King in Yellow"; and *The Long Goodbye* used a small bit from "The Curtain."

word here and there to improve the syntax or vary a mood. More frequently, however, he blew up scenes for the novel. An example is the greenhouse scene, which accounts for approximately 1100 words in "The Curtain," but is enlarged to 2500 words in *The Big Sleep*.

In miniature, the transformation developed as follows: forty-two words from "The Curtain":

> The air steamed. The walls and ceiling of the glass house dripped. In the half light enormous tropical plants spread their blooms and branches all over the place, and the smell of them was almost as overpowering as the smell of boiling alcohol.

became eighty-two words in *The Big Sleep*:

> The air was thick, wet, steamy and larded with the cloying smell of tropical orchids in bloom. The glass walls and roof were heavily misted and big drops of moisture splashed down on the plants. The light had an unreal greenish color, like light filtered through an aquarium tank. The plants filled the place, a forest of them, with nasty meaty leaves and stalks like the newly washed fingers of dead men. They smelled as overpowering as boiling alcohol under a blanket.

Both passages are intense and vivid. The selection from "The Curtain" achieves its effectiveness through terseness, while the selection from the novel allowed the author to create a mood through the use of hyperbole and striking similes.[1]

---

[1] *Farewell, My Lovely* and *The Lady in the Lake* were put together in a manner quite like that described here for *The Big Sleep*. The technique, of course, was worked with variations. When, for example, Chandler incorporated the short story "The Lady in the Lake" into the novel of the same name, he gave a completely different twist to a portion of the plot. In the short story Melton was a murderer, but in the novel, as Kingsley, he had nothing to do with murder. In "Try the Girl," as another example, Mrs. Marineau shot Skalla, who died with Beulah holding his hand. When this story was developed in *Farewell, My Lovely*, Beulah (Velma)—who had already betrayed Skalla (Malloy)—was the one who killed the big man.

When Chandler converted short stories into a novel he needed a greater array of characters for the longer form. The manner in which he adapted, fused, and added characters for *The Big Sleep* was again a test of the author's literary ingenuity. Of the twenty-one characters in *The Big Sleep,* seven were drawn directly from "The Curtain," six were taken from "Killer in the Rain," four were composites from the two stories, and four were new creations.

The fusing of Dade Trevillyan and Carmen Dravec into Carmen Sternwood, and the fusing of General Dade Winslow of "The Curtain" and Tony Dravec of "Killer in the Rain" into General Guy Sternwood of *The Big Sleep* are examples of technical competence.

More important, however, was Chandler's development of the detective-hero. Philip Marlowe, the consistent hero throughout all of his novels, first appeared in *The Big Sleep* in 1939. But he had been conceived in "Blackmailers Don't Shoot" in 1933. The evolution of the character is a point of interest in the eight stories of this volume.

When Chandler published "Killer in the Rain," his fourth story, in 1935, he was still experimenting with his principal character, a nameless first person narrator. In the next of these three stories the detective operated under the name of Carmady, and in the following three he was John Dalmas. By 1941 in "No Crime in the Mountains" he appeared as John Evans, but in the meantime he had become the Philip Marlowe of Chandler's novels.

Throughout these stories it is always obvious that Chandler's protagonist is much more concerned with helping people than he is with making money. He protects the helpless whether or not they have money. In "Try the Girl" Carmady moved in to clean up a messy social situation, after making it clear to the police that he, a free and independent man, had to do a job they could not accomplish. John Dalmas in "Mandarin's Jade" was passionately ethical, one who would not think of accepting money until he had more than earned it. And in "Bay City Blues" the hero exhibited the kind of courage normally found in heroes of the frontier and the Far West.

In each of these stories the hero is "a man fit for adventure." He is a knight whose mission in life is to protect the weak and to make sure that justice is done. It was in the stories in this volume that Chandler developed his detective-hero, the man he wrote about so eloquently in his essay, "The Simple Art of Murder." "He is the hero; he is everything. He must be a complete man and a common man and yet an unusual man. . . . He must be the best man in his world and a good enough man for any world."

It is at this point that the mission of the hero becomes the thematic core of all these stories. Chandler once wrote that "the emotional basis of the standard detective story was and had always been that murder will out and justice will be done." He added, however, that justice will not be done "unless some very determined individual makes it his business to see that justice is done."

The thematic difference between what Chandler called the standard detective story and his own stories is that his hero was motivated less by the desire to solve the mystery of a murder than by the compelling necessity to right social wrongs. There is murder in these stories, to be sure, but the detective risked his life and reputation to correct social injustices of any nature: to protect the weak, to establish ethical standards, to ease pain, or to salvage whatever might be left in fragile human beings. That the murderer was eventually caught and punished was not at all as important as the main theme.

In this sense, with this ever present theme, Chandler went beyond the scope of what is normally thought of as an ordinary detective story. Because the concern for murder, in these stories, was a minor one, and the concern for human misery was a major one, Chandler was using an important theme of what we choose to call "serious" literature.

Now, after a quarter of a century, Raymond Chandler's "cannibalized" stories have been rescued for those readers who did not share the excitement of reading the *Black Mask* and other pulp magazines of the 1930's.

Here are eight stories in which one finds suspense, violence, tragedy, and a knight who cared about human lives. And one sees the city of Los Angeles—sometimes "a big dry sunny place with ugly homes and no style, but good-hearted and peaceful" and sometimes "a hard-boiled city with no more personality than a paper cup"—vividly spread out there in Southern California, just as Raymond Chandler saw it.

PHILIP DURHAM

University of California, Los Angeles.

KILLER IN THE RAIN

KILLER IN THE RAIN

I

WE were sitting in a room at the Berglund. I was on the side of the bed, and Dravec was in the easy chair. It was my room.

Rain beat very hard against the windows. They were shut tight and it was hot in the room and I had a little fan going on the table. The breeze from it hit Dravec's face high up, lifted his heavy black hair, moved the longer bristles in the fat path of eyebrow that went across his face in a solid line. He looked like a bouncer who had come into money.

He showed me some of his gold teeth and said: "What you got on me?"

He said it importantly, as if anyone who knew anything would know quite a lot about him.

"Nothing," I said. "You're clean, as far as I know."

He lifted a large hairy hand and stared at it solidly for a minute.

"You don't get me. A feller named M'Gee sent me here. Violets M'Gee."

"Fine. How is Violets these days?" Violets M'Gee was a homicide dick in the sheriff's office.

He looked at his large hand and frowned. "No—you still don't get it. I got a job for you."

"I don't go out much any more," I said. "I'm getting kind of frail."

He looked around the room carefully, bluffing a bit, like a man not naturally observant.

1

"Maybe it's money," he said.

"Maybe it is," I said.

He had a belted suede raincoat on. He tore it open carelessly and got out a wallet that was not quite as big as a bale of hay. Currency stuck out of it at careless angles. When he slapped it down on his knee it made a fat sound that was pleasant to the ear. He shook money out of it, selected a few bills from the bunch, stuffed the rest back, dropped the wallet on the floor and let it lie, arranged five century notes like a tight poker hand and put them under the base of the fan on the table.

That was a lot of work. It made him grunt.

"I got lots of sugar," he said.

"So I see. What do I do for that, if I get it?"

"You know me now, huh?"

"A little better."

I got an envelope out of an inside pocket and read to him aloud from some scribbling on the back.

"Dravec, Anton or Tony. Former Pittsburgh steelworker, truck guard, all-round muscle stiff. Made a wrong pass and got shut up. Left town, came West. Worked on an avocado ranch at El Seguro. Came up with a ranch of his own. Sat right on the dome when the El Seguro oil boom burst. Got rich. Lost a lot of it buying into other people's dusters. Still has enough. Serbian by birth, six feet, two hundred and forty, one daughter, never known to have had a wife. No police record of any consequence. None at all since Pittsburgh."

I lit a pipe.

"Jeeze," he said. "Where you promote all that?"

"Connections. What's the angle?"

He picked the wallet off the floor and moused around inside it with a couple of square fingers for a while, with his tongue sticking out between his thick lips. He finally got out a slim brown card and some crumpled slips of paper. He pushed them at me.

The card was in golf type, very delicately done. It said: "Mr. Harold Hardwicke Steiner," and very small in the corner, "Rare Books and De Luxe Editions." No address or phone number.

The white slips, three in number, were simple I O U's for

a thousand dollars each, signed: "Carmen Dravec" in a sprawling, moronic handwriting.

I gave it all back to him and said: "Blackmail?"

He shook his head slowly and something gentle came into his face that hadn't been there before.

"It's my little girl—Carmen. This Steiner, he bothers her. She goes to his joint all the time, makes whoopee. He makes love to her, I guess. I don't like it."

I nodded. "How about the notes?"

"I don't care nothin' about the dough. She plays games with him. The hell with that. She's what you call man-crazy. You go tell this Steiner to lay off Carmen. I break his neck with my hands. See?"

All this in a rush, with deep breathing. His eyes got small and round, and furious. His teeth almost chattered.

I said: "Why have me tell him? Why not tell him yourself?"

"Maybe I get mad and kill the ——— !" he yelled.

I picked a match out of my pocket and prodded the loose ash in the bowl of my pipe. I looked at him carefully for a moment, getting hold of an idea.

"Nerts, you're scared to," I told him.

Both fists came up. He held them shoulder high and shook them, great knots of bone and muscle. He lowered them slowly, heaved a deep honest sigh, and said: "Yeah. I'm scared to. I dunno how to handle her. All the time some new guy and all the time a punk. A while back I gave a guy called Joe Marty five grand to lay off her. She's still mad at me."

I stared at the window, watched the rain hit it, flatten out, and slide down in a thick wave, liked melted gelatin. It was too early in the fall for that kind of rain.

"Giving them sugar doesn't get you anywhere," I said. "You could be doing that all your life. So you figure you'd like to have me get rough with this one, Steiner."

"Tell him I break his neck!"

"I wouldn't bother," I said. "I know Steiner. I'd break his neck for you myself, if it would do any good."

He leaned forward and grabbed my hand. His eyes got childish. A gray tear floated in each of them.

"Listen, M'Gee says you're a good guy. I tell you something I ain't told nobody—ever. Carmen—she's not my kid at all. I just picked her up in Smoky, a little baby in the street. She didn't have nobody. I guess maybe I steal her, huh?"

"Sounds like it," I said, and had to fight to get my hand loose. I rubbed feeling back into it with the other one. The man had a grip that would crack a telephone pole.

"I go straight then," he said grimly, and yet tenderly. "I come out here and make good. She grows up. I love her."

I said: "Uh-huh. That's natural."

"You don't get me. I wanta marry her."

I stared at him.

"She gets older, get some sense. Maybe she marry me, huh?"

His voice implored me, as if I had the settling of that.

"Ever ask her?"

"I'm scared to," he said humbly.

"She soft on Steiner, do you think?"

He nodded. "But that don't mean nothin'."

I could believe that. I got off the bed, threw a window up and let the rain hit my face for a minute.

"Let's get this straight," I said, lowering the window again and going back to the bed. "I can take Steiner off your back. That's easy. I just don't see what it buys you."

He grabbed for my hand again, but I was a little too quick for him this time.

"You came in here a little tough, flashing your wad," I said. "You're going out soft. Not from anything I've said. You knew it already. I'm not Dorothy Dix, and I'm only partly a prune. But I'll take Steiner off you, if you really want that."

He stood up clumsily, swung his hat and stared down at my feet.

"You take him off my back, like you said. He ain't her sort, anyway."

"It might hurt your back a little."

"That's okay. That's what it's for," he said.

He buttoned himself up, dumped his hat on his big shaggy head, and rolled on out. He shut the door carefully, as if he was going out of a sickroom.

I thought he was as crazy as a pair of waltzing mice, but I liked him.

I put his goldbacks in a safe place, mixed myself a long

drink, and sat down in the chair that was still warm from him.

While I played with the drink I wondered if he had any idea what Steiner's racket was.

Steiner had a collection of rare and half-rare smut books which he loaned out as high as ten dollars a day—to the right people.

II

It rained all the next day. Late in the afternoon I sat parked in a blue Chrysler roadster, diagonally across the Boulevard from a narrow store front, over which a green neon sign in script letters said: "H. H. Steiner."

The rain splashed knee-high off the sidewalks, filled the gutters, and big cops in slickers that shone like gun barrels had a lot of fun carrying little girls in silk stockings and cute little rubber boots across the bad places, with a lot of squeezing.

The rain drummed on the hood of the Chrysler, beat and tore at the taut material of the top, leaked in at the buttoned places, and made a pool on the floorboards for me to keep my feet in.

I had a big flask of Scotch with me. I used it often enough to keep interested.

Steiner did business, even in that weather; perhaps especially in that weather. Very nice cars stopped in front of his store, and very nice people dodged in, then dodged out again with wrapped parcels under their arms. Of course they could have been buying rare books and de luxe editions.

At five-thirty a pimply-faced kid in a leather windbreaker came out of the store and sloped up the side street at a fast trot. He came back with a neat cream-and-gray coupé. Steiner came out and got into the coupé. He wore a dark green leather raincoat, a cigarette in an amber holder, no

hat. I couldn't see his glass eye at that distance but I knew
he had one. The kid in the windbreaker held an umbrella
over him across the sidewalk, then shut it up and handed
it into the coupé.

Steiner drove west on the Boulevard. I drove west on the
Boulevard. Past the business district, at Pepper Canyon, he
turned north, and I tailed him easily from a block back. I
was pretty sure he was going home, which was natural.

He left Pepper Drive and took a curving ribbon of wet
cement called La Verne Terrace, climbed up it almost to the
top. It was a narrow road with a high bank on one side and
a few well-spaced cabinlike houses built down the steep slope
on the other side. Their roofs were not much above road
level. The front of them were masked by shrubs. Sodden
trees dripped all over the landscape.

Steiner's hideaway had a square box hedge in front of it,
more than window-high. The entrance was a sort of maze,
and the house door was not visible from the road. Steiner
put his gray-and-cream coupé in a small garage, locked up,
went through the maze with his umbrella up, and light went
on in the house.

While he was doing this I had passed him and gone to
the top of the hill. I turned around there and went back
and parked in front of the next house above his. It seemed
to be closed up or empty, but had no signs on it. I went into a conference with my flask of Scotch, and then just sat.

At six-fifteen lights bobbed up the hill. It was quite dark
by then. A car stopped in front of Steiner's hedge. A slim,
tall girl in a slicker got out of it. Enough light filtered out
through the hedge for me to see that she was dark-haired
and possibly pretty.

Voices drifted on the rain and a door shut. I got out of
the Chrysler and strolled down the hill, put a pencil flash
into the car. It was a dark maroon or brown Packard con-
vertible. Its licence read to Carmen Dravec, 3596 Lucerne
Avenue. I went back to my heap.

A solid, slow-moving hour crawled by. No more cars
came up or down the hill. It seemed to be a very quiet
neighborhood.

Then a single flash of hard white light leaked out of
Steiner's house, like a flash of summer lightning. As the
darkness fell again a thin tinkling scream trickled down the

darkness and echoed faintly among the wet trees. I was out of the Chrysler and on my way before the last echo of it died.

There was no fear in the scream. It held the note of a half-pleasurable shock, an accent of drunkenness, and a touch of pure idiocy.

The Steiner mansion was perfectly silent when I hit the gap in the hedge, dodged around the elbow that masked the front door, and put my hand up to bang on the door.

At that exact moment, as if somebody had been waiting for it, three shots racketed close together behind the door. After that there was a long, harsh sigh, a soft thump, rapid steps, going away into the back of the house.

I wasted time hitting the door with my shoulder, without enough start. It threw me back like a kick from an army mule.

The door fronted on a narrow runway, like a small bridge, that led from the banked road. There was no side porch, no way to get at the windows in a hurry. There was no way around to the back except through the house or up a long flight of wooden steps that went up to the back door from the alleylike street below. On these steps I now heard a clatter of feet.

That gave me the impulse and I hit the door again, from the feet up. It gave at the lock and I pitched down two steps into a big, dim, cluttered room. I didn't see much of what was in the room then. I wandered through to the back of the house.

I was pretty sure there was death in it.

A car throbbed in the street below as I reached the back porch. The car went away fast, without lights. That was that. I went back to the living room.

III

THAT room reached all the way across the front of the house and had a low, beamed ceiling, walls painted brown. Strips of tapestry hung all around the walls. Books filled low shelves. There was a thick, pinkish rug on which some light fell from two standing lamps with pale green shades. In the middle of the rug there was a big, low desk and a black chair with a yellow satin cushion at it. There were books all over the desk.

On a sort of dais near one end wall there was a teakwood chair with arms and a high back. A dark-haired girl was sitting in the chair, on a fringed red shawl.

She sat very straight, with her hands on the arms of the chair, her knees close together, her body stiffly erect, her chin level. Her eyes were wide open and mad and had no pupils.

She looked unconscious of what was going on, but she didn't have the pose of unconsciousness. She had a pose as if she was doing something very important and making a lot of it.

Out of her mouth came a tinny chuckling noise, which didn't change her expression or move her lips. She didn't seem to see me at all.

She was wearing a pair of long jade earrings, and apart from those she was stark naked.

I looked away from her to the other end of the room.

Steiner was on his back on the floor, just beyond the edge of the pink rug, and in front of a thing that looked like a small totem pole. It had a round open mouth in which the lens of a camera showed. The lens seemed to be aimed at the girl in the teakwood chair.

There was a flashbulb apparatus on the floor beside Steiner's outflung hand in a loose silk sleeve. The cord of the flashbulb went behind the totem pole thing.

Steiner was wearing Chinese slippers with thick white felt soles. His legs were in black satin pajamas and the upper part of him in an embroidered Chinese coat. The front of it was mostly blood. His glass eye shone brightly and was the most lifelike thing about him. At a glance none of the three shots had missed.

The flashbulb was the sheet lightning I had seen leak out of the house and the half-giggling scream was the doped and naked girl's reaction to that. The three shots had been somebody else's idea of how the proceedings ought to be punctuated. Presumably the idea of the lad who had gone very fast down the back steps.

I could see something in his point of view. At that stage I thought it was a good idea to shut the front door and fasten it with the short chain that was on it. The lock had been spoiled by my violent entrance.

A couple of thin purple glasses stood on a red lacquer tray on one end of the desk. Also a potbellied flagon of something brown. The glasses smelled of ether and laudanum, a mixture I had never tried, but it seemed to fit the scene pretty well.

I found the girl's clothes on a divan in the corner, picked up a brown sleeved dress to begin with, and went over to her. She smelled of ether also, at a distance of several feet.

The tinny chuckling was still going on and a little froth was oozing down her chin. I slapped her face, not very hard. I didn't want to bring her out of whatever kind of trance she was in, into a screaming fit.

"Come on," I said brightly. "Let's be nice. Let's get dressed."

She said: "G-g-go—ta—hell," without any emotion that I could notice.

I slapped her a little more. She didn't mind the slaps, so I went to work getting the dress on her.

She didn't mind the dress either. She let me hold her arms up but she spread her fingers wide, as if that was very cute. It made me do a lot of finagling with the sleeves. I finally got the dress on. I got her stockings on, and her shoes, and then got her up on her feet.

"Let's take a little walk," I said. "Let's take a nice little walk."

We walked. Part of the time her earrings banged against

my chest and part of the time we looked like a couple of adagio dancers doing the splits. We walked over to Steiner's body and back. She didn't pay any attention to Steiner and his bright glass eye.

She found it amusing that she couldn't walk and tried to tell me about it, but only bubbled. I put her arm on the divan while I wadded her underclothes up and shoved them into a deep pocket of my raincoat, put her handbag in my other deep pocket. I went through Steiner's desk and found a little blue notebook written in code that looked interesting. I put that in my pocket, too.

Then I tried to get at the back of the camera in the totem pole, to get the plate, but couldn't find the catch right away. I was getting nervous, and I figured I could build up a better excuse if I ran into the law when I came back later to look for it than for any reason I could give if caught there now.

I went back to the girl and got her slicker on her, nosed around to see if anything else of hers was there, wiped away a lot of fingerprints I probably hadn't made, and at least some of those Miss Dravec must have made. I opened the door and put out both the lamps.

I got my left arm around her again and we struggled out into the rain and piled into her Packard. I didn't like leaving my own bus there very well, but that had to be. Her keys were in her car. We drifted off down the hill.

Nothing happened on the way to Lucerne Avenue except that Carmen stopped bubbling and giggling and went to snoring. I couldn't keep her head off my shoulder. It was all I could do to keep it out of my lap. I had to drive rather slowly and it was a long way anyhow, clear over to the west edge of the city.

The Dravec home was a large old-fashioned brick house in large grounds with a wall around them. A gray composition driveway went through iron gates and up a slope past flower beds and lawns to a big front door with narrow leaded panels on each side of it. There was dim light behind the panels as if nobody much was home.

I pushed Carmen's head into the corner and shed her belongings in the seat, and got out.

A maid opened the door. She said Mr. Dravec wasn't in and she didn't know where he was. Downtown somewhere.

She had a long, yellowish, gentle face, a long nose, no chin and large wet eyes. She looked like a nice old horse that had been turned out to pasture after long service, and as if she would do the right thing by Carmen.

I pointed into the Packard and growled: "Better get her to bed. She's lucky we don't throw her in the can—drivin' around with a tool like that on her."

She smiled sadly and I went away.

I had to walk five blocks in the rain before a narrow apartment house let me into its lobby to use a phone. Then I had to wait another twenty-five minutes for a taxi. While I waited I began to worry about what I hadn't completed.

I had yet to get the used plate out of Steiner's camera.

IV

I PAID the taxi off on Pepper Drive, in front of a house where there was company, and walked back up the curving hill of La Verne Terrace to Steiner's house behind its shrubbery.

Nothing looked any different. I went in through the gap in the hedge, pushed the door open gently, and smelled cigarette smoke.

It hadn't been there before. There had been a complicated set of smells, including the sharp memory of smokeless powder. But cigarette smoke hadn't stood out from the mixture.

I closed the door and slipped down on one knee and listened, holding my breath. I didn't hear anything but the sound of the rain on the roof. I tried throwing the beam of my pencil flash along the floor. Nobody shot at me.

I straightened up, found the dangling tassel of one of the lamps and made light in the room.

The first thing I noticed was that a couple of strips of tapestry were gone from the wall. I hadn't counted them, but the spaces where they had hung caught my eye.

Then I saw Steiner's body was gone from in front of the totem pole thing with the camera eye in its mouth. On the floor below, beyond the margin of the pink rug, somebody had spread down a rug over the place where Steiner's body had been. I didn't have to lift the rug to know why it had been put there.

I lit a cigarette and stood there in the middle of the dimly lighted room and thought about it. After a while I went to the camera in the totem pole. I found the catch this time. There wasn't any plate-holder in the camera.

My hand went towards the mulberry-colored phone on Steiner's low desk, but didn't take hold of it.

I crossed into the little hallway beyond the living room and poked into a fussy-looking bedroom that looked like a woman's room more than a man's. The bed had a long cover with a flounced edge. I lifted that and shot my flash under the bed.

Steiner wasn't under the bed. He wasn't anywhere in the house. Somebody had taken him away. He couldn't very well have gone by himself.

It wasn't the law, or somebody would have been there still. It was only an hour and a half since Carmen and I left the place. And there was none of the mess police photographers and fingerprint men would have made.

I went back to the living room, pushed the flashbulb apparatus around the back of the totem pole with my foot, switched off the lamp, left the house, got into my rain-soaked car and choked it to life.

It was all right with me if somebody wanted to keep the Steiner kill hush-hush for a while. It gave me a chance to find out whether I could tell it leaving Carmen Dravec and the nude photo angle out.

It was after ten when I got back to the Berglund and put my heap away and went upstairs to the apartment. I stood under a shower, then put pajamas on and mixed up a batch of hot grog. I looked at the phone a couple of times, thought about calling to see if Dravec was home yet, thought it might be a good idea to let him alone until the next day.

I filled a pipe and sat down with my hot grog and Steiner's little blue notebook. It was in code, but the arrangement of the entries and the indented leaves made it a list of names and addresses. There were over four hundred and fifty of them. If this was Steiner's sucker list, he had a gold mine—quite apart from the blackmail angles.

Any name on the list might be a prospect as the killer. I didn't envy the cops their job when it was handed to them.

I drank too much whisky trying to crack the code. About midnight I went to bed, and dreamed about a man in a Chinese coat with blood all over the front who chased a naked girl with long jade earrings while I tried to photograph the scene with a camera that didn't have any plate in it.

V

VIOLETS M'GEE called me up in the morning, before I was dressed, but after I had seen the paper and not found anything about Steiner in it. His voice had the cheerful sound of a man who had slept well and didn't owe too much money.

"Well, how's the boy?" he began.

I said I was all right except that I was having a little trouble with my Third Reader. He laughed a little absently, and then his voice got too casual.

"This guy Dravec that I sent over to see you—done anything for him yet?"

"Too much rain," I answered, if that was an answer.

"Uh-huh. He seems to be a guy that things happens to. A car belongin' to him is washin' about in the surf off Lido fish pier."

I didn't say anything. I held the telephone very tightly.

"Yeah," M'Gee went on cheerfully. "A nice new Cad all messed up with sand and sea water. . . . Oh, I forgot. There's a guy inside it."

I let my breath out slowly, very slowly. "Dravec?" I whispered.

"Naw. A young kid. I ain't told Dravec yet. It's under the fedora. Wanta run down and look at it with me?"

I said I would like to do that.

"Snap it up. I'll be in my hutch," M'Gee told me and hung up.

Shaved, dressed and lightly breakfasted I was at the County Building in half an hour or so. I found M'Gee staring at a yellow wall and sitting at a little yellow desk on which there was nothing but M'Gee's hat and one of the M'Gee feet. He took both of them off the desk and we went down to the official parking lot and got into a small black sedan.

The rain had stopped during the night and the morning was all blue and gold. There was enough snap in the air to make life simple and sweet, if you didn't have too much on your mind. I had.

It was thirty miles to Lido, the first ten of them through city traffic. M'Gee made it in three-quarters of an hour. At the end of that time we skidded to a stop in front of a stucco arch beyond which a long black pier extended. I took my feet out of the floorboards and we got out.

There were a few cars and people in front of the arch. A motorcycle officer was keeping the people off the pier. M'Gee showed him a bronze star and we went out along the pier, into a loud smell that even two days' rain had failed to wash away.

"There she is—on the tug," M'Gee said.

A low black tug crouched off the end of the pier. Something large and green and nickeled was on its deck in front of the wheelhouse. Men stood around it.

We went down slimy steps to the deck of the tug.

M'Gee said hello to a deputy in green khaki and another man in plain clothes. The tug crew of three moved over to the wheelhouse, and set their backs against it, watching us.

We looked at the car. The front bumper was bent, and one headlight and the radiator shell. The paint and the nickel were scratched up by sand and the upholstery was sodden and black. Otherwise the car wasn't much the worse for wear. It was a big job in two tones of green, with a wine-colored stripe and trimming.

M'Gee and I looked into the front part of it. A slim,

dark-haired kid who had been good-looking was draped around the steering post, with his head at a peculiar angle to the rest of his body. His face was bluish white. His eyes were a faint dull gleam under the lowered lids. His open mouth had sand in it. There were traces of blood on the side of his head which the sea water hadn't quite washed away.

M'Gee backed away slowly, made a noise in his throat and began to chew on a couple of the violet-scented breath purifiers that gave him his nickname.

"What's the story?" he asked quietly.

The uniformed deputy pointed up to the end of the pier. Dirty white railings made of two-by-fours had been broken through in a wide space and the broken wood showed up yellow and bright.

"Went through there. Must have hit pretty hard, too. The rain stopped early down here, about nine, and the broken wood is dry inside. That puts it after the rain stopped. That's all we know except she fell in plenty of water not to be banged up worse: at least half-tide, I'd say. That would be right after the rain stopped. She showed under the water when the boys came down to fish this morning. We got the tug to lift her out. Then we find the dead guy."

The other deputy scuffed at the deck with the toe of his shoe. M'Gee looked sideways at me with foxy little eyes. I looked blank and didn't say anything.

"Pretty drunk that lad," M'Gee said gently. "Showin' off all alone in the rain. I guess he must have been fond of driving. Yeah—pretty drunk."

"Drunk, hell," the plainclothes deputy said. "The hand throttle's set halfway down and the guy's been sapped on the side of the head. Ask me and I'll call it murder."

M'Gee looked at him politely, then at the uniformed man. "What you think?"

"It could be suicide, I guess. His neck's broke and he could have hurt his head in the fall. And his hand could have knocked the throttle down. I kind of like murder myself, though."

M'Gee nodded, said: "Frisked him? Know who he is?"

The two deputies looked at me, then at the tug crew.

"Okay. Save that part," M'Gee said. "I *know* who he is."

A small man with glasses and a tired face and a black bag came slowly along the pier and down the slimy steps. He picked out a fairly clean place on the deck and put his bag down. He took his hat off and rubbed the back of his neck and smiled wearily.

"'Lo, Doc. There's your patient," M'Gee told him. "Took a dive off the pier last night. That's all we know now."

The medical examiner looked in at the dead man morosely. He fingered the head, moved it around a little, felt the man's ribs. He lifted one lax hand and stared at the fingernails. He let it fall, stepped back and picked his bag up again.

"About twelve hours," he said. "Broken neck, of course. I doubt if there's any water in him. Better get him out of there before he starts to get stiff on us. I'll tell you the rest when I get him on a table."

He nodded around, went back up the steps and along the pier. An ambulance was backing into position beside the stucco arch at the pier head.

The two deputies grunted and tugged to get the dead man out of the car and lay him down on the deck, on the side of the car away from the beach.

"Let's go," M'Gee told me. "That ends this part of the show."

We said goodbye and M'Gee told the deputies to keep their chins buttoned until they heard from him. We went back along the pier and got into the small black sedan and drove back towards the city along a white highway washed clean by the rain, past low rolling hills of yellow-white sand terraced with moss. A few gulls wheeled and swooped over something in the surf. Far out to sea a couple of white yachts on the horizon looked as if they were suspended in the sky.

We laid a few miles behind us without saying anything to each other. Then M'Gee cocked his chin at me and said: "Got ideas?"

"Loosen up," I said. "I never saw the guy before. Who is he?"

"Hell, I thought you were going to tell me about it."

"Loosen up, Violets," I said.

He growled, shrugged, and we nearly went off the road into the loose sand.

"Dravec's chauffeur. A kid named Carl Owen. How do I know? We had him in the cooler a year ago on a Mann Act rap. He run Dravec's hotcha daughter off to Yuma. Dravec went after them and brought them back and had the guy heaved in the goldfish bowl. Then the girl gets to him, and next morning the old man steams downtown and begs the guy off. Says the kid meant to marry her, only she wouldn't. Then, by heck, the kid goes back to work for him and been there ever since. What you think of that?"

"It sounds just like Dravec," I said.

"Yeah—but the kid could have had a relapse."

M'Gee had silvery hair and a knobby chin and a little pouting mouth made to kiss babies with. I looked at his face sideways, and suddenly I got his idea. I laughed.

"You think maybe Dravec killed him?" I asked.

"Why not? The kid makes another pass at the girl and Dravec cracks down at him too hard. He's a big guy and could break a neck easy. Then he's scared. He runs the car down to Lido in the rain and lets it slide off the end of the pier. Thinks it won't show. Maybe don't think at all. Just rattled."

"It's a kick in the pants," I said. "Then all he had to do was walk home thirty miles in the rain."

"Go on. Kid me."

"Dravec killed him, sure," I said. "But they were playing leapfrog. Dravec fell on him."

"Okay, pal. Some day you'll want to play with *my* catnip mouse."

"Listen, Violets," I said seriously. "If the kid was murdered—and you're not sure it's murder at all—it's not Dravec's kind of crime. He might kill a man in a temper—but he'd let him lay. He wouldn't go to all that fuss."

We shuttled back and forth across the road while M'Gee thought about that.

"What a pal," he complained. "I have me a swell theory and look what you done to it. I wish the hell I hadn't brought you. Hell with you. I'm goin' after Dravec just the same."

"Sure," I agreed. "You'd have to do that. But Dravec

never killed that boy. He's too soft inside to cover up on
it."

It was noon when we got back to town. I hadn't had any
dinner but whisky the night before and very little breakfast
that morning. I got off on the Boulevard and let M'Gee go
on alone to see Dravec.

I was interested in what had happened to Carl Owen;
but I wasn't interested in the thought that Dravec might
have murdered him.

I ate lunch at a counter and looked casually at an early
afternoon paper. I didn't expect to see anything about
Steiner in it, and I didn't.

After lunch I walked along the Boulevard six blocks to
have a look at Steiner's store.

VI

IT was a half-store frontage, the other half being occupied
by a credit jeweler. The jeweler was standing in his entrance, a big, white-haired, black-eyed Jew with about nine
carats of diamond on his hand. A faint, knowing smile
curved his lips as I went past him into Steiner's.

A thick blue rug paved Steiner's from wall to wall. There
were blue leather easy chairs with smoke stands beside them.
A few sets of tooled leather books were put out on narrow
tables. The rest of the stock was behind glass. A paneled
partition with a single door in it cut off a back part of the
store, and in the corner by this a woman sat behind a
small desk with a hooded lamp on it.

She got up and came towards me, swinging lean thighs
in a tight dress of some black material that didn't reflect
any light. She was an ash-blonde, with greenish eyes under
heavily mascaraed lashes. There were large jet buttons in
the lobes of her ears; her hair waved back smoothly from
behind them. Her fingernails were silvered.

She gave me what she thought was a smile of welcome, but what I thought was a grimace of strain.

"Was it something?"

I pulled my hat low over my eyes and fidgeted. I said: "Steiner?"

"He won't be in today. May I show you—"

"I'm selling," I said. "Something he's wanted for a long time."

The silvered fingernails touched the hair over one ear. "Oh, a salesman. . . . Well, you might come in tomorrow."

"He sick? I could go up to the house," I suggested hopefully. "He'd want to see what I have."

That jarred her. She had to fight for her breath for a minute. But her voice was smooth enough when it came.

"That—that wouldn't be any use. He's out of town today."

I nodded, looked properly disappointed, touched my hat and started to turn away when the pimply-faced kid of the night before stuck his head through the door in the paneling. He went back as soon as he saw me, but not before I saw some loosely packed cases of books behind him on the floor of the back room.

The cases were small and open and packed any old way. A man in very new overalls was fussing with them. Some of Steiner's stock was being moved out.

I left the store and walked down to the corner, then back to the alley. Behind Steiner's stood a small black truck with wire sides. It didn't have any lettering on it. Boxes showed through the wire sides and, as I watched, the man in overalls came out with another one and heaved it up.

I went back to the Boulevard. Half a block on, a fresh-faced kid was reading a magazine in a parked Green Top. I showed him money and said: "Tail job?"

He looked me over, swung his door open, and stuck his magazine behind the rear-vision mirror.

"My meat, boss," he said brightly.

We went around to the end of the alley and waited beside a fireplug.

There were about a dozen boxes on the truck when the man in the very new overalls got up in front and gunned his motor. He went down the alley fast and turned left on the street at the end. My driver did the same. The truck went north to Garfield, then east. It went very fast and there was a lot of traffic on Garfield. My driver tailed from too far back.

I was telling him about that when the truck turned north off Garfield again. The street at which it turned was called Brittany. When we got to Brittany there wasn't any truck.

The fresh-faced kid who was driving me made comforting sounds through the glass panel of the cab and we went up Brittany at four miles an hour looking for the truck behind bushes. I refused to be comforted.

Brittany bore a little to the east two blocks up and met the next street, Randall Place, in a tongue of land on which there was a white apartment house with its front on Randall Place and its basement garage entrance on Brittany, a story lower. We were going past that and my driver was telling me the truck couldn't be very far away when I saw it in the garage.

We went around to the front of the apartment house and I got out and went into the lobby.

There was no switchboard. A desk was pushed back against the wall, as if it wasn't used any more. Above it names were on a panel of gilt mailboxes.

The name that went with Apartment 405 was Joseph Marty. Joe Marty was the name of the man who played with Carmen Dravec until her papa gave him five thousand dollars to go away and play with some other girl. It could be the same Joe Marty.

I went down steps and pushed through a door with a wired glass panel into the dimness of the garage. The man in the very new overalls was stacking boxes in the automatic elevator.

I stood near him and lit a cigarette and watched him. He didn't like it very well, but he didn't say anything. After a while I said: "Watch the weight, buddy. She's only tested for half a ton. Where's it goin'?"

"Marty, four-o-five," he said, and then looked as if he was sorry he had said it.

"Fine," I told him. "It looks like a nice lot of reading."

I went back up the steps and out of the building, got into my Green Top again.

We drove back downtown to the building where I have an office. I gave the driver too much money and he gave me a dirty card which I dropped into the brass spittoon beside the elevators.

Dravec was holding up the wall outside the door of my office.

VII

AFTER the rain, it was warm and bright but he still had the belted suede raincoat on. It was open down the front, as were his coat, and vest underneath. His tie was under one ear. His face looked like a mask of gray putty with a black stubble on the lower part of it.

He looked awful.

I unlocked the door and patted his shoulder and pushed him in and got him into a chair. He breathed hard but didn't say anything. I got a bottle of rye out of the desk and poured a couple of ponies. He drank both of them without a word. Then he slumped in the chair and blinked his eyes and groaned and took a square white envelope out of an inner pocket. He put it down on the desk top and held his big hairy hand over it.

"Tough about Carl," I said. "I was with M'Gee this morning."

He looked at me emptily. After a little while he said:

"Yeah. Carl was a good kid. I ain't told you about him much."

I waited, looking at the envelope under his hand. He looked down at it himself.

"I gotta let you see it," he mumbled. He pushed it slowly across the desk and lifted his hand off it as if with the movement he was giving up most everything that made life worth living. Two tears welled up in his eyes and slid down his unshaven cheeks.

I lifted the square envelope and looked at it. It was addressed to him at his house, in neat pen-and-ink printing, and bore a Special Delivery stamp. I opened it and looked at the shiny photograph that was inside.

Carmen Dravec sat in Steiner's teakwood chair, wearing her jade earrings. Her eyes looked crazier, if anything, than as I had seen them. I looked at the back of the photo, saw that it was blank, and put the thing face down on my desk.

"Tell me about it," I said carefully.

Dravec wiped the tears off his face with his sleeve, put his hands flat on the desk and stared down at the dirty nails. His fingers trembled on the desk.

"A guy called me," he said in a dead voice. "Ten grand for the plate and the prints. The deal's got to be closed tonight, or they give the stuff to some scandal sheet."

"That's a lot of hooey," I said. "A scandal sheet couldn't use it, except to back up a story. What's the story?"

He lifted his eyes slowly, as if they were very heavy. "That ain't all. The guy say there's a jam to it. I better come through fast, or I'd find my girl in the cooler."

"What's the story?" I asked again, filling my pipe. "What does Carmen say?"

He shook his big shaggy head. "I ain't asked her. I ain't got the heart. Poor little girl. No clothes on her. . . . No, I ain't got the heart. . . . You ain't done nothin' on Steiner yet, I guess."

"I didn't have to," I told him. "Somebody beat me to it."

He stared at me open-mouthed, uncomprehending. It was obvious he knew nothing about the night before.

"Did Carmen go out at all last night?" I asked carelessly.

He was still staring with his mouth open, groping in his mind.

"No. She's sick. She's sick in bed when I get home. She don't go out at all. . . . What you mean—about Steiner?"

I reached for the bottle of rye and poured us each a drink. Then I lit my pipe.

"Steiner's dead," I said. "Somebody got tired of his tricks and shot him full of holes. Last night, in the rain."

"Jeeze," he said wonderingly. "You was there?"

I shook my head. "Not me. Carmen was there. That's the jam your man spoke of. She didn't do the shooting, of course."

Dravec's face got red and angry. He balled his fists. His breath made a harsh sound and a pulse beat visibly in the side of his neck.

"That ain't true! She's sick. She don't go out at all. She's sick in bed when I get home!"

"You told me that," I said. *"That's* not true. I brought Carmen home myself. The maid knows, only she's trying to be decent about it. Carmen was at Steiner's house and I was watching outside. A gun went off and someone ran away. I didn't see him. Carmen was too drunk to see him. That's why she's sick."

His eyes tried to focus on my face, but they were vague and empty, as if the light behind them had died. He took hold of the arms of the chair. His big knuckles strained and got white.

"She don't tell me," he whispered. "She don't tell me. Me, that would do anything for her." There was no emotion in his voice; just the dead exhaustion of despair.

He pushed his chair back a little. "I go get the dough," he said. "The ten grand. Maybe the guy don't talk."

Then he broke. His big rough head came down on the desk and sobs shook his whole body. I stood up and went around the desk and patted his shoulder, kept on patting it, not saying anything. After a while he lifted his face smeared with tears and grabbed for my hand.

"Jeeze, you're a good guy," he sobbed.

"You don't know the half of it."

I pulled my hand away from him and got a drink into his paw, helped him lift it and down it. Then I took the empty glass out of his hand and put it back on the desk. I sat down again.

"You've got to brace up," I told him grimly. "The law doesn't know about Steiner yet. I brought Carmen home and kept my mouth shut. I wanted to give you and Carmen a break. That puts me in a jam. You've got to do your part."

He nodded slowly, heavily. "Yeah, I do what you say—anything you say."

"Get the money," I said. "Have it ready for the call. I've got ideas and you may not have to use it. But it's no time to get foxy. . . . Get the money and sit tight and keep your mouth shut. Leave the rest to me. Can you do that?"

"Yeah," he said. "Jeeze, you're a good guy."

"Don't talk to Carmen," I said. "The less she remembers out of her drunk, the better. This picture—" I touched the back of the photo on the desk—"shows somebody was working with Steiner. We've got to get him and get him quick—even if it costs ten grand to do it."

He stood up slowly. "That's nothin'. That's just dough. I go get it now. Then I go home. You do it like you want to. Me, I do just like you say."

He grabbed for my hand again, shook it, and went slowly out of the office. I heard his heavy steps drag down the hall.

I drank a couple of drinks fast and mopped my face.

VIII

I DROVE my Chrysler slowly up La Verne Terrace towards Steiner's house.

In the daylight, I could see the steep drop of the hill and the flight of wooden steps down which the killer had made his escape. The street below was almost as narrow as an alley. Two small houses fronted on it, not very near Steiner's place. With the noise the rain had been making it was doubtful if anyone in them had paid much attention to the shots.

Steiner's looked peaceful under the afternoon sun. The unpainted shingles of the roof were still damp from the rain. The trees on the other side of the street had new leaves on them. There were no cars on the street.

Something moved behind the square growth of box hedge that screened Steiner's front door.

Carmen Dravec, in a green and white checkered coat and no hat, came out through the opening, stopped suddenly, looked at me wild-eyed, as if she hadn't heard the car. She went back quickly behind the hedge. I drove on and parked in front of the empty house.

I got out and walked back. In the sunlight it felt like an exposed and dangerous thing to do.

I went in through the hedge and the girl stood there very straight and silent against the half-open house door. One hand went slowly to her mouth, and her teeth bit at a funny-looking thumb that was like an extra finger. There were deep purple-black smudges under her frightened eyes.

I pushed her back into the house without saying anything, shut the door. We stood looking at each other inside. She dropped her hand slowly and tried to smile. Then all expression went out of her white face and it looked as intelligent as the bottom of a shoe box.

I got gentleness into my voice and said: "Take it easy. I'm pals. Sit down in that chair by the desk. I'm a friend of your father's. Don't get panicky."

She went and sat down in the yellow cushion in the black chair at Steiner's desk.

The place looked decadent and off-color by daylight. It still stank of the ether.

Carmen licked the corners of her mouth with the tip of a whitish tongue. Her dark eyes were stupid and stunned rather than scared now. I rolled a cigarette around in my fingers and pushed some books out of the way to sit on the edge of the desk. I lit my cigarette, puffed it slowly for a moment, then asked: "What are you doing here?"

She picked at the material of her coat, didn't answer. I tried again.

"How much do you remember about last night?"

She answered that. "Remember what? I was sick last night—at home." Her voice was a cautious, throaty sound that only just reached my ears.

"Before that," I said. "Before I brought you home. Here."

A slow flush crept up her throat and her eyes widened. "You—you were the one?" she breathed, and began to chew on her funny thumb again.

"Yeah, I was the one. How much of it all stays with you?"

She said: "Are you the police?"

"No. I told you I was a friend of your father's."

"You're not the police?"

"No."

It finally registered. She let out a long sigh. "What—what do you want?"

"Who killed him?"

Her shoulders jerked in the checkered coat, but nothing changed much in her face. Her eyes slowly got furtive.

"Who—who else knows?"

"About Steiner? I don't know. Not the police, or someone would be here. Maybe Marty."

It was just a stab in the dark, but it got a sudden, sharp cry out of her.

"Marty!"

We were both silent for a minute. I puffed on my cigarette and she chewed on her thumb.

"Don't get clever," I said. "Did Marty kill him?"

Her chin came down an inch. "Yes."

"Why did he do it?"

"I—I don't know," very dully.

"Seen much of him lately?"

Her hands clenched. "Just once or twice."

"Know where he lives?"

"Yes!" She spat it at me.

"What's the matter? I thought you liked Marty."

"I hate him!" she almost yelled.

"Then you'd like him for the spot," I said.

She was blank to that. I had to explain it. "I mean, are you willing to tell the police it was Marty?"

Sudden panic flamed in her eyes.

"If I kill the nude photo angle," I said soothingly.

She giggled.

That gave me a nasty feeling. If she had screeched, or turned white, or even keeled over, that would have been fairly natural. But she just giggled.

I began to hate the sight of her. Just looking at her made me feel dopey.

Her giggles went on, ran around the room like rats. They gradually got hysterical. I got off the desk, took a step towards her, and slapped her face.

"Just like last night," I said.

The giggling stopped at once and the thumb-chewing started again. She still didn't mind my slaps apparently. I sat on the end of the desk once more.

"You came here to look for the camera plate—for the birthday suit photo," I told her.

Her chin went up and down again.

"Too late. I looked for it last night. It was gone then. Probably Marty has it. You're not kidding me about Marty?"

She shook her head vigorously. She got out of the chair slowly. Her eyes were narrow and sloe-black and as shallow as an oyster shell.

"I'm going now," she said, as if we had been having a cup of tea.

She went over to the door and was reaching out to open it when a car came up the hill and stopped outside the house. Somebody got out of the car.

She turned and stared at me, horrified.

The door opened casually and a man looked in at us.

IX

HE was a hatchet-faced man in a brown suit and a black felt hat. The cuff of his left sleeve was folded under and pinned to the side of his coat with a big black safety pin.

He took his hat off, closed the door by pushing it with his shoulder, looked at Carmen with a nice smile. He had close-cropped black hair and a bony skull. He fitted his clothes well. He didn't look tough.

"I'm Guy Slade," he said. "Excuse the casual entrance. The bell didn't work. Is Steiner around?"

He hadn't tried the bell. Carmen looked at him blankly, then at me, then back at Slade. She licked her lips but didn't say anything.

I said: "Steiner isn't here, Mr. Slade. We don't know just where he is."

He nodded and touched his long chin with the brim of his hat.

"You friends of his?"

"We just dropped by for a book," I said, and gave him back his smile. "The door was half open. We knocked, then stepped inside. Just like you."

"I see," Slade said thoughtfully. "Very simple."

I didn't say anything. Carmen didn't say anything. She was staring fixedly at his empty sleeve.

"A book, eh?" Slade went on. The way he said it told me things. He knew about Steiner's racket, maybe.

I moved over towards the door. "Only *you* didn't knock," I said.

He smiled with faint embarrassment. "That's right. I ought to have knocked. Sorry."

"We'll trot along now," I said carelessly. I took hold of Carmen's arm.

"Any message—if Steiner comes back?" Slade asked softly.

"We won't bother you."

"That's too bad," he said, with too much meaning.

I let go of Carmen's arm and took a slow step away from her. Slade still had his hat in his hand. He didn't move. His deep-set eyes twinkled pleasantly.

I opened the door again.

Slade said: "The girl can go. But I'd like to talk to you a little."

I stared at him, trying to look very blank.

"Kidder, eh?" Slade said nicely.

Carmen made a sudden sound at my side and ran out through the door. In a moment I heard her steps going down the hill. I hadn't seen her car, but I guessed it was around somewhere.

I began to say: "What the hell—"

"Save it," Slade interrupted coldly. "There's something wrong here. I'll just find out what it is."

He began to walk around the room carelessly—too carelessly. He was frowning, not paying much attention to me. That made me thoughtful. I took a quick glance out of the window, but I couldn't see anything but the top of his car above the hedge.

Slade found the potbellied flagon and the two thin purple glasses on the desk. He sniffed at one of them. A disgusted smile wrinkled his thin lips.

"The lousy pimp," he said tonelessly.

He looked at the books on the desk, touched one or two of them, went on around the back of the desk and was in front of the totem pole thing. He stared at that. Then his eyes went down to the floor, to the thin rug that was over the place where Steiner's body had been. Slade moved the rug with his foot and suddenly tensed, staring down.

It was a good act—or else Slade had a nose I could have used in my business. I wasn't sure which—yet, but I was giving it a lot of thought.

He went slowly down to the floor on one knee. The desk partly hid him from me.

I slipped a gun out from under my arm and put both hands behind my body and leaned against the wall.

There was a sharp, swift exclamation, then Slade shot to his feet. His arm flashed up. A long, black Luger slid into it expertly. I didn't move. Slade held the Luger in long, pale fingers, not pointing it at me, not pointing it at anything in particular.

"Blood," he said quietly, grimly, his deep-set eyes black and hard now. "Blood on the floor there, under a rug. A lot of blood."

I grinned at him. "I noticed it," I said. "It's old blood. Dried blood."

He slid sideways into the black chair behind Steiner's desk and raked the telephone towards him by putting the Luger around it. He frowned at the telephone, then frowned at me.

"I think we'll have some law," he said.

"Suits me."

Slade's eyes were narrow and as hard as jet. He didn't like my agreeing with him. The veneer had flaked off him, leaving a well-dressed hard boy with a Luger. Looking as if he could use it.

"Just who the hell are you?" he growled.

"A shamus. The name doesn't matter. The girl is my client. Steiner's been riding her with some blackmail dirt. We came to talk to him. He wasn't here."

"Just walk in, huh?"

"Correct. So what? Think we gunned Steiner, Mr. Slade?"

He smiled slightly, thinly, but said nothing.

"Or do you think Steiner gunned somebody and ran away?" I suggested.

"Steiner didn't gun anybody," Slade said. "Steiner didn't have the guts of a sick cat."

I said: "You don't see anybody here, do you? Maybe Steiner had chicken for dinner, and liked to kill his chickens in the parlor."

"I don't get it. I don't get your game."

I grinned again. "Go ahead and call your friends downtown. Only you won't like the reaction you'll get."

He thought that over without moving a muscle. His lips went back against his teeth.

"Why not?" he asked finally, in a careful voice.

I said: "I know you, Mr. Slade. You run the Aladdin Club down on the Palisades. Flash gambling. Soft lights and evening clothes and a buffet supper on the side. You know Steiner well enough to walk into his house without knocking. Steiner's racket needed a little protection now and then. You could be that."

Slade's finger tightened on the Luger, then relaxed. He put the Luger down on the desk, kept his fingers on it. His mouth became a hard white grimace.

"Somebody got to Steiner," he said softly, his voice and the expression on his face seeming to belong to two different people. "He didn't show at the store today. He didn't answer his phone. I came up to see about it."

"Glad to hear you didn't gun Steiner yourself," I said.

The Luger swept up again and made a target of my chest. I said:

"Put it down, Slade. You don't know enough to pop off yet. Not being bullet-proof is an idea I've had to get used to. Put it down. I'll tell you something—if you don't know it. Somebody moved Steiner's books out of his store today —the books he did his real business with."

Slade put his gun down on the desk for the second time. He leaned back and wrestled an amiable expression onto his face.

"I'm listening," he said.

"I think somebody got to Steiner too," I told him. "I think that blood is his blood. The books being moved out from Steiner's store gives us a reason for moving his body away from here. Somebody is taking over the racket and doesn't want Steiner found till he's all set. Whoever it was ought to have cleaned up the blood. He didn't."

Slade listened silently. The peaks of his eyebrows made sharp angles against the white skin of his indoor forehead.

I went on: "Killing Steiner to grab his racket was a dumb trick, and I'm not sure it happened that way. But I *am* sure that whoever took the books knows about it, and that the blonde down in the store is scared stiff about something."

"Any more?" Slade asked evenly.

"Not right now. There's a piece of scandal dope I want to trace. If I get it, I might tell you where. That will be your muscler in."

"Now would be better," Slade said. Then he drew his lips back against his teeth and whistled sharply, twice.

I jumped. A car door opened outside. There were steps.

I brought the gun around from behind my body. Slade's face convulsed and his hand snatched for the Luger that lay in front of him, fumbled at the butt.

I said: "Don't touch it!"

He came to his feet rigid, leaning over, his hand on the gun, but the gun not in his hand. I dodged past him into the hallway and turned as two men came into the room.

One had short red hair, a white, lined face, unsteady eyes. The other was an obvious pug; a good-looking boy except for a flattened nose and one ear as thick as a club steak.

Neither of the newcomers had a gun in sight. They stopped, stared.

I stood behind Slade in the doorway. Slade leaned over the desk in front of me, didn't stir.

The pug's mouth opened in a wide snarl, showing sharp, white teeth. The redhead looked shaky and scared.

Slade had plenty of guts. In a smooth, low, but very clear voice he said:

"This heel gunned Steiner, boys. Take him!"

The redhead took hold of his lower lip with his teeth and snatched for something under his left arm. He didn't get it. I was all set and braced. I shot him through the right shoulder, hating to do it. The gun made a lot of noise in the closed room. It seemed to me that it would be heard all over the city. The redhead went down on the floor and writhed and threshed about as if I had shot him in the belly.

The pug didn't move. He probably knew there wasn't enough speed in his arm. Slade grabbed his Luger up and started to whirl. I took a step and slammed him behind the ear. He sprawled forward over the desk and the Luger shot against a row of books.

Slade didn't hear me say: "I hate to hit a one-armed man from behind, Slade. And I'm not crazy about the show-off. You made me do it."

The pug grinned at me and said: "Okay, pal. What next?"

"I'd like to get out of here, if I can do it without any more shooting. Or I can stick around for some law. It's all one to me."

He thought it over calmly. The redhead was making moaning noises on the floor. Slade was very still.

The pug put his hands up slowly and clasped them behind his neck. He said coolly: "I don't know what it's all about, but I don't give a good ——— damn where you go or what you do when you get there. And this ain't my idea of a spot for a lead party. Drift!"

"Wise boy. You've more sense than your boss."

I edged around the desk, edged over towards the open door. The pug turned slowly, facing me, keeping his hands behind his neck. There was a wry but almost good-natured grin on his face.

I skinned through the door and made a fast break through the gap in the hedge and up the hill, half expecting lead to fly after me. None came.

I jumped into the Chrysler and chased it up over the brow of the hill and away from that neighborhood.

X

IT was after five when I stopped opposite the apartment house on Randall Place. A few windows were lit up already and radios bleated discordantly on different programs. I rode the automatic elevator to the fourth floor. Apartment 405 was at the end of a long hall that was carpeted in green and paneled in ivory. A cool breeze blew through the hall from open doors to the fire escape.

There was a small ivory push button beside the door marked 405. I pushed it.

After a long time a man opened the door a foot or so. He was a long-legged, thin man with dark brown eyes in a very brown face. Wiry hair grew far back on his head, giving him a great deal of domed brown forehead. His brown eyes probed at me impersonally.

I said: "Steiner?"

Nothing in the man's face changed. He brought a cigarette from behind the door and put it slowly between tight brown lips. A puff of smoke came towards me, and behind it words in a cool, unhurried voice, without inflection. "You said what?"

"Steiner. Harold Hardwicke Steiner. The guy that has the books."

The man nodded. He considered my remark without haste. He glanced at the tip of his cigarette, said: "I think I know him. But he doesn't visit here. Who sent you?"

I smiled. He didn't like that. I said: "You're Marty?"

The brown face got harder. "So what? Got a grift—or just amusin' yourself?"

I moved my left foot casually, enough so that he couldn't slam the door.

"You got the books," I said. "I got the sucker list. How's to talk it over?"

Marty didn't shift his eyes from my face. His right hand went behind the panel of the door again, and his shoulder had a look as if he was making motions with a hand. There was a faint sound in the room behind him—very faint. A curtain ring clicked lightly on a rod.

Then he opened the door wide. "Why not? If you think you've got something," he said coolly.

I went past him into the room. It was a cheerful room, with good furniture and not too much of it. French windows in the end wall looked across a stone porch at the foothills, already getting purple in the dusk. Near the windows a door was shut. Another door in the same wall at the near end of the room had curtains drawn across it, on a brass rod below the lintel.

I sat down on a davenport against the wall in which there

were no doors. Marty shut the door and walked sideways to a tall oak writing desk studded with square nails. A cedar-wood cigar box with gilt hinges rested on the lowered leaf of the desk. Marty picked it up without taking his eyes off me, carried it to a low table beside an easy chair. He sat down in the easy chair.

I put my hat beside me and opened the top button of my coat and smiled at Marty.

"Well—I'm listening," he said.

He snubbed his cigarette out, lifted the lid of the cigar box and took out a couple of fat cigars.

"Cigar?" he suggested casually, and tossed one at me.

I reached for it and that made me a sap. Marty dropped the other cigar back into the box and came up very swiftly with a gun.

I looked at the gun politely. It was a black police Colt, a .38. I had no argument against it at the moment.

"Stand up a minute," Marty said. "Come forward just about two yards. You might grab a little air while you're doing that." His voice was elaborately casual.

I was mad inside, but I grinned at him. I said: "You're the second guy I've met today that thinks a gun in the hand means the world by the tail. Put it away, and let's talk."

Marty's eyebrows came together and he pushed his chin forward a little. His brown eyes were vaguely troubled.

We stared at each other. I didn't look at the pointed black slipper that showed under the curtains across the doorway to my left.

Marty was wearing a dark blue suit, a blue shirt and a black tie. His brown face looked somber above the dark colors. He said softly, in a lingering voice: "Don't get me wrong. I'm not a tough guy—just careful. I don't know hell's first thing about you. You might be a life-taker for all I know."

"You're not careful enough," I said. "The play with the books was lousy."

He drew a long breath and let it out silently. Then he leaned back and crossed his long legs and rested the Colt on his knee.

"Don't kid yourself I won't use this, if I have to. What's your story?"

"Tell your friend with the pointed shoes to come on in," I said. "She gets tired holding her breath."

Without turning his head Marty called out: "Come on in, Agnes."

The curtains over the door swung aside and the green-eyed blonde from Steiner's store joined us in the room. I wasn't very much surprised to see her there. She looked at me bitterly.

"I knew damn well you were trouble," she told me angrily. "I told Joe to watch his step."

"Save it," Marty snapped. "Joe's watchin' his step plenty. Put some light on so I can see to pop this guy, if it works out that way."

The blonde lit a large floor lamp with a square red shade. She sat down under it, in a big velours chair and held a fixed painful smile on her face. She was scared to the point of exhaustion.

I remembered the cigar I was holding and put it in my mouth. Marty's Colt was very steady on me while I got matches out and lit it.

I puffed smoke and said through the smoke: "The sucker list I spoke of is in code. So I can't read the names yet, but there's about five hundred of them. You got twelve boxes of books, say three hundred. There'll be that many more out on loan. Say five hundred altogether, just to be conservative. If it's a good active list and you could run it around all the books, that would be a quarter of a million rentals. Put the average rental low—say a dollar. That's too low, but say a dollar. That's a lot of money these days. Enough to spot a guy for."

The blonde yelped sharply: "You're crazy, if you—"

"Shut up!" Marty swore at her.

The blonde subsided and put her head back against the back of her chair. Her face was tortured with strain.

"It's no racket for bums," I went on telling them. "You've got to get confidence and keep it. Personally I think the blackmail angles are a mistake. I'm for shedding all that."

Marty's dark brown stare held coldly on my face. "You're a funny guy," he drawled smoothly. "Who's got this lovely racket?"

"You have," I said. "Almost."

Marty didn't say anything.

"You shot Steiner to get it," I said. "Last night in the rain. It was good shooting weather. The trouble is, he wasn't alone when it happened. Either you didn't see that, or you got scared. You ran out. But you had nerve enough to come back and hide the body somewhere—so you could tidy up on the books before the case broke."

The blonde made one strangled sound and then turned her face and stared at the wall. Her silvered fingernails dug into her palms. Her teeth bit her lip tightly.

Marty didn't bat an eye. He didn't move and the Colt didn't move in his hand. His brown face was as hard as a piece of carved wood.

"Boy, you take chances," he said softly, at last. "It's lucky as all hell for you I didn't kill Steiner."

I grinned at him, without much cheer. "You might step off for it just the same," I said.

Marty's voice was a dry rustle of sound. "Think you've got me framed for it?"

"Positive."

"How come?"

"There's somebody who'll tell it that way."

Marty swore then. "That—damned little—! She would—just that—damn her!"

I didn't say anything. I let him chew on it. His face cleared slowly, and he put the Colt down on the table, kept his hand near it.

"You don't sound like chisel as I know chisel," he said slowly, his eyes a tight shine between dark narrowed lids. "And I don't see any coppers here. What's your angle?"

I drew on my cigar and watched his gun hand. "The plate that was in Steiner's camera. All the prints that have been made. Right here and right now. You've got it—because that's the only way you could have known who was there last night."

Marty turned his head slightly to look at Agnes. Her face was still to the wall and her fingernails were still spearing her palms. Marty looked back at me.

"You're cold as a night watchman's feet on that one, guy," he told me.

I shook my head. "No. You're a sap to stall, Marty. You can be pegged for the kill easy. It's a natural. If the girl has to tell her story, the pictures won't matter. But she don't want to tell it."

"You a shamus?" he asked.

"Yeah."

"How'd you get to me?"

"I was working on Steiner. He's been working on Dravec. Dravec leaks money. You had some of it. I tailed the books here from Steiner's store. The rest was easy when I had the girl's story."

"She say I gunned Steiner?"

I nodded. "But she could be mistaken."

Marty sighed. "She hates my guts," he said. "I gave her the gate. I got paid to do it, but I'd have done it anyway. She's too screwy for me."

I said: "Get the pictures, Marty."

He stood up slowly, looked down at the Colt, put it in his side pocket. His hand moved slowly up to his breast pocket.

Somebody rang the door buzzer and kept on ringing it.

XI

MARTY didn't like that. His lower lip went in under his teeth and his eyebrows drew down at the corners. His whole face got mean.

The buzzer kept on buzzing.

The blonde stood up quickly. Nerve tension made her face old and ugly.

Watching me, Marty jerked a small drawer open in the tall desk and got a small, white-handled automatic out of it. He held it out to the blonde. She went to him and took it gingerly, not liking it.

"Sit down next to the shamus," he rasped. "Hold the gun on him. If he gets funny, feed him a few."

The blonde sat down on the davenport about three feet

from me, on the side away from the door. She lined the gun on my leg. I didn't like the jerky look in her green eyes.

The door buzzer stopped and somebody started a quick, light, impatient rapping on the panel. Marty went across and opened the door. He slid his right hand into his coat pocket and opened the door with his left hand, threw it open quickly.

Carmen Dravec pushed him back into the room with the muzzle of a small revolver against his brown face.

Marty backed away from her smoothly, lightly. His mouth was open and an expression of panic was on his face. He knew Carmen pretty well.

Carmen shut the door, then bored ahead with her little gun. She didn't look at anyone but Marty, didn't seem to see anything but Marty. Her face had a dopey look.

The blonde shivered the full length of her body and swung the white-handled automatic up and towards Carmen. I shot my hand out and grabbed her hand, closed my fingers down over it quickly, thumbed the safety to the on position, and held it there. There was a short tussle, which neither Marty nor Carmen paid any attention to. Then I had the gun.

The blonde breathed deeply and stared at Carmen Dravec. Carmen looked at Marty with doped eyes and said: "I want my pictures."

Marty swallowed and tried to smile at her. He said: "Sure, kid, sure," in a small, flat voice that wasn't like the voice he had used in talking to me.

Carmen looked almost as crazy as she had looked in Steiner's chair. But she had control of her voice and muscles this time. She said: "You shot Hal Steiner."

"Wait a minute, Carmen!" I yelped.

Carmen didn't turn her head. The blonde came to life with a rush, ducked her head at me as if she was going to butt me, and sank her teeth in my right hand, the one that had her gun in it.

I yelped some more. Nobody minded that either.

Marty said: "Listen, kid, I didn't—"

The blonde took her teeth out of my hand and spat my own blood at me. Then she threw herself at my leg and tried to bite that. I cracked her lightly on the head with the barrel of the gun and tried to stand up. She rolled down my legs and wrapped her arms around my ankles. I fell back on the davenport again. The blonde was strong with the madness of fear.

Marty grabbed for Carmen's gun with his left hand, missed. The little revolver made a dull, heavy sound that was not loud. A bullet missed Marty and broke glass in one of the folded-back french windows.

Marty stood perfectly still again. He looked as if all his muscles had gone back on him.

"Duck and knock her off her feet, you damn' fool!" I yelled at him.

Then I hit the blonde on the side of the head again, much harder, and she rolled off my feet. I got loose and slid away from her.

Marty and Carmen were still facing each other like a couple of images.

Something very large and heavy hit the outside of the door and the panel split diagonally from top to bottom.

That brought Marty to life. He jerked the Colt out of his pocket and jumped back. I snapped a shot at his right shoulder and missed, not wanting to hurt him much. The heavy thing hit the door again with a crash that seemed to shake the whole building.

I dropped the little automatic and got my own gun loose as Dravec came in with the smashed door.

He was wild-eyed, raging drunk, berserk. His big arms were flailing. His eyes were glaring and bloodshot and there was froth on his lips.

He hit me very hard on the side of the head without even looking at me. I fell against the wall, between the end of the davenport and the broken door.

I was shaking my head and trying to get level again when Marty began to shoot.

Something lifted Dravec's coat away from his body behind, as if a slug had gone clean through him. He stumbled, straightened immediately, charged like a bull.

I lined my gun and shot Marty through the body. It shook him, but the Colt in his hand continued to leap and roar. Then Dravec was between us and Carmen was knocked out of the way like a dead leaf and there was nothing more that anybody could do about it.

Marty's bullets couldn't stop Dravec. Nothing could. If he had been dead, he would still have got Marty.

He got him by the throat as Marty threw his empty gun in the big man's face. It bounced off like a rubber ball. Marty yelled shrilly, and Dravec took him by the throat and lifted him clean off his feet.

For an instant Marty's brown hands fought for a hold on the big man's wrists. Something cracked sharply, and Marty's hands fell away limply. There was another, duller crack. Just before Dravec let go of Marty's neck I saw that Marty's face was a purple-black color. I remembered, almost casually, that men whose necks are broken sometimes swallow their tongues before they die.

Then Marty fell down in the corner and Dravec started to back away from him. He backed like a man losing his balance, not able to keep his feet under his center of gravity. He took four clumsy backward steps like that. Then his big body tipped over backwards and he fell on his back on the floor with his arms flung out wide.

Blood came out of his mouth. His eyes strained upwards as if to see through a fog.

Carmen Dravec went down beside him and began to wail like a frightened animal.

There was noise outside in the hall, but nobody showed at the open door. Too much casual lead had been flipped around.

I went quickly over to Marty and leaned over him and got my hand into his breast pocket. I got out a thick, square envelope that had something stiff and hard in it. I straightened up with it and turned.

Far off the wail of a siren sounded faintly on the evening air, seemed to be getting louder. A white-faced man peeped cautiously in through the doorway. I knelt down beside Dravec.

He tried to say something, but I couldn't hear the words. Then the strained look went out of his eyes and they were aloof and indifferent like the eyes of a man looking at something a long way off, across a wide plain.

Carmen said stonily: "He was drunk. He made me tell him where I was going. I didn't know he followed me."

"You wouldn't," I said emptily.

I stood up again and broke the envelope open. There

were a few prints in it and a glass negative. I dropped the plate on the floor and ground it to pieces with my heel. I began to tear up the prints and let the pieces flutter down out of my hands.

"They'll print plenty of photos of you now, girlie," I said. "But they won't print this one."

"I didn't know he was following me," she said again, and began to chew on her thumb.

The siren was loud outside the building now. It died to a penetrating drone and then stopped altogether, just about the time I finished tearing up the prints.

I stood still in the middle of the room and wondered why I had taken the trouble. It didn't matter any more now.

XII

LEANING his elbow on the end of the big walnut table in Inspector Isham's office, and holding a burning cigarette idly between his fingers, Guy Slade said, without looking at me:

"Thanks for putting me on the pan, shamus. I like to see the boys at Headquarters once in a while." He crinkled the corners of his eyes in an unpleasant smile.

I was sitting at the long side of the table across from Isham. Isham was lanky and gray and wore nose glasses. He didn't look, act or talk copper. Violets M'Gee and a merry-eyed Irish dick named Grinnell were in a couple of round-backed chairs against a glass-topped partition wall that cut part of the office off into a reception room.

I said to Slade: "I figured you found that blood a little too soon. I guess I was wrong. My apologies, Mr. Slade."

"Yeah. That makes it just like it never happened." He stood up, picked a malacca cane and one glove off the table. "That all for me, Inspector?"

"That's all tonight, Slade." Isham's voice was dry, cool, sardonic.

Slade caught the crook of his cane over his wrist to open the door. He smiled around before he strolled out. The last thing his eyes rested on was probably the back of my neck, but I wasn't looking at him.

Isham said: "I don't have to tell you how a police department looks at that kind of a cover-up on a murder."

I sighed. "Gunfire," I said. "A dead man on the floor. A naked, doped girl in a chair not knowing what had happened. A killer I couldn't have caught and you couldn't have caught—then. Behind all this a poor old roughneck that was breaking his heart trying to do the right thing in a miserable spot. Go ahead—stick it into me. I'm not sorry."

Isham waved all that aside. "Who did kill Steiner?"

"The blonde girl will tell you."

"I want you to tell me."

I shrugged. "If you want me to guess—Dravec's driver, Carl Owen."

Isham didn't look too surprised. Violets M'Gee grunted loudly.

"What makes you think so?" Isham asked.

"I thought for a while it could be Marty, partly because the girl said so. But that doesn't mean anything. She didn't know, and jumped at the chance to stick a knife into Marty. And she's a type that doesn't let loose of an idea very easily. But Marty didn't act like a killer. And a man as cool as Marty wouldn't have run out that way. I hadn't even banged on the door when the killer started to scram.

"Of course I thought of Slade, too. But Slade's not quite the type either. He packs two gunmen around with him, and they'd have made some kind of a fight of it. And Slade seemed genuinely surprised when he found the blood on the floor this afternoon. Slade was in with Steiner and keeping tabs on him, but he didn't kill him, didn't have any reason to kill him, and wouldn't have killed him that way, in front of a witness, if he had a reason.

"But Carl Owen would. He was in love with the girl once, probably never got over it. He had chances to spy on her, find out where she went and what she did. He lay for Steiner, got in the back way, saw the nude photo stunt and blew his top. He let Steiner have it. Then the panic got him and he just ran."

"Ran all the way to Lido pier, and then off the end of

that," Isham said dryly. "Aren't you forgetting that the Owen boy had a sap wound on the side of his head?"

I said: "No. And I'm not forgetting that somehow or other Marty knew what was on that camera plate—or nearly enough to make him go in and get it and then hide a body in Steiner's garage to give him room."

Isham said: "Get Agnes Laurel in here, Grinnell."

Grinnell heaved up out of his chair and strolled the length of the office, disappeared through a door.

Violets M'Gee said: "Baby, are you a pal!"

I didn't look at him. Isham pulled the loose skin in front of his Adam's apple and looked down at the fingernails of his other hand.

Grinnell came back with the blonde. Her hair was untidy above the collar of her coat. She had taken the jet buttons out of her ears. She looked tired but she didn't look scared any more. She let herself down slowly into the chair at the end of the table where Slade had sat, folded her hands with the silvered nails in front of her.

Isham said quietly: "All right, Miss Laurel. We'd like to hear from you now."

The girl looked down at her folded hands and talked without hesitation, in a quiet, even voice.

"I've known Joe Marty about three months. He made friends with me because I was working for Steiner, I guess. I thought it was because he liked me. I told him all I knew about Steiner. He already knew a little. He had been spending money he had got from Carmen Dravec's father, but it was gone and he was down to nickels and dimes, ready for something else. He decided Steiner needed a partner and he was watching him to see if he had any tough friends in the background.

"Last night he was in his car down on the street back of Steiner's house. He heard the shots, saw the kid tear down the steps, jump into a big sedan and take it on the lam. Joe chased him. Halfway to the beach, he caught him and ran him off the road. The kid came up with a gun, but his nerve was bad and Joe sapped him down. While he was out Joe went through him and found out who he was. When he came around Joe played copper and the kid broke and gave him the story. While Joe was wondering what to do about it the kid came to life and knocked him off the car and scrammed again. He drove like a crazy guy and Joe let him go. He went back to Steiner's house. I guess you know the rest. When Joe had the plate developed and saw what he had he went for a quick touch so we could get out of town before the law found Steiner. We were going to take some of Steiner's books and set up shop in another city."

Agnes Laurel stopped talking. Isham tapped with his fingers, said: "Marty told you everything, didn't he?"

"Uh-huh."

"Sure he didn't murder this Carl Owen?"

"I wasn't there. Joe didn't act like he'd killed anybody."

Isham nodded. "That's all for now, Miss Laurel. We'll want all that in writing. We'll have to hold you, of course."

The girl stood up. Grinnell took her out. She went out without looking at anyone.

Isham said: "Marty couldn't have known Carl Owen was dead. But he was sure he'd try to hide out. By the time we got to him Marty would have collected from Dravec and moved on. I think the girl's story sounds reasonable."

Nobody said anything. After a moment Isham said to me: "You made one bad mistake. You shouldn't have mentioned Marty to the girl until you were sure he was your man. That got two people killed quite unnecessarily."

I said: "Uh-huh. Maybe I better go back and do it over again."

"Don't get tough."

"I'm not tough. I was working for Dravec and trying to save him from a little heartbreak. I didn't know the girl was as screwy as all that, or that Dravec would have a brainstorm. I wanted the pictures. I didn't care a lot about trash like Steiner or Joe Marty and his girl friend, and still don't."

"Okay. Okay," Isham said impatiently. "I don't need you any more tonight. You'll probably be panned plenty at the inquest."

He stood up and I stood up. He held out his hand.

"But that will do you a hell of a lot more good than harm," he added dryly.

I shook hands with him and went out. M'Gee came out after me. We rode down in the elevator together without speaking to each other. When we got outside the building

M'Gee went around to the right side of my Chrysler and got into it.

"Got any liquor at your dump?"

"Plenty," I said.

"Let's go get some of it."

I started the car and drove west along First Street, through a long echoing tunnel. When we were out of that, M'Gee said: "Next time I send you a client I won't expect you to snitch on him, boy."

We went on through the quiet evening to the Berglund. I felt tired and old and not much use to anybody.

THE MAN WHO
LIKED DOGS

I

THERE was a brand-new aluminum-gray DeSoto sedan in front of the door. I walked around that and went up three white steps, through a glass door and up three more carpeted steps. I rang a bell on the wall.

Instantly a dozen dog voices began to shake the roof. While they bayed and howled and yapped I looked at a small alcove office with a rolltop desk and a waiting room with mission leather chairs and three diplomas on the wall, at a mission table scattered with copies of the *Dog Fancier's Gazette*.

Somebody quieted the dogs out back, then an inner door opened and a small pretty-faced man in a tan smock came in on rubber soles, with a solicitous smile under a pencil-line mustache. He looked around and under me, didn't see a dog. His smile got more casual.

He said: "I'd like to break them of that, but I can't. Every time they hear a buzzer they start up. They get bored and they know the buzzer means visitors."

I said: "Yeah," and gave him my card. He read it, turned it over and looked at the back, turned it back and read the front again.

"A private detective," he said softly, licking his moist lips. "Well—I'm Dr. Sharp. What can I do for you?"

"I'm looking for a stolen dog."

His eyes flicked at me. His soft little mouth tightened. Very slowly his whole face flushed. I said: "I'm not suggesting *you* stole the dog, Doc. Almost anybody could plant an animal in a place like this and you wouldn't think about that chance they didn't own it, would you?"

"One doesn't just like the idea," he said stiffly. "What kind of dog?"

"Police dog."

He scuffed a toe on the thin carpet, looked at a corner of the ceiling. The flush went off his face, leaving it with a sort of shiny whiteness. After a long moment he said: "I have only one police dog here, and I know the people he belongs to. So I'm afraid—"

"Then you won't mind my looking at him," I cut in, and started towards the inner door.

Dr. Sharp didn't move. He scuffed some more. "I'm not sure that's convenient," he said softly. "Perhaps later in the day."

"Now would be better for me," I said, and reached for the knob.

He scuttled across the waiting room to his little rolltop desk. His small hand went around the telephone there.

"I'll—I'll just call the police if you want to get tough," he said hurriedly.

"That's jake," I said. "Ask for Chief Fulwider. Tell him Carmady's here. I just came from his office."

Dr. Sharp took his hand away from the phone. I grinned at him and rolled a cigarette around in my fingers.

"Come on, Doc," I said. "Shake the hair out of your eyes and let's go. Be nice and maybe I'll tell you the story."

He chewed both his lips in turn, stared at the brown blotter on his desk, fiddled with a corner of it, stood up and crossed the room in his white bucks, opened the door in front of me and we went along a narrow gray hallway. An operating table showed through an open door. We went through a door farther along, into a bare room with a concrete floor, a gas heater in the corner with a bowl of water beside it, and all along one wall two tiers of stalls with heavy wire mesh doors.

Dogs and cats stared at us silently, expectantly, behind the mesh. A tiny chihuahua snuffled under a big red Persian with a wide sheep-skin collar around its neck. There was a sour-faced Scottie and a mutt with all the skin off one leg and a silky-gray Angora and a Sealyham and two more mutts and a razor-sharp fox terrier with a barrel snout and just the right droop to the last two inches of it.

Their noses were wet and their eyes were bright and they wanted to know whose visitor I was.

I looked them over. "These are toys, Doc," I growled. "I'm talking police dog. Gray and black, no brown. A male. Nine years old. Swell points all around except that his tail is too short. Do I bore you?"

He stared at me, made an unhappy gesture. "Yes, but—" he mumbled. "Well, this way."

We went back out of the room. The animals looked disappointed, especially the chihuahua, which tried to climb through the wire mesh and almost made it. We went back out of a rear door into a cement yard with two garages fronting on it. One of them was empty. The other, with its door open a foot, was a box of gloom at the back of which a big dog clanked a chain and put his jaw down flat on the old comforter that was his bed.

"Be careful," Sharp said. "He's pretty savage at times. I had him inside, but he scared the others."

I went into the garage. The dog growled. I went towards him and he hit the end of his chain with a bang. I said: "Hello there, Voss. Shake hands."

He put his head back down on the comforter. His ears came forward halfway. He was very still. His eyes were wolfish, black-rimmed. Then the curved, too-short tail began to thump the floor slowly. I said: "Shake hands, boy," and put mine out. In the doorway behind me the little vet was telling me to be careful. The dog came up slowly on his big rough paws, swung his ears back to normal and lifted his left paw. I shook it.

The little vet complained: "This is a great surprise to me, Mr.—Mr.—"

"Carmady," I said. "Yeah, it would be."

I patted the dog's head and went back out of the garage.

We went into the house, into the waiting room. I pushed magazines out of the way and sat on a corner of the mission table, looked the pretty little man over.

"Okay," I said. "Give. What's the name of his folks and where do they live?"

He thought it over sullenly. "Their name is Voss. They've

moved East and they are to send for the dog when they're settled."

"Cute at that," I said. "The dog's named Voss after a German war flier. The folks are named after the dog."

"You think I'm lying," the little man said hotly.

"Uh-uh. You scare too easy for a crook. I think somebody wanted to ditch the dog. Here's my story. A girl named Isobel Snare disappeared from her home in San Angelo, two weeks ago. She lives with her great-aunt, a nice old lady in gray silk who isn't anybody's fool. The girl had been stepping out with some pretty shady company in the night spots and gambling joints. So the old lady smelled a scandal and didn't go to the law. She didn't get anywhere until a girl friend of the Snare girl happened to see the dog in your joint. She told the aunt. The aunt hired me—because when the niece drove off in her roadster and didn't come back she had the dog with her."

I mashed out my cigarette on my heel and lit another. Dr. Sharp's little face was as white as dough. Perspiration twinkled in his cute little mustache.

I added gently: "It's not a police job yet. I was kidding you about Chief Fulwider. How's for you and me to keep it under the hat?"

"What—what do you want me to do?" the little man stammered.

"Think you'll hear anything more about the dog?"

"Yes," he said quickly. "The man seemed very fond of him. A genuine dog lover. The dog was gentle with him."

"Then you'll hear from him," I said. "When you do I want to know. What's the guy look like?"

"He was tall and thin with very sharp black eyes. His wife is tall and thin like him. Well-dressed, quiet people."

"The Snare girl is a little runt," I said. "What made it so hush-hush?"

He stared at his foot and didn't say anything.

"Okay," I said. "Business is business. Play ball with me and you won't get any adverse publicity. Is it a deal?" I held my hand out.

"I'll play with you," he said softly, and put a moist fishy little paw in mine. I shook it carefully, so as not to bend it.

I told him where I was staying and went back out to the sunny street and walked a block down to where I had left my Chrysler. I got into it and poked it forward from around the corner, far enough so that I could see the DeSoto and the front of Sharp's place.

I sat like that for half an hour. Then Dr. Sharp came out of his place in street clothes and got into the DeSoto. He drove it off around the corner and swung into the alley that ran behind his yard.

I got the Chrysler going and shot up the block the other way, took a plant at the other end of the alley.

A third of the way down the block I heard growling, barking, snarling. This went on for some time. Then the DeSoto backed out of the concrete yard and came towards me. I ran away from it to the next corner.

The DeSoto went south to Arguello Boulevard, then east on that. A big police dog with a muzzle on his head was chained in the back of the sedan. I could just see his head straining at the chain.

I trailed the DeSoto.

II

CAROLINA STREET was away off at the edge of the little beach city. The end of it ran into a disused interurban right of way, beyond which stretched a waste of Japanese truck farms. There were just two houses in the last block, so I hid behind the first, which was on the corner, with a weedy grass plot and a high dusty red and yellow lantana fighting with a honeysuckle vine against the front wall.

Beyond that two or three burned over lots with a few weed stalks sticking up out of the charred grass and then a ramshackle mud-colored bungalow with a wire fence. The DeSoto stopped in front of that.

Its door slammed open and Dr. Sharp dragged the muzzled dog out of the back and fought him through a gate and up the walk. A big barrel-shaped palm tree kept me from seeing him at the front door of the house. I backed my Chrysler and turned it in the shelter of the corner house, went three blocks over and turned along a street parallel to Carolina. This street also ended at the right of way. The rails were rusted in a forest of weeds, came down the other side on to a dirt road, and started back towards Carolina.

The dirt road dropped until I couldn't see over the embankment. When I had gone what felt like three blocks I pulled up and got out, went up the side of the bank and sneaked a look over it.

The house with the wire gate was half a block from me. The DeSoto was still in front of it. Boomingly on the afternoon air came the deep-toned woof-woofing of the police dog. I put my stomach down in the weeds and sighted on the bungalow and waited.

Nothing happened for about fifteen minutes except that the dog kept right on barking. Then the barking suddenly got harder and harsher. Then somebody shouted. Then a man screamed.

I picked myself out of the weeds and sprinted across the right of way, down the other side to the street end. As I got near the house I heard the low, furious growling of the dog worrying something, and behind it the staccato rattle of a woman's voice in anger, more than in fear.

Behind the wire gate was a patch of lawn mostly dandelions and devil grass. There was a shred of cardboard hanging from the barrel-shaped palm, the remains of a sign. The roots of the tree had wrecked the walk, cracked it wide open and lifted the rough edges into steps.

I went through the gate and thumped up wooden steps to a sagging porch. I banged on the door.

The growling was still going on inside, but the scolding voice had stopped. Nobody came to the door.

I tried the knob, opened the door and went in. There was a heavy smell of chloroform.

In the middle of the floor, on a twisted rug, Dr. Sharp lay spread-eagled on his back, with blood pumping out of the side of his neck. The blood had made a thick glossy pool around his head. The dog leaned away from it, crouched on his forelegs, his ears flat to his head, fragments of a torn muzzle hanging about his neck. His throat bristled and the hair on his spine stood up and there was a low pulsing growl deep in his throat.

Behind the dog a closet door was smashed back against the wall and on the floor of the closet a big wad of cotton-wool sent sickening waves of chloroform out on the air.

A dark handsome woman in a print house dress held a big automatic pointed at the dog and didn't fire it.

She threw a quick glance at me over her shoulder, started to turn. The dog watched her, with narrow, black-rimmed eyes. I took my Luger out and held it down at my side.

Something creaked and a tall black-eyed man in faded blue overalls and a blue work shirt came through the swing door at the back with a sawed-off double-barrel shotgun in his hands. He pointed it at me.

"Hey, you! Drop that gat!" he said angrily.

I moved my jaw with the idea of saying something. The man's finger tightened on the front trigger. My gun went off—without my having much to do with it. The slug hit the stock of the shotgun, knocked it clean out of the man's hands. It pounded on the floor and the dog jumped sideways about seven feet and crouched again.

With an utterly incredulous look on his face the man put his hands up in the air.

I couldn't lose. I said: "Down yours too, lady."

She worked her tongue along her lips and lowered the automatic to her side and walked away from the body on the floor.

The man said: "Hell, don't shoot him. I can handle him."

I blinked, then I got the idea. He had been afraid I was going to shoot the dog. He hadn't been worrying about himself.

I lowered the Luger a little. "What happened?"

"That—tried to chloroform—*him*, a fighting dog!"

I said: "Yeah. If you've got a phone, you'd better call an ambulance. Sharp won't last long with that tear in his neck."

The woman said tonelessly: "I thought *you* were law."

I didn't say anything. She went along the wall to a window seat full of crumpled newspapers, reached down for a phone at one end of it.

I looked down at the little vet. The blood had stopped

coming out of his neck. His face was the whitest face I had ever seen.

"Never mind the ambulance," I told the woman. "Just call Police Headquarters."

The man in the overalls put his hands down and dropped on one knee, began to pat the floor and talk soothingly to the dog.

"Steady, old-timer. Steady. We're all friends now—all friends. Steady, Voss."

The dog growled and swung his hind end a little. The man kept on talking to him. The dog stopped growling and the hackles on his back went down. The man in overalls kept on crooning to him.

The woman on the window seat put the phone aside and said: "On the way. Think you can handle it, Jerry?"

"Sure," the man said, without taking his eyes off the dog.

The dog let his belly touch the floor now and opened his mouth and let his tongue hang out. The tongue dripped saliva, pink saliva with blood mixed in it. The hair at the side of the dog's mouth was stained with blood.

III

THE man called Jerry said: "Hey, Voss. Hey, Voss old kid. You're fine now. You're fine."

The dog panted, didn't move. The man straightened up and went close to him, pulled one of the dog's ears. The dog turned his head sideways and let his ear be pulled. The man stroked his head, unbuckled the chewed muzzle and got it off.

He stood up with the end of the broken chain and the dog came up on his feet obediently, went out through the swing door into the back part of the house, at the man's side.

I moved a little, out of line with the swing door. Jerry

might have more shotguns. There was something about Jerry's face that worried me. As if I had seen him before, but not very lately, or in a newspaper photo.

I looked at the woman. She was a handsome brunette in her early thirties. Her print house dress didn't seem to belong with her finely arched eyebrows and her long soft hands.

"How did it happen?" I asked casually, as if it didn't matter very much.

Her voice snapped at me, as if she was aching to turn it loose. "We've been in the house about a week. Rented it furnished, I was in the kitchen, Jerry in the yard. The car stopped out front and the little guy marched in just as if he lived here. The door didn't happen to be locked, I guess. I opened the swing door a crack and saw him pushing the dog into the closet. Then I smelled the chloroform. Then things began to happen all at once and I went for a gun and called Jerry out of the window. I got back in here about the time you crashed in. Who are you?"

"It was all over then?" I said. "He had Sharp chewed up on the floor?"

"Yes—if Sharp is his name."

"You and Jerry didn't know him?"

"Never saw him before. Or the dog. But Jerry loves dogs."

"Better change a little of that," I said. "Jerry knew the dog's name. Voss."

Her eyes got tight and her mouth got stubborn. "I think you must be mistaken," she said in a sultry voice. "I asked you who you were, mister."

"Who's Jerry?" I asked. "I've seen him somewhere. Maybe on a reader. Where'd he get the sawed-off? You going to let the cops see that?"

She bit her lip, then stood up suddenly, went towards the fallen shotgun. I let her pick it up, saw she kept her hand away from the triggers. She went back to the window seat and pushed it under the pile of newspapers.

She faced me. "Okay, what's the pay-off?" she asked grimly.

I said slowly: "The dog is stolen. His owner, a girl, happens to be missing. I'm hired to find her. The people Sharp said he got the dog from sounded like you and Jerry. Their name was Voss. They moved East. Ever heard of a lady called Isobel Snare?"

The woman said "No," tonelessly, and stared at the end of my chin.

The man in overalls came back through the swing door wiping his face on the sleeve of his blue work shirt. He didn't have any fresh guns with him. He looked me over without much concern.

I said: "I could do you a lot of good with the law, if you had any ideas about this Snare girl."

The woman stared at me, curled her lips. The man smiled, rather softly, as if he held all the cards. Tires squealed, taking a distant corner in a hurry.

"Aw, loosen up," I said quickly. "Sharp was scared. He brought the dog back to where he got him. He must have thought the house was empty. The chloroform idea wasn't so good, but the little guy was all rattled."

They didn't make a sound, either of them. They just stared at me.

"Okay," I said, and stepped over to the corner of the room. "I think you're a couple of lamsters. If whoever's coming isn't law, I'll start shooting. Don't ever think I won't."

The woman said very calmly: "Suit yourself, kibitzer."

Then a car rushed along the block and ground to a harsh stop before the house. I sneaked a quick glance out, saw the red spotlight on the windshield, the P.D. on the side. Two big bruisers in plain clothes tumbled out and slammed through the gate, up the steps.

A fist pounded the door. "It's open," I shouted.

The door swung wide and the two dicks charged in, with drawn guns.

They stopped dead, stared at what lay on the floor. Their guns jerked at Jerry and me. The one who covered me was a big red-faced man in a baggy gray suit.

"Reach—and reach empty!" he yelled in a large tough voice.

I reached, but held on to my Luger. "Easy," I said. "A dog killed him, not a gun. I'm a private dick from San Angelo. I'm on a case here."

"Yeah?" He closed in on me heavily, bored his gun into my stomach. "Maybe so, bud. We'll know all that later on."

He reached up and jerked my gun loose from my hand, sniffed at it, leaning his gun into me.

"Fired, huh? Sweet! Turn around."

"Listen—"

"Turn around, bud."

I turned around slowly. Even as I turned he was dropping his gun into a side pocket and reaching for his hip.

That should have warned me, but it didn't. I may have heard the swish of the blackjack. Certainly I must have felt it. There was a sudden pool of darkness at my feet. I dived into it and dropped . . . and dropped . . . and dropped . . .

IV

WHEN I came to the room was full of smoke. The smoke hung in the air, in thin lines straight up and down, like a bead curtain. Two windows seemed to be open in an end wall, but the smoke didn't move. I had never seen the room before.

I lay a little while thinking, then I opened my mouth and yelled: "Fire!" at the top of my lungs.

Then I fell back on the bed and started laughing. I didn't like the sound I made laughing. It had a goofy ring, even to me.

Steps ran along somewhere and a key turned in the door and the door opened. A man in a short white coat looked in at me, hard-eyed. I turned my head a little and said: "Don't count that one, Jack. It slipped out."

He scowled sharply. He had a hard small face, beady eyes. I didn't know him.

"Maybe you want some more strait jacket," he sneered.

"I'm fine, Jack," I said. "Just fine. I'm going to have me a short nap now."

"Better be just that," he snarled.

The door shut, the key turned, the steps went away.

I lay still and looked at the smoke. I knew now that there wasn't any smoke there really. It must have been night because a porcelain bowl hanging from the ceiling on three chains had light behind it. It had little colored lumps around the edge, orange and blue alternating. While I watched them they opened like tiny portholes and heads stuck out of them, tiny heads like the heads on dolls, but alive heads. There was a man in a yachting cap and a large fluffy blonde and a thin man with a crooked bow tie who kept saying: "Would you like your steak rare or medium, sir?"

I took hold of the corner of the rough sheet and wiped the sweat off my face. I sat up, put my feet down on the floor. They were bare. I was wearing canton flannel pajamas. There was no feeling in my feet when I put them down. After a while they began to tingle and then got full of pins and needles.

Then I could feel the floor. I took hold of the side of the bed and stood up and walked.

A voice that was probably my own was saying to me: "You have the D.T.s . . . you have the D.T.s . . . you have the D.T.s . . ."

I saw a bottle of whisky on a small white table between the two windows. I started towards it. It was a Johnnie Walker bottle, half full. I got it up, took a long drink from the neck. I put the bottle down again.

The whisky had a funny taste. While I was realizing that it had a funny taste I saw a washbowl in the corner. I just made it to the washbowl before I vomited.

I got back to the bed and lay there. The vomiting had made me very weak, but the room seemed a little more real, a little less fantastic. I could see bars on the two windows, a heavy wooden chair, no other furniture but the white table with the doped whisky on it. There was a closet door, shut, probably locked.

The bed was a hospital bed and there were two leather straps attached to the sides, about where a man's wrists would be. I knew I was in some kind of prison ward.

My left arm suddenly began to feel sore. I rolled up the loose sleeve, looked at half a dozen pinpricks on the upper arm, and a black and blue circle around each one.

I had been shot so full of dope to keep me quiet that I was having the French fits coming out of it. That accounted for the smoke and the little heads on the ceiling light. The doped whisky was probably part of somebody else's cure.

I got up again and walked, kept on walking. After a while I drank a little water from the tap, kept it down, drank more. Half an hour or more of that and I was ready to talk to somebody.

The closet door was locked and the chair was too heavy for me. I stripped the bed, slid the mattress to one side. There was a mesh spring underneath, fastened at the top and bottom by heavy coil springs about nine inches long. It took me half an hour and much misery to work one of these loose.

I rested a little and drank a little more cold water and went over to the hinge side of the door.

I yelled "Fire!" at the top of my voice, several times.

I waited, but not long. Steps ran along the hallway outside. The key jabbed into the door, the lock clicked. The hard-eyed little man in the short white coat dodged in furiously, his eyes on the bed.

I laid the coil spring on the angle of his jaw, then on the back of his head as he went down. I got him by the throat. He struggled a good deal. I used a knee on his face. It hurt my knee.

He didn't say how his face felt. I got a blackjack out of his right hip pocket and reversed the key in the door and locked it from the inside. There were other keys on the ring. One of them unlocked my closet. I looked in at my clothes.

I put them on slowly, with fumbling fingers. I yawned a great deal. The man on the floor didn't move.

I locked him in and left him.

V

FROM a wide silent hallway, with a parquetry floor and a narrow carpet down its middle, flat white oak banisters swept down in long curves to the entrance hall. There were closed doors, big, heavy, old-fashioned. No sounds behind them. I went down the carpet runner, walking on the balls of my feet.

There were stained glass inner doors to a vestibule from which the front door opened. A telephone rang as I got that far. A man's voice answered it, from behind a half-open door through which light came out into the dim hall.

I went back, sneaked a glance around the edge of the open door, saw a man at a desk, talking into the phone. I waited until he hung up. Then I went in.

He had a pale, bony, high-crowned head, across which a thin wave of brown hair curled and was plastered to his skull. He had a long, pale, joyless face. His eyes jumped at me. His hand jumped towards a button on his desk.

I grinned, growled at him: "Don't. I'm a desperate man, warden." I showed him the blackjack.

His smile was as stiff as a frozen fish. His long pale hands made gestures like sick butterflies over the top of his desk. One of them began to drift towards a side drawer of the desk.

He worked his tongue loose—"You've been a very sick man, sir. A very sick man. I wouldn't advise—"

I flicked the blackjack at his wandering hand. It drew into itself like a slug on a hot stone. I said: "Not sick, warden, just doped within an inch of my reason. Out is what I want, and some clean whisky. Give."

He made vague motions with his fingers. "I'm Dr. Sundstrand," he said. "This is a private hospital—not a jail."

"Whisky," I croaked. "I get all the rest. Private funny house. A lovely racket. Whisky."

"In the medicine cabinet," he said with a drifting, spent breath.

"Put your hands behind your head."

"I'm afraid you'll regret this." He put his hands behind his head.

I got to the far side of the desk, opened the drawer his hand had wanted to reach, took an automatic out of it. I put the blackjack away, went back round the desk to the medicine cabinet on the wall. There was a pint bottle of bond bourbon in it, three glasses. I took two of them.

I poured two drinks. "You first, warden."

"I—I don't drink. I'm a total abstainer," he muttered, his hands still behind his head.

I took the blackjack out again. He put a hand down quickly, gulped from one of the glasses. I watched him. It didn't seem to hurt him. I smelled my dose, then put it down my throat. It worked, and I had another, then slipped the bottle into my coat pocket.

"Okay," I said. "Who put me in here? Shake it up. I'm in a hurry."

"The—the police, of course."

"What police?"

He hunched his shoulders down in the chair. He looked sick. "A man named Galbraith signed as complaining witness. Strictly legal, I assure you. He is an officer."

I said: "Since when can a cop sign as complaining witness on a psycho case?"

He didn't say anything.

"Who gave me the dope in the first place?"

"I wouldn't know that. I presume it has been going on a long time."

I felt my chin. "All of two days," I said. "They ought to have gunned me. Less kickback in the long run. So long, warden."

"If you go out of here," he said thinly, "you will be arrested at once."

"Not just for going out," I said softly.

As I went out he still had his hands behind his head.

There was a chain and a bolt on the front door, beside the lock. But nobody tried to stop me from opening it. I crossed a big old-fashioned porch, went down a wide path fringed with flowers. A mockingbird sang in a dark tree. There was a white picket fence on the street. It was a corner house, on Twenty-ninth and Descanso.

I walked four blocks east to a bus line and waited for a bus. There was no alarm, no cruising car looking for me. The bus came and I rode downtown, went to a Turkish Bath establishment, had a steam bath, a needle shower, a rubdown, a shave, and the rest of the whisky.

I could eat then. I ate and went to a strange hotel, registered under a fake name. It was half past eleven. The local paper, which I read over more whisky and water, informed me that one Dr. Richard Sharp, who had been found dead in a vacant furnished house on Carolina Street, was still causing the police much headache. They had no clue to the murderer as yet.

The date on the paper informed me that over forty-eight hours had been abstracted from my life without my knowledge or consent.

I went to bed and to sleep, had nightmares and woke up out of them covered with cold sweat. That was the last of the withdrawal symptoms. In the morning I was a well man.

VI

CHIEF OF POLICE FULWIDER was a hammered down, fattish heavyweight, with restless eyes and that shade of red hair that is almost pink. It was cut very short and his pink scalp glistened among the pink hairs. He wore a fawn-colored flannel suit with patch pockets and lapped seams, cut as every tailor can't cut flannel.

He shook hands with me and turned his chair sideways and crossed his legs. That showed me French lisle socks at three or four dollars a pair, and hand-made English walnut brogues at fifteen to eighteen, depression prices.

I figured that probably his wife had money.

"Ah, Carmady," he said, chasing my card over the glass top of his desk, "with two *a*'s, eh? Down here on a job?"

"A little trouble," I said. "You can straighten it out, if you will."

He stuck his chest out, waved a pink hand and lowered his voice a couple of notches.

"Trouble," he said, "is something our little town don't have a lot of. Our little city is small, but very, very clean. I look out of my west window and I see the Pacific Ocean. Nothing cleaner than that. On the north Arguello Boulevard and the foothills. On the east the finest little business section you would want to see and beyond it a paradise of well-kept homes and gardens. On the south—if I had a south window, which I don't have—I would see the finest little yacht harbor in the world, for a small yacht harbor."

"I brought my trouble with me," I said. "That is, some of it. The rest went on ahead. A girl named Isobel Snare ran off from home in the big city and her dog was seen here. I found the dog, but the people who had the dog went to a lot of trouble to sew me up."

"Is that so?" the chief asked absently. His eyebrows crawled around on his forehead. I wasn't sure whether I was kidding him or he was kidding me.

"Just turn the key in the door, will you?" he said. "You're a younger man than I am."

I got up and turned the key and sat down again and got a cigarette out. By that time the chief had a right-looking bottle and two pony glasses on the desk, and a handful of cardamom seeds.

We had a drink and he cracked three or four of the cardamom seeds and we chewed them and looked at one another.

"Just tell me about it," he said then. "I can take it now."

"Did you ever hear of a guy called Farmer Saint?"

"*Did* I?" He banged his desk and the cardamom seeds jumped. "Why there's a thousand berries on that bimbo. A bank stickup, ain't he?"

I nodded, trying to look behind his eyes without seeming to. "He and his sister work together. Diana is her name. They dress up like country folks and smack down small-town banks, state banks. That's why he's called Farmer Saint. There's a grand on the sister too."

"I would certainly like to put the sleeves on that pair," the chief said firmly.

"Then why the hell didn't you?" I asked him.

He didn't quite hit the ceiling, but he opened his mouth so wide I was afraid his lower jaw was going to fall in his lap. His eyes stuck out like peeled eggs. A thin trickle of saliva showed in the fat crease at the corner. He shut his mouth with all the deliberation of a steam shovel.

It was a great act, if it was an act.

"Say that again," he whispered.

I opened a folded newspaper I had with me and pointed to a column.

"Look at this Sharp killing. Your local paper didn't do so good on it. It says some unknown rang the department and the boys ran out and found a dead man in an empty house. That's a lot of noodles. I was there. Farmer Saint and his sister were there. Your cops were there when we were there."

"Treachery!" he shouted suddenly. "Traitors in the department." His face was now as gray as arsenic flypaper. He poured two more drinks, with a shaking hand.

It was my turn to crack the cardamom seeds.

He put his drink down in one piece and lunged for a mahogany call box on his desk. I caught the name Galbraith. I went over and unlocked the door.

We didn't wait very long, but long enough for the chief to have two more drinks. His face got a better color.

Then the door opened and the big red-faced dick who had sapped me loafed through it, with a bulldog pipe clamped in his teeth and his hands in his pockets. He shouldered the door shut, leaned against it casually.

I said: "Hello, Sarge."

He looked at me as if he would like to kick me in the face and not have to hurry about it.

"Badge!" the fat chief yelled. "Badge! Put it on the desk. You're fired!"

Galbraith went over to the desk slowly and put an elbow down on it, put his face about a foot from the chief's nose.

"What was that crack?" he asked thickly.

"You had Farmer Saint under your hand and let him go," the chief yelled. "You and that saphead Duncan. You let him stick a shotgun in your belly and get away. You're through. Fired. You ain't got no more job than a canned oyster. Gimme your badge!"

"Who the hell is Farmer Saint?" Galbraith asked, unimpressed, and blew pipe smoke in the chief's face.

"He don't know," the chief whined at me. "He don't know. That's the kind of material I got to work with."

"What do you mean, work?" Galbraith inquired loosely.

The fat chief jumped as though a bee had stung the end of his nose. Then he doubled a meaty fist and hit Galbraith's jaw with what looked like a lot of power. Galbraith's head moved about half an inch.

"Don't do that," he said. "You'll bust a gut and then where would the department be?" He shot a look at me, looked back at Fulwider. "Should I tell him?"

Fulwider looked at me, to see how the show was going over. I had my mouth open and a blank expression on my face, like a farm boy at a Latin lesson.

"Yeah, tell him," he growled. shaking his knuckles back and forth.

Galbraith stuck a thick leg over a corner of the desk and knocked his pipe out, reached for the whisky and poured himself a drink in the chief's glass. He wiped his lips, grinned. When he grinned he opened his mouth wide, and he had a mouth a dentist could have got both hands in, up to the elbows.

He said calmly: "When me and Dunc crash the joint you was cold on the floor and the lanky guy was over you with a sap. The broad was on a window seat, with a lot of newspapers around her. Okay. The lanky guy starts to tell us some yarn when a dog begins to howl out back and we look that way and the broad slips a sawed-off 12-gauge out of the newspapers and shows it to us. Well, what could we do except be nice? She couldn't have missed and we could. So the guy gets more guns out of his pants and they tie knots around us and stick us in a closet that has enough chloroform in it to make us quiet, without the ropes. After a while we hear 'em leave, in two cars. When we get loose the stiff has the place to hisself. So we fudge it a bit for the papers. We don't get no new line yet. How's it tie to yours?"

"Not bad," I told him. "As I remember the woman phoned for some law herself. But I could be mistaken. The rest of it ties in with me being sapped on the floor and not knowing anything about it."

Galbraith gave me a nasty look. The chief looked at his thumb.

"When I came to," I said, "I was in a private dope and hooch cure out on Twenty-ninth. Run by a man named Sundstrand. I was shot so full of hop myself I could have been Rockefeller's pet dime trying to spin myself."

"That Sundstrand," Galbraith said heavily. "That guy's been a flea in our pants for a long time. Should we go out and push him in the face, Chief?"

"It's a cinch Farmer Saint put Carmady in there," Fulwider said solemnly. "So there must be some tie-up. I'd say yes, and take Carmady with you. Want to go?" he asked me.

"Do I?" I said heartily.

Galbraith looked at the whisky bottle. He said carefully: "There's a grand each on this Saint and his sister. If we gather them in, how do we cut it?"

"You cut me out," I said. "I'm on a straight salary and expenses."

Galbraith grinned again. He teetered on his heels, grinning with thick amiability.

"Okydoke. We got your car in the garage downstairs. Some Jap phoned in about it. We'll use that to go in—just you and me."

"Maybe you ought to have more help, Gal," the chief said doubtfully.

"Uh-uh. Just me and him's plenty. He's a tough baby or he wouldn't be walkin' around."

"Well, all right," the chief said brightly. "And we'll just have a little drink on it."

But he was still rattled. He forgot the cardamom seeds.

VII

IT was a cheerful spot by daylight. Tea-rose begonias made a solid mass under the front windows and pansies were a round carpet about the base of an acacia. A scarlet climbing rose covered a trellis to one side of the house, and a bronze-green hummingbird was prodding delicately in a mass of sweet peas that grew up the garage wall.

It looked like the home of a well-fixed elderly couple who had come to the ocean to get as much sun as possible in their old age.

Galbraith spat on my runningboard and shook his pipe out and tickled the gate open, stamped up the path and flattened his thumb against a neat copper bell.

We waited. A grill opened in the door and a long sallow face looked out at us under a starched nurse's cap.

"Open up. It's the law," the big cop growled.

A chain rattled and ˋa bolt slid back. The door opened. The nurse was a six-footer with long arms and big hands, an ideal torturer's assistant. Something happened to her face and I saw she was smiling.

"Why, it's Mr. Galbraith," she chirped, in a voice that was high-pitched and throaty at the same time. "How are you, Mr. Galbraith? Did you want to see Doctor?"

"Yeah, and sudden," Galbraith growled, pushing past her.

We went along the hall. The door of the office was shut. Galbraith kicked it open, with me at his heels and the big nurse chirping at mine.

Dr. Sundstrand, the total abstainer, was having a morning bracer out of a fresh quart bottle. His thin hair was stuck in wicks with perspiration and his bony mask of a face seemed to have a lot of lines in it that hadn't been there the night before.

He took his hand off the bottle hurriedly and gave us his

frozen-fish smile. He said fussily: "What's this? What's this? I thought I gave orders—"

"Aw, pull your belly in," Galbraith said, and yanked a chair near the desk. "Dangle, sister."

The nurse chirped something more and went back through the door. The door was shut. Dr. Sundstrand worked his eyes up and down my face and looked unhappy.

Galbraith put both his elbows on the desk and took hold of his bulging jowls with his fists. He stared fixedly, venomously, at the squirming doctor.

After what seemed a very long time he said, almost softly: "Where's Farmer Saint?"

The doctor's eyes popped wide. His Adam's apple bobbled above the neck of his smock. His greenish eyes began to look bilious.

"Don't stall!" Galbraith roared. "We know all about your private hospital racket, the crook hideout you're runnin', the dope and women on the side. You made one slip too many when you hung a snatch on this shamus from the big town. Your big city protection ain't going to do you no good on this one. Come on, where is Saint? And where's that girl?"

I remembered, quite casually, that I had not said anything about Isobel Snare in front of Galbraith—if that was the girl he meant.

Dr. Sundstrand's hand flopped about on his desk. Sheer astonishment seemed to be adding a final touch of paralysis to his uneasiness.

"Where are they?" Galbraith yelled again.

The big door opened and the big nurse fussed in again. "Now, Mr. Galbraith, the patients. Please remember the patients, Mr. Galbraith."

"Go climb up your thumb," Galbraith told her, over his shoulder.

She hovered by the door. Sundstrand found his voice at last. It was a mere wisp of a voice. It said wearily: "As if you didn't know."

Then his darting hand swept into his smock, and out again, with a gun glistening in it. Galbraith threw himself sideways, clean out of the chair. The doctor shot at him twice, missed twice. My hand touched a gun, but didn't draw it. Galbraith laughed on the floor and his big right hand snatched at his armpit, came up with a Luger. It looked like my Luger. It went off, just once.

Nothing changed in the doctor's long face. I didn't see where the bullet hit him. His head came down and hit the desk and his gun made a thud on the floor. He lay with his face on the desk, motionless.

Galbraith pointed his gun at me, and got up off the floor. I looked at the gun again. I was sure it was my gun.

"That's a swell way to get information," I said aimlessly.

"Hands down, shamus. You don't want to play."

I put my hands down. "Cute," I said. "I suppose this whole scene was framed just to put the chill on Doc."

"He shot first, didn't he?"

"Yeah," I said thinly. "He shot first."

The nurse was sidling along the wall towards me. No sound had come from her since Sundstrand pulled his act. She was almost at my side. Suddenly, much too late, I saw the flash of knuckles on her good right hand, and hair on the back of the hand.

I dodged, but not enough. A crunching blow seemed to split my head wide open. I brought up against the wall, my knees full of water and my brain working hard to keep my right hand from snatching at a gun.

I straightened. Galbraith leered at me.

"Not so very smart," I said. "You're still holding my Luger. That sort of spoils the plant, doesn't it?"

"I see you get the idea, shamus."

The chirpy-voiced nurse said, in a blank pause: "Jeeze, the guy's got a jaw like a elephant's foot. Damn if I didn't split a knuck on him."

Galbraith's little eyes had death in them. "How about upstairs?" he asked the nurse.

"All out last night. Should I try one more swing?"

"What for? He didn't go for his gat, and he's too tough for you, baby. Lead is his meat."

I said: "You ought to shave baby twice a day on this job."

The nurse grinned, pushed the starched cap and the stringy blond wig askew on a bullet head. She—or more properly he—reached a gun from under the white nurse's uniform.

Galbraith said: "It was self-defense, see? You tangled with Doc, but he shot first. Be nice and me and Dunc will try to remember it that way."

I rubbed my jaw with my left hand. "Listen, Sarge. I can take a joke as well as the next fellow. You sapped me in that house on Carolina Street and didn't tell about it. Neither did I. I figured you had reasons and you'd let me in on them at the right time. Maybe I can guess what the reasons are. I think you know where Saint is, or can find out. Saint knows where the Snare girl is, because he had her dog. Let's put a little more into this deal, something for both of us."

"We've got ours, sappo. I promised Doc I'd bring you back and let him play with you. I put Dunc in here in the nurse's rig to handle you for him. But *he* was the one we really wanted to handle."

"All right," I said. "What do I get out of it?"

"Maybe a little more living."

I said: "Yeah. Don't think I'm kidding you—but look at that little window in the wall behind you."

Galbraith didn't move, didn't take his eyes off me. A thick sneer curved his lips.

Duncan, the female impersonator, looked—and yelled.

A small, square, tinted glass window high up in the corner of the back wall had swung open quite silently. I was looking straight at it, past Galbraith's ear, straight at the black snout of a tommy gun, on the sill, at the two hard black eyes behind the gun.

A voice I had last heard soothing a dog said: "How's to drop the rod, sister? And you at the desk—grab a cloud."

VIII

THE big cop's mouth sucked for air. Then his whole face tightened and he jerked around and the Luger gave one hard, sharp cough.

I dropped to the floor as the tommy gun cut loose in a short burst. Galbraith crumpled beside the desk, fell on his back with his legs twisted. Blood came out of his nose and mouth.

The cop in nurse's uniform turned as white as the starched cap. His gun bounced. His hands tried to claw at the ceiling.

There was a queer, stunned silence. Powder smoke reeked. Farmer Saint spoke downward from his perch at the window, to somebody outside the house.

A door opened and shut distinctly and running steps came along the hall. The door of our room was pushed wide. Diana Saint came in with a brace of automatics in her hands. A tall, handsome woman, neat and dark, with a rakish black hat, and two gloved hands holding guns.

I got up off the floor, keeping my hands in sight. She tossed her voice calmly at the window, without looking towards it.

"Okay, Jerry. I can hold them."

Saint's head and shoulders and his submachine gun went away from the frame of the window, leaving blue sky and the thin, distant branches of a tall tree.

There was a thud, as if feet dropped off a ladder to a wooden porch. In the room we were five statues, two fallen.

Somebody had to move. The situation called for two more killings. From Saint's angle I couldn't see it any other way. There had to be a cleanup.

The gag hadn't worked when it wasn't a gag. I tried it again when it was. I looked past the woman's shoulder, kicked a hard grin on to my face, said hoarsely:

"Hello, Mike. Just in time."

It didn't fool her, of course, but it made her mad. She stiffened her body and snapped a shot at me from the right-hand gun. It was a big gun for a woman and it jumped. The other gun jumped with it. I didn't see where the shot went. I went in under the guns.

My shoulder hit her thigh and she tipped back and hit her head against the jamb of the door. I wasn't too nice about knocking the guns out of her hands. I kicked the door shut, reached up and yanked the key around, then scrambled back from a high-heeled shoe that was doing its best to smash my nose for me.

Duncan said: "Keeno," and dived for his gun on the floor.

"Watch that little window, if you want to live," I snarled at him.

Then I was behind the desk, dragging the phone away from Dr. Sundstrand's dead body, dragging it as far from the line of the door as the cord would let me. I lay down on the floor with it and started to dial, on my stomach.

Diana's eyes came alive on the phone. She screeched: "They've got me, Jerry! They've got me!"

The machine gun began to tear the door apart as I bawled into the ear of a bored desk sergeant.

Pieces of plaster and wood flew like fists at an Irish wedding. Slugs jerked the body of Dr. Sundstrand as though a chill was shaking him back to life. I threw the phone away from me and grabbed Diana's guns and started in on the door for our side. Through a wide crack I could see cloth. I shot at that.

I couldn't see what Duncan was doing. Then I knew. A shot that couldn't have come through the door smacked Diana Saint square on the end of her chin. She went down again, stayed down.

Another shot that didn't come through the door lifted my hat. I rolled and yelled at Duncan. His gun moved in a stiff arc, following me. His mouth was an animal snarl. I yelled again.

Four round patches of red appeared in a diagonal line across the nurse uniform, chest high. They spread even in the short time it took Duncan to fall.

There was a siren somewhere. It was my siren, coming my way, getting louder.

The tommy gun stopped and a foot kicked at the door. It shivered, but held at the lock. I put four more slugs into it, well away from the lock.

The siren got louder. Saint had to go. I heard his step running away down the hall. A door slammed. A car started out back in an alley. The sound of its going got less as the approaching siren screeched into a crescendo.

I crawled over to the woman and looked at blood on her face and hair and soft soggy places on the front of her coat. I touched her face. She opened her eyes slowly, as if the lids were very heavy.

"Jerry—" she whispered.

"Dead," I lied grimly. "Where's Isobel Snare, Diana?"

The eyes closed. Tears glistened, the tears of the dying.

"Where's Isobel, Diana?" I pleaded. "Be regular and tell me. I'm no cop. I'm her friend. Tell me, Diana."

I put tenderness and wistfulness into it, everything I had.

The eyes half opened. The whisper came again: "Jerry—" then it trailed off and the eyes shut. Then the lips moved once more, breathed a word that sounded like "Monty."

That was all. She died.

I stood up slowly and listened to the sirens.

IX

It was getting late and lights were going on here and there in a tall office building across the street. I had been in Fulwider's office all the afternoon. I had told my story twenty times. It was all true—what I told.

Cops had been in and out, ballistics and print men, record men, reporters, half a dozen city officials, even an A.P. correspondent. The correspondent didn't like his handout and said so.

The fat chief was sweaty and suspicious. His coat was off and his armpits were black and his short red hair curled as if it had been singed. Not knowing how much or little I knew he didn't dare lead me. All he could do was yell at me and whine at me by turns, and try to get me drunk in between.

I was getting drunk and liking it.

"Didn't nobody say anything at all!" he wailed at me for the hundredth time.

I took another drink, flopped my hand around, looked silly. "Not a word, Chief," I said owlishly. "I'm the boy that would tell you. They died too sudden."

He took hold of his jaw and cranked it. "Damn funny," he sneered. "Four dead ones on the floor and you not even nicked."

"I was the only one," I said, "that lay down on the floor while still healthy."

He took hold of his right ear and worried that. "You been here three days," he howled. "In them three days we got more crime than in three years before you come. It ain't human. I must be having a nightmare."

"You can't blame me, Chief," I grumbled. "I came down here to look for a girl. I'm still looking for her. I didn't tell Saint and his sister to hide out in your town. When I spotted him I tipped you off, though your own cops didn't. I didn't shoot Doc Sundstrand before anything could be got out of him. I still haven't any idea why the phony nurse was planted there."

"Nor me," Fulwider yelled. "But it's my job that's shot full of holes. For all the chance I got to get out of this I might as well go fishin' right now."

I took another drink, hiccupped cheerfully. "Don't say that, Chief," I pleaded. "You cleaned the town up once and you can do it again. This one was just a hot grounder that took a bad bounce."

He took a turn around the office and tried to punch a hole in the end wall, then slammed himself back in his chair. He eyed me savagely, grabbed for the whisky bottle, then didn't touch it—as though it might do him more good in my stomach.

"I'll make a deal with you," he growled. "You run

on back to San Angelo and I'll forget it was your gun croaked Sundstrand."

"That's not a nice thing to say to a man that's trying to earn his living, Chief. You know how it happened to be my gun."

His face looked gray again, for a moment. He measured me for a coffin. Then the mood passed and he smacked his desk, said heartily:

"You're right, Carmady. I couldn't do that, could I? You still got to find that girl, ain't you? Okay, you run on back to the hotel and get some rest. I'll work on it tonight and see you in the A.M."

I took another short drink, which was all there was left in the bottle. I felt fine. I shook hands with him twice and staggered out of his office. Flash bulbs exploded all over the corridor.

I went down the City Hall steps and around the side of the building to the police garage. My blue Chrysler was home again. I dropped the drunk act and went on down the side streets to the ocean front, walked along the wide cement walk towards the two amusement piers and the Grand Hotel.

It was getting dusk now. Lights on the piers came out. Masthead lights were lit on the small yachts riding at anchor behind the yacht harbor breakwater. In a white barbecue stand a man tickled wienies with a long fork and droned: "Get hungry, folks. Nice hot doggies here. Get hungry, folks."

I lit a cigarette and stood there looking out to sea. Very suddenly, far out, lights shone from a big ship. I watched them, but they didn't move. I went over to the hot dog man.

"Anchored?" I asked him, pointing.

He looked around the end of his booth, wrinkled his nose with contempt.

"Hell, that's the gambling boat. The Cruise to Nowhere, they call the act, because it don't go no place. If Tango ain't crooked enough, try that. Yes, sir, that's the good ship *Montecito*. How about a nice warm puppy?"

I put a quarter on his counter. "Have one yourself," I said softly. "Where do the taxis leave from?"

I had no gun. I went on back to the hotel to get my spare.

The dying Diana Saint had said "Monty."

Perhaps she just hadn't lived long enough to say "Montecito."

At the hotel I lay down and fell asleep as though I had been anaesthetized. It was eight o'clock when I woke up, and I was hungry.

I was tailed from the hotel, but not very far. Of course the clean little city didn't have enough crime for the dicks to be very good shadows.

X

IT was a long ride for forty cents. The water taxi, an old speedboat without trimmings, slid through the anchored yachts and rounded the breakwater. The swell hit us. All the company I had besides the tough-looking citizen at the wheel was two spooning couples who began to peck at each other's faces as soon as the darkness folded down.

I stared back at the lights of the city and tried not to bear down too hard on my dinner. Scattered diamond points at first, the lights drew together and became a jeweled wristlet laid out in the show window of the night. Then they were a soft orange yellow blur above the top of the swell. The taxi smacked in the invisible waves and bounced like a surf boat. There was cold fog in the air.

The portholes of the *Montecito* got large and the taxi swept out in a wide turn, tipped to an angle of forty-five degrees and careened neatly to the side of a brightly lit stage. The taxi engine idled down and backfired in the fog.

A sloe-eyed boy in a tight blue mess jacket and a gangster mouth handed the girls out, swept their escorts with a keen glance, sent them on up. The look he gave me told me somethting about him. The way he bumped into my gun holster told me more.

"Nix," he said softly. "Nix."

He jerked his chin at the taxi man. The taxi man dropped a short noose over a bitt, turned his wheel a little and climbed on the stage. He got behind me.

"Nix," the one in the mess jacket purred. "No gats on this boat, mister. Sorry."

"Part of my clothes," I told him. "I'm a private dick. I'll check it."

"Sorry, bo. No checkroom for gats. On your way."

The taxi man hooked a wrist through my right arm. I shrugged.

"Back in the boat," the taxi man growled behind me. "I owe you forty cents, mister. Come on."

I got back into the boat.

"Okay," I sputtered at Mess Jacket. "If you don't want my money, you don't want it. This is a hell of a way to treat a visitor. This is—"

His sleek, silent smile was the last thing I saw as the taxi cast off and hit the swell on the way back. I hated to leave that smile.

The way back seemed longer. I didn't speak to the taxi man and he didn't speak to me. As I got out on to the float at the pier he sneered at my back: "Some other night when we ain't so busy, shamus."

Half a dozen customers waiting to go out stared at me. I went past them, past the door of the waiting room on the float, towards the steps at the landward end.

A big redheaded roughneck in dirty sneakers and tarry pants and a torn blue jersey straightened from the railing and bumped into me casually.

I stopped, got set. He said softly: " 's matter, dick? No soap on the hell ship?"

"Do I have to tell you?"

"I'm a guy that can listen."

"Who are you?"

"Just call me Red."

"Out of the way, Red. I'm busy."

He smiled sadly, touched my left side. "The gat's kind of bulgy under the light suit," he said. "Want to get on board? It can be done, if you got a reason."

"How much is the reason?" I asked him.

"Fifty bucks. Ten more if you bleed in my boat."

I started away. "Twenty-five out," he said quickly. "Maybe you come back with friends, huh?"

I went four steps away from him before I half turned, said: "Sold," and went on.

At the foot of the bright amusement pier there was a flaring Tango Parlor, jammed full even at that still early hour. I went into it, leaned against a wall and watched a couple of numbers go up on the electric indicator, watched a house player with an inside straight give the high sign under the counter with his knee.

A large blueness took form beside me and I smelled tar. A soft, deep, sad voice said: "Need help out there?"

"I'm looking for a girl, but I'll look alone. What's your racket?" I didn't look at him.

"A dollar here, a dollar there. I like to eat. I was on the cops but they bounced me."

I liked his telling me that. "You must have been leveling," I said, and watched the house player slip his card across with his thumb over the wrong number, watched the counter man get his own thumb in the same spot and hold the card up.

I could feel Red's grin. "I see you been around our little city. Here's how it works. I got a boat with an underwater bypass. I know a loading port I can open. I take a load out for a guy once in a while. There ain't many guys below decks. That suit you?"

I got my wallet out and slipped a twenty and a five from it, passed them over in a wad. They went into a tarry pocket.

Red said: "Thanks," softly, and walked away. I gave him a small start and went after him. He was easy to follow by his size, even in a crowd.

We went past the yacht harbor and the second amusement pier and beyond that the lights got fewer and the crowd thinned to nothing. A short black pier stuck out into the water with boats moored all along it. My man turned out that.

He stopped almost at the end, at the head of a wooden ladder.

"I'll bring her down to here," he said. "Got to make noise warmin' up."

"Listen," I said urgently. "I have to phone a man. I forgot."

"Can do. Come on."

He led the way farther along the pier, knelt, rattled keys on a chain, and opened a padlock. He lifted a small trap and took a phone out, listened to it.

"Still working," he said with a grin in his voice. "Must belong to some crooks. Don't forget to snap the lock back on."

He slipped away silently into the darkness. For ten minutes I listened to water slapping the piles of the pier, the occasional whirr of a seagull in the gloom. Then far off a motor roared and kept on roaring for minutes. Then the noise stopped abruptly. More minutes passed. Something thudded at the foot of the ladder and a low voice called up to me: "All set."

I hurried back to the phone, dialed a number, asked for Chief Fulwider. He had gone home. I dialed another number, got a woman, asked her for the chief, said I was headquarters.

I waited again. Then I heard the fat chief's voice. It sounded full of baked potato.

"Yeah? Can't a guy even eat? Who is it?"

"Carmady, Chief. Saint is on the *Montecito*. Too bad that's over your line."

He began to yell like a wild man. I hung up in his face, put the phone back in its zinc-lined cubbyhole and snapped the padlock. I went down the ladder to Red.

His big black speedboat slid out over the oily water. There was no sound from its exhaust but a steady bubbling along the side of the shell.

The city lights again became a yellow blur low on the black water and the ports of the good ship *Montecito* again got large and bright and round out to sea.

XI

THERE were no floodlights on the seaward side of the ship. Red cut his motor to half of nothing and curved in under the overhang of the stern, sidled up to the greasy plates as coyly as a clubman in a hotel lobby.

Double iron doors loomed high over us, forward a little from the slimy links of a chain cable. The speedboat scuffed the *Montecito*'s ancient plates and the sea water slapped loosely at the bottom of the speedboat under our feet. The shadow of the big ex-cop rose over me. A coiled rope flicked against the dark, caught on something, and fell back into the boat. Red pulled it tight, made a turn around something on the engine cowling.

He said softly: "She rides as high as a steeplechaser. We gotta climb them plates."

I took the wheel and held the nose of the speedboat against the slippery hull, and Red reached for an iron ladder flat to the side of the ship, hauled himself up into the darkness, grunting, his big body braced at right angles, his sneakers slipping on the wet metal rungs.

After a while something creaked up above and feeble yellow light trickled out into the foggy air. The outline of a heavy door showed, and Red's crouched head against the light.

I went up the ladder after him. It was hard work. It landed me panting in a sour, littered hold full of cases and barrels. Rats skittered out of sight in the dark corners. The big man put his lips to my ear: "From here we got an easy way to the boiler-room catwalk. They'll have steam up in one auxiliary, for hot water and the generators. That means one guy. I'll handle him. The crew doubles in brass upstairs. From the boiler room I'll show you a ventilator with no grating in it. Goes to the boat deck. Then it's all yours."

"You must have relatives on board," I said.

"Never no mind. A guy gets to know things when he's on the beach. Maybe I'm close to a bunch that's set to knock the tub over. Will you come back fast?"

"I ought to make a good splash from the boat deck," I said. "Here."

I fished more bills out of my wallet, pushed them at him.

He shook his red head. "Uh-uh. That's for the trip back."

"I'm buying it now," I said. "Even if I don't use it. Take the dough before I bust out crying."

"Well—thanks, pal. You're a right guy."

We went among the cases and barrels. The yellow light came from a passage beyond, and we went along the passage to a narrow iron door. That led to the catwalk. We sneaked along it, down an oily steel ladder, heard the slow hiss of oil burners and went among mountains of iron towards the sound.

Around a corner we looked at a short, dirty Italian in a purple silk shirt who sat in a wired-together office chair, under a naked bulb, and read the paper with the aid of steel-rimmed spectacles and a black forefinger.

Red said gently: "Hi, Shorty. How's all the little bambinos?"

The Italian opened his mouth and reached swiftly. Red hit him. We put him down on the floor and tore his purple shirt into shreds for ties and a gag.

"You ain't supposed to hit a guy with glasses on," Red said. "But the idea is you make a hell of a racket goin' up a ventilator—to a guy down here. Upstairs they won't hear nothing."

I said that was the way I would like it, and we left the Italian bound up on the floor and found the ventilator that had no grating in it. I shook hands with Red, said I hoped to see him again, and started up the ladder inside the ventilator.

It was cold and black and the foggy air rushed down it and the way up seemed a long way. After three minutes that felt like an hour I reached the top and poked my head out cautiously. Canvas-sheeted boats loomed near by on the boat-deck davits. There was a soft whispering in the dark between a pair of them. The heavy throb of music pulsed up from below. Overhead a masthead light, and through the thin, high layers of the mist a few bitter stars stared down.

I listened, but didn't hear any police-boat sirens. I got out of the ventilator, lowered myself to the deck.

The whispering came from a necking couple huddled under a boat. They didn't pay any attention to me. I went along the deck past the closed doors of three or four cabins. There was a little light behind the shutters of two of them. I listened, didn't hear anything but the merrymaking of the customers down below on the main deck.

I dropped into a dark shadow, took a lungful of air and let it out in a howl—the snarling howl of a gray timber wolf, lonely and hungry and far from home, and mean enough for seven kinds of trouble.

The deep-toned woof-woofing of a police dog answered me. A girl squealed along the dark deck and a man's voice said: "I thought all the shellac drinkers was dead."

I straightened and unshipped my gun and ran towards the barking. The noise came from a cabin on the other side of the deck.

I put an ear to the door, listened to a man's voice soothing the dog. The dog stopped barking and growled once or twice, then was silent. A key turned in the door I was touching.

I dropped away from it, down on one knee. The door opened a foot and a sleek head came forward past its edge. Light from a hooded deck lamp made a shine on the black hair.

I stood up and slammed the head with my gun barrel. The man fell softly out of the doorway into my arms. I dragged him back into the cabin, pushed him down on a made-up berth.

I shut the door again, locked it. A small, wide-eyed girl crouched on the other berth. I said: "Hello, Miss Snare. I've had a lot of trouble finding you. Want to go home?"

Farmer Saint rolled over and sat up, holding his head. Then he was very still, staring at me with his sharp black eyes. His mouth had a strained smile, almost good-humored.

I ranged the cabin with a glance, didn't see where the

dog was, but saw an inner door behind which he could
be. I looked at the girl again.

She was not much to look at, like most of the people
that make most of the trouble. She was crouched on the
berth with her knees drawn up and hair falling over one
eye. She wore a knitted dress and golf socks and sport
shoes with wide tongues that fell down over the instep.
Her knees were bare and bony under the hem of the dress.
She looked like a schoolgirl.

I went over Saint for a gun, didn't find one. He grinned
at me.

The girl lifted her hand and threw her hair back. She
looked at me as if I was a couple of blocks away. Then
her breath caught and she began to cry.

"We're married," Saint said softly. "She thinks you're
set to blow holes in me. That was a smart trick with the
wolf howl."

I didn't say anything. I listened. No noises outside.

"How'd you know where to come?" Saint asked.

"Diana told me—before she died," I said brutally.

His eyes looked hurt. "I don't believe it, shamus."

"You ran out and left her in the ditch. What would you
expect?"

"I figured the cops wouldn't bump a woman and I could
make some kind of a deal on the outside. Who got her?"

"One of Fulwider's cops. You got him."

His head jerked back and a wild look came over his
face, then went away. He smiled sideways at the weeping
girl.

"Hello, sugar. I'll get you clear." He looked back at me.
"Suppose I come in without a scrap. Is there a way for her
to get loose?"

"What do you mean, scrap?" I sneered.

"I got plenty friends on this boat, shamus. You ain't
even started yet."

"You got her into it," I said. "You can't get her out.
That's part of the pay-off."

XII

HE nodded slowly, looked down at the floor between his feet. The girl stopped crying long enough to mop at her cheeks, then started in again.

"Fulwider know I'm here?" Saint asked me slowly.

"Yeah."

"You give him the office?"

"Yeah."

He shrugged. "That's okay from your end. Sure. Only I'll never get to talk, if Fulwider pinches me. If I could get to talk to a D.A. I could maybe convince him *she's* not hep to my stuff."

"You could have thought of that, too," I said heavily. "You didn't have to go back to Sundstrand's and cut loose with your stutter gun."

He threw his head back and laughed. "No? Suppose you paid a guy ten grand for protection and he crossed you up by grabbing your wife and sticking her in a crooked dope hospital and telling you to run along far away and be good, or the tide would wash her up on the beach? What would you do—smile, or trot over with some heavy iron to talk to the guy?"

"She wasn't there then," I said. "You were just kill-screwy. And if you hadn't hung on to that dog until he killed a man, the protection wouldn't have been scared into selling you out."

"I like dogs," Saint said quietly. "I'm a nice guy when I'm not workin', but I can get shoved around just so much."

I listened. Still no noises on deck outside.

"Listen," I said quickly. "If you want to play ball with me, I've got a boat at the back door and I'll try to get the girl home before they want her. What happens to you is past me. I wouldn't lift a finger for you, even if you do like dogs."

The girl said suddenly, in a shrill, little-girl voice: "I don't want to go home! I won't go home!"

"A year from now you'll thank me," I snapped at her.

"He's right, sugar," Saint said. "Better beat it with him."

"I won't," the girl shrilled angrily. "I just won't. That's all."

Out of the silence on the deck something hard slammed the outside of the door. A grim voice shouted: "Open up! It's the law!"

I backed swiftly to the door, keeping my eyes on Saint. I spoke back over my shoulder: "Fulwider there?"

"Yeah," the chief's fat voice growled. "Carmady?"

"Listen, Chief. Saint's in here and he's ready to surrender. There's a girl here with him, the one I told you about. So come in easy, will you?"

"Right," the chief said. "Open the door."

I twisted the key, jumped across the cabin and put my back against the inner partition, beside the door behind which the dog was moving around now, growling a little.

The outer door whipped open. Two men I hadn't seen before charged in with drawn guns. The fat chief was behind them. Briefly, before he shut the door, I caught a glimpse of ship's uniforms.

The two dicks jumped on Saint, slammed him around, put cuffs on him. Then they stepped back beside the chief. Saint grinned at them, with blood trickling down his lower lip.

Fulwider looked at me reprovingly and moved a cigar around in his mouth. Nobody seemed to take an interest in the girl.

"You're a hell of a guy, Carmady. You didn't give me no idea where to come," he growled.

"I didn't know," I said. "I thought it was outside your jurisdiction, too."

"Hell with that. We tipped the Feds. They'll be out."

One of the dicks laughed. "But not too soon," he said roughly. "Put the heater away, shamus."

"Try and make me," I told him.

He started forward, but the chief waved him back. The other dick watched Saint, looked at nothing else.

"How'd you find him then?" Fulwider wanted to know.

"Not by taking his money to hide him out," I said.

Nothing changed in Fulwider's face. His voice became almost lazy. "Oh, oh, you've been peekin'," he said very gently.

I said disgustedly. "Just what kind of a sap did you and your gang take me for? Your clean little town stinks. It's the well-known whited sepulcher. A crook sanctuary where the hot rods can lie low—if they pay off nice and don't pull any local capers—and where they can jump off for Mexico in a fast boat, if the finger waves towards them."

The chief said very carefully: "Any more?"

"Yeah," I shouted. "I've saved it for you too damn long. *You* had me doped until I was half goofy and stuck me in a private jail. When that didn't hold me *you* worked a plant up with Galbraith and Duncan to have my gun kill Sundstrand, your helper, and then have me killed resisting some arrest. Saint spoiled that party for you and saved my life. Not intending to, perhaps, but he did it. *You* knew all along where the little Snare girl was. She was Saint's wife and you were holding her yourself to make him stay in line. Hell, why do you suppose I tipped you he was out here? That was something you *didn't* know!"

The dick who had tried to make me put up my gun said: "Now, Chief. We better make it fast. Those Feds—"

Fulwider's jaw shook. His face was gray and his ears were far back in his head. The cigar twitched in his fat mouth.

"Wait a minute," he said thickly, to the man beside. Then to me: "Well—why did you tip me?"

"To get you where you're no more law than Billy the Kid," I said, "and see if you have the guts to go through with murder on the high seas."

Saint laughed. He shot a low, snarling whistle between his teeth. A tearing animal growl answered him. The door beside me crashed open as though a mule had kicked it. The big police dog came through the opening in a looping spring that carried him clear across the cabin. The gray body twisted in mid-air. A gun banged harmlessly.

"Eat 'em up, Voss!" Saint yelled. "Eat 'em alive, boy!"

The cabin filled with gunfire. The snarling of the dog blended with a thick, choked scream. Fulwider and one of the dicks were down on the floor and the dog was at Fulwider's throat.

The girl screamed and plunged her face into a pillow. Saint slid softly down from the bunk and lay on the floor with blood running slowly down his neck in a thick wave.

The dick who hadn't gone down jumped to one side, almost fell headlong on the girl's berth, then caught his balance and pumped bullets into the dog's long gray body —wildly without pretense of aim.

The dick on the floor pushed at the dog. The dog almost bit his hand off. The man yelled. Feet pounded on the deck. Yelling outside. Something was running down my face that tickled. My head felt funny, but I didn't know what had hit me.

The gun in my hand felt large and hot. I shot the dog, hating to do it. The dog rolled off Fulwider and I saw where a stray bullet had drilled the chief's forehead between the eyes, with the delicate exactness of pure chance.

The standing dick's gun hammer clicked on a discharged shell. He cursed, started to reload frantically.

I touched the blood on my face and looked at it. It seemed very black. The light in the cabin seemed to be failing.

The bright corner of an axe blade suddenly split the cabin door, which was wedged shut by the chief's body, and that of the groaning man beside him. I stared at the bright metal, watched it go away and reappear in another place.

Then all the lights went out very slowly, as in a theater just as the curtain goes up. Just as it got quite dark my head hurt me, but I didn't know then that a bullet had fractured my skull.

I woke up two days later in the hospital. I was there three weeks. Saint didn't live long enough to hang, but he lived long enough to tell his story. He must have told it well, because they let Mrs. Jerry (Farmer) Saint go home to her aunt.

By that time the County Grand Jury had indicted half the police force of the little beach city. There were a lot of new faces around the City Hall, I heard. One of them was a big redheaded detective-sergeant named Norgard who said he owed me twenty-five dollars but had had to use it to buy a new suit when he got his job back. He said he would pay me out of his first check. I said I would try to wait.

THE CURTAIN

I

THE first time I ever saw Larry Batzel he was drunk outside Sardi's in a secondhand Rolls-Royce. There was a tall blonde with him who had eyes you wouldn't forget. I helped her argue him out from under the wheel so that she could drive.

The second time I saw him he didn't have any Rolls-Royce or any blonde or any job in pictures. All he had was the jitters and a suit that needed pressing. He remembered me. He was that kind of drunk.

I bought him enough drinks to do him some good and gave him half my cigarettes. I used to see him from time to time "between pictures." I got to lending him money. I don't know just why. He was a big, handsome brute with eyes like a cow and something innocent and honest in them. Something I don't get much of in my business.

The funny part was he had been a liquor runner for a pretty hard mob before Repeal. He never got anywhere in pictures, and after a while I didn't see him around any more.

Then one day out of the clear blue I got a check for all he owed me and a note that he was working on the tables—gambling not dining—at the Dardanella Club, and to come out and look him up. So I knew he was back in the rackets.

I didn't go to see him, but I found out somehow or other that Joe Mesarvey owned the place, and that Joe Mesarvey was married to the blonde with the eyes, the one Larry Batzel had been with in the Rolls that time. I still didn't go out there.

Then very early one morning there was a dim figure standing by my bed, between me and the windows. The blinds had been pulled down. That must have been what wakened me. The figure was large and had a gun.

I rolled over and rubbed my eyes.

"Okay," I said sourly. "There's twelve bucks in my pants and my wrist watch cost twenty-seven fifty. You couldn't get anything on that."

The figure went over to the window and pulled a blind aside an inch and looked down at the street. When he turned again I saw that it was Larry Batzel.

His face was drawn and tired and he needed a shave. He had dinner clothes on still and a dark double-breasted overcoat with a dwarf rose drooping in the lapel.

He sat down and held the gun on his knee for a moment before he put it away, with a puzzled frown, as if he didn't know how it got into his hand.

"You're going to drive me to Berdoo," he said. "I've got to get out of town. They've put the pencil on me."

"Okay," I said. "Tell me about it."

I sat up and felt the carpet with my toes and lit a cigarette. It was a little after five-thirty.

"I jimmied your lock with a piece of celluloid," he said. "You ought to use your night latch once in a while. I wasn't sure which was your flop and I didn't want to rouse the house."

"Try the mailboxes next time," I said. "But go ahead. You're not drunk, are you?"

"I'd like to be, but I've got to get away first. I'm just rattled. I'm not so tough as I used to be. You read about the O'Mara disappearance of course."

"Yeah."

"Listen, anyway. If I keep talking I won't blow up. I don't think I'm spotted here."

"One drink won't hurt either of us," I said. "The Scotch is on the table there."

He poured a couple of drinks quickly and handed me one. I put on a bathrobe and slippers. The glass rattled against his teeth when he drank.

He put his empty glass down and held his hands tight together.

"I used to know Dud O'Mara pretty well. We used to run stuff together down from Hueneme Point. We even carried the torch for the same girl. She's married to Joe Mesarvey now. Dud married five million dollars. He married General Dade Winslow's rickety-rackety divorcée daughter."

"I know all that," I said.

"Yeah. Just listen. She picked him out of a speak, just like I'd pick up a cafeteria tray. But he didn't like the life. I guess he used to see Mona. He got wise Joe Mesarvey and Lash Yeager had a hot car racket on the side. They knocked him off."

"The hell they did," I said. "Have another drink."

"No. Just listen. There's just two points. The night O'Mara pulled down the curtain—no, the night the papers got it —Mona Mesarvey disappeared too. Only she didn't. They hid her out in a shack a couple of miles beyond Realito in the orange belt. Next door to a garage run by a heel named Art Huck, a hot car drop. I found out. I trailed Joe there."

"What made it your business?" I asked.

"I'm still soft on her. I'm telling you this because you were pretty swell to me once. You can make something of it after I blow. They hid her out there so it would look as if Dud had blown with her. Naturally the cops were not too dumb to see Joe after the disappearance. But they didn't find Mona. They have a system on disappearances and they play the system."

He got up and went over to the window again, looked through the side of the blind.

"There's a blue sedan down there I think I've seen before," he said. "But maybe not. There's a lot like it."

He sat down again. I didn't speak.

"This place beyond Realito is on the first side road north from the Foothill Boulevard. You can't miss it. It stands all alone, the garage and the house next door. There's an old cyanide plant up above there. I'm telling you this—"

"That's point one," I said. "What was the second point?"

"The punk that used to drive for Lash Yeager lit out a couple of weeks back and went East. I lent him fifty bucks.

He was broke. He told me Yeager was out to the Winslow estate the night Dud O'Mara disappeared."

I stared at him. "It's interesting, Larry. But not enough to break eggs over. After all we do have a police department."

"Yeah. Add this. I got drunk last night and told Yeager what I knew. Then I quit the job at the Dardanella. So somebody shot at me outside where I live when I got home. I've been on the dodge ever since. Now, will you drive me to Berdoo?"

I stood up. It was May but I felt cold. Larry Batzel looked cold, even with his overcoat on.

"Absolutely," I said. "But take it easy. Later will be much safer than now. Have another drink. You don't *know* they knocked O'Mara off."

"If he found out about the hot car racket, with Mona married to Joe Mesarvey, they'd have to knock him off. He was that kind of guy."

I stood up and went towards the bathroom. Larry went over to the window again.

"It's still there," he said over his shoulder. "You might get shot at riding with me."

"I'd hate that," I said.

"You're a good sort of heel, Carmady. It's going to rain. I'd hate like hell to be buried in the rain, wouldn't you?"

"You talk too damn much," I said, and went into the bathroom.

It was the last time I ever spoke to him.

II

I HEARD him moving around while I was shaving, but not after I got under the shower, of course. When I came out he was gone. I padded over and looked into the kitchenette. He wasn't in there. I grabbed a bathrobe and peeked

out into the hall. It was empty except for a milkman start-
ing down the back stairs with his wiry tray of bottles,
and the fresh folded papers leaning against the shut doors.

"Hey," I called out to the milkman, "did a guy just come
out of here and go by you?"

He looked back at me from the corner of the wall and
opened his mouth to answer. He was a nice-looking boy
with fine large white teeth. I remember his teeth well,
because I was looking at them when I heard the shots.

They were not very near or very far. Out back of the
apartment house, by the garages, or in the alley, I thought.
There were two quick, hard shots and then the riveting
machine. A burst of five or six, all a good chopper should
ever need. Then the roar of the car going away.

The milkman shut his mouth as if a winch controlled it.
His eyes were huge and empty looking at me. Then he very
carefully set his bottles down on the top step and leaned
against the wall.

"That sounded like shots," he said.

All this took a couple of seconds and felt like half an hour.
I went back into my place and threw clothes on, grabbed
odds and ends off the bureau, barged out into the hall. It
was still empty, even of the milkman. A siren was dying
somewhere near. A bald head with a hangover under it
poked out of a door and made a snuffling noise.

I went down the back stairs.

There were two or three people out in the lower hall.
I went out back. The garages were in two rows facing each
other across a cement space, then two more at the end,
leaving a space to go out to the alley. A couple of kids were
coming over a fence three houses away.

Larry Batzel lay on his face, with his hat a yard away
from his head, and one hand flung out to within a foot
of a big black automatic. His ankles were crossed, as if
he had spun as he fell. Blood was thick on the side of his
face, on his blond hair, especially on his neck. It was also
thick on the cement yard.

Two radio cops and the milk driver and a man in a
brown sweater and bibless overalls were bending over him.
The man in overalls was our janitor.

I went up to them, about the same time the two kids
from over the fence hit the yard. The milk driver looked

at me with a queer, strained expression. One of the cops straightened up and said: "Either of you guys know him? He's still got half his face."

He wasn't talking to me. The milk driver shook his head and kept on looking at me from the corner of his eyes. The janitor said: "He ain't a tenant here. He might of been a visitor. Kind of early for visitors, though, ain't it?"

"He's got party clothes on. You know your flophouse better'n I do," the cop said heavily. He got out a notebook.

The other cop straightened up too and shook his head and went towards the house, with the janitor trotting beside him.

The cop with the notebook jerked a thumb at me and said harshly: "You was here first after these two guys. Anything from you?"

I looked at the milkman. Larry Batzel wouldn't care, and a man has a living to earn. It wasn't a story for a prowl car anyway.

"I just heard the shots and came running," I said.

The cop took that for an answer. The milk driver looked up at the lowering gray sky and said nothing.

After a while I got back into my apartment and finished my dressing. When I picked my hat up off the window table by the Scotch bottle there was a small rosebud lying on a piece of scrawled paper.

The note said: "You're a good guy, but I think I'll go it alone. Give the rose to Mona, if you ever should get a chance. Larry."

I put those things in my wallet, and braced myself with a drink.

III

ABOUT three o'clock that afternoon I stood in the main hallway of the Winslow place and waited for the butler to come
back. I had spent most of the day not going near my
office or apartment, and not meeting any homicide men.
It was only a question of time until I had to come
through, but I wanted to see General Dade Winslow first.
He was hard to see.

Oil paintings hung all around me, mostly portraits. There
were a couple of statues and several suits of time-darkened
armor on pedestals of dark wood. High over the huge marble
fireplace hung two bullet-torn—or moth-eaten—cavalry pen-
nants crossed in a glass case, and below them the painted
likeness of a thin, spry-looking man with a black beard
and mustachios and full regimentals of about the time of
the Mexican War. This might be General Dade Winslow's
father. The general himself, though pretty ancient, couldn't
be quite that old.

Then the butler came back and said General Winslow was
in the orchid house and would I follow him, please.

We went out of the french doors at the back and
across the lawns to a big glass pavilion well beyond the
garages. The butler opened the door into a sort of vestibule
and shut it when I was inside, and it was already hot. Then
he opened the inner door and it was really hot.

The air steamed. The walls and ceiling of the green-
house dripped. In the half light enormous tropical plants
spread their blooms and branches all over the place, and
the smell of them was almost as overpowering as the smell
of boiling alcohol.

The butler, who was old and thin and very straight and
white-haired, held branches of the plants back for me to
pass, and we came to an opening in the middle of the place.
A large reddish Turkish rug was spread down on the hex-

agonal flagstones. In the middle of the rug, in a wheel chair, a very old man sat with a traveling rug around his body and watched us come.

Nothing lived in his face but the eyes. Black eyes, deepset, shining, untouchable. The rest of his face was the leaden mask of death, sunken temples, a sharp nose, outward-turning ear lobes, a mouth that was a thin white slit. He was wrapped partly in a reddish and very shabby bathrobe and partly in the rug. His hands had purple fingernails and were clasped loosely, motionless on the rug. He had a few scattered wisps of white hair on his skull.

The butler said: "This is Mr. Carmady, General."

The old man stared at me. After a while a sharp, shrewish voice said: "Place a chair for Mr. Carmady."

The butler dragged a wicker chair out and I sat down. I put my hat on the floor. The butler picked it up.

"Brandy," the general said. "How do you like your brandy, sir?"

"Any way at all," I said.

He snorted. The butler went away. The general stared at me with his unblinking eyes. He snorted again.

"I always take champagne with mine," he said. "A third of a glass of brandy under the champagne, and the champagne as cold as Valley Forge. Colder, if you can get it colder."

A noise that might have been a chuckle came out of him.

"Not that I was at Valley Forge," he said. "Not quite that bad. You may smoke, sir."

I thanked him and said I was tired of smoking for a while. I got a handkerchief out and mopped my face.

"Take your coat off, sir. Dud always did. Orchids require heat, Mr. Carmady—like sick old men."

I took my coat off, a raincoat I had brought along. It looked like rain. Larry Batzel had said it was going to rain.

"Dud is my son-in-law. Dudley O'Mara. I believe you had something to tell me about him."

"Just hearsay," I said. "I wouldn't want to go into it, unless I had your O.K., General Winslow."

The basilisk eyes stared at me. "You are a private detective. You want to be paid, I suppose."

"I'm in that line of business," I said. "But that doesn't mean I have to be paid for every breath I draw. It's just something I heard. You might like to pass it on yourself to the Missing Persons Bureau."

"I see," he said quietly. "A scandal of some sort."

The butler came back before I could answer. He wheeled a tea wagon in through the jungle, set it at my elbow and mixed me a brandy and soda. He went away.

I sipped the drink. "It seems there was a girl," I said. "He knew her before he knew your daughter. She's married to a racketeer now. It seems—"

"I've heard all that," he said. "I don't give a damn. What I want to know is where he is and if he's all right. If he's happy."

I stared at him popeyed. After a moment I said weakly: "Maybe I could find the girl, or the boys downtown could, with what I could tell them."

He plucked at the edge of his rug and moved his head about an inch. I think he was nodding. Then he said very slowly: "Probably I'm talking too much for my health, but I want to make something clear. I'm a cripple. I have two ruined legs and half my lower belly. I don't eat much or sleep much. I'm a bore to myself and a damn nuisance to everybody else. So I miss Dud. He used to spend a lot of time with me. Why, God only knows."

"Well—" I began.

"Shut up. You're a young man to me, so I can be rude to you. Dud left without saying goodbye to me. That wasn't like him. He drove his car away one evening and nobody has heard from him since. If he got tired of my fool daughter and her brat, if he wanted some other woman, that's all right. He got a brainstorm and left without saying goodbye to me, and now he's sorry. That's why I don't hear from him. Find him and tell him I understand. That's all—unless he needs money. If he does, he can have all he wants."

His leaden cheeks almost had a pink tinge now. His black eyes were brighter, if possible. He leaned back very slowly and closed his eyes.

I drank a lot of my drink in one long swallow. I said: "Suppose he's in a jam. Say, on account of the girl's husband. This Joe Mesarvey."

He opened his eyes and winked. "Not an O'Mara," he said. "It's the other fellow would be in a jam."

"Okay. Shall I just pass on to the Bureau where I heard this girl was?"

"Certainly not. They've done nothing. Let them go on doing it. Find him yourself. I'll pay you a thousand dollars —even if you only have to walk across the street. Tell him everything is all right here. The old man's doing fine and sends his love. That's all."

I couldn't tell him. Suddenly I couldn't tell him anything Larry Batzel had told me, or what had happened to Larry, or anything about it. I finished my drink and stood up and put my coat back on. I said: "That's too much money for the job, General Winslow. We can talk about that later. Have I your authority to represent you in my own way?"

He pressed a bell on his wheel chair. "Just tell him," he said. "I want to know he's all right and I want him to know I'm all right. That's all—unless he needs money. Now you'll have to excuse me. I'm tired."

He closed his eyes. I went back through the jungle and the butler met me at the door with my hat.

I breathed in some cool air and said: "The general wants me to see Mrs. O'Mara."

IV

THIS room had a white carpet from wall to wall. Ivory drapes of immense height lay tumbled casually on the white carpet inside the many windows. The windows stared towards the dark foothills, and the air beyond the glass was dark too. It hadn't started to rain yet, but there was a feeling of pressure in the atmosphere.

Mrs. O'Mara was stretched out on a white chaise longue with both her slippers off and her feet in the net stockings they don't wear any more. She was tall and dark, with a sulky mouth. Handsome, but this side of beautiful.

She said: "What in the world can *I* do for you? It's all known. Too damn known. Except that I don't know you, do I?"

"Well, hardly," I said. "I'm just a private copper in a small way of business."

She reached for a glass I hadn't noticed but would have looked for in a moment, on account of her way of talking and the fact she had her slippers off. She drank languidly, flashing a ring.

"I met him in a speakeasy," she said with a sharp laugh. "A very handsome bootlegger, with thick curly hair and an Irish grin. So I married him. Out of boredom. As for him, the bootlegging business was even then uncertain—if there were no other attractions."

She waited for me to say there were, but not as if she cared a lot whether I came through. I just said: "You didn't see him leave on the day he disappeared?"

"No. I seldom saw him leave, or come back. It was like that." She drank some more of her drink.

"Huh," I grunted. "But, of course, you didn't quarrel." They never do.

"There are so many ways of quarreling, Mr. Carmady."

"Yeah. I like your saying that. Of course you knew about the girl."

"I'm glad I'm being properly frank to an old family detective. Yes, I knew about the girl." She curled a tendril of inky hair behind her ear.

"Did you know about her before he disappeared?" I asked politely.

"Certainly."

"How?"

"You're pretty direct, aren't you? Connections, as they say. I'm an old speak fancier. Or didn't you know that?"

"Did you know the bunch at the Dardanella?"

"I've been there." She didn't look startled, or even surprised. "In fact I practically lived there for a week. That's where I met Dudley O'Mara."

"Yeah. Your father married pretty late in life, didn't he?"

I watched color fade in her cheeks. I wanted her mad, but there was nothing doing. She smiled and the color came back and she rang a push bell on a cord down in the swansdown cushions of the chaise longue.

"Very late," she said, "if it's any of your business."

"It's not," I said.

A coy-looking maid came in and mixed a couple of drinks at a side table. She gave one to Mrs. O'Mara, put one down beside me. She went away again, showing a nice pair of legs under a short skirt.

Mrs. O'Mara watched the door shut and then said: "The whole thing has got Father into a mood. I wish Dud would wire or write or something."

I said slowly: "He's an old, old man, crippled, half buried already. One thin thread of interest held him to life. The thread snapped and nobody gives a damn. He tries to act as if he didn't give a damn himself. I don't call that a mood. I call that a pretty swell display of intestinal fortitude."

"Gallant," she said, and her eyes were daggers. "But you haven't touched your drink."

"I have to go," I said. "Thanks all the same."

She held a slim, tinted hand out and I went over and touched it. The thunder burst suddenly behind the hills and she jumped. A gust of air shook the windows.

I went down a tiled staircase to the hallway and the butler appeared out of a shadow and opened the door for me.

I looked down a succession of terraces decorated with flower beds and imported trees. At the bottom a high metal railing with gilded spearheads and a six-foot hedge inside. A sunken driveway crawled down to the main gates and a lodge inside them.

Beyond the estate the hill sloped down to the city and the old oil wells of La Brea, now partly a park, partly a deserted stretch of fenced-in wild land. Some of the wooden derricks still stood. These had made the wealth of the Winslow family and then the family had run away from them up the hill, far enough to get away from the smell of the sumps, not too far for them to look out of the front windows and see what made them rich.

I walked down brick steps between the terraced lawns. On one of them a dark-haired, pale-faced kid of ten or eleven was throwing darts at a target hung on a tree. I went along near him.

"You young O'Mara?" I asked.

He leaned against a stone bench with four darts in his hand and looked at me with cold, slaty eyes, old eyes.

"I'm Dade Winslow Trevillyan," he said grimly.

"Oh, then Dudley O'Mara's not your dad."

"Of course not." His voice was full of scorn. "Who are you?"

"I'm a detective. I'm going to find your—I mean, Mr. O'Mara."

That didn't bring us any closer. Detectives were nothing to him. The thunder was tumbling about in the hills like a bunch of elephants playing tag. I had another idea.

"Bet you can't put four out of five into the gold at thirty feet."

He livened up sharply. "With these?"

"Uh-huh."

"How much you bet?" he snapped.

"Oh, a dollar."

He ran to the target and cleaned darts off it, came back and took a stance by the bench.

"That's not thirty feet," I said.

He gave me a sour look and went a few feet behind the bench. I grinned, then I stopped grinning.

His small hand darted so swiftly I could hardly follow it. Five darts hung in the gold center of the target in less than that made seconds. He stared at me triumphantly.

"Gosh, you're pretty good, Master Trevillyan," I grunted, and got my dollar out.

His small hand snapped at it like a trout taking the fly. He had it out of sight like a flash.

"That's nothing," he chuckled. "You ought to see me on our target range back of the garages. Want to go over there and bet some more?"

I looked back up the hill and saw part of a low white building backed up to a bank.

"Well, not today," I said. "Next time I visit here maybe. So Dud O'Mara is not your dad. If I find him anyway, will it be all right with you?"

He shrugged his thin, sharp shoulders in a maroon sweater. "Sure. But what can you do the police can't do?"

"It's a thought," I said, and left him.

I went on down the brick walk to the bottom of the lawns and along inside the hedge towards the gatehouse. I could see glimpses of the street through the hedge. When I was halfway to the lodge I saw the blue sedan outside. It was a small neat car, low-slung, very clean, lighter than a police car, but about the same size. Over beyond it I could see my roadster waiting under the pepper tree.

I stood looking at the sedan through the hedge. I could see the drift of somebody's cigarette smoke against the windshield inside the car. I turned my back to the lodge and looked up the hill. The Trevillyan kid had gone somewhere out of sight, to salt his dollar down maybe, though a dollar shouldn't have meant much to him.

I bent over and unsheathed the 7.65 Luger I was wearing that day and stuck it nose-down inside my left sock, inside my shoe. I could walk that way, if I didn't walk too fast. I went on to the gates.

They kept them locked and nobody got in without identification from the house. The lodge keeper, a big husky with a gun under his arm, came out and let me through a small postern at the side of the gates. I stood talking to him through the bars for a minute, watching the sedan.

It looked all right. There seemed to be two men in it. It was about a hundred feet along in the shadow of the high wall on the other side. It was a very narrow street, without sidewalks. I didn't have far to go to my roadster.

I walked a little stiffly across the dark pavement and got in, grabbed quickly down into a small compartment in the front part of the seat where I kept a spare gun. It was a police Colt. I slid it inside my under-arm holster and started the car.

I eased the brake off and pulled away. Suddenly the rain let go in big splashing drops and the sky was as black as Carrie Nation's bonnet. Not so black but that I saw the sedan wheel away from the curb behind me.

I started the windshield wiper and built up to forty miles an hour in a hurry. I had gone about eight blocks when they gave me the siren. That fooled me. It was a quiet street, deadly quiet. I slowed down and pulled over to the curb. The sedan slid up beside me and I was looking at the black snout of a submachine gun over the sill of the rear door.

Behind it a narrow face with reddened eyes, a fixed mouth. A voice above the sound of the rain and the windshield wiper and the noise of the two motors said: "Get in here with us. Be nice, if you know what I mean."

They were not cops. It didn't matter now. I shut off the ignition, dropped my car keys on the floor and got out on the running board. The man behind the wheel of the sedan didn't look at me. The one behind kicked a door open and slid away along the seat, holding the tommy gun nicely.

I got into the sedan.

"Okay, Louie. The frisk."

The driver came out from under his wheel and got behind me. He got the Colt from under my arm, tapped my hips and pockets, my belt line.

"Clean," he said, and got back into the front of the car.

The man with the tommy reached forward with his left hand and took my Colt from the driver, then lowered the tommy to the floor of the car and draped a brown rug over it. He leaned back in the corner again, smooth and relaxed, holding the Colt on his knee.

"Okay, Louie. Now let's ride."

V

WE rode—idly, gently, the rain drumming on the roof and streaming down the windows on one side. We wound along curving hill streets, among estates that covered acres, whose houses were distant clusters of wet gables beyond blurred trees.

A tang of cigarette smoke floated under my nose and the red-eyed man said: "What did he tell you?"

"Little enough," I said. "That Mona blew town the night the papers got it. Old Winslow knew it already."

"He wouldn't have to dig very deep for that," Red-eyes said. "The buttons didn't. What else?"

"He said he'd been shot at. He wanted me to ride him out

of town. At the last moment he ran off alone. I don't know why."

"Loosen up, peeper," Red-eyes said dryly. "It's your only way out."

"That's all there is," I said, and looked out of the window at the driving rain.

"You on the case for the old guy?"

"No. He's tight."

Red-eyes laughed. The gun in my shoe felt heavy and unsteady, and very far away. I said: "That might be all there is to know about O'Mara."

The man in the front seat turned his head a little and growled: "Where the hell did you say that street was?"

"Top of Beverly Glen, stupid. Mulholland Drive."

"Oh, that. Jeeze, that ain't paved worth a damn."

"We'll pave it with the peeper," Red-eyes said.

The estates thinned out and scrub oak took possession of the hillsides.

"You ain't a bad guy," Red-eyes said. "You're just tight, like the old man. Don't you get the idea? We want to know *everything* he said, so we'll know whether we got to blot you or no."

"Go to hell," I said. "You wouldn't believe me anyway."

"Try us. This is just a job to us. We just do it and pass on."

"It must be nice work," I said. "While it lasts."

"You'll crack wise once too often, guy."

"I did—long ago, while you were still in Reform School. I'm still getting myself disliked."

Red-eyes laughed again. There seemed to be very little bluster about him.

"Far as we know you're clean with the law. Didn't make no cracks this morning. That right?"

"If I say yes, you can blot me right now. Okay."

"How about a grand pin money and forget the whole thing?"

"You wouldn't believe that either."

"Yeah, we would. Here's the idea. We do the job and pass on. We're an organization. But you live here, you got goodwill and a business. You'd play ball."

"Sure," I said. "I'd play ball."

"We don't," Red-eyes said softly, "never knock off a legit. Bad for the trade."

He leaned back in the corner, the gun on his right knee, and reached into an inner pocket. He spread a large tan wallet on his knee and fished two bills out of it, slid them folded along the seat. The wallet went back into his pocket.

"Yours," he said gravely. "You won't last twenty-four hours if you slip your cable."

I picked the bills up. Two five hundreds. I tucked them in my vest. "Right," I said. "I wouldn't be a legit any more then, would I?"

"Think that over, dick."

We grinned at each other, a couple of nice lads getting along in a harsh, unfriendly world. Then Red-eyes turned his head sharply.

"Okay, Louie. Forget the Mulholland stuff. Pull up."

The car was halfway up a long bleak twist of hill. The rain drove in gray curtains down the slope. There was no ceiling, no horizon. I could see a quarter of a mile and I could see nothing outside our car that lived.

The driver edged over to the side of the bank and shut his motor off. He lit a cigarette and draped an arm on the back seat.

He smiled at me. He had a nice smile—like an alligator.

"We'll have a drink on it," Red-eyes said. "I wish I could make me a grand that easy. Just tyin' my nose to my chin."

"You ain't got no chin," Louie said, and went on smiling.

Red-eyes put the Colt down on the seat and drew a flat half-pint out of his side pocket. It looked like good stuff, green stamp, bottled in bond. He unscrewed the top with his teeth, sniffed at the liquor and smacked his lips.

"No Crow McGee in this," he said. "This is the company spread. Tilt her."

He reached along the seat and gave me the bottle. I could have had his wrist, but there was Louie, and I was too far from my ankle.

I breathed shallowly from the top of my lungs and held the bottle near my lips, sniffed carefully. Behind the charred smell of the bourbon there was something else, very faint, a fruity odor that would have meant nothing to me in another place. Suddenly and for no reason at all I remembered something Larry Batzel had said, something like: "East of

Realito, towards the mountains, near the old cyanide plant."
Cyanide. That was the word.

There was a swift tightness in my temples as I put the
bottle to my mouth. I could feel my skin crawling, and the
air was suddenly cold on it. I held the bottle high up around
the liquor level and took a long gurgling drag at it. Very
hearty and relaxing. About half a teaspoonful went into my
mouth and none of that stayed there.

I coughed sharply and lurched forward gagging. Red-eyes
laughed.

"Don't say you're sick from just one drink, pal."

I dropped the bottle and sagged far down in the seat, gagging violently. My legs slid way to the left, the left one
underneath. I sprawled down on top of them, my arms
limp. I had the gun.

I shot him under my left arm, almost without looking.
He never touched the Colt except to knock it off the seat.
The one shot was enough. I heard him lurch. I snapped
a shot upward towards where Louie would be.

Louie wasn't there. He was down behind the front seat.
He was silent. The whole car, the whole landscape was silent. Even the rain seemed for a moment to be utterly silent
rain.

I still didn't have time to look at Red-eyes, but he wasn't
doing anything. I dropped the Luger and yanked the tommy gun out from under the rug, got my left hand on the
front grip, got it set against my shoulder low down. Louie
hadn't made a sound.

"Listen, Louie," I said softly, "I've got the stutter gun.
How's about it?"

A shot came through the seat, a shot that Louie knew
wasn't going to do any good. It starred a frame of unbreak-
able glass. There was more silence. Louie said thickly: "I
got a pineapple here. Want it?"

"Pull the pin and hold it," I said. "It will take care of
both of us."

"Hell!" Louie said violently. "Is he croaked? I ain't got
no pineapple."

I looked at Red-eyes then. He looked very comfortable in
the corner of the seat, leaning back. He seemed to have
three eyes, one of them redder even than the other two.

For under-arm shooting that was something to be almost bashful about. It was too good.

"Yeah, Louie, he's croaked," I said. "How do we get together?"

I could hear his hard breathing now, and the rain had stopped being silent. "Get out of the heap," he growled. "I'll blow."

"You get out, Louie. I'll blow."

"Jeeze, I can't walk home from here, pal."

"You won't have to, Louie. I'll send a car for you."

"Jeeze, I ain't done nothing. All I done was drive."

"Then reckless driving will be the charge, Louie. You can fix that—you and your organization. Get out before I uncork this popgun."

A door latch clicked and feet thumped on the running board, then on the roadway. I straightened up suddenly with the chopper. Louie was in the road in the rain, his hands empty and the alligator smile still on his face.

I got out past the dead man's neatly shod feet, got my Colt and the Luger off the floor, laid the heavy twelve-pound tommy gun back on the car floor. I got handcuffs off my hip, motioned to Louie. He turned around sulkily and put his hands behind him.

"You got nothing on me," he complained. "I got protection."

I clicked the cuffs on him and went over him for guns, much more carefully than he had gone over me. He had one besides the one he had left in the car.

I dragged Red-eyes out of the car and let him arrange himself on the wet roadway. He began to bleed again, but he was quite dead. Louie eyed him bitterly.

"He was a smart guy," he said. "Different. He liked tricks. Hello, smart guy."

I got my handcuff key out and unlocked one cuff, dragged it down and locked it to the dead man's lifted wrist.

Louie's eyes got round and horrified and at last his smile went away.

"Jeeze," he whined. "Holy—! Jeeze. You ain't going to leave me like this, pal?"

"Goodbye, Louie," I said. "That was a friend of mine you cut down this morning."

"Holy—!" Louie whined.

I got into the sedan and started it, drove on to a place where I could turn, drove back down the hill past him. He stood stiffly as a scorched tree, his face as white as snow, with the dead man at his feet, one linked hand reaching up to Louie's hand. There was the horror of a thousand nightmares in his eyes.

I left him there in the rain.

It was getting dark early. I left the sedan a couple of blocks from my own car and locked it up, put the keys in the oil strainer. I walked back to my roadster and drove downtown.

I called the homicide detail from a phone booth, asked for a man named Grinnell, told him quickly what had happened and where to find Louie and the sedan. I told him I thought they were the thugs that machine-gunned Larry Batzel. I didn't tell him anything about Dud O'Mara.

"Nice work," Grinnell said in a queer voice. "But you better come in fast. There's a tag out for you, account of what some milk driver phoned in an hour ago."

"I'm all in," I said. "I've got to eat. Keep me off the air and I'll come in after a while."

"You better come in, boy. I'm sorry, but you better."

"Well, okay," I said.

I hung up and left the neighborhood without hanging around. I had to break it now. I had to, or get broken myself.

I had a meal down near the Plaza and started for Realito.

VI

At about eight o'clock two yellow vapor lamps glowed high up in the rain and a dim stencil sign strung across the highway read: "Welcome to Realito."

Frame houses on the main street, a sudden knot of stores, the lights of the corner drugstore behind fogged glass, a flying-cluster of cars in front of a tiny movie palace, and a dark bank on another corner, with a knot of men standing in front of it in the rain. That was Realito. I went on. Empty fields closed in again.

This was past the orange country; nothing but the empty fields and the crouched foothills, and the rain.

It was a smart mile, more like three, before I spotted a side road and a faint light on it, as if from behind drawn blinds in a house. Just at that moment my left front tire let go with an angry hiss. That was cute. Then the right rear let go the same way.

I stopped almost exactly at the intersection. Very cute indeed. I got out, turned my raincoat up a little higher, unshipped a flash, and looked at a flock of heavy galvanized tacks with heads as big as dimes. The flat shiny butt of one of them blinked at me from my tire.

Two flats and one spare. I tucked my chin down and started towards the faint light up the side road.

It was the place all right. The light came from the tilted skylight on the garage roof. Big double doors in front were shut tight, but light showed at the cracks, strong white light. I tossed the beam of the flash up and read: "Art Huck— Auto Repairs and Refinishing."

Beyond the garage a house sat back from the muddy road behind a thin clump of trees. That had light too. I saw a small buttoned-up coupé in front of the wooden porch.

The first thing was the tires, if it could be worked, and they didn't know me. It was a wet night for walking.

I snapped the flash out and rapped on the doors with it. The light inside went out. I stood there licking rain off my upper lip, the flash in my left hand, my right inside my coat. I had the Luger back under my arm again.

A voice spoke through the door, and didn't sound pleased. "What you want? Who are you?"

"Open up," I said. "I've got two flat tires on the highway and only one spare. I need help."

"We're closed up, mister. Realito's a mile west of here."

I started to kick the door. There was swearing inside, then another, much softer voice.

"A wise guy, huh? Open up, Art."

A bolt squealed and half of the door sagged inward. I snapped the flash again and it hit a gaunt face. Then an arm swept and knocked it out of my hand. A gun had just peeked at me from the flailing hand.

I dropped low, felt around for the flash and was still. I just didn't pull a gun.

"Kill the spot, mister. Guys get hurt that way."

The flash was burning down in the mud. I snapped it off, stood up with it. Light went on inside the garage, outlined a tall man in coveralls. He backed inward and his gun held on me.

"Come on in and shut the door."

I did that. "Tacks all over the end of your street," I said. "I thought you wanted the business."

"Ain't you got any sense? A bank job was pulled at Realito this afternoon."

"I'm a stranger here," I said, remembering the knot of men in front of the bank in the rain.

"Okay, okay. Well there was and the punks are hid out somewhere in the hills, they say. You stepped on their tacks, huh?"

"So it seems." I looked at the other man in the garage.

He was short, heavy-set, with a cool brown face and cool brown eyes. He wore a belted raincoat of brown leather. His brown hat had the usual rakish tilt and was dry. His hands were in his pockets and he looked bored.

There was a hot sweetish smell of pyroxylin paint on the air. A big sedan over in the corner had a paint gun lying on its fender. It was a Buick, almost new. It didn't need the paint it was getting.

The man in coveralls tucked his gun out of sight through a flap in the side of his clothes. He looked at the brown man. The brown man looked at me and said gently: "Where you from, stranger?"

"Seattle," I said.

"Going west—to the big city?" He had a soft voice, soft and dry, like the rustle of well-worn leather.

"Yes. How far is it?"

"About forty miles. Seems farther in this weather. Come the long way, didn't you? By Tahoe and Lone Pine?"

"Not Tahoe," I said. "Reno and Carson City."

"Still the long way." A fleeting smile touched the brown lips.

"Take a jack and get his flats, Art."

"Now, listen, Lash—" the man in the coveralls growled, and stopped as though his throat had been cut from ear to ear.

I could have sworn that he shivered. There was dead silence. The brown man didn't move a muscle. Something looked out of his eyes, and then his eyes lowered, almost shyly. His voice was the same soft, dry rustle of sound.

"Take two jacks, Art. He's got two flats."

The gaunt man swallowed. Then he went over to a corner and put a coat on, and a cap. He grabbed up a socket wrench and a handjack and wheeled a dolly jack over to the doors.

"Back on the highway, is it?" he asked me almost tenderly.

"Yeah. You can use the spare for one spot, if you're busy," I said.

"He's not busy," the brown man said and looked at his fingernails.

Art went out with his tools. The door shut again. I looked at the Buick. I didn't look at Lash Yeager. I knew it was Lash Yeager. There wouldn't be two men called Lash that came to that garage. I didn't look at him because I would be looking across the sprawled body of Larry Batzel, and it would show in my face. For a moment, anyway.

He glanced towards the Buick himself. "Just a panel job to start with," he drawled. "But the guy that owns it has dough and his driver needed a few bucks. You know the racket."

"Sure," I said.

The minutes passed on tiptoe. Long, sluggish minutes. Then feet crunched outside and the door was pushed open. The light hit pencils of rain and made silver wires of them. Art trundled two muddy flats in sulkily, kicked the door shut, let one of the flats fall on its side. The rain and fresh air had given him his nerve back. He looked at me savagely.

"Seattle," he snarled. "Seattle, my eye!"

The brown man lit a cigarette as if he hadn't heard. Art peeled his coat off and yanked my tire up on a rim spreader, tore it loose viciously, had the tube out and cold-patched in nothing flat. He strode scowling over to the wall near me and grabbed an air hose, let enough air into the tube to give it body, and hefted it in both hands to dip it in a washtub of water.

I was a sap, but their teamwork was very good. Neither had looked at the other since Art came back with my tires.

Art tossed the air-stiffened tube up casually, caught it with both hands wide, looked it over sourly beside the washtub of water, took one short easy step and slammed it down over my head and shoulders.

He jumped behind me in a flash, leaned his weight down on the rubber, dragged it tight against my chest and arms. I could move my hands, but I couldn't get near my gun.

The brown man brought his right hand out of his pocket and tossed a wrapped cylinder of nickels up and down on his palm as he stepped lithely across the floor.

I heaved back hard, then suddenly threw all my weight forward. Just as suddenly Art let go of the tube, and kneed me from behind.

I sprawled, but I never knew when I reached the floor. The fist with the weighted tube of nickels met me in midflight. Perfectly timed, perfectly weighted, and with my own weight to help it out.

I went out like a puff of dust in a draft.

VII

IT seemed there was a woman and she was sitting beside a lamp. Light shone on my face, so I shut my eyes again and tried to look at her through my eyelashes. She was so platinumed that her head shone like a silver fruit bowl.

She wore a green traveling dress with a mannish cut to it and a broad white collar falling over the lapels. A sharp-angled glossy bag stood at her feet. She was smoking, and a drink was tall and pale at her elbow.

I opened my eye wider and said: "Hello there."

Her eyes were the eyes I remembered, outside Sardi's in a secondhand Rolls-Royce. Very blue eyes, very soft and lovely. Not the eyes of a hustler around the fast money boys.

"How do you feel?" Her voice was soft and lovely too.

"Great," I said. "Except somebody built a filling station on my jaw."

"What did you expect, Mr. Carmady? Orchids?"

"So you know my name."

"You slept well. They had plenty of time to go through your pockets. They did everything but embalm you."

"Right," I said.

I could move a little, not very much. My wrists were behind my back, handcuffed. There was a little poetic justice in that. From the cuffs a cord ran to my ankles, and tied them, and then dropped down out of sight over the end of the davenport and was tied somewhere else. I was almost as helpless as if I had been screwed up in a coffin.

"What time is it?"

She looked sideways down at her wrist, beyond the spiral of her cigarette smoke.

"Ten-seventeen. Got a date?"

"Is this the house next the garage? Where are the boys—digging a grave?"

"You wouldn't care, Carmady. They'll be back."

"Unless you have the key to these bracelets you might spare me a little of that drink."

She rose all in one piece and came over to me, with the tall amber glass in her hand. She bent over me. Her breath was delicate. I gulped from the glass craning my neck up.

"I hope they don't hurt you," she said distantly, stepping back. "I hate killing."

"And you Joe Mesarvey's wife. Shame on you. Gimme some more of the hooch."

She gave me some more. Blood began to move in my stiffened body.

"I kind of like you," she said. "Even if your face does look like a collision mat."

"Make the most of it," I said. "It won't last long even this good."

She looked around swiftly and seemed to listen. One of the two doors was ajar. She looked towards that. Her face seemed pale. But the sounds were only the rain.

She sat down by the lamp again.

"Why did you come here and stick your neck out?" she asked slowly, looking at the floor.

The carpet was made of red and tan squares. There were bright green pine trees on the wallpaper and the curtains were blue. The furniture, what I could see of it, looked as if it came from one of those places that advertise on bus benches.

"I had a rose for you," I said. "From Larry Batzel."

She lifted something off the table and twirled it slowly, the dwarf rose he had left for her.

"I got it," she said quietly. "There was a note, but they didn't show me that. Was it for me?"

"No, for me. He left it on my table before he went out and got shot."

Her face fell apart like something you see in a nightmare. Her mouth and eyes were black hollows. She didn't make a sound. And after a moment her face settled back into the same calmly beautiful lines.

"They didn't tell me that either," she said softly.

"He got shot," I said carefully, "because he found out what Joe and Lash Yeager did to Dud O'Mara. Bumped him off."

That one didn't faze her at all. "Joe didn't do anything to Dud O'Mara," she said quietly. "I haven't seen Dud in two years. That was just newspaper hooey, about me seeing him."

"It wasn't in the papers," I said.

"Well, it was hooey wherever it was. Joe is in Chicago. He went yesterday by plane to sell out. If the deal goes through, Lash and I are to follow him. Joe is no killer."

I stared at her.

Her eyes got haunted again. "Is Larry—is he—?"

"He's dead," I said. "It was a professional job, with a tommy gun. I didn't mean they did it personally."

She took hold of her lip and held it for a moment tight between her teeth. I could hear her slow, hard breathing. She jammed her cigarette in an ashtray and stood up.

"Joe didn't do it!" she stormed. "I know damn well he didn't. He—" She stopped cold, glared at me, touched her hair, then suddenly yanked it off. It was a wig. Underneath her own hair was short like a boy's, and streaked yellow and whitish brown, with darker tints at the roots. It couldn't make her ugly.

I managed a sort of laugh. "You just came out here to molt, didn't you, Silver-Wig? And I thought they were hiding you out—so it would look as if you had skipped with Dud O'Mara."

She kept on staring at me. As if she hadn't heard a word I said. Then she strode over to a wall mirror and put the wig back on, straightened it, turned and faced me.

"Joe didn't kill anybody," she said again, in a low, tight voice. "He's a heel—but not that kind of heel. He doesn't know anything more about where Dud O'Mara went than I do. And I don't know anything."

"He just got tired of the rich lady and scrammed," I said dully.

She stood near me now, her white fingers down at her sides, shining in the lamplight. Her head above me was almost in shadow. The rain drummed and my jaw felt large and hot and the nerve along the jawbone ached, ached.

"Lash has the only car that was here," she said softly. "Can you walk to Realito, if I cut the ropes?"

"Sure. Then what?"

"I've never been mixed up in a murder. I won't now. I won't ever."

She went out of the room very quickly, and came back with a long kitchen knife and sawed the cord that tied my ankles, pulled it off, cut the place where it was tied to the handcuffs. She stopped once to listen, but it was just the rain again.

I rolled up to a sitting position and stood up. My feet were numb, but that would pass. I could walk. I could run, if I had to.

"Lash has the key of the cuffs," she said dully.

"Let's go," I said. "Got a gun?"

"No. I'm not going. You beat it. He may be back any minute. They were just moving stuff out of the garage."

I went over close to her. "You're going to stay here after turning me loose? Wait for that killer? You're nuts. Come on, Silver-Wig, you're going with me."

"No."

"Suppose," I said, "he did kill O'Mara? Then he also killed Larry. It's got to be that way."

"Joe never killed anybody," she almost snarled at me.

"Well, suppose Yeager did."

"You're lying, Carmady. Just to scare me. Get out. I'm not afraid of Lash Yeager. I'm his boss's wife."

"Joe Mesarvey is a handful of mush," I snarled back. "The only time a girl like you goes for a wrong gee is when he's a handful of mush. Let's drift."

"Get out!" she said hoarsely.

"Okay." I turned away from her and went through the door.

She almost ran past me into the hallway and opened the front door, looked out into the black wetness. She motioned me forward.

"Goodbye," she whispered. "I hope you find Dud. I hope you find who killed Larry. But it wasn't Joe."

I stepped close to her, almost pushed her against the wall with my body.

"You're still crazy, Silver-Wig. Goodbye."

She raised her hands quickly and put them on my face. Cold hands, icy cold. She kissed me swiftly on the mouth with cold lips.

"Beat it, strong guy. I'll be seeing you some more. Maybe in heaven."

I went through the door and down the dark slithery wooden steps of the porch, across gravel to the round grass plot and the clump of thin trees. I came past them to the roadway, went back along it towards Foothill Boulevard. The rain touched my face with fingers of ice that were no colder than her fingers.

The curtained roadster stood just where I had left it, leaned over, the left front axle on the tarred shoulder of the highway. My spare and one stripped rim were thrown in the ditch.

They had probably searched it, but I still hoped. I crawled in backwards and banged my head on the steering post and rolled over to get the manacled hands into my little secret gun pocket. They touched the barrel. It was still there.

I got it out, got myself out of the car, got hold of the gun by the right end and looked it over.

I held it tight against my back to protect it a little from the rain and started back towards the house.

VIII

I WAS halfway there when he came back. His lights turning quickly off the highway almost caught me. I flopped into the ditch and put my nose in the mud and prayed.

The car hummed past. I heard the wet rasp of its tires shouldering the gravel in front of the house. The motor died and lights went off. The door slammed. I didn't hear the house door shut, but I caught a feeble fringe of light through the trees as it opened.

I got up on my feet and went on. I came up beside the car, a small coupé, rather old. The gun was down at my side, pulled around my hip as far as the cuffs would let it come.

The coupé was empty. Water gurgled in the radiator. I listened and heard nothing from the house. No loud voices, no quarrel. Only the heavy bong-bong-bong of the raindrops hitting the elbows at the bottom of rain gutters.

Yeager was in the house. She had let me go and Yeager was in there with her. Probably she wouldn't tell him anything. She would just stand and look at him. She was his boss's wife. That would scare Yeager to death.

He wouldn't stay long, but he wouldn't leave her behind, alive or dead. He would be on his way and take her with him. What happened to her later on was something else.

All I had to do was wait for him to come out. I didn't do it.

I shifted the gun into my left hand and leaned down to scoop up some gravel. I threw it against the front window. It was a weak effort. Very little even reached the glass.

I ran back behind the coupé and got its door open and saw the keys in the ignition lock. I crouched down on the running board, holding on to the door post.

The house had already gone dark, but that was all. There wasn't any sound from it. No soap. Yeager was too cagy.

I reached it with my foot and found the starter, then strained back with one hand and turned the ignition key. The warm motor caught at once, throbbed gently against the pounding rain.

I got back to the ground and slid along to the rear of the car, crouched down.

The sound of the motor got him. He couldn't be left there without a car.

A darkened window slid up an inch, only some shifting of light on the glass showing it moved. Flame spouted from it, the racket of three quick shots. Glass broke in the coupé.

I screamed and let the scream die into a gurgling groan. I was getting good at that sort of thing. I let the groan die in a choked gasp. I was through, finished. He had got me. Nice shooting, Yeager.

Inside the house a man laughed. Then silence again, except for the rain and the quietly throbbing motor of the coupé.

Then the house door inched open. A figure showed in it. She came out on the porch, stiffly, the white showing at her collar, the wig showing a little but not so much. She came down the steps like a wooden woman. I saw Yeager crouched behind her.

She started across the gravel. Her voice said slowly, without any tone at all:

"I can't see a thing, Lash. The windows are all misted."

She jerked a little, as if a gun had prodded her, and came on. Yeager didn't speak. I could see him now past her shoulder, his hat, part of his face. But no kind of a shot for a man with cuffs on his wrists.

She stopped again, and her voice was suddenly horrified.

"He's behind the wheel!" she yelled. "Slumped over!"

He fell for it. He knocked her to one side and started to blast again. More glass jumped around. A bullet hit a tree on my side of the car. A cricket whined somewhere. The motor kept right on humming.

He was low, crouched against the black, his face a grayness without form that seemed to come back very slowly after the glare of the shots. His own fire had blinded him too—for a second. That was enough.

I shot him four times, straining the pulsing Colt against my ribs.

He tried to turn and the gun slipped away from his hand. He half snatched for it in the air, before both his hands suddenly went against his stomach and stayed there. He sat down on the wet gravel and his harsh panting dominated every other sound of the wet night.

I watched him lie down on his side, very slowly, without taking his hands away from his stomach. The panting stopped.

It seemed like an age before Silver-Wig called out to me. Then she was beside me, grabbing my arm.

"Shut the motor off!" I yelled at her. "And get the key of these damn irons out of his pocket."

"You d-darn fool," she babbled. "W-what did you come back for?"

IX

CAPTAIN AL ROOF of the Missing Persons Bureau swung in his chair and looked at the sunny window. This was another day, and the rain had stopped long since.

He said gruffly: "You're making a lot of mistakes, brother. Dud O'Mara just pulled down the curtain. None of those people knocked him off. The Batzel killing had nothing to do with it. They've got Mesarvey in Chicago and he looks clean. The Heeb you anchored to the dead guy don't even know who they were pulling the job for. Our boys asked him enough to be sure of that."

"I'll bet they did," I said. "I've been in the same bucket all night and I couldn't tell them much either."

He looked at me slowly, with large, bleak, tired eyes. "Killing Yeager was all right, I guess. And the chopper. In the circumstances. Besides I'm not homicide. I couldn't link any of that to O'Mara—unless you could."

I could, but I hadn't. Not yet. "No," I said. "I guess not."

I stuffed and lit my pipe. After a sleepless night it tasted better.

"That all that's worrying you?"

"I wondered why you didn't find the girl, at Realito. It couldn't have been very hard—for you."

"We just didn't. We should have. I admit it. We didn't. Anything else?"

I blew smoke across his desk. "I'm looking for O'Mara because the general told me to. It wasn't any use my telling him you would do everything that could be done. He could afford a man with all his time on it. I suppose you resent that."

He wasn't amused. "Not at all, if he wants to waste money. The people that resent you are behind a door marked Homicide Bureau."

He planted his feet with a slap and elbowed his desk.

"O'Mara had fifteen grand in his clothes. That's a lot of jack but O'Mara would be the boy to have it. So he could take it out and have his old pals see him with it. Only they wouldn't think it was fifteen grand of real dough. His wife says it was. Now with any other guy but an ex-legger in the gravy that might indicate an intention to disappear. But not O'Mara. He packed it all the time."

He bit a cigar and put a match to it. He waved a large finger. "See?"

I said I saw.

"Okay. O'Mara had fifteen grand, and a guy that pulls down the curtain can keep it down only so long as his wad lasts. Fifteen grand is a good wad. I might disappear myself, if I had that much. But after it's gone we get him. He cashes a check, lays down a marker, hits a hotel or store for credit, gives a reference, writes a letter or gets one. He's in a new town and he's got a new name, but he's got the same old appetite. He has to get back into the fiscal system one way or another. A guy can't have friends everywhere, and if he had, they wouldn't all stay clammed forever. Would they?"

"No, they wouldn't," I said.

"He went far," Roof said. "But the fifteen grand was all the preparation he made. No baggage, no boat or rail or plane reservation, no taxi or private rental hack to a point out of town. That's all checked. His own car was found a dozen blocks from where he lived. But that means nothing. He knew people who would ferry him several hundred miles and keep quiet about it, even in the face of a reward. Here, but not everywhere. Not new friends."

"But you'll get him," I said.

"When he gets hungry."

"That could take a year or two. General Winslow may not live a year. That is a matter of sentiment, not whether you have an open file when you retire."

"You attend to the sentiment, brother." His eyes moved and bushy reddish eyebrows moved with them. He didn't like me. Nobody did, in the police department, that day.

"I'd like to," I said and stood up. "Maybe I'd go pretty far to attend to that sentiment."

"Sure," Roof said, suddenly thoughtful. "Well, Winslow is a big man. Anything I can do let me know."

"You could find out who had Larry Batzel gunned," I said. "Even if there isn't any connection."

"We'll do that. Glad to," he guffawed and flicked ash all over his desk. "You just knock off the guys who can talk and we'll do the rest. We like to work that way."

"It was self-defense," I growled. "I couldn't help myself."

"Sure. Take the air, brother. I'm busy."

But his large bleak eyes twinkled at me as I went out.

X

THE morning was all blue and gold and the birds in the ornamental trees of the Winslow estate were crazy with song after the rain.

The gatekeeper let me in through the postern and I walked up the driveway and along the top terrace to the huge carved Italian front door. Before I rang the bell I looked down the hill and saw the Trevillyan kid sitting on his stone bench with his head cupped in his hands, staring at nothing.

I went down the brick path to him. "No darts today, son?"

He looked up at me with his lean, slaty, sunken eyes.

"No. Did you find him?"

"Your dad? No, sonny, not yet."

He jerked his head. His nostrils flared angrily. "He's not my dad I told you. And don't talk to me as if I was four years old. My dad he's—he's in Florida or somewhere."

"Well, I haven't found him yet, whoever's dad he is," I said.

"Who smacked your jaw?" he asked, staring at me.

"Oh, a fellow with a roll of nickels in his hand."

"Nickels?"

"Yeah. That's as good as brass knuckles. Try it sometime, but not on me." I grinned.

"You won't find him," he said bitterly, staring at my jaw. "Him, I mean. My mother's husband."

"I bet I do."

"How much you bet?"

"More money than even you've got in your pants."

He kicked viciously at the edge of a red brick in the walk. His voice was still sulky, but more smooth. His eyes speculated.

"Want to bet on something else? C'mon over to the range. I bet you a dollar I can knock down eight out of ten pipes in ten shots."

I looked back towards the house. Nobody seemed impatient to receive me.

"Well," I said, "we'll have to make it snappy. Let's go."

We went along the side of the house under the windows. The orchid green-house showed over the tops of some bushy trees far back. A man in neat whipcord was polishing the chromium on a big car in front of the garages. We went past there to the low white building against the bank.

The boy took a key out and unlocked the door and we went into close air that still held traces of cordite fumes. The boy clicked a spring lock on the door.

"Me first," he snapped.

The place looked something like a small beach shooting gallery. There was a counter with a .22 repeating rifle on it and a long, slim target pistol. Both well oiled but dusty. About thirty feet beyond the counter was a waist-high, solid-looking partition across the building, and behind that a simple layout of clay pipes and ducks and two round white targets marked off with black rings and stained by lead bullets.

The clay pipes ran in an even line across the middle, and there was a big skylight, and a row of hooded overhead lights.

The boy pulled a cord on the wall and a thick canvas blind slid across the skylight. He turned on the hooded lights and then the place really looked like a beach shooting gallery.

He picked up the .22 rifle and loaded it quickly from a cardboard box of shells, .22 shorts.

"A dollar I get eight out of ten pipes?"

"Blast away," I said, and put my money on the counter.

He took aim almost casually, fired too fast, showing off. He missed three pipes. It was pretty fancy shooting at that. He threw the rifle down on the counter.

"Gee, go set up some more. Let's not count that one. I wasn't set."

"You don't aim to lose any money, do you, son? Go set 'em up yourself. It's your range."

His narrow face got angry and his voice got shrill. "You do it! I've got to relax, see. I've got to relax."

I shrugged at him, lifted a flap in the counter and went along the whitewashed side wall, squeezed past the end of the low partition. The boy clicked his reloaded rifle shut behind me.

"Put that down," I growled back at him. "Never touch a gun when there's anyone in front of you."

He put it down, looking hurt.

I bent down and grabbed a handful of clay pipes out of the sawdust in a big wooden box on the floor. I shook the yellow grains of wood off them and started to straighten up.

I stopped with my hat above the barrier, just the top of my hat. I never knew why I stopped. Blind instinct.

The .22 cracked and the lead bullet bonged into the target in front of my head. My hat stirred lazily on my head, as though a blackbird had swooped at it during the nesting season.

A nice kid. He was full of tricks, like Red-eyes. I dropped the pipes and took hold of my hat by the brim, lifted it straight up off my head a few inches. The gun cracked again. Another metallic bong on the target.

I let myself fall heavily to the wooden flooring, among the pipes.

A door opened and shut. That was all. Nothing else. The hard glare from the hooded lights beat down on me. The sun peeked in at the edges of the skylight blind. There were two bright new splashes on the nearest target, and there were four small round holes in my hat, two and two, on each side.

I crawled to the end of the barrier and peeked around it. The boy was gone. I could see the small muzzles of the two guns on the counter.

I stood up and went back along the wall, switched the lights off, turned the knob of the spring lock and went out. The Winslow chauffeur whistled at his polish job around in front of the garages.

I crushed my hat in my hand and went back along the side of the house, looking for the kid. I didn't see him. I rang the front door bell.

I asked for Mrs. O'Mara. I didn't let the butler take my hat.

XI

SHE was in an oyster-white something, with white fur at the cuffs and collar and around the bottom. A breakfast table on wheels was pushed to one side of her chair and she was flicking ashes among the silver.

The coy-looking maid with the nice legs came and took the table out and shut the tall white door. I sat down.

Mrs. O'Mara leaned her head back against a cushion and looked tired. The line of her throat was distant, cold. She stared at me with a cool, hard look, in which there was plenty of dislike.

"You seemed rather human yesterday," she said. "But I see you are just a brute like the rest of them. Just a brutal cop."

"I came to ask you about Lash Yeager," I said.

She didn't even pretend to be amused. "And why should you think of asking me?"

"Well—if you lived a week at the Dardanella Club—" I waved my crunched-together hat.

She looked at her cigarette fixedly. "Well, I did meet him, I believe. I remember the rather unusual name."

"They all have names like that, those animals," I said. "It seems that Larry Batzel—I guess you read in your paper about him too—was a friend of Dud O'Mara's once. I didn't tell you about him yesterday. Maybe that was a mistake."

A pulse began to throb in her throat. She said softly: "I have a suspicion you are about to become very insolent, that I may even have to have you thrown out."

"Not before I've said my piece," I said. "It seems that Mr. Yeager's driver—they have drivers as well as unusual names, those animals—told Larry Batzel that Mr. Yeager was out this way the night O'Mara disappeared."

The old army blood had to be good for something in her. She didn't move a muscle. She just froze solid.

I got up and took the cigarette from between her frozen fingers and killed it in a white jade ashtray. I laid my hat carefully on her white satin knee. I sat down again.

Her eyes moved after a while. They moved down and looked at the hat. Her face flushed very slowly, in two vivid patches over the cheekbones. She fought around with her tongue and lips.

"I know," I said. "It's not much of a hat. I'm not making you a present of it. But just look at the bullet holes in it once."

Her hand became alive and snatched at the hat. Her eyes became flames.

She spread the crown out, looked at the holes, and shuddered.

"Yeager?" she asked, very faintly. It was a wisp of a voice, an old voice.

I said very slowly: "Yeager wouldn't use a .22 target rifle, Mrs. O'Mara."

The flame died in her eyes. They were pools of darkness, much emptier than darkness.

"You're his mother," I said. "What do you want to do about it?"

"Merciful God! Dade! He . . . shot at you!"

"Twice," I said.

"But why? . . . Oh, why?"

"You think I'm a wise guy, Mrs. O'Mara. Just another hard-eyed boy from the other side of the tracks. It would be easy in this spot, if I was. But I'm not that at all, really. Do I have to tell why he shot at me!"

She didn't speak. She nodded slowly. Her face was a mask now.

"I'd say he probably can't help it," I said. "He didn't want me to find his stepfather, for one thing. Then he's a little lad that likes money. That seems small, but it's part of the picture. He almost lost a dollar to me on his shooting. It seems small, but he lives in a small world. Most of all, of course, he's a crazy little sadist with an itchy trigger finger."

"How dare you!" she flared. It didn't mean anything. She forgot it herself instantly.

"How dare I? I do dare. Let's not bother figuring why he shot at *me*. I'm not the first, am I? You wouldn't have known what I was talking about, you wouldn't have assumed he did it on purpose."

She didn't move or speak. I took a deep breath.

"So let's talk about why he shot Dud O'Mara," I said.

If I thought she would yell even this time, I fooled myself. The old man in the orchid house had put more into her than her tallness and her dark hair and her reckless eyes.

She pulled her lips back and tried to lick them, and it made her look like a scared little girl, for a second. The lines of her cheeks sharpened and her hand went up like an artificial hand moved by wires and took hold of the white fur at her throat and pulled it tight and squeezed it until her knuckles looked like bleached bone. Then she just stared at me.

Then my hat slid off her knee on to the floor, without her moving. The sound it made falling was one of the loudest sounds I had ever heard.

"Money," she said in a dry croak. "Of course you want money."

"How much money do I want?"

"Fifteen thousand dollars."

I nodded, stiff-necked as a floorwalker trying to see with his back.

"That would be about right. That would be the established retainer. That would be about what he had in his pockets and what Yeager got for getting rid of him."

"You're too—damned smart," she said horribly. "I could kill you myself and like it."

I tried to grin. "That's right. Smart and without a feeling in the world. It happened something like this. The boy got O'Mara where he got me, by the same simple ruse. I don't think it was a plan. He hated his stepfather, but he wouldn't exactly plan to kill him."

"He hated him," she said.

"So they're in the little shooting gallery and O'Mara is dead on the floor, behind the barrier, out of sight. The shots, of course, meant nothing there. And very little blood, with a head shot, small caliber. So the boy goes out and locks the door and hides. But after a while he has to tell somebody. He has to. He tells you. You're his mother. You're the one to tell."

"Yes," she breathed. "He did just that." Her eyes had stopped hating me.

"You think about calling it an accident, which is okay, except for one thing. The boy's not a normal boy, and you know it. The general knows it, the servants know. There must be other people that know it. And the law, dumb as you think they are, are pretty smart with subnormal types. They get to handle so many of them. And I think he would have talked. I think, after a while, he would even have bragged."

"Go on," she said.

"You wouldn't risk that," I said. "Not for your son and not for the sick old man in the orchid house. You'd do any awful criminal callous thing rather than risk that. You did it. You knew Yeager and you hired him to get rid of the body. That's all—except that hiding the girl, Mona Mesarvey, helped to make it look like a deliberate disappearance."

"He took him away after dark, in Dud's own car," she said hollowly.

I reached down and picked my hat off the floor. "How about the servants?"

"Norris knows. The butler. He'd die on the rack before he told."

"Yeah. Now you know why Larry Batzel was knocked off and why I was taken for a ride, don't you?"

"Blackmail," she said. "It hadn't come yet, but I was waiting for it. I would have paid anything, and he would know that."

"Bit by bit, year by year, there was a quarter of a million in it for him, easy. I don't think Joe Mesarvey was in it at all. I know the girl wasn't."

She didn't say anything. She just kept her eyes on my face.

"Why in hell," I groaned, "didn't you take the guns away from him?"

"He's worse than you think. That would have started something worse. I'm—I'm almost afraid of him myself."

"Take him away," I said. "From here. From the old man. He's young enough to be cured, by the right handling. Take him to Europe. Far away. Take him now. It would kill the general out of hand to know his blood was in that."

She got up draggingly and dragged herself across to the windows. She stood motionless, almost blending into the heavy white drapes. Her hands hung at her sides, very motionless also. After a while she turned and walked past me. When she was behind me she caught her breath and sobbed just once.

"It was very vile. It was the vilest thing I ever heard of. Yet I would do it again. Father would not have done it. He would have spoken right out. It would, as you say, have killed him."

"Take him away," I pounded on. "He's hiding out there now. He thinks he got me. He's hiding somewhere like an animal. Get him. He can't help it."

"I offered you money," she said, still behind me. "That's nasty. I wasn't in love with Dudley O'Mara. That's nasty too. I can't thank you. I don't know what to say."

"Forget it," I said. "I'm just an old workhorse. Put *your* work on the boy."

"I promise. Goodbye, Mr. Carmady."

We didn't shake hands. I went back down the stairs and the butler was at the front door as usual. Nothing in his face but politeness.

"You will not want to see the general today, sir?"

"Not today, Norris."

I didn't see the boy outside. I went through the postern and got into my rented Ford and drove on down the hill, past where the old oil wells were.

Around some of them, not visible from the street, there were still sumps in which waste water lay and festered with a scum of oil on top.

They would be ten or twelve feet deep, maybe more. There would be dark things in them. Perhaps in one of them—

I was glad I had killed Yeager.

On the way back downtown I stopped at a bar and had a couple of drinks. They didn't do me any good.

All they did was make me think of Silver-Wig, and I never saw her again.

THE big guy wasn't any of my business. He never was, then or later, least of all then.

I was over on Central, which is the Harlem of Los Angeles, on one of the "mixed" blocks, where there were still both white and colored establishments. I was looking for a little Greek barber named Tom Aleidis whose wife wanted him to come home and was willing to spend a little money to find him. It was a peaceful job. Tom Aleidis was not a crook.

I saw the big guy standing in front of Shamey's, an all-colored drink and dice second-floor, not too savory. He was looking up at the broken stencils in the electric sign, with a sort of rapt expression, like a hunky immigrant looking at the Statue of Liberty, like a man who had waited a long time and come a long way.

He wasn't just big. He was a giant. He looked seven feet high, and he wore the loudest clothes I ever saw on a really big man.

Pleated maroon pants, a rough grayish coat with white billiard balls for buttons, brown suede shoes with explosions in white kid on them, a brown shirt, a yellow tie, a large red carnation, and a front-door handkerchief the color of the Irish flag. It was neatly arranged in three points, under the red carnation. On Central Avenue, not the quietest dressed street in the world, with that size and that make-up he looked about as unobtrusive as a tarantula on a slice of angel food.

He went over and swung back the doors into Shamey's. The doors didn't stop swinging before they exploded outward again. What sailed out and landed in the gutter and made a high, keening noise, like a wounded rat, was a slick-haired colored youth in a pinchback suit. A "brown," the color of coffee with rather thin cream in it. His face, I mean.

It still wasn't any of my business. I watched the colored boy creep away along the walls. Nothing more happened. So I made my mistake.

I moved along the sidewalk until I could push the swing door myself. Just enough to look in. Just too much.

A hand I could have sat in took hold of my shoulder and hurt and lifted me through the doors and up three steps.

A deep, soft voice said in my ear easily, "Smokes in here, pal. Can you tie that?"

I tried for a little elbow room to get to my sap. I wasn't wearing a gun. The little Greek barber business hadn't seemed to be that sort of job.

He took hold of my shoulder again.

"It's that kind of place," I said quickly.

"Don't say that, pal. Beulah used to work here. Little Beulah."

"Go on up and see for yourself."

He lifted me up three more steps.

"I'm feeling good," he said. "I wouldn't want anybody to bother me. Let's you and me go on up and maybe nibble a drink."

"They won't serve you," I said.

"I ain't seen Beulah in eight years, pal," he said softly, tearing my shoulder to pieces without noticing what he was doing. "She ain't even wrote in six. But she'll have a reason. She used to work here. Let's you and me go on up."

"All right," I said. "I'll go up with you. Just let me walk. Don't carry me. I'm fine. Carmady's the name. I'm all grown up. I go to the bathroom alone and everything. Just don't carry me."

"Little Beulah used to work here," he said softly. He wasn't listening to me.

We went on up. He let me walk.

A crap table was in the far corner beyond the bar, and scattered tables and a few customers were here and there. The whiny voices chanting around the crap table stopped instantly. Eyes looked at us in that dead, alien silence of another race.

A large Negro was leaning against the bar in shirt-sleeves with pink garters on his arms. An ex-pug who had been hit by everything but a concrete bridge. He pried himself loose from the bar edge and came towards us in a loose fighter's crouch.

He put a large brown hand against the big man's gaudy chest. It looked like a stud there.

"No white folks, brother. Jes' fo' the colored people. I'se sorry."

"Where's Beulah?" the big man asked in his deep, soft voice that went with his big white face and his depthless black eyes.

The Negro didn't quite laugh. "No Beulah, brother. No hooch, no gals, jes' the scram, brother. Jes' the scram."

"Kind of take your goddam mitt off me," the big man said.

The bouncer made a mistake, too. He hit him. I saw his shoulder drop, his body swing behind the punch. It was a good clean punch. The big man didn't even try to block it.

He shook his head and took hold of the bouncer by the throat. He was quick for his size. The bouncer tried to knee him. The big man turned him and bent him, took hold of the back of his belt. That broke. So the big man just put his huge hand flat against the bouncer's spine and threw him, clear across the narrow room. The bouncer hit the wall on the far side with a crash that must have been heard in Denver. Then he slid softly down the wall and lay there, motionless.

"Yeah," the big man said. "Let's you and me nibble one."

We went over to the bar. The barman swabbed the bar hurriedly. The customers, by ones and twos and threes, drifted out, silent across the bare floor, silent down the dim uncarpeted stairs. Their departing feet scarcely rustled.

"Whisky sour," the big man said.

We had whisky sours.

"You know where Beulah is?" the big man asked the barman impassively, licking his whisky sour down the side of the thick glass.

"Beulah, you says?" the barman whined. "I ain't seen her roun' heah lately. Not right lately, no suh."

"How long you been here?"

" 'Bout a yeah, Ah reckon. 'Bout a yeah. Yes suh. 'Bout—"

"How long's this coop been a dinge box?"

"Says which?"

The big man made a fist down at his side, about the size of a bucket.

"Five years anyway," I put in. "This fellow wouldn't know anything about a white girl named Beulah."

The big man looked at me as if I had just hatched out. His whisky sour didn't seem to improve his temper.

"Who the hell asked you to stick your face in?"

I smiled. I made it a big, friendly smile. "I'm the fellow came in here with you. Remember?"

He grinned back, a flat, white grin. "Whisky sour," he told the barman. "Get them fleas outa your pants. Service."

The barman scuttled around, hating us with the whites of his eyes.

The place was empty now, except for the two of us and the barman, and the bouncer over against the far wall.

The bouncer groaned and stirred. He rolled over and began to crawl softly along the baseboard, like a fly with one wing. The big man paid no attention to him.

"There ain't nothing left of the joint," he complained. "They was a stage and a band and cute little rooms where you could have fun. Beulah did some warbling. A redhead. Awful cute. We was to of been married when they hung the frame on me."

We had two more whisky sours before us now. "What frame?" I asked.

"Where you figure I been them eight years I told you about?"

"In somebody's Stony Lonesome," I said.

"Right." He prodded his chest with a thumb like a baseball bat. "Steve Skalla. The Great Bend job in Kansas. Just me. Forty grand. They caught up with me right here. I was what that—hey!"

The bouncer had made a door at the back and fallen through it. A lock clicked.

"Where's that door lead to?" the big man demanded.

"Tha—tha's Mistah Montgom'ry's office, suh. He's the boss. He's got his office back—"

"He might know," the big man said. He wiped his mouth

on the Irish flag handkerchief and arranged it carefully back in his pocket. "He better not crack wise neither. Two more whisky sours."

He crossed the room to the door behind the crap table. The lock gave him a little argument for a moment, then a piece of the panel dropped off and he went through, shut the door after him.

It was very silent in Shamey's now. I looked at the barman.

"This guy's tough," I said quickly. "And he's liable to go mean. You can see the idea. He's looking for an old sweetie who used to work here when it was a place for whites. Got any artillery back there?"

"I thought you was with him," the barman said suspiciously.

"Couldn't help myself. He dragged me up. I didn't feel like being thrown over any houses."

"Shuah. Ah got me a shotgun," the barman said, still suspicious.

He began to stoop behind the bar, then stayed in that position rolling his eyes.

There was a dull flat sound at the back of the place, behind the shut door. It might have been a slammed door. It might have been a gun. Just the one sound. No other followed it.

The barman and I waited too long, wondering what the sound was. Not liking to think what it could be.

The door at the back opened and the big man came through quickly, with a Colt army .45 automatic looking like a toy in his hand.

He looked the room over with one swift glance. His grin was taut. He looked like the man who could take forty grand singlehanded from the Great Bend Bank.

He came over to us in swift, almost soundless steps, for all his size.

"Rise up, nigger!"

The barman came up slowly, gray; his hands empty, high.

The big man felt me over, stepped away from us.

"Mr. Montgomery didn't know where Beulah was either," he said softly. "He tried to tell me—with this." He waggled the gun. "So long, punks. Don't forget your rubbers."

He was gone, down the stairs, very quickly, very quietly.

I jumped around the bar and took the sawed-off shotgun that lay there, on the shelf. Not to use on Steve Skalla. That was not my job. So the barman wouldn't use it on me. I went back across the room and through that door.

The bouncer lay on the floor of a hall with a knife in his hand. He was unconscious. I took the knife out of his hand and stepped over him through a door marked Office.

Mr. Montgomery was in there, behind a small scarred desk, close to a partly boarded-up window. Just folded, like a handkerchief or a hinge.

A drawer was open at his right hand. The gun would have come from there. There was a smear of oil on the paper that lined it.

Not a smart idea, but he would never have a smarter one —not now.

Nothing happened while I waited for the police.

When they came both the barman and the bouncer were gone. I had locked myself in with Mr. Montgomery and the shotgun. Just in case.

Hiney got it. A lean-jawed, complaining, overslow detective lieutenant, with long yellow hands that he held on his knees while he talked to me in his cubicle at Headquarters. His shirt was darned under the points of his old-fashioned stiff collar. He looked poor and sour and honest.

This was an hour or so later. They knew all about Steve Skalla then, from their own records. They even had a ten-year-old photo that made him look as eyebrowless as a French roll. All they didn't know was where he was.

"Six foot six and a half," Hiney said. "Two hundred sixty-four pounds. A guy that size can't get far, not in them fancy duds. He couldn't buy anything else in a hurry. Whyn't you take him?"

I handed the photo back and laughed.

Hiney pointed one of his long yellow fingers at me bitterly. "Carmady, a tough shamus, huh? Six feet of man, and a jaw you could break rocks on. Whyn't you take him?"

"I'm getting a little gray at the temples," I said. "And I didn't have a gun. He had. I wasn't on a gun-toting job over there. Skalla just picked me up. I'm kind of cute sometimes."

Hiney glared at me.

"All right," I said. "Why argue? I've seen the guy. He

could wear an elephant in his vest pocket. And I didn't know he'd killed anybody. You'll get him all right."

"Yeah," Hiney said. "Easy. But I just don't like to waste my time on these shine killings. No pix. No space. Not even three lines in the want-ad section. Heck, they was five smokes—five, mind you—carved Harlem sunsets all over each other over on East Eight-four one time. All dead. Cold meat. And the —— newshawks wouldn't even go out there."

"Pick him up nice," I said. "Or he'll knock off a brace of prowlies for you. Then you'll get space."

"And I wouldn't have the case then neither," Hiney jeered. "Well, the hell with him. I got him on the air. Ain't nothing else to do but just sit."

"Try the girl," I said. "Beulah. Skalla will. That's what he's after. That's what started it all. Try her."

"You try her," Hiney said. "I ain't been in a joy house in twenty years."

"I suppose I'd be right at home in one. How much will you pay?"

"Jeeze, guy, coppers don't hire private dicks. What with?" He rolled a cigarette out of a can of tobacco. It burned down one side like a forest fire. A man yelled angrily into a telephone in the next cubbyhole. Hiney made another cigarette with more care and licked it and lighted it. He clasped his bony hands on his bony knees again.

"Think of your publicity," I said. "I bet you twenty-five I find Beulah before you put Skalla under glass."

He thought it over. He seemed almost to count his bank balance on his cigarette puffs.

"Ten is top," he said. "And she's all mine—private."

I stared at him.

"I don't work for that kind of money," I said. "But if I can do it in one day—and you let me alone—I'll do it for nothing. Just to show you why you've been a lieutenant for twenty years."

He didn't like that crack much better than I liked his about the joy house. But we shook hands on it.

I got my old Chrysler roadster out of the official parking lot and drove back towards the Central Avenue district.

Shamey's was closed up, of course. An obvious plain-clothes man sat in a car in front of it, reading a paper with one eye. I didn't know why. Nobody there knew anything about Skalla.

I parked around the corner and went into the diagonal lobby of a Negro hotel called the Hotel Sans Souci. Two rows of hard, empty chairs stared at each other across a strip of fiber carpet. Behind a desk a bald-headed man had his eyes shut and his hands clasped on the desk top. He dozed. He wore an ascot tie that had been tied about 1880, and the green stone in his stickpin was not quite as large as a trash barrel. His large, loose chin folded down on it gently, and his brown hands were soft, peaceful, and clean.

A metal embossed sign at his elbow said: *This Hotel Is Under the Protection of the International Consolidated Agencies, Inc.*

When he opened one eye I pointed to the sign and said: "H.P.D. man checking up. Any trouble here?"

H.P.D. means Hotel Protective Department, which is the part of a large agency that looks after check bouncers and people who move out by the back stairs, leaving second-hand suitcases full of bricks.

"Trouble, brother," he said, in a high, sonorous voice, "is something we is fresh out of." He lowered the voice four or five notches and added, "We don't take no checks."

I leaned on the counter across from his folded hands and started to spin a quarter on the bare, scarred wood.

"Heard what happened over at Shamey's this morning?"

"Brother, I forgit." Both his eyes were open now and he was watching the blur of light made by the spinning quarter.

"The boss got bumped off," I said. "Montgomery. Got his neck broken."

"May the Lawd receive his soul, brother." The voice went down again. "Cop?"

"Private—on a confidential lay. And I know a man who can keep one that way when I see one."

He looked me over, closed his eyes again. I kept spinning the quarter. He couldn't resist looking at it.

"Who done it?" he asked softly. "Who fixed Sam?"

"A tough guy out of the jailhouse got sore because it wasn't a white joint. It used to be. Remember?"

He didn't say anything. The coin fell over with a light whirr and lay still.

"Call your play," I said. "I'll read you a chapter of the Bible or buy you a drink. Either one."

"Brother," he said sonorously, "I kinda like to read my Bible in the seclusion of my family." Then he added swiftly, in his business voice, "Come around to this side of the desk."

I went around there and pulled a pint of bonded bourbon off my hip and handed it to him in the shelter of the desk. He poured two small glasses, quickly, sniffed his with a smooth, expert manner, and tucked it away.

"What you want to know?" he asked. "Ain't a crack in the sidewalk I don't know. Mebbe I ain't tellin' though. This liquor's been in the right company."

"Who ran Shamey's before it was a colored place?"

He stared at me, surprised. "The name of that pore sinner was Shamey, brother."

I groaned. "What have I been using for brains?"

"He's daid, brother, gathered to the Lawd. Died in nineteen and twenty-nine. A wood alcohol case, brother. And him in the business." He raised his voice to the sonorous level. "The same year the rich folks lost their goods and chattels, brother." The voice went down again. "I didn't lose me a nickel."

"I'll bet you didn't. Pour some more. He leave any folks —anybody that's still around?"

He poured another small drink, corked the bottle firmly. "Two is all—before lunch," he said. "I thank you, brother. Yo' method of approach is soothin' to a man's dignity." He cleared his throat. "Had a wife," he said. "Try the phone book."

He wouldn't take the bottle. I put it back on my hip. He shook hands with me, folded his on the desk once more and closed his eyes.

The incident, for him, was over.

There was only one Shamey in the phone book. Violet Lu Shamey, 1644 West Fifty-fourth Place. I spent a nickel in a booth.

After a long time a dopey voice said, "Uh-huh. Wh-what is it?"

"Are you the Mrs. Shamey whose husband once ran a place on Central Avenue—a place of entertainment?"

"Wha—what? My goodness sakes alive! My husband's been gone these seven years. Who did you say you was?"

"Detective Carmady. I'll be right out. It's important."

"Wh-who did you say—"

It was a thick, heavy, clogged voice.

It was a dirty brown house with a dirty brown lawn in front of it. There was a large bare patch around a tough-looking palm tree. On the porch stood one lonely rocker.

The afternoon breeze made the unpruned shoots of last year's poinsettias tap-tap against the front wall. A line of stiff, yellowish, half-washed clothes jittered on a rusty wire in the side yard.

I drove on a little way and parked my roadster across the street, and walked back.

The bell didn't work, so I knocked. A woman opened the door blowing her nose. A long yellow face with weedy hair growing down the sides of it. Her body was shapeless in a flannel bathrobe long past all color and design. It was just something around her. Her toes were large and obvious in a pair of broken man's slippers.

I said, "Mrs. Shamey?"

"You the—?"

"Yeah. I just called you."

She gestured me in wearily. "I ain't had time to get cleaned up yet," she whined.

We sat down in a couple of dingy mission rockers and looked at each other across a living room in which everything was junk except a small new radio droning away behind its dimly lighted panel.

"All the company I got," she said. Then she tittered. "Bert ain't done nothing, has he? I don't get cops calling on me much."

"Bert?"

"Bert Shamey, mister. My husband."

She tittered again and flopped her feet up and down. In her titter was a loose alcoholic overtone. It seemed I was not to get away from it that day.

"A joke, mister," she said. "He's dead. I hope to Christ there's enough cheap blondes where he is. He never got enough of them here."

"I was thinking more about a redhead," I said.

"I guess he'd use one of those too." Her eyes, it seemed to me, were not so loose now. "I don't call to mind. Any special one?"

"Yeah. A girl named Beulah. I don't know her last name. She worked at the Club on Central. I'm trying to trace her for her folks. It's a colored place now and, of course, the people there never heard of her."

"I never went there," the woman yelled, with unexpected violence. "I wouldn't know."

"An entertainer," I said. "A singer. No chance you'd know her, eh?"

She blew her nose again, on one of the dirtiest handkerchiefs I ever saw. "I got a cold."

"You know what's good for it," I said.

She gave me a swift, raking glance. "I'm fresh out of that."

"I'm not."

"Gawd," she said. "You're no cop. No cop ever bought a drink."

I brought out my pint of bourbon and balanced it on my knee. It was almost full still. The clerk at the Hotel Sans Souci was no reservoir. The woman's seaweed-colored eyes jumped at the bottle. Her tongue coiled around her lips.

"Man, that's liquor," she sighed. "I don't care who you are. Hold it careful, mister."

She heaved up and waddled out of the room and came back with two thick, smeared glasses.

"No fixin's," she said. "Just what you brought." She held the glasses out.

I poured her a slug that would have made me float over a wall. A smaller one for me. She put hers down like an aspirin tablet and looked at the bottle. I poured her another. She took that over to her chair. Her eyes had turned two shades browner.

"This stuff dies painless with me," she said. "It never knows what hit it. What was we talkin' about?"

"A red-haired girl named Beulah. Used to work at the joint. Remember better now?"

"Yeah." She used her second drink. I went over and stood the bottle on the table beside her. She used some out of that.

"Hold on to your chair and don't step on no snakes," she said. "I got me a idea."

She got up out of the chair, sneezed, almost lost her bathrobe, slapped it back against her stomach and stared at me coldly.

"No peekin'," she said, and wagged a finger at me and went out of the room again, hitting the side of the door casement on her way.

From the back of the house presently there were various types of crashes. A chair seemed to be kicked over. A bureau drawer was pulled out too far and smashed to the floor. There was fumbling and thudding and loud language. After a while, then, there was the slow click of a lock and what seemed to be the screech of a trunk top going up. More fumbling and banging things around. A tray landed on the floor, I thought. Then a chortle of satisfaction.

She came back into the room holding a package tied with faded pink tape. She threw it in my lap.

"Look 'em over, Lou. Photos. Newspaper stills. Not that them tramps ever got in no newspapers except by way of the police blotter. They're people from the joint. By God, they're all the —— left me. Them and his old clothes."

She sat down and reached for the whisky again.

I untied the tape and looked through a bunch of shiny photos of people in professional poses. Not all of them were women. The men had foxy faces and racetrack clothes or make-up. Hoofers and comics from the filling-station circuits. Not many of them ever got west of Main Street. The women had good legs and displayed them more than Will Hays would have liked. But their faces were as threadbare as a bookkeeper's coat. All but one.

She wore a Pierrot costume, at least from the waist up. Under the high conical white hat her fluffed-out hair might have been red. Her eyes had laughter in them. I won't say her face was unspoiled. I'm not that good at faces. But it wasn't like the others. It hadn't been kicked around. Somebody had been nice to that face. Perhaps just a tough mug like Steve Skalla. But he had been nice. In the laughing eyes there was still hope.

I threw the others aside and carried this one over to the sprawled, glassy-eyed woman in the chair. I poked it under her nose.

"This one," I said. "Who is she? What happened to her?"
She stared at it fuzzily, then chuckled.
"Tha's Steve Skalla's girl, Lou. Heck, I forgot her name."

"Beulah," I said. "Beulah's her name."

She watched me under her tawny, mangled eyebrows. She wasn't so drunk.

"Yeah?" she said. "Yeah?"

"Who's Steve Skalla?" I rapped.

"Bouncer down at the joint, Lou." She giggled again. "He's in the pen."

"Oh no, he isn't," I said. "He's in town. He's out. I know him. He just got in."

Her face went to pieces like a clay pigeon. Instantly I knew who had turned Skalla up to the local law. I laughed. I couldn't miss. Because she knew. If she hadn't known, she wouldn't have bothered to be cagey about Beulah. She couldn't have forgotten Beulah. Nobody could.

Her eyes went far back into her head. We stared into each other's faces. Then her hand snatched at the photo.

I stepped back and tucked it away in an inside pocket.

"Have another drink," I said. I handed her the bottle.

She took it, lingered over it, gurgled it slowly down her throat, staring at the faded carpet.

"Yeah," she said whisperingly. "I turned him in but he never knew. Money in the bank he was. Money in the bank."

"Give me the girl," I said. "And Skalla knows nothing from me."

"She's here," the woman said. "She's in radio. I heard her once on KLBL. She's changed her name, though. I dunno."

I had another hunch. "You do know," I said. "You're bleeding her still. Shamey left you nothing. What do you live on? You're bleeding her because she pulled herself up in the world, from people like you and Skalla. That's it, isn't it?"

"Money in the bank," she croaked. "Hundred a month. Reg'lar as rent. Yeah."

The bottle was on the floor again. Suddenly, without being touched, it fell over on its side. Whisky gurgled out. She didn't move to get it.

"Where is she?" I pounded on. "What's her name?"

"I dunno, Lou. Part of the deal. Get the money in a cashier's check. I dunno. Honest."

"The hell you don't!" I snarled. "Skalla—"

She came to her feet in a surge and screamed at me, "Get

out, you! Get out before I call a cop! Get out, you ———
——!"

"Okay, okay." I put a hand out soothingly. "Take it easy.
I won't tell Skalla. Just take it easy."

She sat down again slowly and retrieved the almost empty
bottle. After all I didn't have to have a scene now. I could
find out other ways.

She didn't even look towards me as I went out. I went
out into the crisp fall sunlight and got into my car. I was
a nice boy, trying to get along. Yes, I was a swell guy. I
liked knowing myself. I was the kind of guy who chiseled
a sodden old wreck out of her life secrets to win a ten-
dollar bet.

I drove down to the neighborhood drugstore and shut
myself in its phone booth to call Hiney.

"Listen," I told him, "the widow of the man that ran
Shamey's when Skalla worked there is still alive. Skalla
might call to see her, if he thinks he dares."

I gave him the address. He said sourly, "We almost got
him. A prowl car was talkin' to a Seventh Street conductor
at the end of the line. He mentioned a guy that size and
with them clothes. He got off at Third and Alexandria, the
conductor says. What he'll do is break into some big house
where the folks is away. So we got him bottled."

I told him that was fine.

KLBL was on the western fringe of that part of the city
that melts into Beverly Hills. It was housed in a flat stucco
building, quite unpretentious, and there was a service station in the form of a Dutch windmill on the corner of the
lot. The call letters of the station revolved in neon letters
on the sails of the windmill.

I went into a ground-floor reception room, one side of
which was glass and showed an empty broadcasting studio
with a stage and ranged chairs for an audience. A few people sat around the reception room trying to look magnetic,
and the blond receptionist was spearing chocolates out of a
large box with nails that were almost royal purple in color.

I waited half an hour and then got to see a Mr. Dave
Marineau, studio manager. The station manager and the day-
program manager were both too busy to see me. Marineau
had a small sound-proofed office behind the organ. It was
papered with signed photographs.

Marineau was a handsome tall man, somewhat in the Levantine style, with red lips a little too full, a tiny silky mustache, large limpid brown eyes, shiny black hair that might or might not have been marceled, and long, pale, nicotined fingers.

He read my card while I tried to find my Pierrot girl on his wall and didn't.

"A private detective, eh? What can we do for you?"

I took my Pierrot out and placed it down on his beautiful brown blotter. It was fun watching him stare at it. All sorts of minute things happened to his face, none of which he wanted known. The sum total of them was that he knew the face and that it meant something to him. He looked up at me with a bargaining expression.

"Not very recent," he said. "But nice. I don't know whether we could use it or not. Legs, aren't they?"

"It's at least eight years old," I said. "What would you use it for?"

"Publicity, of course. We get one in the radio column about every second month. We're a small station still."

"Why?"

"You mean you don't know who it is?"

"I know who she was," I said.

"Vivian Baring, of course. Star of our Jumbo Candy Bar program. Don't you know it? A triweekly serial, half an hour."

"Never heard of it," I said. "A radio serial is my idea of the square root of nothing."

He leaned back and lit a cigarette, although one was burning on the edge of his glass-lined tray.

"All right," he said sarcastically. "Stop being fulsome and get to business. What is it you want?"

"I'd like her address."

"I can't give you that, of course. And you won't find it in any phone book or directory. I'm sorry." He started to gather papers together and then saw the second cigarette and that made him feel like a sap. So he leaned back again.

"I'm in a spot," I said. "I have to find the girl. Quickly. And I don't want to look like a blackmailer."

He licked his very full and very red lips. Somehow I got the idea he was pleased at something.

He said softly, "You mean you know something that might hurt Miss Baring—and incidentally the program?"

"You can always replace a star in radio, can't you?"

He licked his lips some more. Then his mouth tried to get tough. "I seem to smell something nasty," he said.

"It's your mustache burning," I said.

It wasn't the best gag in the world, but it broke the ice. He laughed. Then he did wingovers with his hands. He leaned forward and got as confidential as a tipster.

"We're going at this wrong," he said. "Obviously. You're probably on the level—you look it—so let me make my play." He grabbed a leatherbound pad and scribbled on it, tore the leaf off and passed it across.

I read: *1737 North Flores Avenue.*

"That's her address," he said. "I won't give the phone number without her O.K. Now treat me like a gentleman. That is, if it concerns the station."

I tucked his paper into my pocket and thought it over. He had suckered me neatly, put me on my few remaining shreds of decency. I made my mistake.

"How's the program going?"

"We're promised network audition. It's simple, everyday stuff called 'A Street in Our Town,' but it's done beautifully. It'll wow the country some day. And soon." He wiped his hand across his fine white brow. "Incidentally, Miss Baring writes the scripts herself,"

"Ah," I said. "Well, here's your dirt. She had a boy friend in the big house. That is he used to be. She got to know him in a Central Avenue joint where she worked once. He's out and he's looking for her and he's killed a man. Now wait a minute—"

He hadn't turned as white as a sheet, because he didn't have the right skin. But he looked bad.

"Now wait a minute," I said. "It's nothing against the girl and you know it. She's okay. You can see that in her face. It might take a little counterpublicity, if it all came out. But that's nothing. Look how they gild some of those tramps in Hollywood."

"It costs money," he said. "We're a poor studio. And the network audition would be off." There was something faintly dishonest about his manner that puzzled me.

"Nuts," I said, leaning forward and pounding the desk. "The real thing is to protect her. This tough guy—Steve Skalla is his name—is in love with her. He kills people with his bare hands. He won't hurt her, but if she has a boy friend or a husband—"

"She's not married," Marineau put in quickly, watching the rise and fall of my pounding hand.

"He might wring his neck for him. That would put it a little too close to her. Skalla doesn't know where she is. He's on the dodge, so it's harder for him to find out. The cops are your best bet, if you have enough drag to keep them from feeding it to the papers."

"Nix," he said. "Nix on the cops. You want the job, don't you?"

'When do you need her here again?"

"Tomorrow night. She's not on tonight."

"I'll hide her for you until then," I said. "If you want me to. That's as far as I'd go alone."

He grabbed my card again, read it, dropped it into a drawer.

"Get out there and dig her out," he snapped. "If she's not home, stick till she is. I'll get a conference upstairs and then we'll see. Hurry it!"

I stood up. "Want a retainer?" he snapped.

"That can wait."

He nodded, made some more wingovers with his hands and reached for his phone.

That number on Flores would be up near Sunset Towers, across town from where I was. Traffic was pretty thick, but I hadn't gone more than twelve blocks before I was aware that a blue coupé which had left the studio parking lot behind me was still behind me.

I jockeyed around in a believable manner, enough to feel sure it was following me. There was one man in it. Not Skalla. The head was a foot too low over the steering wheel.

I jockeyed more and faster and lost it. I didn't know who it was, and at the moment, I hadn't time to bother figuring it out.

I reached the Flores Avenue place and tucked my roadster into the curb.

Bronze gates opened into a nice bungalow court, and two rows of bungalows with steep roofs of molded shingles gave an effect a little like the thatched cottages in old English sporting prints. A very little.

The grass was almost too well kept. There was a wide walk and an oblong pool framed in colored tiles and stone benches along its sides. A nice place. The late sun made interesting shadows over its lawns, and except for the motor horns, the distant hum of traffic up on Sunset Boulevard wasn't unlike the drone of bees.

My number was the last bungalow on the left. Nobody answered the bell, which was set in the middle of the door so that you would wonder how the juice got to where it had to go. That was cute too. I rang time after time, then I started back to the stone benches by the pool to sit down and wait.

A woman passed me walking fast, not in a hurry, but like a woman who always walks fast. She was a thin, sharp brunette in burnt-orange tweeds and a black hat that looked like a pageboy's hat. It looked like the devil with the burnt-orange tweeds. She had a nose that would be in things and tight lips and she swung a key container.

She went up to my door, unlocked it, went in. She didn't look like Beulah.

I went back and pushed the bell again. The door opened at once. The dark, sharp-faced woman gave me an up-and-down look and said: "Well?"

"Miss Baring? Miss Vivian Baring?"

"Who?" It was like a stab.

"Miss Vivian Baring—of KLBL," I said. "I was told—"

She flushed tightly and her lips almost bit her teeth. "If this is a gag, I don't care for it," she said. She started the door towards my nose.

I said hurriedly, "Mr. Marineau sent me."

That stopped the door closing. It opened again, very wide. The woman's mouth was as thin as a cigarette paper. Thinner.

"I," she said very distinctly, "happen to be Mr. Marineau's wife. This happens to be Mr. Marineau's residence. I wasn't aware that this—this—"

"Miss Vivian Baring," I said. But it wasn't uncertainty about the name that had stopped her. It was plain, cold fury.

"—that this Miss Baring," she went on, exactly as though

I had not said a word, "had moved in here. Mr. Marineau must be feeling very amusing today."

"Listen, lady. This isn't—"

The slamming door almost made a wave in the pool down the walk. I looked at it for a moment, and then I looked at the other bungalows. If we had an audience, it was keeping out of sight. I rang the bell again.

The door jumped open this time. The brunette was livid. "Get off my porch!" she yelled. "Get off before I have you thrown off!"

"Wait a minute," I growled. "This may be a gag for him, but it's no gag to the police."

That got her. Her whole expression got soft and interested. "Police?" she cooed.

"Yeah. It's serious. It involves a murder. I've got to find this Miss Baring. Not that she, you understand—"

The brunette dragged me into the house and shut the door and leaned against it, panting.

"Tell me," she said breathlessly. "Tell me. Has that red-headed something got herself mixed up in a murder?" Suddenly her mouth snapped wide open and her eyes jumped at me.

I slapped a hand over her mouth. "Take it easy!" I pleaded. "It's not your Dave. Not Dave, lady."

"Oh." She got rid of my hand and let out a sigh and looked silly. "No, of course. Just for a moment . . . Well, who is it?"

"Nobody you know. I can't broadcast things like that, anyway. I want Miss Baring's address. Have you got it?"

I didn't know any reason why she would have. Or rather, I might be able to think of one, if I shook my brains hard enough.

"Yes," she said. "Yes, I have. Indeed, I have. Mister Smarty doesn't know that. Mister Smarty doesn't know as much as he thinks he knows, does Mister Smarty? He—"

"The address is all I can use right now," I growled. "And I'm in a bit of a hurry, Mrs. Marineau. Later on—" I gave her a meaning look. "I'm sure I'll want to talk to you."

"It's on Heather Street," she said. "I don't know the number. But I've been there. I've been past there. It's only a short street, with four or five houses, and only one of them on the downward side of the hill." She stopped, added, "I don't think the house has a number. Heather Street is at the top of Beachwood Drive."

"Has she a phone?"

"Of course, but a restricted number. She would have. They all do, those ——. If I knew it—"

"Yeah," I said. "You'd call her up and chew her ear off. Well, thank you very much, Mrs. Marineau. This is confidential, of course. I mean confidential."

"Oh, by all means!"

She wanted to talk longer but I pushed past her out of the house and went back down the flagged walk. I could feel her eyes on me all the way, so I didn't do any laughing.

The lad with the restless hands and the full red lips had had what he thought was a very cute idea. He had given me the first address that came into his head, his own. Probably he had expected his wife to be out. I didn't know. It looked awfully silly, however I thought about it—unless he was pressed for time.

Wondering why he should be pressed for time, I got careless. I didn't see the blue coupé double-parked almost at the gates until I also saw the man step from behind it.

He had a gun in his hand.

He was a big man, but not anything like Skalla's size. He made a sound with his lips and held his left palm out and something glittered in it. It might have been a piece of tin or a police badge.

Cars were parked along both sides of Flores. Half a dozen people should have been in sight. There wasn't one—except the big man with the gun and myself.

He came closer, making soothing noises with his mouth.

"Pinched," he said. "Get in my hack and drive it, like a nice lad." He had a soft, husky voice, like an overworked rooster trying to croon.

"You all alone?"

"Yeah, but I got the gun," he sighed. "Act nice and you're as safe as the bearded woman at a Legion convention. Safer."

He was circling slowly, carefully. I saw the metal thing now.

"That's a special badge," I said. "You've got no more right to pinch me than I have to pinch you."

"In the hack, bo. Be nice or your guts lie on this here

street. I got orders." He started to pat me gently. "Hell, you ain't even rodded."

"Skip it!" I growled. "Do you think you could take me if I was?"

I walked over to his blue coupé and slid under its wheel. The motor was running. He got in beside me and put his gun in my side and we went on down the hill.

"Take her west on Santa Monica," he husked. "Then up, say, Canyon Drive to Sunset. Where the bridle path is."

I took her west on Santa Monica, past the bottom of Holloway, then a row of junk yards and some stores. The street widened and became a boulevard past Doheny. I let the car out a little to feel it. He stopped me doing that. I swung north to Sunset and then west again. Lights were being lit in big houses up the slopes. The dusk was full of radio music.

I eased down and took a look at him before it got too dark. Even under the pulled-down hat on Flores I had seen the eyebrows, but I wanted to be sure. So I looked again. They were the eyebrows, all right.

They were almost as even, almost as smoothly black, and fully as wide as a half-inch strip of black plush pasted across his broad face above the eyes and nose. There was no break in the middle. His nose was large and coarse-grained and had hung out over too many beers.

"Bub McCord," I said. "Ex-copper. So you're in the snatch racket now. It's Folsom for you this time, baby."

"Aw, can it." He looked hurt and leaned back in the corner. Bub McCord, caught in a graft tangle, had done a three in Quentin. Next time he would go to the recidivist prison, which is Folsom in our state.

He leaned his gun on his left thigh and cuddled the door with his fat back. I let the car drift and he didn't seem to mind. It was betweentimes, after the homeward rush of the office man, before the evening crowd came out.

"This ain't no snatch," he complained. "We just don't want no trouble. You can't expect to go up against an organization like KLBL with a two-bit shakedown, and get no kickback. It ain't reasonable." He spat out of the window without turning his head. "Keep her rollin', bo."

"What shakedown?"

"You wouldn't know, would you? Just a wandering peeper

with his head stuck in a knothole, huh? That's you. Innocent, as the guy says."

"So you work for Marineau. That's all I wanted to know. Of course I knew it already, after I back-alleyed you, and you showed up again."

"Neat work, bo—but keep her rollin'. Yeah, I had to phone in. Just caught him."

"Where do we go from here?"

"I take care of you till nine-thirty. After that we go to a place."

"What place?"

"It ain't nine-thirty. Hey, don't go to sleep in that there corner."

"Drive it yourself, if you don't like my work."

He pushed the gun at me hard. It hurt. I kicked the coupé out from under him and set him back in his corner, but he kept his gun in a good grip. Somebody called out archly on somebody's front lawn.

Then I saw a red light winking ahead, and a sedan just passing it, and through the rear window of the sedan two flat caps side by side.

"You'll get awfully tired of holding that gun," I told McCord. "You don't dare use it anyway. You're copper-soft. There's nothing so soft as a copper who's had his badge torn off. Just a big heel. Copper-soft."

We weren't near to the sedan, but I wanted his attention. I got it. He slammed me over the head and grabbed the wheel and yanked the brake on. We ground to a stop. I shook my head woozily. By the time I came out of it he was away from me again, in his corner.

"Next time," he said thinly, for all his huskiness, "I put you to sleep in the rumble. Just try it, bo. Just try it. Now roll—and keep the wisecracks down in your belly."

I drove ahead, between the hedge that bordered the bridle path and the wide parkway beyond the curbing. The cops in the sedan tooled on gently, drowsing, listening with half an ear to their radio, talking of this and that. I could almost hear them in my mind, the sort of thing they would be saying.

"Besides," McCord growled. "I don't need no gun to handle you. I never see the guy I couldn't handle without no gun."

"I saw one this morning," I said. I started to tell him about Steve Skalla.

Another red stoplight showed. The sedan ahead seemed loath to leave it. McCord lit a cigarette with his left hand, bending his head a little.

I kept telling him about Skalla and the bouncer at Shamey's.

Then I tramped on the throttle.

The little car shot ahead without a quiver. McCord started to swing his gun at me. I yanked the wheel hard to the right and yelled: "Hold tight! It's a crash!"

We hit the prowl car almost on the left rear fender. It waltzed around on one wheel, apparently, and loud language came out of it. It slewed, rubber screamed, metal made a grinding sound, the left taillight splintered and probably the gas tank bulged.

The little coupé sat back on its heels and quivered like a scared rabbit.

McCord could have cut me in half. His gun muzzle was inches from my ribs. But he wasn't a hard guy, really. He was just a broken cop who had done time and got himself a cheap job after it and was on an assignment he didn't understand.

He tore the right-hand door open, and jumped out of the car.

One of the cops was out by this time, on my side. I ducked down under the wheel. A flash beam burned across the top of my hat.

It didn't work. Steps came near and the flash jumped into my face.

"Come on out of that," a voice snarled. "What the hell you think this is—a racetrack?"

I got out sheepishly. McCord was crouched somewhere behind the coupé, out of sight.

"Lemme smell of your breath."

I let him smell my breath.

"Whisky," he said. "I thought so. Walk, baby. Walk." He prodded me with the flashlight.

I walked.

The other cop was trying to jerk his sedan loose from the coupé. He was swearing, but he was busy with his own troubles.

"You don't walk like no drunk," the cop said. "What's the matter? No brakes?" The other cop had got the bumpers free and was climbing back under his wheel.

I took my hat off and bent my head. "Just an argument," I said. "I got hit. It made me woozy for a minute."

McCord made a mistake. He started running when he heard that. He vaulted across the parkway, jumped the wall and crouched. His footsteps thudded on turf.

That was my cue. "Holdup!" I snapped at the cop who was questioning me. "I was afraid to tell you!"

"Jeeze, the howling—!" he yelled, and tore a gun out of his holster. "Why'n't you say so?" He jumped for the wall. "Circle the heap! We want that guy!" he yelled at the man in the sedan.

He was over the wall. Grunts. More feet pounding on the turf. A car stopped half a block away and a man started to get out of it but kept his foot on the running board. I could barely see him behind his dimmed headlights.

The cop in the prowl car charged at the hedge that bordered the bridle path, backed furiously, swung around and was off with screaming siren.

I jumped into McCord's coupé, and jerked the starter.

Distantly there was a shot, then two shots, then a yell. The siren died at a corner and picked up again.

I gave the coupé all it had and left the neighborhood. Far off, to the north, a lonely sound against the hills, a siren kept on wailing.

I ditched the coupé half a block from Wilshire and took a taxi in front of the Beverly-Wilshire. I knew I could be traced. That wasn't important. The important thing was how soon.

From a cocktail bar in Hollywood I called Hiney. He was still on the job and still sour.

"Anything new on Skalla?"

"Listen," he said nastily, "was you over to talk to that Shamey woman? Where are you?"

"Certainly I was," I said. "I'm in Chicago."

"You better come on home. Why was you there?"

"I thought she might know Beulah, of course. She did. Want to raise that bet a little?"

"Can the comedy. She's dead."

"Skalla—" I started to say.

"That's the funny side," he grunted. "He was there. Some nosy old —— next door seen him. Only there ain't a mark on her. She died natural. I kind of got tied up here, so I didn't get over to see her."

"I know how busy you are," I said in what seemed to me a dead voice.

"Yeah. Well, hell, the doc don't even know what she died of. Not yet."

"Fear," I said. "She's the one that turned Skalla up eight years ago. Whisky may have helped a little."

"Is that so?" Hiney said. "Well, well. We got him now anyways. We make him at Girard, headed north in a rent hack. We got the county and state law in on it. If he drops over to the Ridge, we nab him at Castaic. She was the one turned him up, huh? I guess you better come in, Carmady."

"Not me," I said. "Beverly Hills wants me for a hit-and-run. I'm a criminal myself now."

I had a quick snack and some coffee before I took a taxi to Las Flores and Santa Monica and walked up to where I had left my roadster parked.

Nothing was happening around there except that some kid in the back of a car was strumming a ukelele.

I pointed my roadster towards Heather Street.

Heather Street was a gash in the side of a steep flat slope, at the top of Beachwood Drive. It curved around the shoulder enough so that even by daylight you couldn't have seen much more than half a block of it at one time while you were on it.

The house I wanted was built downward, one of those clinging-vine effects, with a front door below the street level, a patio on the roof, a bedroom or two possibly in the basement, and a garage as easy to drive into as an olive bottle.

The garage was empty, but a big shiny sedan had its two right wheels off the road, on the shoulder of the bank. There were lights in the house.

I drove around the curb, parked, walked back along the smooth, hardly used cement and poked a fountain pen flash into the sedan. It was registered to one David Marineau, 1737 North Flores Avenue, Hollywood, California. That made me go back to my heap and get a gun out of a locked pocket.

I repassed the sedan, stepped down three rough stone steps and looked at the bell beside a narrow door topped by a lancet arch.

I didn't push it, I just looked at it. The door wasn't quite shut. A fairly wide crack of dim light edged around its panel. I pushed it an inch. Then I pushed it far enough to look in.

Then I listened. The silence of that house was what made me go in. It was one of those utterly dead silences that come after an explosion. Or perhaps I hadn't eaten enough dinner. Anyway I went in.

The long living room went clear to the back, which wasn't very far as it was a small house. At the back there were french doors and the metal railing of a balcony showed through the glass. The balcony would be very high above the slope of the hill, built as the house was.

There were nice lamps, nice chairs with deep sides, nice tables, a thick apricot-colored rug, two small cozy davenports, one facing and one right-angled to a fireplace with an ivory mantel and a miniature Winged Victory on that. A fire was laid behind the copper screen, but not lit.

The room had a hushed, warm smell. It looked like a room where people got made comfortable. There was a bottle of Vat 69 on a low table with glasses and a copper bucket, and tongs.

I fixed the door about as I had found it and just stood. Silence. Time passed. It passed in the dry whirr of an electric clock on a console radio, in the far-off hoot of an auto horn down on Beachwood half a mile below, in the distant hornet drone of a night-flying plane, in the metallic wheeze of a cricket under the house.

Then I wasn't alone any longer.

Mrs. Marineau slid into the room at the far end, by a door beside the french doors. She didn't make any more noise than a butterfly. She still wore the pillbox black hat and the burnt-orange tweeds, and they still looked like hell together. She had a small glove in her hand wrapped around the butt of a gun. I don't know why. I never did find that out.

She didn't see me at once and when she did it didn't mean anything much. She just lifted the gun a little and slid along the carpet towards me, her lip clutched back so far that I couldn't even see the teeth that clutched it.

But I had a gun out now myself. We looked at each other across our guns. Maybe she knew me. I hadn't any idea from her expression.

I said, "You got them, huh?"

She nodded a little. "Just him," she said.

"Put the gun down. You're all through with it."

She lowered it a little. She hadn't seemed to notice the Colt I was pushing through the air in her general direction. I lowered that too.

She said, "She wasn't here."

Her voice had a dry, impersonal sound, flat, without timbre.

"Miss Baring wasn't here?" I asked.

"No."

"Remember me?"

She took a better look at me but her face didn't light up with any pleasure.

"I'm the guy that was looking for Miss Baring," I said. "You told me where to come. Remember? Only Dave sent a loogan to put the arm on me and ride me around while he came up here himself and promoted something. I couldn't guess what."

The brunette said, "You're no cop. Dave said you were a fake."

I made a broad, hearty gesture and moved a little closer to her, unobtrusively. "Not a city cop," I admitted. "But a cop. And that was a long time ago. Things have happened since then. Haven't they?"

"Yes," she said. "Especially to Dave. Hee, hee."

It wasn't a laugh. It wasn't meant to be a laugh. It was just a little steam escaping through a safety valve.

"Hee, hee," I said. We looked at each other like a couple of nuts being Napoleon and Josephine.

The idea was to get close enough to grab her gun. I was still too far.

"Anybody here besides you?" I asked.

"Just Dave."

"I had an idea Dave was here." It wasn't clever, but it was good for another foot.

"Oh, Dave's here," she agreed. "Yes. You'd like to see him?"

"Well—if it isn't too much trouble."

"Hee, hee," she said. "No trouble at all. Like this."

She jerked the gun up and snapped the trigger at me. She did it without moving a muscle of her face.

The gun not going off puzzled her, in a sort of vague, week-before-last manner. Nothing immediate or important. I wasn't there any more. She lifted the gun up, still being very careful about the black kid glove wrapped about its butt, and peered into the muzzle. That didn't get her anywhere. She shook the gun. Then she was aware of me again. I hadn't moved. I didn't have to, now.

"I guess it's not loaded," she said.

"Maybe just all used up," I said. "Too bad. These little ones only hold seven. My shells won't fit, either. Let's see if I can do anything?"

She put the gun in my hand. Then she dusted her hands together. Her eyes didn't seem to have any pupils, or to be all pupils. I wasn't sure which.

The gun wasn't loaded. The magazine was quite empty. I sniffed the muzzle. The gun hadn't been fired since it was last cleaned.

That got me. Up to that point it had looked fairly simple, if I could get by without any more murder. But this threw it. I hadn't any idea what either of us was talking about now.

I dropped her pistol into my side pocket and put mine back on my hip and chewed my lip for a couple of minutes, to see what might turn up. Nothing did.

The sharp-faced Mrs. Marineau merely stood still and stared at a spot between my eyes, fuzzily, like a rather blotto tourist seeing a swell sunset on Mount Whitney.

"Well," I said at last, "let's kind of look through the house and see what's what."

"You mean Dave?"

"Yeah, we could take that in."

"He's in the bedroom." She tittered. "He's at home in bedrooms."

I touched her arm and turned her around. She turned obediently, like a small child.

"But this one will be the last one he'll be at home in," she said. "Hee, hee."

"Oh, yeah. Sure," I said.

My voice sounded to me like the voice of a midget.

Dave Marineau was dead all right—if there had been any doubt about it.

A white bowl lamp with raised figures shone beside a large bed in a green and silver bedroom. It was the only light in the room. It filtered a hushed kind of light down at his face. He hadn't been dead long enough to get the corpse look.

He lay sprawled casually on the bed, a little sideways, as though he had been standing in front of it when he was shot. One arm was flung out as loose as a strand of kelp and the other was under him. His open eyes were flat and shiny and almost seemed to hold a self-satisfied expression. His mouth was open a little and the lamplight glistened on the edges of his upper teeth.

I didn't see the wound at all at first. It was high up, on the right side of his head, in the temple, but back rather far, almost far enough to drive the petrosal bone through the brain. It was powder-burned, rimmed with dusky red, and a fine trickle spidered down from it and got browner as it got thinner against his cheek.

"Hell, that's a contact wound," I snapped at the woman. "A suicide wound."

She stood at the foot of the bed and stared at the wall above his head. If she was interested in anything besides the wall, she didn't show it.

I lifted his still limp right hand and sniffed at the place where the base of the thumb joins the palm. I smelled cordite, then I didn't smell cordite, then I didn't know whether I smelled cordite or not. It didn't matter, of course. A paraffin test would prove it one way or the other.

I put the hand down again, carefully, as though it were a fragile thing of great value. Then I plowed around on the bed, went down on the floor, got halfway under the bed, swore, got up again and rolled the dead man to one side enough to look under him. There was a bright, brassy shell-case but no gun.

It looked like murder again. I liked that better. He wasn't the suicide type.

"See any gun?" I asked her.

"No." Her face was as blank as a pie pan.

"Where's the Baring girl? What are you supposed to be doing here?"

She bit the end of her left little finger. "I'd better confess," she said. "I came here to kill them both."

"Go on," I said.

"Nobody was here. Of course, after I phoned him and he told me you were not a real cop and there was no murder and you were a blackmailer and just trying to scare me out of the address—" She stopped and sobbed once, hardly more than a sniff, and moved her line of sight to a corner of the ceiling.

Her words had a tumbled arrangement, but she spoke them like a drugstore Indian

"I came here to kill both of them," she said. "I don't deny that."

"With an empty gun?"

"It wasn't empty two days ago. I looked. Dave must have emptied it. He must have been afraid."

"That listens," I said. "Go on."

"So I came here. That was the last insult—his sending you to me to get her *address*. That was more than I would—"

"The story," I said. "I know how you felt. I've read it in the love mags myself."

"Yes. Well, he said there was something about Miss Baring he had to see her about on account of the studio and it was nothing personal, never had been, never would be—"

"My Gawd," I said, "I know that too. I know what he'd feed you. We've got a dead man lying around here. We've got to do something, even if he was just your husband."

"You ——," she said.

"Yeah," I said. "That's better than the dopey talk. Go on."

"The door wasn't shut. I came in. That's all. Now, I'm going. And you're not going to stop me. You know where I live, you ——." She called me the same name again.

"We'll talk to some law first," I said. I went over and shut the door and turned the key on the inside of it and took it out. Then I went over to the french doors. The woman gave me looks, but I couldn't hear what her lips were calling me now.

French doors on the far side of the bed opened on the

same balcony as the living room. The telephone was in a niche in the wall there, by the bed, where you could yawn and reach out for it in the morning and order a tray of diamond necklaces sent up to try on.

I sat down on the side of the bed and reached for the phone, and a muffled voice came to me through the glass and said: "Hold it, pal! Just hold it!"

Even muffled by the glass it was a deep, soft voice. I had heard it before. It was Skalla's voice.

I was in line with the lamp. The lamp was right behind me. I dived off the bed on to the floor, clawing at my hip.

A shot roared and glass sprinkled the back of my neck. I couldn't figure it. Skalla wasn't on the balcony. I had looked.

I rolled over and started to snake away along the floor away from the french doors, my only chance with the lamp where it was.

Mrs. Marineau did just the right thing—for the other side. She jerked a slipper off and started slamming me with the heel of it. I grabbed for her ankles and we wrestled around and she cut the top of my head to pieces.

I threw her over. It didn't last long. When I started to get up Skalla was in the room, laughing at me. The .45 still had a home in his fist. The french door and the locked screen outside looked as though a rogue elephant had passed that way.

"Okay," I said. "I give up."

"Who's the twist? She sure likes you, pal."

I got up on my feet. The woman was over in a corner somewhere. I didn't even look at her.

"Turn around, pal, while I give you the fan."

I hadn't worked my gun loose yet. He got that. I didn't say anything about the door key, but he took it. So he must have been watching from somewhere. He left me my car keys. He looked at the little empty gun and dropped it back in my pocket.

"Where'd you come from?" I asked.

"Easy. Clumb up the balcony and held on, looking through the grill at you. Cinch to an old circus man. How you been, pal?"

Blood from the top of my head was leaking down my

face. I got a handkerchief out and mopped at it. I didn't answer him.

"Jeeze, you sure was funny on the bed grabbin' for the phone with the stiff at your back."

"I was a scream," I growled. "Take it easy. He's her husband."

He looked at her. "She's his woman?"

I nodded and wished I hadn't.

"That's tough. If I'd a known—but I couldn't help meself. The guy asked for it."

"You—" I started to say, staring at him. I heard a queer, strained whine behind me, from the woman.

"Who else, pal? Who else? Let's all go back in that livin' room. Seems to me they was a bottle of nice-looking hooch there. And you need some stuff on that head."

"You're crazy to stick around here," I growled. "There's a general pickup out for you. The only way out of this canyon is back down Beachwood or over the hills—on foot."

Skalla looked at me and said very quietly, "Nobody's phoned no law from here, pal."

Skalla watched me while I washed and put some tape on my head in the bathroom. Then we went back to the living room. Mrs. Marineau, curled up on one of the davenports, looked blankly at the unlit fire. She didn't say anything.

She hadn't run away because Skalla had her in sight all the time. She acted resigned, indifferent, as if she didn't care what happened now.

I poured three drinks from the Vat 69 bottle, handed one to the brunette. She held her hand out for the glass, half smiled at me, crumpled off the davenport to the floor with the smile still on her face.

I put the glass down, lifted her and put her back on the davenport with her head low. Skalla stared at her. She was out cold, as white as paper.

Skalla took his drink, sat down on the other davenport and put the .45 beside him. He drank his drink looking at the woman, with a queer expression on his big pale face.

"Tough," he said. "Tough. But the louse was cheatin' on her anyways. The hell with him." He reached for another drink, swallowed it, sat down near her on the other davenport right-angled to the one she lay on.

"So you're a dick," he said.

"How'd you guess?"

"Lu Shamey told me about a guy goin' there. He sounded like you. I been around and looked in your heap outside. I walk silent."

"Well—what now?" I asked.

He looked more enormous than ever in the room in his sports clothes. The clothes of a smart-aleck kid. I wondered how long it had taken him to get them together. They couldn't have been ready-made. He was much too big for that.

His feet were spread wide on the apricot rug, he looked down sadly at the white kid explosions on the suede. They were the worst-looking shoes I ever saw.

"What you doin' here?" he asked gruffly.

"Looking for Beulah. I thought she might need a little help. I had a bet with a city cop I'd find her before he found you. But I haven't found her yet."

"You ain't seen her, huh?"

I shook my head, slowly, very carefully.

He said softly, "Me neither, pal. I been around for hours. She ain't been home. Only the guy in the bedroom come here. How about the dinge manager up at Shamey's?"

"That's what the tag's for."

"Yeah. A guy like that. They would. Well, I gotta blow. I'd like to take the stiff, account of Beulah. Can't leave him around to scare her. But I guess it ain't any use now. The dinge kill queers that."

He looked at the woman at his elbow on the other little davenport. Her face was still greenish white, her eyes shut. There was a movement of her breast.

"Without her," he said, "I guess I'd clean up right and button you good." He touched the .45 at his side. "No hard feelings, of course. Just for Beulah. But the way it is— heck, I can't knock the frail off."

"Too bad," I snarled, feeling my head.

He grinned. "I guess I'll take your heap. For a short ways. Throw them keys over."

I threw them over. He picked them up and laid them beside the big Colt. He leaned forward a little. Then he reached back into one of his patch pockets and brought out a small pearl-handled gun, about .25 caliber. He held it on the flat of his hand.

"This done it," he said. "I left a rent hack I had on the street below and come up the bank and around the house. I hear the bell ring. This guy is at the front door. I don't come up far enough for him to see me. Nobody answers. Well, what do you think? The guy's got a key. A key to Beulah's house!"

His huge face became one vast scowl. The woman on the davenport was breathing a little more deeply, and I thought I saw one of her eyelids twitch.

"What the hell," I said. "He could get that a dozen ways. He's a boss at KLBL where she works. He could get at her bag, take an impression. Hell, she didn't have to give it to him."

"That's right, pal." He beamed. "O' course, she didn't have to give it to the ——. Okay, he went in, and I made it fast after him. But he had the door shut. I opened it my way. After that it didn't shut so good, you might of noticed. He was in the middle of this here room, over there by a desk. He's been here before all right though"—the scowl came back again, although not quite so black—"because he slipped a hand into the desk drawer and come up with this." He danced the pearl-handled thing on his enormous palm.

Mrs. Marineau's face now had distinct lines of tensity.

"So I start for him. He lets one go. A miss. He's scared and runs into the bedroom. Me after. He lets go again. Another miss. You'll find them slugs in the wall somewheres."

"I'll make a point of it," I said.

"Yeah, then I got him. Well, hell, the guy's only a punk in a white muffler. If she's washed up with me, okay. I want it from her, see? Not from no greasy-faced piece of cheese like him. So I'm sore. But the guy's got guts at that."

He rubbed his chin. I doubted the last bit.

"I say: 'My woman lives here, pal. How come?' He says: 'Come back tomorrow. This here is my night.'"

Skalla spread his free left hand in a large gesture. "After that nature's got to take its course, ain't it? I pull his arms and legs off. Only while I'm doing it the damn little gat pops off and he's as limp as—as—" he glanced at the woman and didn't finish what he was going to say. "Yeah, he was dead."

One of the woman's eyelids flickered again. I said, "Then?"

"I scrammed. A guy does. But I come back. I got to thinkin' it's tough on Beulah, with that stiff on her bed. So I'll just go back and ferry him out to the desert and then crawl in a hole for a while. Then this frail comes along and spoils that part."

The woman must have been shamming for quite a long time. She must have been moving her legs and feet and turning her body a fraction of an inch at a time, to get in the right position, to get leverage against the back of the davenport.

The pearl-handled gun still lay on Skalla's flat hand when she moved. She shot off the davenport in a flat dive, gathering herself in the air like an acrobat. She brushed his knees and picked the gun off his hand as neatly as a chipmunk peels a nut.

He stood up and swore as she rolled against his legs. The big Colt was at his side, but he didn't touch it or reach for it. He stooped to take hold of the woman with his big hands empty.

She laughed just before she shot him.

She shot him four times, in the lower belly, then the hammer clicked. She threw the gun at his face and rolled away from him.

He stepped over her without touching her. His big pale face was quite empty for a moment, then it settled into stiff lines of torture, lines that seemed to have been there always.

He walked erectly along the rug towards the front door. I jumped for the big Colt and got it. To keep it from the woman. At the fourth step he took, blood showed on the yellowish nap of the rug. After that it showed at every step he took.

He reached the door and put his big hand flat against the wood and leaned there for a moment. Then he shook his head and turned back. His hand left a bloody smear on the door from where he had been holding his belly.

He sat down in the first chair he came to and leaned forward and held himself tightly with his hands. The blood came between his fingers slowly, like water from an overflowing basin.

"Them little slugs," he said, "hurt just like the big ones, down below anyways."

The dark woman walked towards him like a marionette. He watched her come unblinkingly, under his half-lowered, heavy lids.

When she got close enough she leaned over and spat in his face.

He didn't move. His eyes didn't change. I jumped for her and threw her into a chair. I wasn't nice about it.

"Leave her alone," he grunted at me. "Maybe she loved the guy."

Nobody tried to stop me from telephoning this time.

Hours later I sat on a red stool at Lucca's, at Fifth and Western, and sipped a martini and wondered how it felt to be mixing them all day and never drink one.

I took another martini over and ordered a meal. I guess I ate it. It was late, past one. Skalla was in the prison ward of the General Hospital. Miss Baring hadn't showed up yet, but they knew she would, as soon as she heard Skalla was under glass, and no longer dangerous.

KLBL, who didn't know anything about it at first, had got a nice hush working. They were to have twenty-four clear hours to decide how to release the story.

Lucca's was almost as full as at noon. After a while an Italian brunette with a grand nose and eyes you wouldn't fool with came over and said: "I have a table for you now."

My imagination put Skalla across the table from me. His flat black eyes had something in them that was more than mere pain, something he wanted me to do. Part of the time he was trying to tell me what it was, and part of the time he was holding his belly in one piece and saying again: "Leave her alone. Maybe she loved the guy."

I left there and drove north to Franklin and over Franklin to Beachwood and up to Heather Street. It wasn't staked. They were that sure of her.

I drifted along the street below and looked up the scrubby slope spattered with moonlight and showing her house from behind as if it were three stories high. I could see the metal brackets that supported the porch. They looked high enough off the ground so that a man would need a balloon to reach them. But there was where he had gone up. Always the hard way with him.

He could have run away and had a fight for his money or even bought himself a place to live up in. There were plenty of people in the business, and they wouldn't fool with Skalla. But he had come back instead to climb her balcony, like Romeo, and get his stomach full of slugs. From the wrong woman, as usual.

I drove around a white curve that looked like moonlight itself and parked and walked up the hill the rest of the way. I carried a flash, but I didn't need it to see there was nobody on the doorstep waiting for the milk. I didn't go in the front way. There might just happen to be some snooper with night glasses up on the hill.

I sneaked up the bank from behind, between the house and the empty garage. I found a window I could reach and made not much noise breaking it with a gun inside my hat. Nothing happened except that the crickets and tree frogs stopped for a moment.

I picked a way to the bedroom and prowled my flash around discreetly, after lowering the shades and pulling the drapes across them. The light dropped on a tumbled bed, on daubs of print powder, on cigarette butts on the window sills and heel marks in the nap of the carpet. There was a green and silver toilet set on the dressing table and three suitcases in the closet. There was a built-in bureau back in there with a lock that meant business. I had a chilled-steel screwdriver with me as well as the flash. I jimmied it.

The jewelry wasn't worth a thousand dollars. Perhaps not half. But it meant a lot to a girl in show business. I put it back where I got it.

The living room had shut windows and a queer, unpleasant, sadistic smell. The law enforcement had taken care of the Vat 69, to make it easier for the fingerprint men. I had to use my own. I got a chair that hadn't been bled on into a corner, wet my throat and waited in the darkness.

A shade flapped in the basement or somewhere. That made me wet my throat again. Somebody came out of a house half a dozen blocks away and whooped. A door banged. Silence. The tree frogs started again, then the crickets. Then the electric clock on the radio got louder than all the other sounds together.

Then I went to sleep.

When I woke up the moon had gone from the front windows and a car had stopped somewhere. Light, delicate, careful steps separated themselves from the night. They were outside the front door. A key fumbled in the lock.

In the opening door the dim sky showed a head without a hat. The slope of the hill was too dark to outline any more. The door clicked shut.

Steps rustled on the rug. I already had the lamp cord in my fingers. I yanked it and there was light.

The girl didn't make a sound, not a whisper of sound. She just pointed the gun at me.

I said, "Hello, Beulah."

She was worth waiting for.

Not too tall, not too short; that girl. She had the long legs that can walk and dance. Her hair even by the light of the one lamp was like a brush fire at night. Her face had laughter wrinkles at the corner of the eyes. Her mouth could laugh.

The features were shadowed and had that drawn look that makes some faces more beautiful because it makes them more delicate. I couldn't see her eyes. They might have been blue enough to make you jump, but I couldn't see.

The gun looked about a .32, but had the extreme right-angled grip of a Mauser.

After a while she said very softly, "Police, I suppose."

She had a nice voice, too. I still think of it, at times.

I said, "Let's sit down and talk. We're all alone here. Ever drink out of the bottle?"

She didn't answer. She looked down at the gun she was holding, half smiled, shook her head.

"You wouldn't make two mistakes," I said. "Not a girl as smart as you are."

She tucked the gun into the side pocket of a long ulster-like coat with a military collar.

"Who are you?"

"Just a shamus. Private detective to you. Carmady is the name. Need a lift?"

I held my bottle out. It hadn't grown to my hand yet. I still had to hold it.

"I don't drink. Who hired you?"

"KLBL. To protect you from Steve Skalla."

"So they know," she said. "So they know about him."

I digested that and said nothing.

"Who's been here?" she went on sharply. She was still standing in the middle of the room, with her hands in her coat pockets now, and no hat.

"Everybody but the plumber," I said. "He's a little late, as usual."

"You're one of *those* men." Her nose seemed to curl a little. "Drugstore comics."

"No," I said. "Not really. It's just a way I get talking to the people I have to talk to. Skalla came back again and ran into trouble and got shot up and arrested. He's in the hospital. Pretty bad."

She didn't move. "How bad?"

"He might live if he'd have surgery. Doubtful, even with that. Hopeless without. He has three in the intestines and one in the liver."

She moved at last and started to sit down. "Not in that chair," I said quickly. "Over here."

She came over and sat near me, on one of the davenports. Lights twisted in her eyes. I could see them now. Little twisting lights like Catherine wheels spinning brightly.

She said, "Why did he come back?"

"He thought he ought to tidy up. Remove the body and so on. A nice guy, Skalla."

"Do you think so?"

"Lady, if nobody else in the world thinks so, I do."

"I'll take that drink," she said.

I handed her the bottle. I grabbed it away in a hurry. "Gosh," I said. "You have to break in on this stuff."

She looked towards the side door that led to the bedroom back of me.

"Gone to the morgue," I said. "You can go in there."

She stood up at once and went out of the room. She came back almost at once.

"What have they got on Steve?" she asked. "If he recovers."

"He killed a nigger over on Central this morning. It was more or less self-defense on both sides. I don't know. Except for Marineau he might get a break."

"Marineau?" she said.

"Yeah. You knew he killed Marineau."

"Don't be silly," she said. "I killed Dave Marineau."

"Okay," I said. "But that's not the way Steve wants it."

She stared at me. "You mean Steve came back here deliberately to take the blame?"

"If he had to, I guess. I think he really meant to cart Marineau off to the desert and lose him. Only a woman showed up here—Mrs. Marineau."

"Yes," the girl said tonelessly. "She thinks I was his mistress. That greasy spoon."

"Were you?" I asked.

"Don't try that again," she said. "Even if I did work on Central Avenue once." She went out of the room again.

Sounds of a suitcase being yanked about came into the living room. I went in after her. She was packing pieces of cobweb and packing them as if she liked nice things nicely packed.

"You don't wear that stuff down in the tank," I told her, leaning in the door.

She ignored me some more. "I was going to make a break for Mexico," she said. "Then South America. I didn't mean to shoot him. He roughed me up and tried to blackmail me into something and I went and got the gun. Then we struggled again and it went off. Then I ran away."

"Just what Skalla said he did," I said. "Hell, couldn't you just have shot the —— on purpose?"

"Not for your benefit," she said. "Or any cop. Not when I did eight months in Dalhart, Texas, once for rolling a drunk. Not with that Marineau woman yelling her head off that I seduced him and then got sick of him."

"A lot she'll say," I grunted. "After I tell how she spat in Skalla's face when he had four slugs in him."

She shivered. Her face whitened. She went on taking the things out of the suitcase and putting them in again.

"Did you roll the drunk really?"

She looked up at me, then down. "Yes," she whispered.

I went over nearer to her. "Got any bruises or torn clothes to show?" I asked.

"No."

"Too bad," I said, and took hold of her.

Her eyes flamed at first and then turned to black stone. I tore her coat off, tore her up plenty, put hard fingers into her arms and neck and used my knuckles on her mouth. I let her go, panting. She reeled away from me, but didn't quite fall.

"We'll have to wait for the bruises to set and darken," I said. "Then we'll go downtown."

She began to laugh. Then she went over to the mirror and looked at herself. She began to cry.

"Get out of here while I change my clothes!" she yelled. "I'll give it a tumble. But if it makes any difference to Steve —I'm going to tell it right."

"Aw, shut up and change your clothes," I said.

I went out and banged the door.

I hadn't even kissed her. I could have done that, at least. She wouldn't have minded any more than the rest of the knocking about I gave her.

We rode the rest of the night, first in separate cars to hide hers in my garage, then in mine. We rode up the coast and had coffee and sandwiches at Malibu, then on up and over. We had breakfast at the bottom of the Ridge Route, just north of San Fernando.

Her face looked like a catcher's mitt after a tough season. She had a lower lip the size of a banana and you could have cooked steaks on the bruises on her arms and neck, they were so hot.

With the first strong daylight we went to the City Hall.

They didn't even think of holding her or checking her up. They practically wrote the statement themselves. She signed it blank-eyed, thinking of something else. Then a man from KLBL and his wife came down to get her.

So I didn't get to ride her to a hotel. She didn't get to see Skalla either, not then. He was under morphine.

He died at two-thirty the same afternoon. She was holding one of his huge, limp fingers, but he didn't know her from the Queen of Siam.

MANDARIN'S JADE

I 300 Carats of Fei Tsui

I WAS smoking my pipe and making faces at the back of my name on the glass part of the office door when Violets M'Gee called me up. There hadn't been any business in a week.

"How's the sleuth racket, huh?" Violets asked. He's a homicide dick in the sheriff's office. "Take a little flutter down at the beach? Body guarding or something, it is."

"Anything that goes with a dollar," I said. "Except murder. I get three-fifty for that."

"I bet you do nice neat work too. Here's the lay, John."

He gave me the name, address and telephone number of a man named Lindley Paul who lived at Castellamare, was a socialite and went everywhere except to work, lived alone with a Jap servant, and drove a very large car. The sheriff's office had nothing against him except that he had too much fun.

Castellamare was in the city limits, but didn't look it, being a couple of dozen houses of various sizes hanging by their eyebrows to the side of a mountain, and looking as if a good sneeze would drop them down among the box lunches on the beach. There was a sidewalk café up on the highway, and beside that a cement arch which was really a pedestrian bridge. From the inner end of this a flight of white concrete steps went straight as a ruler up the side of the mountain.

Quinonal Avenue, Mr. Lindley Paul had told me over the phone, was the third street up, if I cared to walk. It was, he said, the easiest way to find his place the first time, the streets being designed in a pattern of interesting but rather intricate curves. People had been known to wander about in them for several hours without making any more yardage than an angleworm in a bait can.

So I parked my old blue Chrysler down below and walked up. It was a fine evening and there was still some sparkle on the water when I started. It had all gone when I reached the top. I sat down on the top step and rubbed my leg muscles and waited for my pulse to come down into the low hundreds. After that I shook my shirt loose from my back and went along to the house, which was the only one in the foreground.

It was a nice enough house, but it didn't look like really important money. There was a salt-tarnished iron staircase going up to the front door and the garage was underneath the house. A long black battleship of a car was backed into it, an immense streamlined boat with enough hood for three cars and a coyote tail tied to the radiator cap. It looked as if it had cost more than the house.

The man who opened the door at the top of the iron stairs wore a white flannel suit with a violet satin scarf arranged loosely inside the collar. He had a soft brown neck, like the neck of a very strong woman. He had pale blue-green eyes, about the color of an aquamarine, features on the heavy side but very handsome, three precise ledges of thick blond hair rising from a smooth brown forehead, an inch more of height than I had—which made him six feet one—and the general look of a guy who would wear a white flannel suit with a violet satin scarf inside the collar.

He cleared his throat, looked over my left shoulder, and said: "Yes?"

"I'm the man you sent for. The one Violets M'Gee recommended."

"Violets? Gracious, what a peculiar nickname. Let me see, your name is—"

He hesitated and I let him work at it until he cleared his throat again and moved his blue-green eyes to a spot several miles beyond my other shoulder.

"Dalmas," I said. "The same as it was this afternoon."

"Oh, come in, Mr. Dalmas. You'll excuse me, I'm sure. My houseboy is away this evening. So I—" He smiled deprecatingly at the closing door, as though opening and closing it himself sort of dirtied him.

The door put us on a balcony that ran around three sides of a big living room, only three steps above it in level. We went down the steps and Lindley Paul pointed with his eyebrows at a pink chair, and I sat down on it and hoped I wouldn't leave a mark.

It was the kind of room where people sit on floor cushions with their feet in their laps and sip absinthe through lumps of sugar and talk from the backs of their throats, and some of them just squeak. There were bookshelves all around the balcony and bits of angular sculpture in glazed clay on pedestals. There were cozy little divans and bits of embroidered silk tossed here and there against the bases of lamps and so on. There was a big rosewood grand piano and on it a very tall vase with just one yellow rose in it, and under its leg there was a peach-colored Chinese rug a gopher could have spent a week in without showing his nose above the nap.

Lindley Paul leaned in the curve of the piano and lit a cigarette without offering me one. He put his head back to blow smoke at the tall ceiling and that made his throat look more than ever like the throat of a woman.

"It's a very slight matter," he said negligently. "Really hardly worth bothering you about. But I thought I might as well have an escort. You must promise not to flash any guns or anything like that. I suppose you do carry a gun."

"Oh, yes," I said. "Yes." I looked at the dimple in his chin. You could have lost a marble in it.

"Well, I won't want you to use it, you know, or anything like that. I'm just meeting a couple of men and buying something from them. I shall be carrying a little money in cash."

"How much money and what for?" I asked, putting one of my own matches to one of my own cigarettes.

"Well, really—" It was a nice smile, but I could have put the heel of my hand in it without feeling bad. I just didn't like the man.

"It's rather a confidential mission I'm undertaking for a friend. I'd hardly care to go into the details," he said.

"You just want me to go along to hold your hat," I suggested.

His hand jerked and some ash fell on his white suit cuff. That annoyed him. He frowned down at it, then he said softly, in the manner of a sultan suggesting a silk noose for a harem lady whose tricks have gone stale: "You are not being impertinent, I hope."

"Hope is what keeps us alive," I said.

He stared at me for a while. "I've a damned good mind to give you a sock on the nose," he said.

"That's more like it," I said. "You couldn't do it without hardening up a bit, but I like the spirit. Now let's talk business."

He was still a bit sore. "I ordered a bodyguard," he said coldly. "If I employed a private secretary I shouldn't tell him all my personal business."

"He'd know it if he worked for you steady. He'd know it upside down and backwards. But I'm just day labor. You've got to tell me. What is it—blackmail?"

After a long time he said: "No. It's a necklace of Fei Tsui jade worth at least seventy-five thousand dollars. Did you ever hear of Fei Tsui jade?"

"No."

"We'll have a little brandy and I'll tell you about it. Yes, we'll have a little brandy."

He leaned away from the piano and went off like a dancer, without moving his body above the waist. I put my cigarette out and sniffed at the air and thought I smelled sandalwood, and then Lindley Paul came back with a nice-looking bottle and a couple of sniffing glasses. He poured a tablespoonful in each and handed me a glass.

I put mine down in one piece and waited for him to get through rolling his spoonful under his nose and talk. He got around to it after a while.

He said in a pleasant enough tone: "Fei Tsui jade is the only really valuable kind. The others are valuable for the workmanship put on them, chiefly. Fei Tsui is valuable in itself. There are no known unworked deposits, very little of it in existence, all the known deposits having been exhausted hundreds of years ago. A friend of mine had a necklace of this jade. Fifty-one carved mandarin beads, perfectly matched, about six carats each. It was taken in a holdup some time ago. It was the only thing taken, and we were warned—I happened to be with this lady, which is one reason why I'm taking the risk of making the pay-off—not to tell the police or any insurance company, but wait for a phone call. The call came in a couple of days, the price was set at ten thousand dollars, and the time is tonight at eleven. I haven't heard the place yet. But it's to be somewhere fairly near here, somewhere along the Palisades."

I looked into my empty sniffing glass and shook it. He put a little more brandy in it for me. I sent that after the first dose and lit another cigarette, one of his this time, a nice Virginia Straight Cut with his monogram on the paper.

"Jewel ransom racket," I said. "Well organized, or they wouldn't know where and when to pull the job. People don't wear valuable jewels out very much, and half of the time, when they do, they're phonies. Is jade hard to imitate?"

"As to material, no," Lindley Paul said. "As to workmanship—that would take a lifetime."

"So the stuff can't be cut," I said. "Which means it can't be fenced except for a small fraction of the value. So the ransom money is the gang's only pay-off. I'd say they'll play ball. You left your bodyguard problem pretty late, Mr. Paul. How do you know they'll stand for a bodyguard?"

"I don't," he said rather wearily. "But I'm no hero. I like company in the dark. If the thing misses—it misses. I thought of going it alone and then I thought, why not have a man hidden in the back of my car, just in case?"

"In case they take your money and give you a dummy package? How could I prevent that? If I start shooting and come out on top and it *is* a dummy package, you'll never see your jade again. The contact men won't know who's behind the gang. And if I don't open up, they'll be gone before you can see what they've left you. They may not even give you anything. They may tell you your stuff will come to you through the mail after the money has been checked for markings. Is it marked?"

"My God, no!"

"It ought to be," I growled. "It can be marked these days so that only a microscope and black light could show the markings up. But that takes equipment, which means cops. Okay. I'll take a flutter at it. My part will cost you fifty bucks. Better give it to me now, in case we don't come back. I like to feel money."

His broad, handsome face seemed to turn a little white

and glistening. He said swiftly: "Let's have some more brandy."

He poured a real drink this time.

We sat around and waited for the phone to ring. I got my fifty bucks to play with.

The phone rang four times and it sounded from his voice as if women were talking to him. The call we wanted didn't come through until ten-forty.

II   I Lose My Client

I DROVE. Or rather I held the wheel of the big black car and let it drive itself. I was wearing a sporty light-colored overcoat and hat belonging to Lindley Paul. I had ten grand in hundred-dollar bills in one of the pockets. Paul was in the back seat. He had a silver-mounted Luger that was a pip to look at, and I hoped he knew how to use it. There wasn't anything about the job I liked.

The meeting place was a hollow at the head of Purissima Canyon, about fifteen minutes from the house. Paul said he knew the spot fairly well and wouldn't have any trouble directing me.

We switchbacked and figure-eighted around on the side of the mountain until I got dizzy and then all of a sudden we were out on the state highway, and the lights of the streaming cars were a solid white beam as far as you could see in either direction. The long-haul trucks were on their way.

We turned inland past a service station at Sunset Boulevard. There was loneliness then, and for a while the smell of kelp, not very strong, and the smell of wild sage dripping down the dark slopes much stronger. A dim, distant yellow window would peek down at us from the crest of some realtor's dream. A car would growl by and its white glare would hide the hills for a moment. There was a half-moon and wisps of cold fog chasing it down the sky.

"Off here is the Bel-Air Beach Club," Paul said. "The next canyon is Las Pulgas and the next after that is Purissima. We turn off at the top of the next rise." His voice was hushed, taut. It didn't have any of the Park Avenue brass of our earlier acquaintance.

"Keep your head down," I growled back at him. "We may be watched all the way. This car sticks out like spats at an Iowa picnic."

The car purred on in front of me until, "Turn right here," he whispered sharply at the top of the next hill.

I swung the black car into a wide, weed-grown boulevard that had never jelled into a traffic artery. The black stumps of unfinished electroliers jutted up from the crusted sidewalk. Brush leaned over the concrete from the waste land behind. I could hear crickets chirp and tree frogs drone behind them. The car was that silent.

There was a house to a block now, all dark. The folks out there went to bed with the chickens it seemed. At the end of this road the concrete stopped abruptly and we slid down a dirt slope to a dirt terrace, then down another slope, and a barricade of what looked like four-by-fours painted white loomed across the dirt road.

I heard a rustling behind me and Paul leaned over the seat, with a sigh in his whispered voice. "This is the spot. You've got to get out and move that barricade and drive on down into the hollow. That's probably so that we can't make a quick exit, as we'd have to back out with this car. They want their time to get away."

"Shut up and keep down unless you hear me yell," I said.

I cut the almost noiseless motor and sat there listening. The crickets and tree frogs got a little louder. I heard nothing else. Nobody was moving nearby, or the crickets would have been still. I touched the cold butt of the gun under my arm, opened the car door and slid out on to the hard clay, stood there. There was brush all around. I could smell the sage. There was enough of it to hide an army. I went towards the barricade.

Perhaps this was just a tryout, to see if Paul did what he was told to do.

I put my hands out—it took both of them—and started to lift a section of the white barrier to one side. It wasn't a tryout. The largest flashlight in the world hit me square in the face from a bush not fifteen feet away.

A thin, high, niggerish voice piped out of the darkness behind the flash: "Two of us with shotguns. Put them mitts up high an' empty. We ain't takin' no chances."

I didn't say anything. For a moment I just stood holding the barricade inches off the ground. Nothing from Paul or the car. Then the weight of the four-by-fours pulled my muscles and my brain said let go and I put the section down again. I put my hands slowly into the air. The flash pinned me like a fly squashed on the wall. I had no particular thought except a vague wonder if there hadn't been a better way for us to work it.

"Tha's fine," the thin, high, whining voice said. "Jes' hold like that until I git aroun' to you."

The voice awakened vague echoes in my brain. It didn't mean anything though. My memory had too many such echoes. I wondered what Paul was doing. A thin, sharp figure detached itself from the fan of light, immediately ceased to be sharp or of any shape at all, and became a vague rustling off to the side. Then the rustling was behind me. I kept my hands in the air and blinked at the glare of the flash.

A light finger touched my back, then the hard end of a gun. The half-remembered voice said: "This may hurt jes' a little."

A giggle and a swishing sound. A white, hot glare jumped through the top of my head. I piled down on the barricade and clawed at it and yelled. My right hand tried to jerk down under my left arm.

I didn't hear the swishing sound the second time. I only saw the white glare get larger and larger, until there was nothing else anywhere but hard, aching white light. Then there was darkness in which something red wriggled like a germ under the microscope. Then there was nothing red and nothing wriggling, just darkness and emptiness, and a falling sensation.

I woke up looking fuzzily at a star and listening to two goblins talking in a black hat.

"Lou Lid."

"What's that?"

"Lou Lid."

"Who's Lou Lid?"

"A tough dinge gunman you saw third-degreed once down at the Hall."

"Oh . . . Lou Lid."

I rolled over and clawed at the ground and crawled up on one knee. I groaned. There wasn't anybody there. I was talking to myself, coming out of it. I balanced myself, holding my hands flat on the ground, listening, not hearing anything. When I moved my hands, dried burrs stuck to the skin and the sticky ooze from the purple sage from which wild bees get most of their honey.

Honey was sweet. Much, much too sweet, and too hard on the stomach. I leaned down and vomited.

Time passed and I gathered my insides together again. I still didn't hear anything but the buzzing in my own ears. I got up very cautiously, like an old man getting out of a tub bath. My feet didn't have much feeling in them and my legs were rubbery. I wobbled and wiped the cold sweat of nausea off my forehead and felt the back of my head. It was soft and pulpy, like a bruised peach. When I touched it I could feel the pain clear down to my ankles. I could feel every pain I ever felt since the first time I got kicked in the rear in grade school.

Then my eyes cleared enough for me to see the outlines of the shallow bowl of wild land, with brush growing on the banks all around like a low wall, and a dirt road, indistinct under the sinking moon, crawling up one side. Then I saw the car.

It was quite close to me, not more than twenty feet away. I just hadn't looked in that direction. It was Lindley Paul's car, lightless. I stumbled over to it and instinctively grabbed under my arm for a gun. Of course there wasn't any gun there now. The whiny guy whose voice reminded me of someone would have seen to that. But I still had a fountain-pen flash. I unshipped it, opened the rear door of the car and poked the light in.

It didn't show anything—no blood, no torn upholstery, no starred or splintered glass, no bodies. The car didn't seem to have been the scene of a battle. It was just empty. The keys hung on the ornate panel. It had been driven down there and left. I pointed my little flash at the ground and began to prowl, looking for him. He'd be around there all right, if the car was.

Then in the cold silence a motor throbbed above the rim of the bowl. The light in my hand went out. Other lights—headlights—tilted up over the frayed bushes. I dropped and crawled swiftly behind the hood of Lindley Paul's car.

The lights tilted down, got brighter. They were coming down the slope of the dirt road into the bowl. I could hear the dull, idling sound of a small motor now.

Halfway down the car stopped. A spotlight at the side of the windshield clicked on and swung to one side. It lowered, held steady on some point I couldn't see. The spot clicked off again and the car came slowly on down the slope.

At the bottom it turned a little so that its headlights raked the black sedan. I took my upper lip between my teeth and didn't feel myself biting it until I tasted the blood.

The car swung a little more. Its lights went out abruptly. Its motor died and once more the night became large and empty and black and silent. Nothing—no movement, except the crickets and tree frogs far off that had been droning all the time, only I hadn't been hearing them. Then a door latch snapped and there was a light, quick step on the ground and a beam of light cut across the top of my head like a sword.

Then a laugh. A girl's laugh—strained, taut as a mandolin wire. And the white beam jumped under the big black car and hit my feet.

The girl's voice said sharply: "All right, you. Come out of there with your hands up—and very damned empty! I've got you covered!"

I didn't move.

The voice stabbed at me again. "Listen, I've got three slugs for your feet, mister, and seven more for your tummy, and spare clips, and I change them plenty fast. Coming?"

"Put that toy up!" I snarled. "Or I'll blow it out of your hand." My voice sounded like somebody else's voice. It was hoarse and thick.

"Oh, a hard-boiled gentleman." There was a little quaver in the voice now. Then it hardened again. "Coming? I'll count three. Look at all the odds I'm giving you—twelve big fat cylinders to hide behind—or is it sixteen? Your feet will hurt you though. And anklebones take years to get well when they've been hurt, and sometimes—"

I straightened up and looked into her flashlight. "I talk too much when I'm scared, too," I said.

"Don't—don't move another inch! Who are you?"

"A bum private dick—detective to you. Who cares?"

I started around the car towards her. She didn't shoot. When I was six feet from her I stopped.

"You stay right there!" she snapped angrily—after I had stopped.

"Sure. What were you looking at back there, with your windshield spotlight?"

"A man."

"Hurt bad?"

"I'm afraid he's dead," she said simply. "And you look half dead yourself."

"I've been sapped," I said. "It always makes me dark under the eyes."

"A nice sense of humor," she said. "Like a morgue attendant."

"Let's look him over," I said gruffly. "You can stay behind me with your popgun, if it makes you feel any safer."

"I never felt safer in my life," she said angrily, and backed away from me.

I circled the little car she had come in. An ordinary little car, nice and clean and shiny under what was left of the moon. I heard her steps behind me but I didn't pay any attention to her. About halfway up the slope a few feet off to the side I saw his foot.

I put my own little flash on him and then the girl added hers. I saw him all. He was smeared to the ground, on his back, at the base of a bush. He was in that bag-of-clothes position that always means the same thing.

The girl didn't speak. She kept away from me and breathed hard and held her light as steadily as any tough old homicide veteran.

One of his hands was flung out in a frozen gesture. The fingers were curled. The other hand was under him and his overcoat was twisted as though he had been thrown out and rolled. His thick blond hair was matted with blood, black as shoe polish under the moon, and there was more of it on his face and there was a gray ooze mixed in with the blood. I didn't see his hat.

Then was when I ought to have got shot. Up to that instant I hadn't even thought of the packet of money in my pocket. The thought came to me so quickly now, jarred me so hard, that I jammed a hand down into my pocket. It must have looked exactly like a hand going for a gun.

The pocket was quite empty. I took the hand out and looked back at her.

"Mister," she half sighed, "if I hadn't made my mind up about your face—"

"I had ten grand," I said. "It was his money. I was carrying it for him. It was a pay-off. I just remembered the money. And you've got the sweetest set of nerves I ever met on a woman. I didn't kill him."

"I didn't think you killed him," she said. "Somebody hated him to smash his head open like that."

"I hadn't known him long enough to hate him," I said. "Hold the flash down again."

I knelt and went through his pockets, trying not to move him much. He had loose silver and bills, keys in a tooled leather case, the usual billfold with the usual window for a driver's licence and the usual insurance cards behind the licence. No money in the folder. I wondered why they had missed his trouser pockets. Panicked by the light, perhaps. Otherwise they'd have stripped him down to his coat lining. I held more stuff up in her light: two fine handkerchiefs as white and crisp as dry snow; half a dozen paper match folders from swank night traps; a silver cigarette case as heavy as a buggy weight and full of his imported straight-cuts; another cigarette case, with a tortoise-shell frame and embroidered silk sides, each side a writhing dragon. I tickled the catch open and there were three long cigarettes under the elastic, Russians, with hollow mouthpieces. I pinched one. It felt old, dry.

"Maybe for ladies," I said. "He smoked others."

"Or maybe jujus," the girl said behind me, breathing on my neck. "I knew a lad who smoked them once. Could I look?"

I passed the case up to her and she poked her flash into it until I growled at her to put it on the ground again. There wasn't anything else to examine. She snapped the case shut and handed it back and I put it in his breast pocket.

"That's all. Whoever tapped him down was afraid to wait and clean up. Thanks."

I stood up casually and turned and speared the little gun out of her hand.

"Darn it, you didn't have to get rough!" she snapped.

"Give," I said. "Who are you, and how come you ride around this place at midnight?"

She pretended I had hurt her hand, put the flash on it and looked at it carefully.

"I've been nice to you, haven't I?" she complained. "I'm burning up with curiosity and scared and I haven't asked you a single question, have I?"

"You've been swell," I said. "But I'm in a spot where I can't fool around. Who are you? And douse the flash now. We don't need light any more."

She put it out and the darkness lightened for us gradually until we could see the outlines of the bushes and the dead man's sprawled body and the glare in the southeastern sky that would be Santa Monica.

"My name is Carol Pride," she said. "I live in Santa Monica. I try to do feature stories for a newspaper syndicate. Sometimes I can't get sleepy at night and I go out riding—just anywhere. I know all this country like a book. I saw your little light flickering around down in the hollow and it seemed to me it was pretty cold for young love—if they use lights."

"I wouldn't know," I said. "I never did. So you have spare clips for this gun. Would you have a permit for it?"

I hefted the little weapon. It felt like a Colt .25 in the dark. It had a nice balance for a small gun. Plenty of good men have been put to sleep with .25's.

"Certainly I have a permit. That was just bluff about the spare clips though."

"Not afraid of things are you, Miss Pride? Or would it be Mrs.?"

"No, it wouldn't. . . . This neighborhood isn't dangerous. People don't even lock their doors around here. I guess some bad men just happened to get wise how lonely it is."

I turned the little gun around and held it out. "Here. It's not my night to be clever. Now if you'll be good enough to

ride me down to Castellamare, I'll take my car there and go
find some law."

"Shouldn't somebody stay with him?"

I looked at the radiolite dial of my wrist watch. "It's a
quarter to one," I said. "We'll leave him with the crickets
and the stars. Let's go."

She tucked the gun in her bag and we went back down
the slope and got into her car. She jockeyed it around without lights and drove it back up the slope. The big black car
looked like a monument standing there behind us.

At the top of the rise I got out and dragged the section of
white barricade back into position across the road. He was
safe for the night now, and likely enough for many nights.

The girl didn't speak until we had come near the first
house. Then she put the lights on and said quietly: "There's
blood on your face, Mr. Whatever-Your-Name-Is, and I
never saw a man who needed a drink worse. Why not go
back to my house and phone West Los Angeles from there?
There's nothing but a fire station in this neighborhood."

"John Dalmas is the name," I said. "I like the blood on
my face. You wouldn't want to be mixed up in a mess like
this. I won't even mention you."

She said: "I'm an orphan and live all alone. It wouldn't
matter in the slightest."

"Just keep going down to the beach," I said. "I'll play it
solo after that."

But we had to stop once before we got to Castellamare.
The movement of the car made me go off into the weeds
and be sick again.

When we came to the place where my car was parked and
the steps started up the hill I said good night to her and sat
in the Chrysler until I couldn't see her taillights any more.

The sidewalk café was still open. I could have gone in
there and had a drink and phoned. But it seemed smarter
to do what I did half an hour later—walk into the West
Los Angeles Police Station cold sober and green, with the
blood still on my face.

Cops are just people. And their whisky is just as good as
what they push across bars at you.

III Lou Lid

I DIDN'T tell it well. It tasted worse all the time. Reavis, the man who came out from the downtown homicide bureau, listened to me with his eyes on the floor, and two plain-clothes men lounged behind him like a bodyguard. A prowl-car unit had gone out long before to guard the body.

Reavis was a thin, narrow-faced, quiet man about fifty, with smooth gray skin and immaculate clothes. His trousers had a knife-edge crease and he pulled them up carefully after he sat down. His shirt and tie looked as if he had put them on new ten minutes ago and his hat looked as if he had bought it on the way over.

We were in the day captain's room at the West Los Angeles Police Station, just off Santa Monica Boulevard, near Sawtelle. There were just the four of us in it. Some drunk in a cell, waiting to go down to the city drunk tank for sunrise court, kept giving the Australian bush call all the time we were talking.

"So I was his bodyguard for the evening," I said at the end. "And a sweet job I made of it."

"I wouldn't give any thought to that," Reavis said care-lessly. "It could happen to anybody. Seems to me they took you for this Lindley Paul, slugged you to save argument and to get plenty of time, perhaps didn't have the stuff with them at all and didn't mean to give it up so cheap. When they found you were not Paul they got sore and took it out on him."

"He had a gun," I said. "A swell Luger, but two shotguns staring at you don't make you warlike."

"About this darktown brother," Reavis said. He reached for a phone on the desk.

"Just a voice in the dark. I couldn't be sure."

"Yeah, but we'll find what he was doing about that time. Lou Lid. A name that would linger."

He lifted the phone off its cradle and told the PBX man: "Desk at headquarters, Joe. . . . This is Reavis out in West L.A. on that stick-up murder. I want a Negro or half-Negro gunman name of Lou Lid. About twenty-two to twenty-four, a lightish brown, neat-appearing, small, say one hundred thirty, cast in one eye, I forget which. There's something on him, but not much, and he's been in and out plenty times. The boys at Seventy-seventh will know him. I want to check his movements for this evening. Give the colored squad an hour, then put him on the air."

He cradled the phone and winked at me. "We got the best shine dicks west of Chicago. If he's in town, they'll pick him off without even looking. Will we move out there now?"

We went downstairs and got into a squad car and went back through Santa Monica to the Palisades.

Hours later, in the cold gray dawn, I got home. I was guzzling aspirin and whisky and bathing the back of my head with very hot water when my phone jangled. It was Reavis.

"Well, we got Lou Lid," he said. "Pasadena got him and a Mex named Fuente. Picked them up on Arroyo Seco Boulevard—not exactly with shovels, but kind of careful."

"Go on," I said, holding the phone tight enough to crack it, "give me the punch line."

"You guessed it already. They found them under the Colorado Street Bridge. Gagged, trussed fore and aft with old wire. And smashed like ripe oranges. Like it?"

I breathed hard. "It's just what I needed to make me sleep like a baby," I said.

The hard concrete pavement of Arroyo Seco Boulevard is some seventy-five feet directly below Colorado Street Bridge —sometimes also known as Suicide Bridge.

"Well," Reavis said after a pause, "it looks like you bit into something rotten. What do you say now?"

"Just for a quick guess I'd say an attempted hijack of the pay-off money by a couple of smart-alecks that got a lead to it somehow, picked their own spot and got smeared with the cash."

"That would need inside help," Reavis said. "You mean guys that knew the beads were taken, but didn't have them.

I like better that they tried to leave town with the whole take instead of passing it to the boss. Or even that the boss thought he had too many mouths to feed."

He said good night and wished me pleasant dreams. I drank enough whisky to kill the pain in my head. Which was more than was good for me.

I got down to the office late enough to be elegant, but not feeling that way. Two stitches in the back of my scalp had begun to draw and the tape over the shaved place felt as hot as a bartender's bunion.

My office was two rooms hard by the coffee-shop smell of the Mansion House Hotel. The little one was a reception room I always left unlocked for a client to go in and wait, in case I had a client and he wanted to wait.

Carol Pride was in there, sniffing at the faded red davenport, the two odd chairs, the small square of carpet and the boy's-size library table with the pre-Repeal magazines on it.

She wore brownish speckled tweeds with wide lapels and a mannish shirt and tie, nice shoes, a black hat that might have cost twenty dollars for all I knew, and looked as if you could have made it with one hand out of an old desk blotter.

"Well, you do get up," she said. "That's nice to know. I was beginning to think perhaps you did all your work in bed."

"Tut, tut," I said. "Come into my boudoir."

I unlocked the communicating door, which looked better than just kicking the lock lightly—which had the same effect —and we went into the rest of the suite, which was a rust-red carpet with plenty of ink on it, five green filing cases, three of them full of California climate, an advertising calendar showing the Dionne quintuplets rolling around on a sky-blue floor, a few near walnut chairs, and the usual desk with the usual heel marks on it and the usual squeaky swivel chair behind it. I sat down in that and put my hat on the telephone.

I hadn't really seen her before, even by the lights down at Castellamare. She looked about twenty-six and as if she hadn't slept very well. She had a tired, pretty little face under fluffed-out brown hair, a rather narrow forehead with more height than is considered elegant, a small inquisitive nose, an upper lip a shade too long and a mouth more than a shade too wide. Her eyes could be very blue if they tried.

She looked quiet, but not mousy-quiet. She looked smart, but not Hollywood-smart.

"I read it in the evening paper that comes out in the morning," she said. "What there was of it."

"And that means the law won't break it as a big story. They'd have held it for the morning sheets."

"Well, anyhow, I've been doing a little work on it for you," she said.

I stared hard at her, poked a flat box of cigarettes across the desk, and filled my pipe. "You're making a mistake," I said. "I'm not on this case. I ate my dirt last night and banged myself to sleep with a bottle. This is a police job."

"I don't think it is," she said. "Not all of it. And anyway you have to earn your fee. Or didn't you get a fee?"

"Fifty bucks," I said. "I'll return it when I know who to return it to. Even my mother wouldn't think I earned it."

"I like you," she said. "You look like a guy who was almost a heel and then something stopped him—just at the last minute. Do you know who that jade necklace belonged to?"

I sat up with a jerk that hurt. "What jade necklace?" I almost yelled. I hadn't told her anything about a jade necklace. There hadn't been anything in the paper about a jade necklace.

"You don't have to be clever. I've been talking to the man on the case—Lieutenant Reavis. I told him about last night. I get along with policemen. He thought I knew more than I did. So he told me things."

"Well—who does it belong to?" I asked, after a heavy silence.

"A Mrs. Philip Courtney Prendergast, a lady who lives in Beverly Hills—part of the year at least. Her husband has a million or so and a bad liver. Mrs. Prendergast is a black-eyed blonde who goes places while Mr. Prendergast stays home and takes calomel."

"Blondes don't like blonds," I said. "Lindley Paul was as blond as a Swiss yodeler."

"Don't be silly. That comes of reading movie magazines. This blonde liked that blond. I *know*. The society editor of the *Chronicle* told me. He weighs two hundred pounds and has a mustache and they call him Giddy Gertie."

"He tell you about the necklace?"

"No. The manager of Blocks Jewelry Company told me about that. I told him I was doing an article on rare jade— for the *Police Gazette*. Now you've got me doing the wise-cracks."

I lit my pipe for the third time and squeaked my chair back and nearly fell over backwards.

"Reavis knows all this?" I asked, trying to stare at her without seeming to.

"He didn't tell me he did. He can find out easily enough. I've no doubt he will. He's nobody's fool."

"Except yours," I said. "Did he tell you about Lou Lid and Fuente the Mex?"

"No. Who are they?"

I told her about them. "Why, that's terrible," she said, and smiled.

"Your old man wasn't a cop by any chance, was he?" I asked suspiciously.

"Police Chief of Pomona for almost fifteen years."

I didn't say anything. I remembered that Police Chief John Pride of Pomona had been shot dead by two kid bandits about four years before.

After a while I said: "I should have thought of that. All right, what next?"

"I'll lay you five to one Mrs. Prendergast didn't get her necklace back and that her bilious husband has enough drag to keep that part of the story and their name out of the papers, and that she needs a nice detective to help her get straightened out—without any scandal."

"What scandal?"

"Oh, I don't know. She's the type that would have a basket of it in her dressing room."

"I suppose you had breakfast with her," I said. "What time did you get up?"

"No, I can't see her till two o'clock. I got up at six."

"My God," I said, and got a bottle out of the deep drawer of my desk. "My head hurts me something terrible."

"Just one," Carol Pride said sharply. "And only because you were beaten up. But I daresay that happens quite often."

I put the drink inside me, corked the bottle but not too tightly, and drew a deep breath.

The girl groped in her brown bag and said: "There's something else. But maybe you ought to handle this part of it yourself."

"It's nice to know I'm still working here," I said.

She rolled three long Russian cigarettes across the desk. She didn't smile.

"Look inside the mouthpieces," she said, "and draw your own conclusions. I swiped them out of that Chinese case last night. They all have that something to make you wonder."

"And you a cop's daughter," I said.

She stood up, wiped a little pipe ash off the edge of my desk with her bag and went towards the door.

"I'm a woman too. Now I've got to go see another society editor and find out more about Mrs. Philip Courtney Prendergast and her love life. Fun, isn't it?"

The office door and my mouth shut at about the same moment.

I picked up one of the Russian cigarettes. I pinched it between my fingers and peeped into the hollow mouthpiece. There seemed to be something rolled up in there, like a piece of paper or card, something that wouldn't have improved the drawing of the cigarette. I finally managed to dig it out with the nail-file blade of my pocketknife.

It was a card all right, a thin ivory calling card, man's size. Three words were engraved on it, nothing else.

Soukesian the Psychic

I looked into the other mouthpieces, found identical cards in each of them. It didn't mean a thing to me. I had never heard of Soukesian the Psychic. After a while I looked him up 'n the phone book. There was a man named Soukesian on West Seventh. It sounded Armenian so I looked him up again under *Oriental Rugs* in the classified section. He was there all right, but that didn't prove anything. You don't have to be a psychic to sell oriental rugs. You only have to be a psychic to buy them. And something told me this Soukesian on the card didn't have anything to do with oriental rugs.

I had a rough idea what his racket would be and what kind of people would be his customers. And the bigger he was the less he would advertise. If you gave him enough time and paid him enough, he would cure anything from a tired husband to a grasshopper plague. He would be an expert in frustrated women, in tricky, tangled, love affairs, in wandering boys who hadn't written home, in whether to sell the property now or hold it another year, in whether this part will hurt my type with my public or improve it. Even men would go to him—guys who bellowed like bulls around their own offices and were all cold mush inside just the same. But most of all, women—women with money, women with jewels, women who could be twisted like silk thread around a lean Asiatic finger.

I refilled my pipe and shook my thoughts around without moving my head too much, and fished for a reason why a man would carry a spare cigarette case, with three cigarettes in it not meant for smoking, and in each of those three cigarettes the name of another man concealed. Who would find that name?

I pushed the bottle to one side and grinned. Anyone would find those cards who went through Lindley Paul's pockets with a fine-tooth comb—carefully and taking time. Who would do that? A cop. And when? If Mr. Lindley Paul died or was badly hurt in mysterious circumstances.

I took my hat off the telephone and called a man named Willy Peters who was in the insurance business, so he said, and did a sideline selling unlisted telephone numbers bribed from maids and chauffeurs. His fee was five bucks. I figured Lindley Paul could afford it out of his fifty.

Willy Peters had what I wanted. It was a Brentwood Heights number.

I called Reavis down at headquarters. He said everything was fine except his sleeping time and for me just to keep my mouth shut and not worry, but I ought really to have told him about the girl. I said that was right but maybe he had a daughter himself and wouldn't be so keen to have a lot of camera hounds jumping out at her. He said he had and the case didn't make me look very good but it could happen to anyone and so long.

I called Violets M'Gee to ask him to lunch some day when he had just had his teeth cleaned and his mouth was sore. But he was up in Ventura returning a prisoner. Then I called the Brentwood Heights number of Soukesian the Psychic.

After a while a slightly foreign woman's voice said: " 'Allo."

"May I speak to Mr. Soukesian?"

"I am ver-ry sor-ry. Soukesian he weel never speak upon the telephone. I am hees secretar-ry. Weel I take the message?"

"Yeah. Got a pencil?"

"But of course I 'ave the pencil. The message, eef you please?"

I gave her my name and address and occupation and telephone number first. I made sure she had them spelled right. Then I said: "It's about the murder of a man named Lindley Paul. It happened last night down on the Palisades near Santa Monica. I'd like to consult Mr. Soukesian."

"He weel be ver-ry pleased." Her voice was as calm as an oyster. "But of course I cannot give you the appointment today. Soukesian he ees always ver-ry busy. Per'aps tomorrow—"

"Next week will be fine," I said heartily. "There's never any hurry about a murder investigation. Just tell him I'll give him two hours before I go to the police with what I know."

There was a silence. Maybe a breath caught sharply and maybe it was just wire noise. Then the slow foreign voice said: "I weel tell him. I do not understand—"

"Give it the rush, angel. I'll be waiting in my office."

I hung up, fingered the back of my head, put the three cards away in my wallet and felt as if I could eat some hot food. I went out to get it.

IV Second Harvest

THE INDIAN smelled. He smelled clear across my little reception room when I heard the outer door open and got up to see who it was. He stood just inside the door looking as if he had been cast in bronze. He was a big man from the waist up and had a big chest.

Apart from that he looked like a bum. He wore a brown

suit, too small for him. His hat was at least two sizes too small, and had been perspired in freely by someone it fitted better than it fitted him. He wore it about where a house wears a weathercock. His collar had the snug fit of a horse collar and was about the same shade of dirty brown. A tie dangled from it, outside his buttoned coat, and had apparently been tied with a pair of pliers in a knot the size of a pea. Around his bare throat above the collar he wore what looked like a piece of black ribbon.

He had a big, flat face, a big, high-bridged, fleshy nose that looked as hard as the prow of a cruiser. He had lidless eyes, drooping jowls, the shoulders of a blacksmith. If he had been cleaned up a little and dressed in a white nightgown, he would have looked like a very wicked Roman senator.

His smell was the earthy smell of the primitive man; dirty, but not the dirt of cities. "Huh," he said. "Come quick. Come now."

I jerked my thumb at the inner office and went back into it. He followed me ponderously and made as much noise walking as a fly makes. I sat down behind my desk, pointed at the chair opposite, but he didn't sit down. His small black eyes were hostile.

"Come where?" I wanted to know.

"Huh. Me Second Harvest. Me Hollywood Indian."

"Take a chair, Mr. Harvest."

He snorted and his nostrils got very wide. They had been wide enough for mouseholes in the first place.

"Name Second Harvest. No Mr. Harvest. Nuts."

"What do you want?"

"He say come quick. Big white father say come now. He say—"

"Don't give me any more of that pig Latin," I said. "I'm no schoolmarm at the snake dances."

"Nuts," he said.

He removed his hat with slow disgust and turned it upside down. He rolled a finger around under the sweatband. That turned the sweatband up into view. He removed a paper clip from the edge of the leather and moved near enough to throw a dirty fold of tissue paper on the desk. He pointed at it angrily. His lank, greasy black hair had a shelf all around it, high up, from the too-tight hat.

I unfolded the bit of tissue paper and found a card which read: *Soukesian the Psychic*. It was in thin script, nicely engraved. I had three just like it in my wallet.

I played with my empty pipe, stared at the Indian, tried to ride him with my stare. "Okay. What does he want?"

"He want you come now. Quick."

"Nuts," I said. The Indian liked that. That was the fraternity grip. He almost grinned. "It will cost him a hundred bucks as a retainer," I added.

"Huh?"

"Hundred dollars. Iron men. Bucks to the number one hundred. Me no money, me no come. Savvy?" I began to count by opening and closing both fists.

The Indian tossed another fold of tissue paper on the desk. I unfolded it. It contained a brand-new hundred-dollar bill.

"Psychic is right," I said. "A guy that smart I'm scared of, but I'll go nevertheless."

The Indian put his hat back on his head without bothering to fold the sweatband under. It looked only very slightly more comical that way.

I took a gun from under my arm, not the one I had had the night before unfortunately—I hate to lose a gun—dropped the magazine into the heel of my hand, rammed it home again, fiddled with the safety and put the gun back in its holster.

This meant no more to the Indian than if I had scratched my neck.

"I gottum car," he said. "Big car. Nuts."

"Too bad," I said. "I don't like big cars any more. However, let's go."

I locked up and we went out. In the elevator the Indian smelled very strong indeed. Even the elevator operator noticed it.

The car was a tan Lincoln touring, not new but in good shape, with glass gypsy curtains in the back. It dipped down past a shining green polo field, zoomed up the far side, and the dark, foreign-looking driver swung it into a narrow paved ribbon of white concrete that climbed almost as steeply as Lindley Paul's steps, but not as straight. This was well out of town, beyond Westwood, in Brentwood Heights.

We climbed past two orange groves, rich man's pets, as

that is not orange country, past houses molded flat to the side of the foothills, like bas-reliefs.

Then there were no more houses, just the burnt foothills and the cement ribbon and a sheer drop on the left into the coolness of a nameless canyon, and on the right heat bouncing off the seared clay bank at whose edge a few unbeatable wild flowers clawed and hung on like naughty children who won't go to bed.

And in front of me two backs, a slim, whipcord back with a brown neck, black hair, a vizored cap on the black hair, and a wide, untidy back in an old brown suit with the Indian's thick neck and heavy head above that, and on his head the ancient greasy hat with the sweatband still showing.

Then the ribbon of road twisted into a hairpin, the big tires skidded on loose stones, and the tan Lincoln tore through an open gate and up a steep drive lined with pink geraniums growing wild. At the top of the drive there was an eyrie, an eagle's nest, a hilltop house of white plaster and glass and chromium, as modernistic as a fluoroscope and as remote as a lighthouse.

The car reached the top of the driveway, turned, stopped before a blank white wall in which there was a black door. The Indian got out, glared at me. I got out, nudging the gun against my side with the inside of my left arm.

The black door in the white wall opened slowly, untouched from outside, and showed a narrow passage ending far back. A bulb glowed in the ceiling.

The Indian said: "Huh. Go in, big shot."

"After you, Mr. Harvest."

He went in scowling and I followed him and the black door closed noiselessly of itself behind us. A bit of mumbo-jumbo for the customers. At the end of the narrow passage there was an elevator. I had to get into it with the Indian. We went up slowly, with a gentle purring sound, the faint hum of a small motor. The elevator stopped, its door opened without a whisper and there was daylight.

I got out of the elevator. It dropped down again behind me with the Indian still in it. I was in a turret room that was almost all windows, some of them close-draped against the afternoon glare. The rugs on the floor had the soft colors of old Persians, and there was a desk made of carved panels that probably came out of a church. And behind the desk there was a woman smiling at me, a dry, tight, withered smile that would turn to powder if you touched it.

She had sleek, black, coiled hair, a dark Asiatic face. There were pearls in her ears and rings on her fingers, large, rather cheap rings, including a moonstone and a square-cut emerald that looked as phony as a ten-cent-store slave bracelet. Her hands were little and dark and not young and not fit for rings.

"Ah, Meester Dalmas, so ver-ry good of you to come. Soukesian he weel be so pleased."

"Thanks," I said. I took the new hundred-dollar bill out of my wallet and laid it on her desk, in front of her dark, glittering hands. She didn't touch it or look at it. "My party," I said. "But thanks for the thought."

She got up slowly, without moving the smile, swished around the desk in a tight dress that fitted her like a mermaid's skin, and showed that she had a good figure, if you liked them four sizes bigger below the waist than above it.

"I weel conduct you," she said.

She moved before me to a narrow panelled wall, all there was of the room besides the windows and the tiny elevator shaft. She opened a narrow door beyond which there was a silky glow that didn't seem to be daylight. Her smile was older than Egypt now. I nudged my gun holster again and went in.

The door shut silently behind me. The room was octagonal, draped in black velvet, windowless, with a remote black ceiling. In the middle of the black rug there stood a white octagonal table, and on either side of that a stool that was a smaller edition of the table. Over against the black drapes there was one more such stool. There was a large milky ball on a black stand on the white table. The light came from this. There was nothing else in the room.

I stood there for perhaps fifteen seconds, with that obscure feeling of being watched. Then the velvet drapes parted and a man came into the room and walked straight over to the other side of the table and sat down. Only then did he look at me.

He said: "Be seated opposite me, please. Do not smoke and do not move around or fidget, if you can avoid it. How may I serve you?"

V Soukesian the Psychic

He was a tall man, straight as steel, with the blackest eyes I had ever seen and the palest and finest blond hair I had ever seen. He might have been thirty or sixty. He didn't look any more like an Armenian than I did. His hair was brushed straight back from as good a profile as John Barrymore had at twenty-eight. A matinee idol, and I expected something furtive and dark and greasy that rubbed its hands.

He wore a black double-breasted business suit cut like nobody's business, a white shirt, a black tie. He was as neat as a gift book.

I gulped and said: "I don't want a reading. I know all about this stuff."

"Yes?" he said delicately. "And what do you know about it?"

"Let it pass," I said. "I can figure the secretary because she's a sweet buildup for the shock people get when they see you. The Indian stumps me a bit, but it's none of my business anyhow. I'm not a bunko squad cop. What I came about is a murder."

"The Indian happens to be a natural medium," Soukesian said mildly. "They are much rarer than diamonds and, like diamonds, they are sometimes found in dirty places. That might not interest you either. As to the murder you may inform me. I never read the papers."

"Come, come," I said. "Not even to see who's pulling the big checks at the front office? Oke, here it is."

And I laid it in front of him, the whole damn story, and about his cards and where they had been found.

He didn't move a muscle. I don't mean that he didn't scream or wave his arms or stamp on the floor or bite his nails. I mean he simply didn't move at all, not even an eyelid, not even an eye. He just sat there and looked at me, like a stone lion outside the Public Library.

When I was all done he put his finger right down on the spot. "You kept those cards from the police? Why?"

"You tell me. I just did."

"Obviously the hundred dollars I sent you was not nearly enough."

"That's an idea too," I said. "But I hadn't really got around to playing with it."

He moved enough to fold his arms. His black eyes were as shallow as a cafeteria tray or as deep as a hole to China—whichever you like. They didn't say anything, either way.

He said: "You wouldn't believe me if I said I only knew this man in the most casual manner—professionally?"

"I'd take it under advisement," I said.

"I take it you haven't much faith in me. Perhaps Mr. Paul had. Was anything on those cards besides my name?"

"Yeah," I said. "And you wouldn't like it." This was kindergarten stuff, the kind the cops pull on radio crime dramatizations. He let it go without even looking at it.

"I'm in a sensitive profession," he said. "Even in this paradise of fakers. Let me see one of those cards."

"I was kidding you," I said. "There's nothing on them but your name." I got my wallet out and withdrew one card and laid it in front of him. I put the wallet away. He turned the card over with a fingernail.

"You know what I figure?" I said heartily. "I figure Lindley Paul thought you would be able to find out who did him in, even if the police couldn't. Which means he was afraid of somebody."

Soukesian unfolded his arms and folded them the other way. With him that was probably equivalent to climbing up the light fixture and biting off a bulb.

"You don't think anything of the sort," he said. "How much—quickly—for the three cards and a signed statement that you searched the body before you notified the police?"

"Not bad," I said, "for a guy whose brother is a rug peddler."

He smiled, very gently. There was something almost nice about his smile. "There are honest rug dealers," he said. "But Arizmian Soukesian is not my brother. Ours is a common name in Armenia."

I nodded.

"You think I'm just another faker, of course," he added.

"Go ahead and prove you're not."

"Perhaps it is not money you want after all," he said carefully.

"Perhaps it isn't."

I didn't see him move his foot, but he must have touched a floor button. The black velvet drapes parted and the Indian came into the room. He didn't look dirty or funny any more.

He was dressed in loose white trousers and a white tunic embroidered in black. There was a black sash around his waist and a black fillet around his forehead. His black eyes were sleepy. He shuffled over to the stool beside the drapes and sat down and folded his arms and leaned his head on his chest. He looked bulkier than ever, as if these clothes were over his other clothes.

Soukesian held his hands above the milky globe that was between us on the white table. The light on the remote black ceiling was broken and began to weave into odd shapes and patterns, very faint because the ceiling was black. The Indian kept his head low and his chin on his chest but his eyes turned up slowly and stared at the weaving hands.

The hands moved in a swift, graceful, intricate pattern that meant anything or nothing, that was like Junior Leaguers doing Greek dances, or coils of Christmas ribbon tossed on the floor—whatever you liked.

The Indian's solid jaw rested on his solid chest and slowly, like a toad's eyes, his eyes shut.

"I could have hypnotized him without all that," Soukesian said softly. "It's merely part of the show."

"Yeah." I watched his lean, firm throat.

"Now, something Lindley Paul touched," he said. "This card will do."

He stood up noiselessly and went across to the Indian and pushed the card inside the fillet against the Indian's forehead, left it there. He sat down again.

He began to mutter softly in a guttural language I didn't know. I watched his throat.

The Indian began to speak. He spoke very slowly and heavily, between motionless lips, as though the words were heavy stones he had to drag up hill in a blazing hot sun.

"Lindley Paul bad man. Make love to squaw of chief.

Chief very angry. Chief have necklace stolen. Lindley Paul have to get um back. Bad man kill. *Grrrr*."

The Indian's head jerked as Soukesian clapped his hands. The little lidless black eyes snapped open again. Soukesian looked at me with no expression at all on his handsome face.

"Neat," I said. "And not a darn bit gaudy." I jerked a thumb at the Indian. "He's a bit heavy to sit on your knee, isn't he? I haven't seen a good ventriloquist act since the chorus girls quit wearing tights."

Soukesian smiled very faintly.

"I watched your throat muscles," I said. "No matter. I guess I get the idea. Paul had been cutting corners with somebody's wife. The somebody was jealous enough to have him put away. It has points, as a theory. Because this jade necklace she was wearing wouldn't be worn often and somebody had to know she was wearing it that particular night when the stick-up was pulled off. A husband would know that."

"It is quite possible," Soukesian said. "And since you were not killed perhaps it was not the intent to kill Lindley Paul. Merely to beat him up."

"Yeah," I said. "And here's another idea. I ought to have had it before. If Lindley Paul really did fear somebody and wanted to leave a message, then there might still be something written on those cards—in invisible ink."

That got to him. His smile hung on but it had a little more wrinkle at the corners than at first. The time was short for me to judge that.

The light inside the milky globe suddenly went out. Instantly the room was pitch dark. You couldn't see your own hand. I kicked my stool back and jerked my gun free and started to back away.

A rush of air brought a strong earthy smell with it. It was uncanny. Without the slightest error of timing or space, even in that complete blackness, the Indian hit me from behind and pinned my arms. He started to lift me. I could have jerked a hand up and fanned the room in front of me with blind shots. I didn't try. There wasn't any point in it.

The Indian lifted me with his two hands holding my arms against my sides as though a steam crane was lifting me. He set me down again, hard, and he had my wrists. He had them behind me, twisting them. A knee like the corner of a foundation stone went into my back. I tried to yell. Breath panted in my throat and couldn't get out.

The Indian threw me sideways, wrapped my legs with his legs as we fell, and had me in a barrel. I hit the floor hard, with part of his weight on me.

I still had the gun. The Indian didn't know I had it. At least he didn't act as if he knew. It was jammed down between us. I started to turn it.

The light flicked on again.

Soukesian was standing beyond the white table, leaning on it. He looked older. There was something on his face I didn't like. He looked like a man who had something to do he didn't relish, but was going to do it all the same.

"So," he said softly. "Invisible writing."

Then the curtains swished apart and the thin dark woman rushed into the room with a reeking white cloth in her hands and slapped it around my face, leaning down to glare at me with hot black eyes.

The Indian grunted a little behind me, straining at my arms.

I had to breathe the chloroform. There was too much weight dragging my throat tight. The thick, sweetish reek of it ate into me.

I went away from there.

Just before I went somebody fired a gun twice. The sound didn't seem to have anything to do with me.

I was lying out in the open again, just like the night before. This time it was daylight and the sun was burning a hole in my right leg. I could see the hot blue sky, the lines of a ridge, scrub oak, yuccas in bloom spouting from the side of a hill, more hot blue sky.

I sat up. Then my left leg began to tingle with tiny needle points. I rubbed it. I rubbed the pit of my stomach. The chloroform stank in my nose. I was as hollow and rank as an old oil drum.

I got up on my feet, but didn't stay there. The vomiting was worse than last night. More shakes to it, more chills, and my stomach hurt worse. I got back up on my feet.

The breeze off the ocean lifted up the slope and put a little frail life into me. I staggered around dopily and looked at some tire marks on red clay, then at a big galvanized-iron cross, once white but with the paint flaked off badly.

It was studded with empty sockets for light bulbs, and its base was of cracked concrete with an open door, inside which a verdigris-coated copper switch showed.

Beyond this concrete base I saw the feet.

They stuck out casually from under a bush. They were in hard-toed shoes, the kind college boys used to wear about the year before the war. I hadn't seen shoes like that for years, except once.

I went over there and parted the bushes and looked down at the Indian.

His broad, blunt hands lay at his sides, large and empty and limp. There were bits of clay and dead leaf and wild oyster-plant seeds in his greasy black hair. A tracery of sunlight skimmed along his brown cheek. On his stomach the flies had found a sodden patch of blood. His eyes were like other eyes I had seen—too many of them—half open, clear, but the play behind them was over.

He had his comic street clothes on again and his greasy hat lay near him, with the sweatband still wrong side out. He wasn't funny any more, or tough, or nasty. He was just a poor simple dead guy who had never known what it was all about.

I had killed him, of course. Those were my shots I had heard, from my gun.

I didn't find the gun. I went through my clothes. The other two Soukesian cards were missing. Nothing else. I followed the tire tracks to a deeply rutted road and followed that down the hill. Cars glittered by far below as the sunlight caught their windshields or the curve of a headlight. There was a service station and a few houses down there too. Farther off still the blue of water, piers, the long curve of the shore line towards Point Firmin. It was a little hazy. I couldn't see Catalina Island.

The people I was dealing with seemed to like operating in that part of the country.

It took me half an hour to reach the service station. I phoned for a taxi and it had to come from Santa Monica. I drove all the way home to my place in the Berglund, three blocks above the office, changed clothes, put my last gun in the holster and sat down to the phone.

Soukesian wasn't home. Nobody answered that number. Carol Pride didn't answer her number. I didn't expect her to. She was probably having tea with Mrs. Philip Courtney Prendergast. But police headquarters answered their number, and Reavis was still on the job. He didn't sound pleased to hear from me.

"Anything new on the Lindley Paul killing?" I asked him.

"I thought I told you to forget it. I meant to." His voice was nasty.

"You told me all right, but it keeps worrying at me. I like a clean job. I think her husband had it done."

He was silent for a moment. Then, "Whose husband, smart boy?"

"The husband of the frail that lost the jade beads, naturally."

"And of course you've had to poke your face into who she is."

"It sort of drifted to me," I said. "I just had to reach out."

He was silent again. This time so long that I could hear the loudspeaker on his wall put out a police bulletin on a stolen car.

Then he said very smoothly and distinctly: "I'd like to sell you an idea, shamus. Maybe I can. There's a lot of peace of mind in it. The Police Board gave you a licence once and the sheriff gave you a special badge. Any acting captain with a peeve can get both of them taken away from you overnight. Maybe even just a lieutenant—like me. Now what did you have when you got that licence and that badge? Don't answer, I'm telling you. You had the social standing of a cockroach. You were a snooper for hire. All in the world you had to do then was to spend your last hundred bucks on a down payment on some rent and office furniture and sit on your tail until somebody brought a lion in—so you could put your head in the lion's mouth to see if he would bite. If he bit your ear off, you got sued for mayhem. Are you beginning to get it?"

"It's a good line," I said. "I used it years ago. So you don't want to break the case?"

"If I could trust you, I'd tell you we want to break up a very smart jewel gang. But I can't trust you. Where are you—in a poolroom?"

"I'm in bed," I said. "I've got a telephone jag."

"Well, you just fill yourself a nice hot-water bottle and

put it on your face and go to sleep like a good little boy, will you please?"

"Naw. I'd rather go out and shoot an Indian, just for practice."

"Well, just one Indian, Junior."

"Don't forget that bite," I yelled, and hung the phone in his face.

VI   Lady in Liquor

I HAD a drink on the way down to the boulevard, black coffee laced with brandy, in a place where they knew me. It made my stomach feel like new, but I still had the same shopworn head. And I could still smell chloroform in my whiskers.

I went up to the office and into the little reception room. There were two of them this time, Carol Pride and a blonde. A blonde with black eyes. A blonde to make a bishop kick a hole in a stained-glass window.

Carol Pride stood up and scowled at me and said: "This is Mrs. Philip Courtney Prendergast. She has been waiting quite some time. And she's not used to being kept waiting. She wants to employ you."

The blonde smiled at me and put a gloved hand out. I touched the hand. She was perhaps thirty-five and she had that wide-eyed, dreamy expression, as far as black eyes can have it. Whatever you need, whatever you are—she had it. I didn't pay much attention to her clothes. They were black and white. They were what the guy had put on her and he would know or she wouldn't have gone to him.

I unlocked the door of my private thinking-parlor and ushered them in.

There was a half-empty quart of hooch standing on the corner of my desk.

"Excuse me for keeping you waiting, Mrs. Prendergast," I said. "I had to go out on a little business."

"I don't see why you had to go out," Carol Pride said icily. "There seems to be all you can use right in front of you."

I placed chairs for them and sat down and reached for the bottle and the phone rang at my left elbow.

A strange voice took its time saying: "Dalmas? Okay. We have the gat. I guess you'll want it back, won't you?"

"Both of them. I'm a poor man."

"We only got one," the voice said smoothly. "The one the johns would like to have. I'll be calling you later. Think things over."

"Thanks." I hung up and put the bottle down on the floor and smiled at Mrs. Prendergast.

"I'll do the talking," Carol Pride said. "Mrs. Prendergast has a slight cold. She has to save her voice."

She gave the blonde one of those sidelong looks that women think men don't understand, the kind that feel like a dentist's drill.

"Well—" Mrs. Prendergast said, and moved a little so that she could see along the end of the desk, where I had put the whisky bottle down on the carpet.

"Mrs. Prendergast has taken me into her confidence," Carol Pride said. "I don't know why, unless it is that I have shown her where a lot of unpleasant notoriety can be avoided."

I frowned at her. "There isn't going to be any of that. I talked to Reavis a while ago. He has a hush on it that would make a dynamite explosion sound like a pawnbroker looking at a dollar watch."

"Very funny," Carol Pride said, "for people who dabble in that sort of wit. But it just happens Mrs. Prendergast would like to get her jade necklace back—without Mr. Prendergast knowing it was stolen. It seems he doesn't know yet."

"That's different," I said. (The hell he didn't know!)

Mrs. Prendergast gave me a smile I could feel in my hip pocket. "I just love straight rye," she cooed. "Could we—just a little one?"

I got out a couple of pony glasses and put the bottle up on the desk again. Carol Pride leaned back and lit a cigarette contemptuously and looked at the ceiling. She wasn't

so hard to look at herself. You could look at her longer
without getting dizzy. But Mrs. Prendergast had it all over
her for a quick smash.

I poured a couple of drinks for the ladies. Carol Pride
didn't touch hers at all.

"In case you don't know," she said distantly, "Beverly
Hills, where Mrs. Prendergast lives, is peculiar in some ways.
They have two-way radio cars and only a small territory to
cover and they cover it like a blanket, because there's plenty
of money for police protection in Beverly Hills. In the better homes they even have direct communication with headquarters, over wires that can't be cut."

Mrs. Prendergast put her drink to sleep with one punch
and looked at the bottle. I milked it again.

"That's nothing," she glowed. "We even have photo-cell
connections on our safes and fur closets. We can fix the
house so that even the servants can't go near certain
places without police knocking at the door in about thirty
seconds. Marvelous, isn't it?"

"Yes, marvelous," Carol Pride said. "But that's only in
Beverly Hills. Once outside—and you can't spend your
entire life in Beverly Hills—that is, unless you're an ant—
your jewels are not so safe. So Mrs. Prendergast had a
duplicate of her jade necklace—in soapstone."

I sat up straighter. Lindley Paul had let something drop
about it taking a lifetime to duplicate the workmanship on
Fei Tsui beads—even if material were available.

Mrs. Prendergast fiddled with her second drink, but not
for long. Her smile got warmer and warmer.

"So when she went to a party outside Beverly Hills,
Mrs. Prendergast was supposed to wear the imitation. That
is, when she wanted to wear jade at all. Mr. Prendergast was
very particular about that."

"And he has a lousy temper," Mrs. Prendergast said.

I put some more rye under her hand. Carol Pride watched
me do it and almost snarled at me: "But on the night of
the holdup she made a mistake and was wearing the real
one."

I leered at her.

"I know what you're thinking," she snapped. "Who knew
she had made that mistake? It happened that Mr. Paul
knew it, soon after they left the house. He was her escort."

"He—er—touched the necklace a little," Mrs. Prendergast sighed. "He could tell real jade by the feel of it. I've heard some people can. He knew a lot about jewels."

I leaned back again in my squeaky chair. "Hell," I said disgustedly, "I ought to have suspected that guy long ago. The gang had to have a society finger. How else could they tell when the good things were out of the icebox? He must have pulled a cross on them and they used this chance to put him away."

"Rather wasteful of such a talent, don't you think?" Carol Pride said sweetly. She pushed her little glass along the desk top with one finger. "I don't really care for this, Mrs. Prendergast—if you'd like another—"

"Moths in your ermine," Mrs. Prendergast said, and threw it down the hatch.

"Where and how was the stick-up?" I rapped.

"Well, that seems a little funny too," Carol Pride said, beating Mrs. Prendergast by half a word. "After the party, which was in Brentwood Heights, Mr. Paul wanted to drop in at the Trocadero. They were in his car. At that time they were widening Sunset Boulevard all through the County Strip, if you remember. After they had killed a little time at the Troc—"

"And a few snifters," Mrs. Prendergast giggled, reaching for the bottle. She refilled one of her glasses. That is, some of the whisky went into the glass.

"—Mr. Paul drove her home by way of Santa Monica Boulevard."

"That was the natural way to go," I said. "Almost the only way to go unless you wanted a lot of dust."

"Yes, but it also took them past a certain down-at-the-heels hotel called the Tremaine and a beer parlor across the street from it. Mrs. Prendergast noticed a car pull away from in front of the beer parlor and follow them. She's pretty sure it was that same car that crowded them to the curb a little later—and the holdup men knew just what they wanted. Mrs. Prendergast remembers all this very well."

"Well, naturally," Mrs. Prendergast said. "You don't mean I was drunk, I hope. This baby carries her hooch. You don't lose a string of beads like that every night."

She put her fifth drink down her throat.

"I wouldn't know a darn thing about wha—what those men looked like," she told me a little thickly. "Lin—tha's Mr. Paul—I called him Lin, y'know, felt kinda bad about it. That's why he stuck his neck out."

"It was your money—the ten thousand for the pay-off?" I asked her.

"It wasn't the butler's, honey. And I want those beads back before Court gets wise. How about lookin' over that beer parlor?"

She grabbled around in her black and white bag and pushed some bills across the desk in a lump. I straightened them out and counted them. They added to four hundred and sixty-seven dollars. Nice money. I let them lie.

"Mr. Prendergast," Carol Pride ploughed on sweetly, "whom Mrs. Prendergast calls 'Court,' thinks the imitation necklace was taken. He can't tell one from the other, it seems. He doesn't know anything about last night except that Lindley Paul was killed by some bandits."

"The hell he doesn't." I said it out loud this time, and sourly. I pushed the money back across the desk. "I believe you think you're being blackmailed, Mrs. Prendergast. You're wrong. I think the reason this story hasn't broken in the press the way it happened is because pressure has been brought on the police. They'd be willing anyhow, because what they want is the jewel gang. The punks that killed Paul are dead already."

Mrs. Prendergast stared at me with a hard, bright, alcoholic stare. "I hadn't the slightest idea of bein' blackmailed," she said. She was having trouble with her s's now. "I want my beads and I want them quick. It's not a question of money. Not 'tall. Gimme a drink."

"It's in front of you," I said. She could drink herself under the desk for all I cared.

Carol Pride said: "Don't you think you ought to go out to that beer parlor and see what you can pick up?"

"A piece of chewed pretzel," I said. "Nuts to that idea."

The blonde was waving the bottle over her two glasses. She got herself a drink poured finally, drank it, and pushed the handful of currency around on the desk with a free and easy gesture, like a kid playing with sand.

I took it away from her, put it together again and went around the desk to put it back into her bag.

"If I do anything, I'll let you know," I told her. "I don't need a retainer from *you*, Mrs. Prendergast."

She liked that. She almost took another drink, thought better of it with what she still had to think with, got to her feet and started for the door.

I got to her in time to keep her from opening it with her nose. I held her arm and opened the door for her and there was a uniformed chauffeur leaning against the wall outside.

"Oke," he said listlessly, snapped a cigarette into the distance and took hold of her. "Let's go, baby. I ought to paddle your behind. Damned if I oughtn't."

She giggled and held on to him and they went down the corridor and turned a corner out of sight. I went back into the office and sat down behind my desk and looked at Carol Pride. She was mopping the desk with a dustcloth she had found somewhere.

"You and your office bottle," she said bitterly. Her eyes hated me.

"To hell with her," I said angrily. "I wouldn't trust her with my old socks. I hope she gets raped on the way home. To hell with her beer-parlor angle too."

"Her morals are neither here nor there, Mr. John Dalmas. She has pots of money and she's not tight with it. I've seen her husband and he's nothing but a beanstalk with a checkbook that never runs dry. If any fixing has been done, she has done it herself. She told me she's suspected for some time that Paul was a Raffles. She didn't care as long as he let her alone."

"This Prendergast is a prune, huh? He would be, of course."

"Tall, thin, yellow. Looks as if his first drink of milk soured on his stomach and he could still taste it."

"Paul didn't steal her necklace."

"No?"

"No. And she didn't have any duplicate of it."

Her eyes got narrower and darker. "I suppose Soukesian the Psychic told you all this."

"Who's he?"

She leaned forward a moment and then leaned back and pulled her bag tight against her side.

"I see," she said slowly. "You don't like my work. Excuse me for butting in. I thought I was helping you a little."

"I told you it was none of my business. Go on home and write yourself a feature article. I don't need any help."

"I thought we were friends," she said. "I thought you liked me." She stared at me for a minute with bleak, tired eyes.

"I've got a living to make. I don't make it bucking the police department."

She stood up and looked at me a moment longer without speaking. Then she went to the door and went out. I heard her steps die along the mosaic floor of the corridor.

I sat there for ten or fifteen minutes almost without moving. I tried to guess why Soukesian hadn't killed me. None of it made any sense. I went down to the parking lot and got into my car.

VII I Cross the Bar

THE Hotel Tremaine was far out of Santa Monica, near the junk yards. An interurban right-of-way split the street in half, and just as I got to the block that would have the number I had looked up, a two-car train came racketing by at forty-five miles an hour, making almost as much noise as a transport plane taking off. I speeded up beside it and passed the block, pulled into the cement space in front of a market that had gone out of business. I got out and looked back from the corner of the wall.

I could see the Hotel Tremaine's sign over a narrow door between two store fronts, both empty—an old two-story walk-up. Its woodwork would smell of kerosene, its shades would be cracked, its curtains would be a sleazy cotton lace and its bedsprings would stick into your back. I knew all about places like the Hotel Tremaine, I had slept in them, staked out in them, fought with bitter, scrawny landladies in them, got shot at in them, and might yet get carried out of one of them to the morgue wagon. They are flops where you find the cheap ones, the sniffers and pin-jabbers, the gowed-up runts who shoot you before you can say hello.

The beer parlor was on my side of the street. I went back to the Chrysler and got inside it while I moved my gun to my waistband, then I went along the sidewalk.

There was a red neon sign—BEER—over it. A wide pulled-down shade masked the front window, contrary to the law. The place was just a made-over store, half-frontage. I opened the door and went in.

The barman was playing the pin game on the house's money and a man sat on a stool with a brown hat on the back of his head reading a letter. Prices were scrawled in white on the mirror back of the bar.

The bar was just a plain, heavy wooden counter, and at each end of it hung an old frontier .44 in a flimsy cheap holster no gunfighter would ever have worn. There were printed cards on the walls, about not asking for credit and what to take for a hangover and a liquor breath, and there were some nice legs in photographs.

The place didn't look as if it even paid expenses.

The barkeep left the pin game and went behind the bar. He was fiftyish, sour. The bottoms of his trousers were frayed and he moved as if he had corns. The man on the stool kept right on chuckling over his letter, which was written in green ink on pink paper.

The barkeep put both his blotched hands on the bar and looked at me with the expression of a dead-pan comedian, and I said: "Beer."

He drew it slowly, raking the glass with an old dinner knife.

I sipped my beer and held my glass with my left hand. After a while I said: "Seen Lou Lid lately?" This seemed to be in order. There had been nothing in any paper I had seen about Lou Lid and Fuente the Mex.

The barkeep looked at me blankly. The skin over his eyes was grained like lizard skin. Finally he spoke in a husky whisper. "Don't know him."

There was a thick white scar on his throat. A knife had gone in there once which accounted for the husky whisper.

The man who was reading the letter guffawed suddenly

and slapped his thigh. "I gotta tell this to Moose," he roared. "This is right from the bottom of the bucket."

He got down off his stool and ambled over to a door in the rear wall and went through it. He was a husky dark man who looked like anybody. The door shut behind him.

The barkeep said in his husky whisper: "Lou Lid, huh? Funny moniker. Lots a guys come in here. I dunno their names. Copper?"

"Private," I said. "Don't let it bother you. I'm just drinking beer. This Lou Lid was a shine. Light brown. Young."

"Well, maybe I seen him sometime. I don't recall."

"Who's Moose?"

"Him? That's the boss. Moose Magoon."

He dipped a thick towel down in a bucket and folded it and wrung it out and pushed it along the bar holding it by the ends. That made a club about two inches thick and eighteen inches long. You can knock a man into the next county with a club like that if you know how.

The man with the pink letter came back through the rear door, still chuckling, shoved the letter into his side pocket and strolled to the pin game. That put him behind me. I began to get a little worried.

I finished my beer quickly and stood down off the stool. The barkeep hadn't rung up my dime yet. He held his twisted towel and moved it back and forth slowly.

"Nice beer," I said. "Thanks all the same."

"Come again," he whispered, and knocked my glass over.

That took my eyes for a second. When I looked up again the door at the back was open and a big man stood in it with a big gun in his hand.

He didn't say anything. He just stood there. The gun looked at me. It looked like a tunnel. The man was very broad, very swarthy. He had a build like a wrestler. He looked plenty tough. He didn't look as if his real name was Magoon.

Nobody said anything. The barkeep and the man with the big gun just stared at me fixedly. Then I heard a train coming on the interurban tracks. Coming fast and coming noisy. That would be the time. The shade was down all across the front window and nobody could see into the place. The train would make a lot of noise as it went by. A couple of shots would be lost in it.

The noise of the approaching train got louder. I had to move before it got quite loud enough.

I went head first over the bar in a rolling dive.

Something banged faintly against the roar of the train and something rattled overhead, seemingly on the wall. I never knew what it was. The train went on by in a booming crescendo.

I hit the barkeep's legs and the dirty floor about the same moment. He sat down on my neck.

That put my nose in a puddle of stale beer and one of my ears into some very hard concrete floor. My head began to howl with pain. I was low down along a sort of duckboard behind the bar and half turned on my left side. I jerked the gun loose from my waistband. For a wonder it hadn't slipped and jammed itself down my trouser leg.

The barkeep made a kind of annoyed sound and something hot stung me and I didn't hear any more shots just at the moment. I didn't shoot the barkeep. I rammed the gun muzzle into a part of him where some people are sensitive. He was one of them.

He went up off me like a foul fly. If he didn't yell it was not for want of trying. I rolled a little more and put the gun in the seat of his pants. "Hold it!" I snarled at him. "I don't want to get vulgar with you."

Two more shots roared. The train was off in the distance, but somebody didn't care. These cut through wood. The bar was old and solid but not solid enough to stop .45 slugs. The barkeep sighed above me. Something hot and wet fell on my face. "You've shot me, boys," he whispered, and started to fall down on top of me.

I wriggled away just in time, got to the end of the bar nearest the front of the beer parlor and looked around it. A face with a brown hat over it was about nine inches from my own face, on the same level.

We looked at each other for a fraction of a second that seemed long enough for a tree to grow to maturity in, but was actually so short a time that the barkeep was still foundering in the air behind me.

This was my last gun. Nobody was going to get it. I got it up before the man I was facing had even reacted to the situation. He didn't do anything. He just slid off to one side and as he slid a thick gulp of red came out of his mouth.

I heard this shot. It was so loud it was like the end of the world, so loud that I almost didn't hear the door slam towards the back. I crawled farther around the end of the bar, knocked somebody's gun along the floor peevishly, stuck my hat around the corner of the wood. Nobody shot at it. I stuck one eye and part of my face out.

The door at the back was shut and the space in front of it was empty. I got up on my knees and listened. Another door slammed, and a car motor roared.

I went crazy. I tore across the room, threw the door open and plunged through it. It was a phony. They had slammed the door and started the car just for a come-on. I saw that the flailing arm held a bottle.

For the third time in twenty-four hours I took the count.

I came out of this one yelling, with the harsh bite of ammonia in my nose. I swung at a face. But I didn't have anything to swing with. My arms were a couple of four-ton anchors. I threshed around and groaned.

The face in front of me materialized into the bored yet attentive pan of a man with a white coat, a fast-wagon medico.

"Like it?" he grinned. "Some people used to drink it—with a wine-tonic chaser."

He pulled at me and something nipped at my shoulder and a needle stung me.

"Light shot," he said. "That head of yours is pretty bad. You won't go out."

His face went away. I prowled my eyes. Beyond there was a vagueness. Then I saw a girl's face, hushed, sharp, attentive. Carol Pride.

"Yeah," I said. "You followed me. You would."

She smiled and moved. Then her fingers were stroking my cheek and I couldn't see her.

"The prowl-car boys just made it," she said. "The crooks had you all wrapped up in a carpet—for shipment in a truck out back."

I couldn't see very well. A big red-faced man in blue slid in front of me. He had a gun in his hand with the gate open. Somebody groaned somewhere in the background.

She said: "They had two others wrapped up. But they were dead. Ugh!"

"Go on home," I grumbled woozily. "Go write yourself a feature story."

"You used that one before, sap." She went on stroking my cheek. "I thought you made them up as you went along. Drowsy?"

"That's all taken care of," a voice said sharply. "Get this shot guy down to where you can work on him. I want him to live."

Reavis came towards me as out of a mist. His face formed itself slowly, gray, attentive, rather stern. It lowered, as if he sat down in front of me, close to me.

"So you had to play it smart," he said in a sharp, edgy voice. "All right, talk. The hell with how your head feels. You asked for it and you got it."

"Gimme a drink."

Vague motion, a flicker of bright light, the lip of a flask touched my mouth. Hot strength ran down my throat. Some of it ran cold on my chin and I moved my head away from the flask.

"Thanks. Get Magoon—the biggest one?"

"He's full of lead, but still turning over. On his way downtown now."

"Get the Indian?"

"Huh?" he gulped.

"In some bushes under Peace Cross down on the Palisades. I shot him. I didn't mean to."

"Holy—"

Reavis went away again and the fingers moved slowly and rhythmically on my cheek.

Reavis came back and sat down again. "Who's the Indian?" he snapped.

"Soukesian's strong-arm man. Soukesian the Psychic. He—"

"We know about him," Reavis interrupted bitterly. "You've been out a whole hour, shamus. The lady told us about those cards. She says it's her fault but I don't believe it. Screwy anyhow. But a couple of the boys have gone out there."

"I was there," I said. "At his house. He knows something. I don't know what. He was afraid of me—yet he didn't knock me off. Funny."

"Amateur," Reavis said dryly. "He left that for Moose

Magoon. Moose Magoon was tough—up till lately. A record from here to Pittsburgh. . . . Here. But take it easy. This is *ante mortem* confession liquor. Too damn good for you."

The flask touched my lips again.

"Listen," I said thickly. "This was the stick-up squad. Soukesian was the brains. Lindley Paul was the finger. He must have crossed them on something—"

Reavis said, "Nuts," and just then a phone rang distantly and a voice said: "You, Lieutenant."

Reavis went away. When he came back again he didn't sit down.

"Maybe you're right," he said softly. "Maybe you are, at that. In a house on top of a hill in Brentwood Heights there's a golden-haired guy dead in a chair with a woman crying over him. Dutch act. There's a jade necklace on a table beside him."

"Too much death," I said, and fainted.

I woke up in an ambulance. At first I thought I was alone in it. Then I felt her hand and knew I wasn't. I was stone blind now. I couldn't even see light. It was just bandages.

"The doctor's up front with the driver," she said. "You can hold my hand. Would you like me to kiss you?"

"If it doesn't obligate me to anything."

She laughed softly. "I guess you'll live," she said. She kissed me. "Your hair smells of Scotch. Do you take baths in it? The doctor said you weren't to talk."

"They beaned me with a full bottle. Did I tell Reavis about the Indian?"

"Yes."

"Did I tell him Mrs. Prendergast thought Paul was mixed up—"

"You didn't even mention Mrs. Prendergast," she said quickly.

I didn't say anything to that. After a while she said: "This Soukesian, did he look like a lady's man?"

"The doctor said I wasn't to talk," I said.

VIII   Poison Blonde

It was a couple of weeks later that I drove down to Santa Monica. Ten days of the time I had spent in the hospital, at my own expense, getting over a bad concussion. Moose Magoon was in the prison ward at the County Hospital about the same time, while they picked seven or eight police slugs out of him. At the end of that time they buried him.

The case was pretty well buried by this time, too. The papers had had their play with it and other things had come along and after all it was just a jewel racket that went sour from too much double-crossing. So the police said, and they ought to know. They didn't find any more jewels, but they didn't expect to. They figured the gang pulled just one job at a time, with coolie labor mostly, and sent them on their way with their cut. That way only three people really knew what it was all about: Moose Magoon, who turned out to be an Armenian; Soukesian, who used his connections to find out who had the right kind of jewels; and Lindley Paul, who fingered the jobs and tipped the gang off when to strike. Or so the police said, and they ought to know.

It was a nice warm afternoon. Carol Pride lived on Twenty-fifth Street, in a neat little red brick house trimmed with white with a hedge in front of it.

Her living room had a tan figured rug, white-and-rose chairs, a black marble fireplace with tall brass andirons, very high bookcases built back into the walls, rough cream-colored drapes against shades of the same color.

There was nothing womanish in it except a full-length mirror with a clear sweep of floor in front.

I sat down in a nice soft chair and rested what was left of my head and sipped Scotch and soda while I looked at her fluffed-out brown hair above a high-collar dress that made her face look small, almost childish.

"I bet you didn't get all this writing," I said.

"And my dad didn't get it grafting on the cops either," she snapped. "We had a few lots at Playa Del Rey, if you have to know."

"A little oil," I said. "Nice. I didn't have to know. Don't start snapping at me."

"Have you still got your licence?"

"Oh, yes," I said. "Well, this is nice Scotch. You wouldn't like to go riding in an old car, would you?"

"Who am I to sneer at an old car?" she asked. "The laundry must have put too much starch in your neck."

I grinned at the thin line between her eyebrows.

"I kissed you in that ambulance," she said. "If you remember, don't take it too big. I was just sorry for the way you got your head bashed in."

"I'm a career man," I said. "I wouldn't build on anything like that. Let's go riding. I have to see a blonde in Beverly Hills. I owe her a report."

She stood up and glared at me. "Oh, the Prendergast woman," she said nastily. "The one with the hollow wooden legs."

"They may be hollow," I said.

She flushed and tore out of the room and came back in what seemed about three seconds with a funny little octagonal hat that had a red button on it, and a plaid overcoat with a suede collar and cuffs. "Let's go," she said breathlessly.

The Philip Courtney Prendergasts lived on one of those wide, curving streets where the houses seem to be too close together for their size and the amount of money they represent. A Jap gardener was manicuring a few acres of soft green lawn with the usual contemptuous expression Jap gardeners have. The house had an English slate roof and a porte-cochere, some nice imported trees, a trellis with bougainvillaea. It was a nice place and not loud. But Beverly Hills is Beverly Hills, so the butler had a wing collar and an accent like Alan Mowbray.

He ushered us through zones of silence into a room that was empty at the moment. It had large chesterfields and lounging chairs done in pale yellow leather and arranged around a fireplace, in front of which, on the glossy but not slippery floor, lay a rug as thin as silk and as old as

Aesop's aunt. A jet of flowers in the corner, another jet on a low table, walls of dully painted parchment, silence, comfort, space, coziness, a dash of the very modern and a dash of the very old. A very swell room.

Carol Pride sniffed at it.

The butler swung half of a leather-covered door and Mrs. Prendergast came in. Pale blue, with a hat and bag to match, all ready to go out. Pale blue gloves slapping lightly at a pale blue thigh. A smile, hints of depths in the black eyes, a high color, and even before she spoke a nice edge.

She flung both her hands out at us. Carol Pride managed to miss her share. I squeezed mine.

"Gorgeous of you to come," she cried. "How nice to see you both again. I can still taste that whisky you had in your office. Terrible, wasn't it?"

We all sat down.

I said: "I didn't really need to take up your time by coming in person, Mrs. Prendergast. Everything turned out all right and you got your beads back."

"Yes. That strange man. How curious of him to be what he was. I knew him too. Did you know that?"

"Soukesian? I thought perhaps you knew him," I said.

"Oh, yes. Quite well. I must owe you a lot of money. And your poor head. How is it?"

Carol Pride was sitting close to me.

She said tinnily, between her teeth, almost to herself, but not quite: "Sawdust and creosote. Even at that the termites are getting her."

I smiled at Mrs. Prendergast and she returned my smile with an angel on its back.

"You don't owe me a nickel," I said. "There was just one thing—"

"Impossible. I must. But let's have a little Scotch, shall we?" She held her bag on her knees, pressed something under the chair, said: "A little Scotch and soda, Vernon." She beamed. "Cute, eh? You can't even see the mike. This house is just full of little things like that. Mr. Prendergast loves them. This one talks in the butler's pantry."

Carol Pride said: "I bet the one that talks by the chauffeur's bed is cute too."

Mrs. Prendergast didn't hear her. The butler came in with

a tray and mixed drinks, handed them around and went out.

Over the rim of her glass Mrs. Prendergast said: "You were nice not to tell the police I suspected Lin Paul of being —well, you know. Or that I had anything to do with your going to that awful beer parlor. By the way, how did you explain that?"

"Easy. I told them Paul told me himself. He was with you, remember?"

"But he didn't, of course?" I thought her eyes were a little sly now.

"He told me practically nothing. That was the whole truth. And of course he didn't tell me he'd been black-mailing you."

I seemed to be aware that Carol Pride had stopped breathing. Mrs. Prendergast went on looking at me over the rim of her glass. Her face had, for a brief moment, a sort of half-silly, nymph-surprised-while-bathing expression. Then she put her glass down slowly and opened her bag in her lap and got a handkerchief out and bit it. There was silence.

"That," she said in a low voice, "is rather fantastic, isn't it?"

I grinned at her coldly. "The police are a lot like the news-papers, Mrs. Prendergast. For one reason and another they can't use everything they get. But that doesn't make them dumb. Reavis isn't dumb. He doesn't really think, any more than I do, that this Soukesian person was really running a tough jewel-heist gang. He couldn't have handled people like Moose Magoon for five minutes. They'd have walked all over his face just for exercise. Yet Soukesian did have the necklace. That needs explaining. I think he bought it— from Moose Magoon. For the ten-grand pay-off supplied by you—and for some other little consideration likely paid in advance to get Moose to pull the job."

Mrs. Prendergast lowered her lids until her eyes were almost shut, then she lifted them again and smiled. It was a rather ghastly smile. Carol Pride didn't move beside me.

"Somebody *wanted* Lindley Paul killed," I said. "That's obvious. You might kill a man accidentally with a black-jack, by not knowing how hard to hit with it. But you won't put his brains all over his face. And if you beat him up just to teach him to be good, you wouldn't beat him about the head at all. Because that way he wouldn't know how badly you were hurting him. And you'd want him to know that—if you were just teaching him a lesson."

"Wha—what," the blonde woman asked huskily, "has all this to do with me?"

Her face was a mask. Her eyes held a warm bitterness like poisoned honey. One of her hands was roving around inside her bag. It became quiet, inside the bag.

"Moose Magoon would pull a job like that," I bored on, "if he was paid for it. He'd pull any kind of a job. And Moose was an Armenian, so Soukesian might have known how to reach him. And Soukesian was just the type to go skirt-simple over a roto queen and be willing to do anything she wanted him to do, even have a man killed, especially if that man was a rival, especially if he was the kind of man who rolled around on floor cushions and maybe even took candid camera photos of his lady friends when they got a little too close to the Garden of Eden. That wouldn't be too hard to understand, would it, Mrs. Prendergast?"

"Take a drink," Carol Pride said icily. "You're drooling. You don't have to tell this baby she's a tramp. She knows it. But how the hell could anybody blackmail her? You've got to have a reputation to be blackmailed."

"Shut up!" I snapped. "The less you've got the more you'll pay to keep it." I watched the blond woman's hand move suddenly inside her bag. "Don't bother to pull the gun," I told her. "I know they won't hang you. I just wanted you to know you're not kidding anybody and that that trap in the beer parlor was rigged to finish me off when Soukesian lost his nerve and that you were the one that sent me in there to get what they had for me. The rest of it's dead wood now."

But she pulled the gun out just the same and held it on her pale blue knee and smiled at me.

Carol Pride threw a glass at her. She dodged and the gun went off. A slug went softly and politely into the parchment-covered wall, high up, making no more sound than a finger going into a glove.

The door opened and an enormously tall, thin man strolled into the room.

"Shoot me," he said. "I'm only your husband."

The blonde looked at him. For just a short moment I thought she might be going to take him up on it.

Then she just smiled a little more and put the gun back into her bag and reached for her glass. "Listening in again?" she said dully. "Someday you'll hear something you won't like."

The tall, thin man took a leather checkbook out of his pocket and cocked an eyebrow at me and said: "How much will keep you quiet—permanently?"

I gawked at him. "You heard what I said in here?"

"I think so. The pickup's pretty good this weather. I believe you were accusing my wife of having something to do with somebody's death, was it not?"

I kept on gawking at him.

"Well—how much do you want?" he snapped. "I won't argue with you. I'm used to blackmailers."

"Make it a million," I said. "And she just took a shot at us. That will be four bits extra."

The blonde laughed crazily and the laugh turned into a screech and then into a yell. The next thing she was rolling on the floor screaming and kicking her legs around.

The tall man went over to her quickly and bent down and hit her in the face with his open hand. You could have heard that smack a mile. When he straightened up again his face was a dusky red and the blonde was lying there sobbing.

"I'll show you to the door," he said. "You can call at my office tomorrow."

"What for?" I asked, and took my hat. "You'll still be a sap, even at your office."

I took Carol Pride's arm and steered her out of the room. We left the house silently. The Jap gardener had just pulled a bit of weed root out of the lawn and was holding it up and sneering at it.

We drove away from there, towards the foothills. A red spotlight near the old Beverly Hills Hotel stopped me after a while. I just sat there holding the wheel. The girl beside me didn't move either. She didn't say anything. She just looked straight ahead.

"I didn't get the big warm feeling," I said. "I didn't get to smack anybody down. I didn't make it stick."

"She probably didn't plan it in cold blood," she whispered.

"She just got mad and resentful and somebody sold her an idea. A woman like that takes men and gets tired of them and throws them away and they go crazy trying to get her back. It might have been just between the two lovers—Paul and Soukesian. But Mr. Magoon played rough."

"She sent me to that beer parlor," I said. "That's enough for me. And Paul had ideas about Soukesian. I knew she'd miss. With the gun, I mean."

I grabbed her. She was shivering.

A car came up behind us and the driver stood on his horn. I listened to it for a little while, then I let go of Carol Pride and got out of the roadster and walked back. He was a big man, behind the wheel of a sedan.

"That's a boulevard stop," he said sharply. "Lover's Lane is farther up in the hills. Get out of there before I push you out."

"Blow your horn just once more," I begged him. "Just once. Then tell me which side you want the shiner on."

He took a police captain's badge out of his vest pocket. Then he grinned. Then we both grinned. It wasn't my day.

I got back into the roadster and turned it around and started back towards Santa Monica. "Let's go home and drink some more Scotch," I said. "Your Scotch."

BAY CITY BLUES

I Cinderella Suicide

IT must have been Friday because the fish smell from the Mansion House coffee-shop next door was strong enough to build a garage on. Apart from that it was a nice warm day in spring, the tail of the afternoon, and there hadn't been any business in a week. I had my heels in the groove on my desk and was sunning my ankles in a wedge of sunlight when the phone rang. I took my hat off it and made a yawning sound into the mouthpiece.

A voice said: "I heard that. You oughta be ashamed of yourself, Johnny Dalmas. Ever hear of the Austrian case?"

It was Violets M'Gee, a homicide dick in the sheriff's office and a very nice guy except for one bad habit—passing me cases where I got tossed around and didn't make enough money to buy a secondhand corset.

"No."

"One of those things down at the beach—Bay City. I hear the little burg went sour again the last time they elected themselves a mayor, but the sheriff lives down there and we like to be nice. We ain't tramped on it. They say the gambling boys put up thirty grand campaign money, so now you get a racing form with the bill of fare in the hash houses."

I yawned again.

"I heard that, too," M'Gee barked. "If you ain't interested I'll just bite my other thumbnail and let the whole thing go. The guy's got a little dough to spend, he says."

"What guy?"

"This Matson, the guy that found the stiff."

"What stiff?"

"You don't know nothing about the Austrian case, huh?"

"Didn't I say I didn't?"

"You ain't done nothing but yawn and say 'What.' Okay. We'll just let the poor guy get bumped off and City Homicide can worry about that one, now he's up here in town."

"This Matson? Who's going to bump him off?"

"Well, if he knew that, he wouldn't want to hire no shamus to find out, would he? And him in your own racket until they bust him a while back and now he can't go out hardly, on account of these guys with guns are bothering him."

"Come on over," I said. "My left arm is getting tired."

"I'm on duty."

"I was just going down to the drugstore for a quart of V.O. Scotch."

"That's me you hear knocking on the door," M'Gee said.

He arrived in less than half an hour—a large, pleasant-faced man with silvery hair and a dimpled chin and a tiny little mouth made to kiss babies with. He wore a well-pressed blue suit, polished square-toed shoes, and an elk's tooth on a gold chain hung across his stomach.

He sat down carefully, the way a fat man sits down, and unscrewed the top of the whisky bottle and sniffed it carefully, to make sure I hadn't refilled a good bottle with ninety-eight cent hooch, the way they do in the bars. Then he poured himself a big drink and rolled some of it around on his tongue and pawed my office with his eyes.

"No wonder you sit around waiting for jobs," he said. "You gotta have front these days."

"You could spare me a little," I said. "What about this Matson and this Austrian case?"

M'Gee finished his drink and poured another, not so large. He watched me play with a cigarette.

"A monoxide Dutch," he said. "A blond bim named Austrian, wife of a doctor down at Bay City. A guy that runs around all night keeping movie hams from having pink elephants for breakfast. So the frill went around on her own. The night she croaked herself she was over to Vance Conried's club on the bluff north of there. Know it?"

"Yeah. It used to be a beach club, with a nice private beach down below and the swellest legs in Hollywood in front of the cabañas. She went there to play roulette, huh?"

"Well, if we had any gambling joints in this county," M'Gee said, "I'd say the Club Conried would be one of them and there would be roulette. Say she played roulette. They tell me she had more personal games she played with Conried, but say she played roulette on the side. She loses, which is what roulette is for. That night she loses her shirt and she gets sore and throws a wingding all over the house. Conried gets her into his private room and pages the doc, her husband, through the Physicians' Exchange. So then the doc—"

"Wait a minute," I said. "Don't tell me all this was in evidence—not with the gambling syndicate we would have in this county, if we had a gambling syndicate."

M'Gee looked at me pityingly. "My wife's got a kid brother works on a throw-away paper down there. They didn't have no inquest. Well, the doc steams over to Conried's joint and pokes his wife in the arm with a needle to quiet her down. But he can't take her home on account of he has a babe case in Brentwood Heights. So Vance Conried gets his personal car out and takes her home and meantime the doc has called up his office nurse and asked her to go over to the house and see that his wife is all right. Which is all done, and Conried goes back to his chips and the nurse sees her in bed and leaves, and the maid goes back to bed. This is maybe midnight, or just a little after.

"Well, along about 2 A.M. this Harry Matson happens by. He's running a night-watchman service down there and that night he's out making rounds himself. On the street where Austrian lives he hears a car engine running in a dark garage, and he goes in to investigate. He finds the blond frail on the floor on her back, in peekaboo pajamas and slippers, with soot from the exhaust all over her hair."

M'Gee paused to sip a little more whisky and stare around my office again. I watched the last of the sunlight sneak over my windowsill and drop into the dark slit of the alley.

"So what does the chump do?" M'Gee said, wiping his lips on a silk handkerchief. "He decides the bim is dead, which maybe she is, but you can't always be sure in a gas case, what with this new methylene-blue treatment—"

"For God's sake," I said. "What does he do?"

"He don't call no law," M'Gee said sternly. "He kills the car motor and douses his flash and beats it home to where he lives a few blocks away. He pages the doc from there and after a while they're both back at the garage. The doc says she's dead. He sends Matson in at a side door to call the local chief of police personal, at his home. Which Matson does, and after a while the chief buzzes over with a couple of stooges, and a little while after them the body snatcher from the undertaker, whose turn it is to be deputy coroner that week. They cart the stiff away and some lab man takes a blood sample and says it's full of monoxide. The coroner gives a release and the dame is cremated and the case is closed."

"Well, what's the matter with it?" I asked.

M'Gee finished his second drink and thought about having a third. He decided to have a cigar first. I didn't have any cigars and that annoyed him slightly, but he lit one of his own.

"I'm just a cop," he said, blinking at me calmly through the smoke. "I wouldn't know. All I know is, this Matson got bust loose from his licence and run out of town and he's scared."

"The hell with it," I said. "The last time I muscled into a small-town setup I got a fractured skull. How do I contact Matson?"

"I give him your number. He'll contact you."

"How well do you know him?"

"Well enough to give him your name," M'Gee said. "Of course, if anything comes up I should look into—"

"Sure," I said. "I'll put it on your desk. Bourbon or rye?"

"Go to hell," M'Gee said. "Scotch."

"What does Matson look like?"

"He's medium heavy, five-seven, one-seventy, gray hair."

He had another short, quick drink and left.

I sat there for an hour and smoked too many cigarettes. It got dark and my throat felt dry. Nobody called me up. I went over and switched the lights on, washed my hands, tucked away a small drink and locked the bottle up. It was time to eat.

I had my hat on and was going through the door when the Green Feather messenger boy came along the hallway looking at numbers. He wanted mine. I signed for a small irregular-shaped parcel done up in the kind of flimsy yellowish paper laundries use. I put the parcel on my desk and cut the string. Inside there was tissue paper and an envelope with a sheet of paper and a flat key in it. The note began abruptly:

A friend in the sheriff's office gave me your name as a man I could trust. I have been a heel and am in a jam and all I want now is to get clear. Please come after dark to 524 Tennyson Arms Apartments, Harvard near Sixth, and use key to enter if I am out. Look out for Pat Reel, the manager, as I don't trust him. Please put the slipper in a safe place and keep it clean. P.S. They call him Violets, I never knew why.

I knew why. It was because he chewed violet-scented breath purifiers. The note was unsigned. It sounded a little jittery to me. I unwound the tissue paper. It contained a green velvet pump, size about 4A lined with white kid. The name *Verschoyle* was stamped in flowing gold script on the white kid insole. On the side a number was written very small in indelible ink—S465—where a size number would be, but I knew it wasn't a size number because Verschoyle, Inc., on Cherokee Street in Hollywood made only custom shoes from individual lasts, and theatrical footwear and riding boots.

I leaned back and lit a cigarette and thought about it for a while. Finally I reached for the phone book and looked up the number of Verschoyle, Inc., and dialed it. The phone rang several times before a chirpy voice said: "Hello? Yes?"

"Verschoyle—in person," I said. "This is Peters, Identification Bureau." I didn't say what identification bureau.

"Oh, Mr. Verschoyle has gone home. We're closed, you know. We close at five-thirty. I'm Mr. Pringle, the bookkeeper. Is there anything—"

"Yeah. We got a couple of your shoes in some stolen goods. The mark is S-Four-Six-Five. That mean anything to you?"

"Oh yes, of course. That's a last number. Shall I look it up for you?"

"By all means," I said.

He was back in no time at all. "Oh yes, indeed, that is

Mrs. Leland Austrian's number. Seven-thirty-six Altair Street, Bay City. We made all her shoes. Very sad. Yes. About two months ago we made her two pairs of emerald velvet pumps."

"What do you mean, sad?"

"Oh, she's dead, you know. Committed suicide."

"The hell you say. Two pairs of pumps, huh?"

"Oh yes, both the same you know. People often order delicate colors in pairs like that. You know a spot or stain of any kind—and they might be made to match a certain dress—"

"Well, thanks a lot and take care of yourself," I said, and gave the phone back to him.

I picked up the slipper again and looked it over carefully. It hadn't been worn. There was no sign of rubbing on the buffed leather of the thin sole. I wondered what Harry Matson was doing with it. I put it in my office safe and went out to dinner.

II   Murder on the Cuff

THE TENNYSON ARMS was an old-fashioned dump, about eight stories high, faced with dark red brick. It had a wide center court with palm trees and a concrete fountain and some prissy-looking flower beds. Lanterns hung beside the Gothic door and the lobby inside was paved with red plush. It was large and empty except for a bored canary in a gilt cage the size of a barrel. It looked like the sort of apartment house where widows would live on the life insurance— not very young widows. The elevator was the self-operating kind that opens both doors automatically when it stops.

I walked along the narrow maroon carpet of the fifth-floor hallway and didn't see anybody, hear anybody, or smell anybody's cooking. The place was as quiet as a minister's study. Apartment 524 must have opened on the center court because a stained-glass window was right beside its door. I

knocked, not loud, and nobody came to the door so I used
the flat key and went in, and shut the door behind me.

A mirror glistened in a wall bed across the room. Two
windows in the same wall as the entrance door were shut
and dark drapes were drawn half across them, but enough
light from some apartment across the court drifted in to
show the dark bulk of heavy, overstuffed furniture, ten years
out of date, and the shine of two brass doorknobs. I went
over to the windows and pulled the drapes closed, then used
my pocket flash to find my way back to the door. The light
switch there set off a big cluster of flame-colored candles
in the ceiling fixture. They made the room look like a
funeral-chapel annex. I put the light on in a red standing
lamp, doused the ceiling light and started to give the place
the camera eye.

In the narrow dressing room behind the wall bed there
was a built-in bureau with a black brush and comb on it
and gray hairs in the comb. There was a can of talcum, a
flashlight, a crumpled man's handkerchief, a pad of writing
paper, a bank pen and a bottle of ink on a blotter—about
what one suitcase would hold in the drawers. The shirts had
been bought in a Bay City men's furnishing store. There was
a dark gray suit on a hanger and a pair of black brogues
on the floor. In the bathroom there was a safety razor, a tube
of brushless cream, some blades, three bamboo toothbrushes
in a glass, a few other odds and ends. On the porcelain toilet
tank there was a book bound in red cloth—Dorsey's *Why
We Behave Like Human Beings*. It was marked at page 116
by a rubber band. I had it open and was reading about the
Evolution of Earth, Life and Sex when the phone started
to ring in the living room.

I snicked off the bathroom light and padded across the
carpet to the davenport. The phone was on a stand at one
end. It kept on ringing and a horn tooted outside in the
street, as if answering it. When it had rung eight times I
shrugged and reached for it.

"Pat? Pat Reel?" the voice said.

I didn't know how Pat Reel would talk. I grunted. The
voice at the other end was hard and hoarse at the same time.
It sounded like a tough-guy voice.

"Pat?"

"Sure," I said.

There was silence. It hadn't gone over. Then the voice said: "This is Harry Matson. Sorry as all hell I can't make it back tonight. Just one of those things. That bother you much?"

"Sure," I said.

"What's that?"

"Sure."

"Is 'sure' all the words you know, for God's sake?"

"I'm a Greek."

The voice laughed. It seemed pleased with itself.

I said: "What kind of toothbrushes do you use, Harry?"

"Huh?"

This was a startled explosion of breath—not so pleased now.

"Toothbrushes—the little dinguses some people brush their teeth with. What kind do you use?"

"Aw, go to hell."

"Meet you on the step," I said.

The voice got mad now. "Listen, smart monkey! You ain't pulling nothin', see? We got your name, we got your number, and we got a place to put you if you don't keep your nose clean, see? And Harry don't live there any more, ha, ha."

"You picked him off, huh?"

"I'll say we picked him off. What do you think we done, took him to a picture show?"

"That's bad," I said. "The boss won't like that."

I hung up in his face and put the phone down on the table at the end of the davenport and rubbed the back of my neck. I took the door key out of my pocket and polished it on my handkerchief and laid it down carefully on the table. I got up and walked across to one of the windows and pulled the drapes aside far enough to look out into the court. Across its palm-dotted oblong, on the same floor level I was on, a bald-headed man sat in the middle of a room under a hard, bright light, and didn't move a muscle. He didn't look like a spy.

I let the drapes fall together again and settled my hat on my head and went over and put the lamp out. I put my pocket flash down on the floor and palmed my handkerchief on the doorknob and quietly opened the door.

Braced to the door frame by eight hooked fingers, all but

one of which were white as wax, there hung what was left
of a man.

He had eyes an eighth of an inch deep, china-blue, wide
open. They looked at me but they didn't see me. He had
coarse gray hair on which the smeared blood looked purple.
One of his temples was a pulp, and the tracery of blood from
it reached clear to the point of his chin. The one straining
finger that wasn't white had been pounded to shreds as far
as the second joint. Sharp splinters of bone stuck out of
the mangled flesh. Something that might once have been a
fingernail looked now like a ragged splinter of glass.

The man wore a brown suit with patch pockets, three of
them. They had been torn off and hung at odd angles showing the dark alpaca lining beneath.

He breathed with a faraway unimportant sound, like distant footfalls on dead leaves. His mouth was strained open
like a fish's mouth, and blood bubbled from it. Behind him
the hallway was empty as a new-dug grave.

Rubber heels squeaked suddenly on the bare space of wood
beside the hall runner. The man's straining fingers slipped
from the door frame and his body started to wind up on his
legs. The legs couldn't hold it. They scissored and the body
turned in mid-air, like a swimmer in a wave, and then
jumped at me.

I clamped my teeth hard and spread my feet and caught
him from behind, after his torso had made a half turn. He
weighed enough for two men. I took a step back and nearly
went down, took two more and then I had his dragging heels
clear of the doorway. I let him down on his side as slowly as
I could, crouched over him panting. After a second I straightened, went over to the door and shut and locked it. Then I
switched the ceiling light on and started for the telephone.

He died before I reached it. I heard the rattle, the spent
sigh, then silence. An outflung hand, the good one, twitched
once and the fingers spread out slowly into a loose curve
and stayed like that. I went back and felt his carotid artery,
digging my fingers in hard. Not a flicker of a pulse. I got a
small steel mirror out of my wallet and held it against his
open mouth for a long minute. There was no trace of mist on
it when I took it away. Harry Matson had come home from
his ride.

A key tickled at the outside of the door lock and I moved

fast. I was in the bathroom when the door opened, with a
gun in my hand and my eyes to the crack of the bathroom
door.

This one came in quickly, the way a wise cat goes through
a swing door. His eyes flicked up at the ceiling lights, then
down at the floor. After that they didn't move at all. All
his big body didn't move a muscle. He just stood and looked.

He was a big man in an unbuttoned overcoat, as if he had
just come in or was just going out. He had a gray felt hat
on the back of a thick creamy-white head. He had the heavy
black eyebrows and broad pink face of a boss politician,
and his mouth looked as if it usually had the smile—but not
now. His face was all bone and his mouth jiggled a half-
smoked cigar along his lips with a sucking noise.

He put a bunch of keys back in his pocket and said
"God!" very softly, over and over again. Then he took a step
forward and went down beside the dead man with a slow,
clumsy motion. He put large fingers into the man's neck,
took them away again, shook his head, looked slowly around
the room. He looked at the bathroom door behind which I
was hiding, but nothing changed in his eyes.

"Fresh dead," he said, a little louder. "Beat to a pulp."

He straightened up slowly and rocked on his heels. He
didn't like the ceiling light any better than I had. He put
the standing lamp on and switched the ceiling light off,
rocked on his heels some more. His shadow crawled up the
end wall, started across the ceiling, paused and dropped
back again. He worked the cigar around in his mouth, dug
a match out of his pocket and relit the butt carefully, turning it around and around in the flame. When he blew the
match out he put it in his pocket. He did all this without
once taking his eyes off the dead man on the floor.

He moved sideways over to the davenport and let himself
down on the end of it. The springs squeaked dismally. He
reached for the phone without looking at it, eyes still on the
dead man.

He had the phone in his hand when it started to ring
again. That jarred him. His eyes rolled and his elbows jerked
against the sides of his thick overcoated body. Then he
grinned very carefully and lifted the phone off the cradle
and said in a rich, fruity voice: "Hello. . . . Yeah, this is
Pat."

I heard a dry, inarticulate croaking noise on the wire, and I saw Pat Reel's face slowly congest with blood until it was the color of fresh beef liver. His big hand shook the phone savagely.

"So it's Mister Big Chin!" he blared. "Well, listen here, saphead, you know something? Your stiff is right here on my carpet, that's where he is. . . . How did he get here? How the hell would I know? Ask me, you croaked him here, and lemme tell you something. It's costing you plenty, see, plenty. No murder on the cuff in my house. I spot a guy for you and you knock him off in my lap, damn you! I'll take a grand and not a cent less, and you come and get what's here and I mean get it, see?"

There was more croaking on the wire. Pat Reel listened. His eyes got almost sleepy and the purple died out of his face. He said more steadily: "Okay. Okay. I was only kidding. . . . Call me in half an hour downstairs."

He put down the phone and stood up. He didn't look towards the bathroom door, he didn't look anywhere. He began to whistle. Then he scratched his chin and took a step towards the door, stopped to scratch his chin again. He didn't know there was anybody in the apartment, he didn't know there *wasn't* anybody in the apartment—and he didn't have a gun. He took another step towards the door. Big Chin had told him something and the idea was to get out. He took a third step, then he changed his mind.

"Aw hell," he said out loud. "That screwy mug." Then his eyes ranged round the apartment swiftly. "Tryin' to kid me, huh?"

His hand raised to the chain switch. Suddenly he let it fall and knelt beside the dead man again. He moved the body a little, rolling it without effort on the carpet, and put his face down close to squint at the spot where the head had lain. Pat Reel shook his head in displeasure, got to his feet and put his hands under the dead man's armpits. He threw a glance over his shoulder at the dark bathroom and started to back towards me, dragging the body, grunting, the cigar butt still clamped in his mouth. His creamy-white hair glistened cleanly in the lamplight.

He was still bent over with his big legs spraddled when I stepped out behind him. He may have heard me at the last second but it didn't matter. I had shifted the gun to my left hand and I had a small pocket sap in my right. I laid the sap against the side of his head, just behind his right ear, and I laid it as though I loved it.

Pat Reel collapsed forward across the sprawled body he was dragging, his head down between the dead man's legs. His hat rolled gently off to the side. He didn't move. I stepped past him to the door and left.

III   Gentleman of the Press

OVER on Western Avenue I found a phone booth and called the sheriff's office. Violets M'Gee was still there, just ready to go home.

I said: "What was the name of your kid brother-in-law that works on the throw-away paper down at Bay City?"

"Kincaid. They call him Dolly Kincaid. A little feller."

"Where would he be about now?"

"He hangs around the city hall. Thinks he's got a police beat. Why?"

"I saw Matson," I said. "Do you know where he's staying?"

"Naw. He just called me on the phone. What you think of him?"

"I'll do what I can for him. Will you be home tonight?"

"I don't know why not. Why?"

I didn't tell him why. I got into my car and pointed it towards Bay City. I got down there about nine. The police department was half a dozen rooms in a city hall that belonged in the hookworm-and-Bible belt. I pushed past a knot of smoothies into an open doorway where there was light and a counter. There was a PBX board in the corner and a uniformed man behind it.

I put an arm on the counter and a plainclothes man with his coat off and an under-arm holster looking the size of a wooden leg against his ribs took one eye off his paper and said, "Yeah?" and bonged a spittoon without moving his head more than an inch.

I said: "I'm looking for a fellow named Dolly Kincaid."

"Out to eat. I'm holdin' down his beat," he said in a solid, unemotional voice.

"Thanks. You got a pressroom here?"

"Yeah. Got a toilet, too. Wanta see?"

"Take it easy," I said. "I'm not trying to get fresh with your town."

He bonged the spittoon again. "Pressroom's down the hall. Nobody in it. Dolly's due back, if he don't get drowned in a pop bottle."

A small-boned, delicate-faced young man with a pink complexion and innocent eyes strolled into the room with a half-eaten hamburger sandwich in his left hand. His hat, which looked like a reporter's hat in a movie, was smashed on the back of his small blond head. His shirt collar was unbuttoned at the neck and his tie was pulled to one side. The ends of it hung out over his coat. The only thing the matter with him for a movie newshawk was that he wasn't drunk. He said casually: "Anything stirring, boys?"

The big black-haired plainclothes man bonged his private spittoon again and said: "I hear the mayor changed his underpants, but it's just a rumor."

The small young man smiled mechanically and turned away. The cop said: "This guy wants to see you, Dolly."

Kincaid munched his hamburger and looked at me hopefully. I said: "I'm a friend of Violets'. Where can we talk?"

"Let's go into the pressroom," he said. The black-haired cop studied me as we went out. He had a look in his eyes as if he wanted to pick a fight with somebody, and he thought I would do.

We went along the hall towards the back and turned into a room with a long, bare, scarred table, three or four wooden chairs and a lot of newspapers on the floor. There were two telephones on one end of the table, and a flyblown framed picture in the exact center of each wall—Washington, Lincoln, Horace Greeley, and the other one somebody I didn't recognize. Kincaid shut the door and sat on one end of the table and swung his leg and bit into the last of his sandwich.

I said: "I'm John Dalmas, a private dick from L.A. How's to take a ride over to Seven thirty-six Altair Street and tell me what you know about the Austrian case? Maybe you better call M'Gee up and get him to introduce us." I pushed a card at him.

The pink young man slid down off the table very rapidly and stuffed the card into his pocket without looking at it and spoke close to my ear. "Hold it."

Then he walked softly over to the framed picture of Horace Greeley and lifted it off the wall and pressed on a square of paint behind it. The paint gave—it was painted over fabric. Kincaid looked at me and raised his eyebrows. I nodded. He hung the picture back on the wall and came back to me. "Mike," he said under his breath. "Of course I don't know who listens or when, or even whether the damn thing still works."

"Horace Greeley would have loved it," I said.

"Yeah. The beat's pretty dead tonight. I guess I could go out. Al De Spain will cover for me anyway." He was talking loud now.

"The big black-haired cop?"

"Yeah."

"What makes him sore?"

"He's been reduced to acting patrolman. He ain't even working tonight. Just hangs around and he's so tough it would take the whole damn police force to throw him out."

I looked towards the microphone and raised my eyebrows. "That's okay," Kincaid said. "I gotta feed 'em something to chew on."

He went over to a dirty washbowl in the corner and washed his hands on a scrap of lava soap and dried them on his pocket handkerchief. He was just putting the handkerchief away when the door opened. A small, middle-aged, gray-haired man stood in it, looking at us expressionlessly.

Dolly Kincaid said: "Evening, Chief, anything I can do for you?"

The chief looked at me silently and without pleasure. He had sea-green eyes, a tight, stubborn mouth, a ferret-shaped nose, and an unhealthy skin. He didn't look big enough to be a cop. He nodded very slightly and said: "Who's your friend?"

"He's a friend of my brother-in-law. He's a private dick

from L.A. Let's see—" Kincaid gripped desperately in his pocket for my card. He didn't even remember my name.

The chief said sharply: "What's that? A private detective? What's your business here?"

"I didn't say I was here on business," I told him.

"Glad to hear it," he said. "Very glad to hear it. Good night."

He opened the door and went out quickly and snapped it shut behind him.

"Chief Anders—one swell guy," Kincaid said loudly. "They don't come any better." He was looking at me like a scared rabbit.

"They never have," I said just as loudly. "In Bay City."

I thought for a moment he was going to faint, but he didn't. We went out in the front of the city hall and got into my car and drove away.

I stopped the car on Altair Street across the way from the residence of Dr. Leland Austrian. The night was windless and there was a little fog under the moon. A faint pleasant smell of brackish water and kelp came up the side of the bluff from the beach. Small riding lights pinpointed the yacht harbor and the shimmering lines of three piers. Quite far out to sea a big-masted fishing barge had lights strung between its masts and from the mastheads down to the bow and stern. Other things than fishing probably happened on it.

Altair Street in that block was a dead-end, cut off by a tall, ornamental iron fence that walled a big estate. The houses were on the inland side of the street only, on eighty- or hundred-foot lots, well spaced. On the seaward side there was a narrow sidewalk and a low wall, beyond which the bluff dropped almost straight down.

Dolly Kincaid was pressed back into the corner of the seat, the red tip of a cigarette glowing at intervals in front of his small blurred face. The Austrian house was dark except for a small light over the embrasure in which the front door was set. It was stucco, with a wall across the front yard, iron gates, the garage outside the wall. A cement walk went from a side door of the garage to a side door of the house. There was a bronze plate set into the wall beside the gates and I knew it would read *Leland M. Austrian, M.D.*

"All right," I said. "Now what was the matter with the Austrian case?"

"Nothing was the matter with it," Kincaid said slowly. "Except you're going to get me in a jam."

"Why?"

"Somebody must have heard you mention Austrian's address over that mike. That's why Chief Anders came in to look at you."

"De Spain might have figured me for a dick—just on looks. He might have tipped him off."

"No. De Spain hates the chief's guts. Hell, he was a detective lieutenant up to a week ago. Anders don't want the Austrian case monkeyed with. He wouldn't let us write it up."

"Swell press you got in Bay City."

"We got a swell climate—and the press is a bunch of stooges."

"Okay," I said. "You got a brother-in-law who's a homicide dick in the sheriff's office. All the L.A. papers but one are strong for the sheriff. This town is where he lives, though, and like a lot of other guys he don't keep his own yard clean. So you're scared, huh?"

Dolly Kincaid threw his cigarette out of the window. I watched it fall in a small red arc and lie faintly pink on the narrow sidewalk. I leaned forward and pressed on the starter button. "Excuse it, please," I said. "I won't bother you any more."

I meshed the gears and the car crawled forward a couple of yards before Kincaid leaned over and jerked the parking brake on. "I'm not yellow," he said sharply. "What do you wanta know?"

I cut the motor again and leaned back with my hands on the wheel. "First off, why did Matson lose his licence. He's my client."

"Oh—Matson. They said he tried to put the bite on Dr. Austrian. And they not only took his licence, they run him out of town. A couple of guys with guns shoved him into a car one night and roughed him around and told him to skip the burg or else. He reported it down at headquarters and you could have heard them laugh for blocks. But I don't think it was cops."

"Do you know anybody called Big Chin?"

Dolly Kincaid thought. "No. The mayor's driver, a goof called Moss Lorenz, has a chin you could balance a piano on. But I never heard him called Big Chin. He used to work for Vance Conried. Ever hear of Conried?"

"I'm all caught up on that angle," I said. "Then if this Conried wanted to bump somebody off that was bothering him, and especially somebody that had made a little trouble here in Bay City, this Lorenz would be just the guy. Because the mayor would have to cover for him—up to a point, anyway."

Dolly Kincaid said, "Bump who off?" and his voice was suddenly thick and tense.

"They didn't only run Matson out of town," I told him. "They traced him to an apartment house in L.A. and some guy called Big Chin gave him the works. Matson must have been working still on whatever it was he was working on."

"Geez," Dolly Kincaid whispered. "I didn't get a word on that."

"The L.A. cops neither—when I left. Did you know Matson?"

"A little. Not well."

"Would you call him honest?"

"Well, as honest as—well, yeah, I guess he was all right. Geez, bumped off, huh?"

"As honest as a private dick usually is?" I said.

He giggled, from sudden strain and nervousness and shock —very little from amusement. A car turned into the end of the street and stopped by the curb and its lights went out. Nobody got out.

"How about Dr. Austrian," I said. "Where was he when his wife was murdered?"

Dolly Kincaid jumped. "Jeepers, who said she was murdered?" he gasped.

"I think Matson was trying to say so. But he was trying to get paid for not saying it even harder than he was trying to say it. Either way would have got him disliked, but his way got him chilled with a piece of lead pipe. My hunch is that Conried would have that done because he would not like to have anybody make the pay sign at him, except in the way of legitimate graft. But on the other hand it would be a little better for Conried's club to have Dr. Austrian murder his wife than for her to do a Dutch on account of

losing all her dough at Conried's roulette tables. Maybe not
a lot better, but some better. So I can't figure why Conried
would have Matson bumped off for talking about murder. I
figure he could have been talking about something else as
well."

"Does all this figuring ever get you anywhere?" Dolly Kincaid asked politely.

"No. It's just something to do while I'm patting the cold
cream into my face at night. Now about this lab man that
made the blood sample. Who was he?"

Kincaid lit another cigarette and looked down the block
at the car that had stopped in front of the end house. Its
lights had gone on again now and it was moving forward
slowly.

"A guy named Greb," he said. "He has a small place in
the Physicians and Surgeons Building and works for the
doctors."

"Not official, huh?"

"No, but they don't run to lab men down here. And the
undertakers all take turns being coroner for a week, so what
the hell. The chief handles it the way he likes."

"Why would he want to handle it at all?"

"I guess maybe he might get orders from the mayor, who
might get a hint from the gambling boys that Vance Conried works for, or from Vance Conried direct. Conried
might not like his bosses to know he was mixed up with a
dead frill in a way to make a kickback on the club."

"Right," I said. "That guy down the block don't know
where he lives."

The car was still crawling forward along the curb. It's
lights were out again, but it was still moving.

"And while I'm still healthy," Dolly Kincaid said, "you
might as well know that Doc Austrian's office nurse used
to be Matson's wife. She's a redheaded man-eater with no
looks but a lot of outside curve."

"I like a well-crowded stocking myself," I said. "Get out
of that door and in the back of the car and lie down and
make it fast."

"Geez—"

"Do what I say!" I snapped. "Fast!"

The door on the right clicked open and the little man slid
out like a wisp of smoke. The door clicked shut. I heard

the rear door open and sneaked a look back and saw a dark shape haunched on the floor of the car. I slid over to the right side myself and opened the door again and stepped out on the narrow sidewalk that ran along the rim of the bluff.

The other car was close now. Its lights flared up again and I ducked. The lights swerved so that they swept my car, then swerved back and the car stopped opposite and went quietly dark. It was a small black coupé. Nothing happened for a minute, then its left door opened and a chunky man stepped out and started to stroll over towards my side of the side-paved street. I took my gun from under my arm and tucked it in my belt and buttoned the bottom button of my coat. Then I walked around the rear end of my car to meet him.

He stopped dead when he saw me. His hands hung empty at his sides. There was a cigar in his mouth. "Police," he said briefly. His right hand shaded back slowly towards his right hip. "Nice night ain't it?"

"Swell," I said. "A little foggy, but I like fog. It softens the air up and—"

He cut in on me sharply: "Where's the other guy?"

"Huh?"

"Don't kid me, stranger. I saw a cigarette on the right side of your car."

"That was me," I said. "I didn't know it was against the law to smoke on the right side of a car."

"Oh, a smart monkey. Who are you and what's your business here?" His heavy, greasy face reflected the sifted light in the soft misty air.

"The name's O'Brien," I said. "Just down from San Mateo on a little pleasure trip."

His hand was very close to his hip now. "I'll look at your driver's licence," he said. He came close enough to reach it, if we both stretched out our arms to each other.

"I'll look at what gives you the right to look at it," I said.

His right hand made an abrupt movement. Mine flicked the gun out of my belt and pointed it at his stomach. His hand stopped as though it had been frozen in a block of ice.

"Maybe you're a stick-up," I said. "It's still being done with nickel badges."

He stood there, paralyzed, hardly breathing. He said thickly: "Got a licence for that heater?"

"Every day in the week," I said. "Let's see your badge and I'll put it away. You don't wear the buzzer where you sit down, do you?"

He stood for another frozen minute. Then he looked along the block as if he hoped another car might arrive. Behind me, in the back of my car, there was a soft, sibilant breathing. I didn't know whether the chunky man heard it or not. His own breathing was heavy enough to iron a shirt with.

"Aw, quit your kiddin'," he snarled out with sudden ferocity. "You're nothin' but a lousy two-bit shamus from L.A."

"I upped the rate," I said. "I get thirty cents now."

"Go to hell. We don't want you nosin' around here, see. This time I'm just tellin' you."

He turned on his heel and walked back to his coupé and put a foot on the running board. His thick neck turned slowly and his greasy skin showed again. "Go to hell," he said, "before we send you there in a basket."

"So long, Greasy-Puss," I said. "Nice to have met you with your pants down."

He slammed into his car, started it with a jerk and lurched it around. He was gone down the block in a flash.

I jumped into mine and was only a block behind him when he made the stop for Arguello Boulevard. He turned right. I turned left. Dolly Kincaid came up and put his chin on the back of the seat beside my shoulder.

"Know who that was?" he croaked. "That was Trigger Weems, the chief's right bower. He might have shot you."

"Fanny Brice might have had a pug nose," I said. "It was that close."

I rode around a few blocks and stopped to let him get in beside me. "Where's your car?" I said.

He took his crumpled reporter's hat off and smacked it on his knee and put it back on again. "Why, down at the city hall. In the police yard."

"Too bad," I said. "You'll have to take the bus to L.A. You ought to spend a night with your sister once in a while. Especially tonight."

IV   Redheaded Woman

THE road twisted, dipped, soared along the flank of the foothills, a scatter of lights to the northwest and a carpet of
them to the south. The three piers seemed remote from this
point, thin pencils of light laid out on a pad of black velvet.
There was fog in the canyons and a smell of wild growth,
but no fog on the high ground between the canyons.

I swung past a small, dim service station, closed up for
the night, down into another wide canyon, up past half a
mile of expensive wire fence walling in some invisible estate. Then the scattered houses got still more scattered along
the hills and the air smelled strongly of the sea. I turned
left past a house with a round white turret and drove out between the only electroliers in miles to a big stucco building
on a point above the coast highway. Light leaked from
draped windows and along an arched stucco colonnade, and
shone dimly on a thick cluster of cars parked in diagonal
slots around an oval lawn.

This was the Club Conried. I didn't know exactly what I
was going to do there, but it seemed to be one of the places
where I had to go. Dr. Austrian was still wandering in unknown parts of the town visiting unnamed patients. The
Physicians' Exchange said he usually called in about eleven.
It was now about ten-fifteen.

I parked in a vacant slot and walked along the arched
colonnade. A six-foot-six Negro, in the uniform of a comic-
opera South American field marshal, opened one half of a
wide grilled door from the inside and said: "Card, please,
suh."

I tucked a dollar's worth of folding money into his lilac-
colored palm. Enormous ebony knuckles closed over it like
a dragline over a bucketful of gravel. His other hand picked
a piece of lint off my left shoulder and left a metal tag down

behind my show handkerchief in the outside breast pocket of my jacket.

"New floor boss kinda tough," he whispered. "I thank you, suh."

"You mean sucker," I said, and went in past him.

The lobby—they called it a foyer—looked like an MGM set for a night club in the Broadway Melody of 1980. Under the artificial light, it looked as if it had cost about a million dollars and took up enough space for a polo field. The carpet didn't quite tickle my ankles. At the back there was a chromium gangway like a ship's gangway going up to the dining-room entrance, and at the top of this a chubby Italian captain of waiters stood with a set smile and a two-inch satin stripe on his pants and a bunch of gold-plated menus under his arm.

There was a free-arched stairway with banisters like white-enameled sleigh rails. This would go up to the second-floor gambling rooms. The ceiling had stars in it and they twinkled. Beside the bar entrance, which was dark and vaguely purple, like a half-remembered nightmare, there was a huge round mirror set back in a white tunnel with an Egyptian headdress over the top of it. In front of this a lady in green was preening her metallic blond hair. Her evening gown was cut so low at the back that she was wearing a black beauty patch on her lumbar muscle, about an inch below where her pants would have been, if she had been wearing any pants.

A check girl in peach-bloom pajamas with small black dragons on them came over to take my hat and disapprove of my clothes. She had eyes as black and shiny and expressionless as the toes of patent-leather pumps. I gave her a quarter and kept my hat. A cigarette girl with a tray the size of a five-pound candy box came down the gangway. She wore feathers in her hair, enough clothes to hide behind a three-cent stamp, and one of her long, beautiful, naked legs was gilded and the other was silvered. She had the cold, disdainful expression of a dame who is dated so far ahead that she would have to think twice before accepting a knockdown to a maharajah with a basket of rubies under his arm.

I went into the soft purple twilight of the bar. Glasses tinkled gently. There were quiet voices, chords on a piano off in a corner, and a pansy tenor singing "My Little Buckeroo" as confidentially as a bartender mixing a Mickey Finn. Little by little the purple light got to be something I could see by. The bar was fairly full but not crowded. A man laughed off-key and the pianist expressed his annoyance by doing an Eddie Duchin ripple down the keyboard with his thumbnail.

I spotted an empty table and went and sat behind it, against the cushioned wall. The light grew still brighter for me. I could even see the buckeroo singer now. He had wavy red hair that looked hennaed. The girl at the table next to me had red hair too. It was parted in the middle and strained back as if she hated it. She had large, dark, hungry eyes, awkward features and no make-up except a mouth that glared like a neon sign. Her street suit had too-wide shoulders, too-flaring lapels. An orange undersweater snuggled her neck and there was a black-and-orange quill in her Robin Hood hat, crooked on the back of her head. She smiled at me and her teeth were as thin and sharp as a pauper's Christmas. I didn't smile back.

She emptied her glass and rattled it on the tabletop. A waiter in a neat mess jacket slipped out of nowhere and stood in front of me.

"Scotch and soda," the girl snapped. She had a hard, angular voice with a liquor slur in it.

The waiter looked at her, barely moved his chin and looked back at me. I said: "Bacardi and grenadine."

He went away. The girl said: "That'll make you sicky, big boy."

I didn't look at her. "So you don't want to play," she said loosely. I lit a cigarette and blew a ring in the soft purplish air. "Go chase yourself," the girl said. "I could pick up a dozen gorillas like you on every block on Hollywood Boulevard. Hollywood Boulevard, my foot. A lot of bit players out of work and fish-faced blondes trying to shake a hangover out of their teeth."

"Who said anything about Hollywood Boulevard?" I asked.

"You did. Nobody but a guy from Hollywood Boulevard wouldn't talk back to a girl that insulted him civilly."

A man and a girl at a nearby table turned their heads and stared. The man gave me a short, sympathetic grin. "That goes for you, too," the girl said to him.

"You didn't insult me yet," he said.

"Nature beat me to it, handsome."

The waiter came back with the drinks. He gave me mine first. The girl said loudly: "I guess you're not used to waiting on ladies."

The waiter gave her her Scotch and soda. "I beg your pardon, madam," he said in an icy tone.

"Sure. Come around sometime and I'll give you a manicure, if I can borrow a hoe. Boy friend's paying the ticket on this."

The waiter looked at me. I gave him a bill and a lift of my right shoulder. He made change, took his tip, and faded off among the tables.

The girl picked her drink up and came over to my table. She put her elbows on the table and cupped her chin in her hands. "Well, well, a spender," she said. "I didn't know they made them any more. How do you like me?"

"I'm thinking it over," I said. "Keep your voice down or they'll throw you out."

"I doubt it," she said. "As long as I don't break any mirrors. Besides, me and their boss are like that." She held up two fingers close together. "That is we would be if I could meet him." She laughed tinnily, drank a little of her drink. "Where've I seen you around?"

"Most anywhere."

"Where've you seen me?"

"Hundreds of places."

"Yes," she said. "Just like that. A girl can't hang on to her individuality any more."

"She can't get it back out of a bottle," I said.

"The heck you say. I could name you plenty of big names that go to sleep with a bottle in each hand. And have to get pushed in the arm so they won't wake up yelling."

"Yeah?" I said. "Movie soaks, huh?"

"Yeah. I work for a guy that pushes them in the arm—at ten bucks a push. Sometimes twenty-five or fifty."

"Sounds like a nice racket," I said.

"If it lasts. You think it'll last?"

"You can always go to Palm Springs when they run you out of here."

"Who's going to run who out of where?"

"I don't know," I said. "What were we talking about?"

She had red hair. She was not good-looking, but she had curves. And she worked for a man who pushed people in the arm. I licked my lips.

A big dark man came through the entrance door and stood just inside it, waiting for his eyes to get used to the light. Then he started to look the place over without haste. His glance traveled to the table where I was sitting. He leaned his big body forward and started to walk our way.

"Oh, oh," the girl said. "The bouncer. Can you take it?"

I didn't answer. She stroked her colorless cheek with a strong pale hand and leered at me. The man at the piano struck some chords and began to whine about "We Can Still Dream, Can't We?"

The big, dark man stopped with his hand on the chair across the table from me. He pulled his eyes off the girl and smiled at me. She was the one he had been looking at. She was the one he had come down the room to get near. But I was the one he looked at from now on. His hair was smooth and dark and shiny above cold gray eyes and eyebrows that looked as if they were penciled, and a handsome actorish mouth and a nose that had been broken but well set. He spoke liplessly.

"Haven't seen you around for some time—or is my memory bad?"

"I don't know," I said. "What are you trying to remember?"

"Your name, doc."

I said: "Quit trying. We never met." I fished the metal tag out of my breast pocket and tossed it down. "Here's my ticket in from the drum major on the wicket." I got a card out of my wallet and tossed that down. "Here's my name, age, height, weight, scars if any, and how many times convicted. And my business is to see Conried."

He ignored the tag and read the card twice, turned it over and looked at the back, then looked at the front again, hooked an arm over the chairback and gave me a mealy smile. He didn't look at the girl then or ever. He racked the card edge across the tabletop and made a faint squeak, like a very young mouse. The girl stared at the ceiling and pretended to yawn.

He said dryly: "So you're one of those guys. So sorry. Mr. Conried had to go north on a little business trip. Caught an early plane."

The girl said: "That must have been his stand-in I saw this afternoon at Sunset and Vine, in a gray Cord sedan."

He didn't look at her. He smiled faintly. "Mr. Conried doesn't have a gray Cord sedan."

The girl said: "Don't let him kid you. I bet he's upstairs crooking a roulette wheel right this minute."

The dark man didn't look at her. His not looking at her was more emphatic than if he had slapped her face. I saw her whiten a little, very slowly, and stay white.

I said: "He's not here, he's not here. Thanks for listening. Maybe some other time."

"Oh sure. But we don't use any private eyes in here. So sorry."

"Say that 'so sorry' again and I'll scream. So help me," the red-haired girl said.

The black-haired man put my card in the casual outer pocket of his dinner jacket. He pushed his chair back and stood up.

"You know how it is," he said. "So—"

The girl cackled and threw her drink in his face.

The dark man stepped back jarringly and swept a crisp white handkerchief from his pocket. He mopped his face swiftly, shaking his head. When he lowered the handkerchief there was a big soaked spot on his shirt, limp above the black pearl stud. His collar was a ruin.

"So sorry," the girl said. "Thought you were a spittoon."

He dropped his hand and his teeth glinted edgily. "Get her out," he purred. "Get her out fast."

He turned and walked off very quickly among the tables, holding his handkerchief against his mouth. Two waiters in mess jackets came up close and stood looking at us. Everybody in the place was looking at us.

"Round one," the girl said. "A little slow. Both fighters were cautious."

"I'd hate to be with you when you'd take a chance," I said.

Her head jerked. In that queer purple light the extreme whiteness of her face seemed to leap at me. Even her rouged lips had a drained look. Her hand went up to her mouth, stiff and clawlike. She coughed dryly like a consumptive and reached for my glass. She gulped the bacardi and grenadine down in bubbling swallows. Then she began to shake. She reached for her bag and pushed it over the edge of the table to the floor. It fell open and some stuff came out. A gilt-metal cigarette case slid under my chair. I had to get up and move the chair to reach it. One of the waiters was behind me.

"Can I help?" he asked suavely.

I was stooped over when the glass the girl had drunk from rolled over the edge of the table and hit the floor beside my hand. I picked up the cigarette case, looked at it casually, and saw that a hand-tinted photo of a big-boned, dark man decorated the front of it. I put it back in her bag and took hold of the girl's arm and the waiter who had spoken to me slid around and took her other arm. She looked at us blankly, moving her head from side to side as if trying to limber up a stiff neck.

"Mama's about to pass out," she croaked, and we started down the room with her. She put her feet out crazily, threw her weight from one side to the other as if trying to upset us. The waiter swore steadily to himself in a monotonous whisper. We came out of the purple light into the bright lobby.

"Ladies' Room," the waiter grunted, and pointed with his chin at a door which looked like the side entrance to the Taj Mahal. "There's a colored heavyweight in there can handle anything."

"Nuts to the Ladies' Room," the girl said nastily. "And leggo of my arm, steward. Boy friend's all the transportation I need."

"He's not your boy friend, madam. He don't even know you."

"Beat it, wop. You're either too polite or not polite enough. Beat it before I lose my culture and bong you."

"Okay," I told him. "I'll set her out to cool. She come in alone?"

"I couldn't think of any reason why not," he said, and stepped away. The captain of waiters came halfway down his gangplank and stood glowering, and the vision at the checkroom looked as bored as the referee of a four-round opener.

I pushed my new friend out into the cold, misty air. walked her along the colonnade and felt her body come controlled and steady on my arm.

"You're a nice guy," she said dully. "I played that about as smooth as a handful of tacks. You're a nice guy, mister. I didn't think I'd ever get out of there alive."

"Why?"

"I had a wrong idea about making some money. Forget it. Let it lay with all the other wrong ideas I've been having all my life. Do I get a ride? I came in a cab."

"Sure. Do I get told your name?"

"Helen Matson," she said.

I didn't get any kick out of that now. I had guessed it long ago.

She still leaned on me a little as we walked down the strip of paved road past the parked cars. When we came to mine I unlocked it and held the door for her and she climbed in and fell back in the corner with her head on the cushion.

I shut the door and then I opened it again and said: "Would you tell me something else? Who's that mug on the cigarette case you carry? Seems to me I've seen him somewhere."

She opened her eyes. "An old sweet," she said, "that wore out. He—" Her eyes widened and her mouth snapped open and I barely heard the faint rustle behind me as something hard dug into my back and a muffled voice said: "Hold it, buddy. This is a heist."

Then a naval gun went off in my ear and my head was a large pink firework exploding into the vault of the sky and scattering and falling slow and pale, and then dark, into the waves. Blackness ate me up.

V My Dead Neighbor

I SMELLED of gin. Not just casually, as if I had taken a few drinks, but as if the Pacific Ocean was pure gin and I had been swimming in it with my clothes on. The gin was on my hair, on my eyebrows, on my face and under my chin on my shirt. My coat was off and I was lying flat on somebody's carpet and I was looking up at a framed photograph on the end of a plaster mantel. The frame was some kind of grained wood and the photo was intended to be arty, with a high-light on a long, thin, unhappy face, but all the highlight did was make the face look just that—long and thin and unhappy under some kind of flat, pale hair that might have been paint on a dried skull. There was writing across the corner of the photo behind the glass, but I couldn't read that.

I reached up and pressed the side of my head and I could feel a shoot of pain clear to the soles of my feet. I groaned and made a grunt out of the groan, from professional pride, and then I rolled over slowly and carefully and looked at the foot of a pulled-down twin wall bed. The other twin was still up in the wall with a flourish of design painted on the enameled wood. When I rolled, a gin bottle rolled off my chest and hit the floor. It was water-white, empty. I thought there couldn't have been that much gin in just one bottle.

I got my knees under me and stayed on all fours for a while, sniffing like a dog who can't finish his dinner and yet hates to leave it. I moved my head around on my neck. It hurt. I moved it some more and it still hurt, so I got up on my feet and discovered that I didn't have any shoes on.

It seemed like a nice apartment, not too cheap and not too expensive—the usual furniture, the usual drum lamp, the usual durable carpet. On the bed, which was down, a girl was lying, clothed in a pair of tan silk stockings. There were deep scratches that had bled and there was a thick bath towel across her middle, wadded up almost into a roll. Her eyes were open. The red hair that had been parted and strained back as if she hated it was still that way. But she didn't hate it any more.

She was dead.

Above and inside her left breast there was a scorched place the size of the palm of a man's hand, and in the middle of that there was a thimbleful of blazed blood. Blood had run down her side, but it had dried now.

I saw clothes on a davenport, mostly hers, but including my coat. There were shoes on the floor—mine and hers. I went over, stepping on the balls of my feet as though on very thin ice, and picked up my coat and felt through the pockets. They still held everything I could remember having put in them. The holster that was still strapped around my body was empty, of course. I put my shoes and coat on, pushed the empty holster around under my arm and went over to the bed and lifted the heavy bath towel. A gun fell out of it—my gun. I wiped some blood off the barrel, sniffed the muzzle for no reason at all, and quietly put the gun back under my arm.

Heavy feet came along the corridor outside the apartment door and stopped. There was a mutter of voices, then somebody knocked, a quick, hard, impatient rapping. I looked at the door and wondered how long it would be before they tried it, and if the spring lock would be set so they could walk in, and if it wasn't set how long it would take to get the manager up with a passkey if he wasn't there already. I was still wondering when a hand tried the door. It was locked.

That was very funny. I almost laughed out loud.

I stepped over to another door and glanced into a bathroom. There were two wash rugs on the floor, a bath mat folded neatly over the edge of the tub, a pebbled glass window above it. I eased the bathroom door shut quietly and stood on the edge of the bathtub and pushed up the lower sash of the bathroom window. I put my head out and looked down about six floors to the darkness of a side street lined with trees. To do this I had to look out through a slot formed by two short blank walls, hardly more than an air shaft. The windows were in pairs, all in the same end wall opposite the open end of the slot. I leaned farther out and decided I could make the next window if I tried. I wondered if it was unlocked, and if it would do me any good, and if I'd have time before they could get the door open.

Behind me, beyond the closed bathroom door, the pounding was a little louder and harder and a voice was growling out: "Open it up or we'll bust it in."

That didn't mean anything. That was just routine cop stuff. They wouldn't break it down because they could get a key, and kicking that kind of door in without a fire axe is a lot of work and tough on the feet.

I shut the lower half of the window and pulled down the upper half and took a towel off the rack. Then I opened the bathroom door again and my eyes were looking straight at the face in the photo frame on the mantel. I had to read the inscription on that photo before I left. I went over and scanned it while the pounding on the door went on angrily. The inscription said—*With all my love—Leland.*

That made a sap out of Dr. Austrian, without anything else. I grabbed the photo and went back into the bathroom and shut the door again. Then I shoved the photo under the dirty towels and linen in the cupboard under the bathroom closet. It would take them a little while to find it, if they were good cops. If we were in Bay City, they probably wouldn't find it at all. I didn't know of any reason why we should be in Bay City, except that Helen Matson would very likely live there and the air outside the bathroom window seemed to be beach air.

I squeezed out through the upper half of the window with the towel in my hand and swung my body across to the next window, holding on to the sash of the one I had left. I could reach just far enough to push the next window up, if it was unlocked. It wasn't unlocked. I swung my foot and kicked the glass in just over the catch. It made a noise that ought to have been heard a mile. The distant pounding went on monotonously.

I wrapped the towel around my left hand and stretched my arms for all they had in them and shoved my hand in through the broken place and turned the window catch. Then I swung over to the other sill and reached back to push up the window I had come out of. They could have the fingerprints. I didn't expect to be able to prove I hadn't been in Helen Matson's apartment. All I wanted was a chance to prove how I had got there.

I looked down at the street. A man was getting into a car. He didn't even look up at me. No light had gone on in the apartment I was breaking into. I got the window down and climbed in. There was a lot of broken glass in the bathtub. I got down to the floor and switched the light on and picked the glass out of the bathtub and wrapped it in my towel and hid it. I used somebody else's towel to wipe off the sill and the edge of the bathtub where I'd stood. Then I took my gun out and opened the bathroom door.

This was a larger apartment. The room I was looking at had twin beds with pink dust covers. They were made up nicely and they were empty. Beyond the bedroom there was a living room. All the windows were shut and the place had a close, dusty smell. I lit a floor lamp, then I ran a finger along the arm of a chair and looked at dust on it. There was an armchair radio, a book rack built like a hod, a big bookcase full of novels with the jackets still on them, a dark wood highboy with a siphon and a decanter of liquor on it, and four striped glasses upside down. I sniffed the liquor, which was Scotch, and used a little of it. It made my head feel worse but it made me feel better.

I left the light on and went back to the bedroom and poked into bureau and closets. There were male clothes in one closet, tailor-made, and the name written on the label by the tailor was George Talbot. George's clothes looked a little small for me. I tried the bureau and found a pair of pajamas I thought would do. The closet gave me a bathrobe and slippers. I stripped to the skin.

When I came out of the shower I smelled only faintly of gin. There was no noise or pounding going on anywhere now, so I knew they were in Helen Matson's apartment with their little pieces of chalk and string. I put Mr. Talbot's pajamas and slippers and bathrobe on, used some of Mr. Talbot's tonic on my hair and his brush and comb to tidy up. I hoped Mr. and Mrs. Talbot were having a good time wherever they were and that they would not have to hurry home.

I went back to the living room, used some more Talbot Scotch and lit one of his cigarettes. Then I unlocked the entrance door. A man coughed close by in the hall. I opened the door and leaned against the jamb and looked out. A uniformed man was leaning against the opposite wall—a smallish, blond, sharp-eyed man. His blue trousers were edged like a knife and he looked neat, clean, competent and nosy.

I yawned and said: "What goes on, officer?"

He stared at me with sharp reddish-brown eyes flecked with gold, a color you seldom see with blond hair. "A little trouble next door to you. Hear anything?" His voice was mildly sarcastic.

"The carrot-top?" I said. "Haw, haw. Just the usual big-game hunt. Drink?"

The cop went on with his careful stare. Then he called down the hallway: "Hey, Al!"

A man stepped out of an open door. He was about six feet, weighed around two hundred, and he had coarse black hair and deep-set expressionless eyes. It was Al De Spain whom I had met that evening at Bay City headquarters.

He came down the hall without haste. The uniformed cop said: "Here's the guy lives next door."

De Spain came close to me and looked into my eyes. His own held no more expression than pieces of black slate. He spoke almost softly.

"Name?"

"George Talbot," I said. I didn't quite squeak.

"Hear any noises? I mean, before we got here?"

"Oh, a brawl, I guess. Around midnight. That's nothing new in there." I jerked a thumb towards the dead girl's apartment.

"That so? Acquainted with the dame?"

"No. Doubt if I'd want to know her."

"You won't have to," De Spain said. "She's croaked."

He put a big, hard hand against my chest and pushed me back very gently through the door into the apartment. He kept his hand against my chest and his eyes flicked down sharply to the side pockets of the bathrobe, then back to my face again. When he had me eight feet from the door he said over his shoulder: "Come in and shut the door, Shorty."

Shorty came and shut the door, small, sharp eyes gleaming. "Quite a gag," De Spain said, very casually. "Put a gun on him, Shorty."

Shorty flicked his black belt holster open and had a police

gun in his hand like lightning. He licked his lips. "Oh boy," he said softly. "Oh boy." He snapped his handcuff holder open and half drew the cuffs out. "How'd you know, Al?"

"Know what?" De Spain kept his eyes on my eyes. He spoke to me gently. "What was you goin' to do—go down and buy a paper?"

"Yah," Shorty said. "He's the killer, sure. He come in through the bathroom window and put on clothes belonging to the guy that lives here. The folks are away. Look at the dust. No windows open. Dead air in the place."

De Spain said softly: "Shorty's a scientific cop. Don't let him get you down. He's got to be wrong some day."

I said: "What for is he in uniform, if he's so hot?"

Shorty reddened. De Spain said: "Find his clothes, Shorty. And his gun. And make it fast. This is our pinch, if we make it fast."

"You ain't detailed on the case even," Shorty said.

"What can I lose?"

"*I* can lose this here uniform."

"Take a chance, boy. That lug Reed next door couldn't catch a moth in a shoe box."

Shorty scuttled into the bedroom. De Spain and I stood motionless, except that he took his hand off my chest and dropped it to his side. "Don't tell me," he drawled. "Just let me guess."

We heard Shorty fussing around opening doors. Then we heard a yelp like a terrier's yelp when he smells a rathole. Shorty came back into the room with my gun in his right hand and my wallet in his left. He held the gun by the fore sight, with a handkerchief. "The gat's been fired," he said. "And this guy ain't called Talbot."

De Spain didn't turn his head or change expression. He smiled at me thinly, moving only the extreme corners of his wide, rather brutal mouth.

"You don't say," he said. "You don't say." He pushed me away from him with a hand as hard as a piece of tool steel. "Get dressed, sweetheart—and don't fuss with your necktie. Places want us to go to them."

VI   I Get My Gun Back

WE went out of the apartment and along the hall. Light still came from the open door of Helen Matson's apartment. Two men with a basket stood outside it smoking. There was a sound of wrangling voices inside the dead woman's place.

We went around a bend of the hall and started down the stairs, floor after floor, until we came out in the lobby. Half a dozen people stood around bug-eyed—three women in bathrobes, a bald-headed man with a green eyeshade, like a city editor, two more who hung back in the shadows. Another uniformed man walked up and down just inside the front door, whistling under his breath. We went out past him. He looked completely uninterested. A knot of people clustered on the sidewalk outside.

De Spain said: "This is a big night in our little town."

We walked along to a black sedan that had no police insignia on it and De Spain slid in behind the wheel and motioned me to get in beside him. Shorty got in the back. He'd had his gun back in his holster long since, but he left the flap unbuttoned, and kept his hand close to it.

De Spain put the car into motion with a jerk that threw me back against the cushions. We made the nearest corner on two wheels, going east. A big black car with twin red spotlights was only half a block away and coming fast as we made the turn.

De Spain spat out of the window and drawled: "That's the chief. He'll be late for his own funeral. Boy, did we skin his nose on this one."

Shorty said disgustedly from the back seat: "Yeah—for a thirty-day lay-off."

De Spain said: "Keep that mush of yours in low and you might get back on Homicide."

"I'd rather wear buttons and eat," Shorty said.

De Spain drove the car hard for ten blocks, then slowed a little. Shorty said: "This ain't the way to headquarters."

De Spain said: "Don't be an ass."

He let the car slow to a crawl, turned it left into a quiet, dark, residential street lined with coniferous trees and small exact houses set back from small exact lawns. He braked the car gently, coasted it over to the curb and switched the motor off. Then he threw an arm over the back of the seat and turned to look at the small "sharp-eyed" uniformed man.

"You think this guy plugged her, Shorty?"

"His gun went off."

"Get that big flash outa the pocket and look at the back of his head."

Shorty snorted, fussed around in the back of the car, and then metal clicked and the blinding white beam of a large bell-topped flashlight sprayed over my head. I heard the little man's close breathing. He reached out and pressed the sore place on the back of my head. I yelped. The light went off and the blackness of the dark street jumped at us again.

Shorty said: "I guess he was sapped."

De Spain said without emotion: "So was the girl. It didn't show much but it's there. She was sapped so she could have her clothes pulled off and be clawed up before she was shot, so the scratches would bleed and look like you know what. Then she was shot with a bath towel around the gun. Nobody heard the shot. Who reported it, Shorty?"

"How the hell would I know? A guy called up two-three minutes before you came into the Hall, while Reed was still looking for a cameraman. A guy with a thick voice, the operator said."

"Okay. If you done it, Shorty, how would you get out of there?"

"I'd walk out," Shorty said. "Why not? Hey," he barked at me, "why didn't you?"

I said: "I have to have my little secrets."

De Spain said tonelessly: "You wouldn't climb across no air shaft, would you, Shorty? You wouldn't crash into the next apartment and pretend to be the guy that lived there, would you? And you wouldn't call no law and tell them to take it up there in high and they'd catch the killer, would you?"

"Hell," Shorty said, "this guy call up? No, I wouldn't do any of them things."

"Neither did the killer," De Spain said, "except the last one. He called up."

"Them sex fiends do funny things," Shorty said. "This guy could have had help and the other guy tried to put him in the middle after knocking him out with a sap."

De Spain laughed harshly. "Hello, sex fiend," he said, and poked me in the ribs with a finger as hard as a gun barrel. "Look at us saps, just sitting here and throwing our jobs away—that is, the one of us that has a job—and arguing it out when you, the guy that knows all the answers, ain't told us a damn thing. We don't even know who the dame was."

"A redhead I picked up in the bar of the Club Conried," I said. "No, she picked me up."

"No name or anything?"

"No. She was tight. I helped her out into the air and she asked me to take her away from there and while I was putting her into my car somebody sapped me. I came to on the floor of the apartment and the girl was dead."

De Spain said: "What was you doing in the bar of the Club Conried?"

"Getting my hair cut," I said. "What do you do in a bar? This redhead was tight and seemed scared about something and she threw a drink in the floor boss's face. I felt a little sorry for her."

"I always feel sorry for a redhead, too," De Spain said. "This guy that sapped you must have been an elephant, if he carried you up to that apartment."

I said: "Have you ever been sapped?"

"No," De Spain said. "Have you, Shorty?"

Shorty said he had never been sapped either. He said it unpleasantly.

"All right," I said. "It's like an alcohol drunk. I probably came to in the car and the fellow would have a gun and that would keep me quiet. He would walk me up to the apartment with the girl. The girl may have known him. And when he had me up there he would sap me again and I wouldn't remember anything that happened in between the two sappings."

"I've heard of it," De Spain said. "But I never believed it."

"Well, it's true," I said. "It's got to be true. Because I don't remember and the guy couldn't have carried me up there without help."

"I could," De Spain said. "I've carried heavier guys than you."

"All right," I said. "He carried me up. Now what do we do?"

Shorty said: "I don't get why he went to all that trouble."

"Sapping a guy ain't trouble," De Spain said. "Pass over that heater and wallet."

Shorty hesitated, then passed them over. De Spain smelled the gun and dropped it carelessly into his side pocket, the one next to me. He flipped the wallet open and held it down under the dashlight and then put it away. He started the car, turned it in the middle of the block, and shot back up Arguello Boulevard, turned east on that and pulled up in front of a liquor store with a red neon sign. The place was wide open, even at that hour of the night.

De Spain said over his shoulder: "Run inside and phone the desk, Shorty. Tell the sarge we got a hot lead and we're on our way to pick up a suspect in the Brayton Avenue killing. Tell him to tell the chief his shirt is out."

Shorty got out of the car, slammed the rear door, started to say something, then walked fast across the sidewalk into the store.

De Spain jerked the car into motion and hit forty in the first block. He laughed deep down in his chest. He made it fifty in the next block and then began to turn in and out of streets and finally he pulled to a stop again under a pepper tree outside a schoolhouse.

I got the gun when he reached forward for the parking brake. He laughed dryly and spat out of the open window.

"Okay," he said. "That's why I put it there. I talked to Violets M'Gee. That kid reporter called me up from L.A. They've found Matson. They're sweating some apartment house guy right now."

I slid away from him over to my corner of the car and held the gun loosely between my knees. "We're outside the limits of Bay City, copper," I told him. "What did M'Gee say?"

"He said he gave you a lead to Matson, but he didn't know whether you had contacted him or not. This apartment house guy—I didn't hear his name—was trying to dump a stiff in the alley when a couple of prowlies jumped him. M'Gee said if you had contacted Matson and heard his story you would be down here getting in a jam, and would likely wake up sapped beside some stiff."

"I didn't contact Matson," I said.

I could feel De Spain staring at me under his dark craggy brows. "But you're down here in a jam," he said.

I got a cigarette out of my pocket with my left hand and lit it with the dash lighter. I kept my right hand on the gun. I said: "I got the idea you were on the way out down here. That you weren't even detailed on this killing. Now you've taken a prisoner across the city line. What does that make you?"

"A bucket of mud—unless I deliver something good."

"That's what I am," I said. "I guess we ought to team up and break these three killings."

"Three?"

"Yeah. Helen Matson, Harry Matson and Doc Austrian's wife. They all go together."

"I ditched Shorty," De Spain said quietly, "because he's a little guy and the chief likes little guys and Shorty can put the blame on me. Where do we start?"

"We might start by finding a man named Greb who runs a laboratory in the Physicians and Surgeons Building. I think he turned in a phony report on the Austrian death. Suppose they put out an alarm for you?"

"They use the L.A. air. They won't use that to pick up one of their own cops."

He leaned forward and started the car again.

"You might give me my wallet," I said. "So I can put this gun away."

He laughed harshly and gave it to me.

VII   Big Chin

THE lab man lived on Ninth Street, on the wrong side of town. The house was a shapeless frame bungalow. A large dusty hydrangea bush and some small undernourished plants along the path looked like the work of a man who had spent his life trying to make something out of nothing.

De Spain doused the lights as we glided up front and said: "Whistle, if you need help. If any cops should crowd us, skin over to Tenth and I'll circle the block and pick you up. I don't think they will, though. All they're thinking of tonight is that dame on Brayton Avenue."

I looked up and down the quiet block, walked across the street in foggy moonlight and up the walk to the house. The front door was set at right angles to the street in a front projection that looked like a room which had been added as an afterthought to the rest of the house. I pushed a bell and heard it ring somewhere in the back. No answer. I rang it twice more and tried the front door. It was locked.

I went down off the little porch and around the north side of the house towards a small garage on the back lot. Its doors were shut and locked with a padlock you could break with a strong breath. I bent over and shot my pocket flash under the loose doors. The wheels of a car showed. I went back to the front door of the house and knocked this time—plenty loud.

The window in the front room creaked and came down slowly from the top, about halfway. There was a shade pulled down behind the window and darkness behind the shade. A thick, hoarse voice said: "Yeah?"

"Mr. Greb?"

"Yeah."

"I'd like to speak to you—on important business."

"I gotta get my sleep, mister. Come back tomorrow."

The voice didn't sound like the voice of a laboratory

technician. It sounded like a voice I had heard over the telephone once, a long time ago, early in the evening at the Tennyson Arms Apartments.

I said: "Well, I'll come to your office then, Mr. Greb. What's the address again?"

The voice didn't speak for a moment. Then it said: "Aw, go on, beat it before I come out there and paste you one."

"That's no way to get business, Mr. Greb," I said. "Are you sure you couldn't give me just a few moments, now you're up?"

"Pipe down. You'll wake the wife. She's sick. If I gotta come out there—"

"Good night, Mr. Greb," I said.

I went back down the walk in the soft, foggy moonlight. When I got across to the far side of the dark parked car I said: "It's a two-man job. Some tough guy is in there. I think it's the man I heard called Big Chin over the phone in L.A."

"Geez. The guy that killed Matson, huh?" De Spain came over to my side of the car and stuck his head out and spat clear over a fireplug that must have been eight feet away. I didn't say anything.

De Spain said: "If this guy you call Big Chin is Moss Lorenz, I'll know him. We might get in. Or maybe we walk ourselves into some hot lead."

"Just like the coppers do on the radio," I said.

"You scared?"

"Me?" I said. "Sure I'm scared. The car's in the garage, so either he's got Greb in there and is trying to make up his mind what to do with him—"

"If it's Moss Lorenz, he don't have a mind," De Spain growled. "That guy is screwy except in two places—behind a gun and behind the wheel of a car."

"And behind a piece of lead pipe," I said. "What I was saying was, Greb might be out without his car and this Big Chin—"

De Spain bent over to look at the clock on the dash. "My guess would be he's skipped. He'd be home by now. He's got a tip to scram out of some trouble."

"Will you go in there or won't you?" I snapped. "Who would tip him?"

"Whoever fixed him in the first place, if he was fixed."

De Spain clicked the door open and slid out of the car, stood looking over it across the street. He opened his coat and loosened the gun in his shoulder clip. "Maybe I could kid him," he said. "Keep your hands showing and empty. It's our best chance."

We went back across the street and up the walk, up on the porch. De Spain leaned on the bell.

The voice came growling at us again from the half-open window, behind the frayed dark green shade.

"Yeah?"

"Hello, Moss," De Spain said.

"Huh?"

"This is Al De Spain, Moss. I'm in on the play."

Silence—a long, murderous silence. Then the thick, hoarse voice said: "Who's that with you?"

"A pal from L.A. He's okay."

More silence, then, "What's the angle?"

"You alone in there?"

"Except for a dame. She can't hear you."

"Where's Greb?"

"Yeah—where is he? What's the angle, copper? Snap it up!"

De Spain spoke as calmly as though he had been at home in an armchair, beside the radio. "We're workin' for the same guy, Moss."

"Haw, haw," Big Chin said.

"Matson's been found dead in L.A., and those city dicks have already connected him with the Austrian dame. We gotta step fast. The big shot's up north alibi-ing himself, but what does that do for us?"

The voice said, "Aw, baloney," but there was a note of doubt in it.

"It looks like a stink," De Spain said. "Come on, open up. You can see we don't have anything to hold on you."

"By the time I got around to the door you would have," Big Chin said.

"You ain't that yellow," De Spain sneered.

The shade rustled at the window as if a hand had let go of it and the sash moved up into place. My hand started up.

De Spain growled: "Don't be a sap. This guy is our case. We want him all in one piece."

Faint steps sounded inside the house. A lock turned in

the front door and it opened and a figure stood there, shadowed, a big Colt in his hand. Big Chin was a good name for him. His big, broad jaw stuck out from his face like a cowcatcher. He was a bigger man than De Spain—a good deal bigger.

"Snap it up," he said, and started to move back.

De Spain, his hands hanging loose and empty, palms turned out, took a quiet step forward on his left foot and kicked Big Chin in the groin—just like that—without the slightest hesitation, and against a gun.

Big Chin was still fighting—inside himself—when we got our guns out. His right hand was fighting to press the trigger and hold the gun up. His sense of pain was fighting down everything else but the desire to double up and yell. That internal struggle of his wasted a split second and he had neither shot nor yelled when we slammed him. De Spain hit him on the head and I hit him on the right wrist. I wanted to hit his chin—it fascinated me—but his wrist was nearest the gun. The gun dropped and Big Chin dropped, almost as suddenly, then plunged forward against us. We caught and held him and his breath blew hot and rank in our faces, then his knees went to pieces and we fell into the hallway on top of him.

De Spain grunted and struggled to his feet and shut the door. Then he rolled the big, groaning, half-conscious man over and dragged his hands behind him and snapped cuffs on his wrists.

We went down the hall. There was a dim light in the room to the left, from a small table lamp with a newspaper over it. De Spain lifted the paper off and we looked at the woman on the bed. At least he hadn't murdered her. She lay in sleazy pajamas with her eyes wide open and staring and half mad with fear. Mouth, wrists, ankles and knees were taped and the ends of thick wads of cotton stuck out of her ears. A vague bubbling sound came from behind the slab of two-inch adhesive that plastered her mouth shut. De Spain bent the lampshade a little. Her face was mottled. She had bleached hair, dark at the roots, and a thin, scraped look about the bones of her face.

De Spain said: "I'm a police officer. Are you Mrs. Greb?"

The woman jerked and stared at him agonizingly. I pulled the cotton out of her ears and said: "Try again."

"Are you Mrs. Greb?"

She nodded.

De Spain took hold of the tape at the side of her mouth. Her eyes winced and he jerked it hard and capped a hand down over her mouth at once. He stood there, bending over, the tape in his left hand—a big, dark, dead-pan copper who didn't seem to have any more nerves than a cement mixer.

"Promise not to scream?" he said.

The woman forced a nod and he took his hand away. "Where's Greb?" he asked.

He pulled the rest of the tape off her.

She swallowed and took hold of her forehead with her red-nailed hand and shook her head. "I don't know. He hasn't been home."

"What talk was there when the gorilla came in?"

"There wasn't any," she said dully. "The bell rang and I opened the door and he walked in and grabbed me. Then the big brute tied me up and asked me where my husband was and I said I didn't know and he slapped my face a few times, but after a while he seemed to believe me. He asked me why my husband didn't have the car and I said he always walked to work and never took the car. Then he just sat in the corner and didn't move or speak. He didn't even smoke."

"Did he use the telephone?" De Spain asked.

"No."

"You ever seen him before?"

"No."

"Get dressed," De Spain said. "You gotta find some friends you can go to for the rest of the night."

She stared at him and sat up slowly on the bed and rumpled her hair. Then her mouth opened and De Spain clapped his hand over it again, hard.

"Hold it," he said sharply. "Nothing's happened to him that we know of. But I guess you wouldn't be too damn surprised if it did."

The woman pushed his hand away and stood up off the bed and walked around it to a bureau and took out a pint of whisky. She unscrewed the top and drank from the bottle. "Yeah," she said in a strong, coarse voice. "What would you do, if you had to soap a bunch of doctors for every nickel you made and there was damn few nickels to be made at that?" She took another drink.

De Spain said: "I might switch blood samples."

The woman stared at him blankly. He looked at me and shrugged. "Maybe it's happy powder," he said. "Maybe he peddles a little of that. It must be damn little, to go by how he lives." He looked around the room contemptuously. "Get dressed, lady."

We went out of the room and shut the door. De Spain bent down over Big Chin, lying on his back and half on his side on the floor. The big man groaned steadily with his mouth open, neither completely out nor fully aware of what was going on around him. De Spain, still bending down in the dim light he'd put on in the hall, looked at the piece of adhesive in the palm of his hand and laughed suddenly. He slammed the tape hard over Big Chin's mouth.

"Think we can make him walk?" he asked. "I'd hate like hell to have to carry him."

"I don't know," I said. "I'm just the swamper on this route. Walk to where?"

"Up in the hills where it's quiet and the birds sing," De Spain said grimly.

I sat on the running board of the car with the big bell-shaped flashlight hanging down between my knees. The light wasn't too good, but it seemed to be good enough for what De Spain was doing to Big Chin. A roofed reservoir was just above us and the ground sloped away from that into a deep canyon. There were two hilltop houses about half a mile away, both dark, with a glisten of moonlight on their stucco walls. It was cold up there in the hills, but the air was clear and the stars were like pieces of polished chromium. The light haze over Bay City seemed to be far off, as if in another county, but it was only a fast ten-minute drive.

De Spain had his coat off. His shirt-sleeves were rolled up and his wrists and his big hairless arms looked enormous in the faint hard light. His coat lay on the ground between him and Big Chin. His gun holster lay on the coat, with the gun in the holster, and the butt towards Big Chin. The coat was a little to one side so that between De Spain and Big Chin there was a small space of scuffed moonlit gravel. The gun was to Big Chin's right and to De Spain's left.

After a long silence thick with breathing De Spain said:

"Try again." He spoke casually, as if he were talking to a man playing a pinball game.

Big Chin's face was a mass of blood. I couldn't see it as red, but I had put the flash on it a time or two and I knew it was there. His hands were free and what the kick in the groin had done to him was long ago, on the far side of oceans of pain. He made a croaking noise and turned his left hip suddenly against De Spain and went down on his right knee and lunged for the gun.

De Spain kicked him in the face.

Big Chin rolled back on the gravel and clawed at his face with both hands and a wailing sound came through his fingers. De Spain stepped over and kicked him on the ankle. Big Chin howled. De Spain stepped back to his original position beyond the coat and the holstered gun. Big Chin rolled a little and came up on his knees and shook his head. Big dark drops fell from his face to the gravelly ground. He got up to his feet slowly and stayed hunched over a little.

De Spain said: "Come on up. You're a tough guy. You got Vance Conried behind you and he's got the syndicate behind him. You maybe got Chief Anders behind you. I'm a lousy flatfoot with a ticket to nowhere in my pants. Come up. Let's put on a show."

Big Chin shot out in a diving lunge for the gun. His hand touched the butt but only slewed it around. De Spain came down hard on the hand with his heel and screwed his heel. Big Chin yelled. De Spain jumped back and said wearily: "You ain't overmatched, are you, sweetheart?"

I said thickly: "For God's sake, why don't you let him talk?"

"He don't want to talk," De Spain said. "He ain't the talking kind. He's a tough guy."

"Well, let's shoot the poor devil then."

"Not a chance. I'm not that kind of cop. Hey, Moss, this guy thinks I'm just one of those sadistic cops that has to smack a head with a piece of lead pipe every so often to keep from getting nervous indigestion. You ain't going to let him think that, are you? This is a square fight. You got me shaded twenty pounds and look where the gun is."

Big Chin mumbled: "Suppose I got it. Your pal would blast me."

"Not a chance. Come on, big boy. Just once more. You got a lot of stuff left."

Big Chin got up on his feet again. He got up so slowly that he seemed like a man climbing up a wall. He swayed and wiped blood off his face with his hand. My head ached. I felt sick at my stomach.

Big Chin swung his right foot very suddenly. It looked like something for a fraction of a second, then De Spain picked the foot out of the air and stepped back, pulled on it. He held the leg taut and the big bruiser swayed on his other foot trying to hold his balance.

De Spain said conversationally: "That was okay when I did it because you had plenty of gun in your mitt and I didn't have any gun and you didn't figure on me taking a chance like that. Now you see how wrong the play is in this spot."

He twisted the foot quickly, with both hands. Big Chin's body seemed to leap into the air and dive sideways, and his shoulder and face smashed into the ground, but De Spain held on to the foot. He kept on turning it. Big Chin began to thresh around on the ground and make harsh animal sounds, half stifled in the gravel. De Spain gave the foot a sudden hard wrench. Big Chin screamed like a dozen sheets tearing.

De Spain lunged forward and stepped on the ankle of Big Chin's other foot. He put his weight against the foot he held in his hands and spread Big Chin's legs. Big Chin tried to gasp and yell at the same time and made a sound something like a very large and very old dog barking.

De Spain said: "Guys get paid money for what I'm doing. Not nickels—real dough. I oughta look into it."

Big Chin yelled: "Lemme up! I'll talk! I'll talk!"

De Spain spread the legs some more. He did something to the foot and Big Chin suddenly went limp. It was like a sea lion fainting. It staggered De Spain and he reeled to one side as the leg smacked the ground. Then he reached a handkerchief out of his pocket and slowly mopped his face and hands.

"Soft," he said. "Too much beer. The guy looked healthy. Maybe it's always having his fanny under a wheel."

"And his hand under a gun," I said.

"That's an idea," De Spain said. "We don't want to lose him his self-respect."

He stepped over and kicked Big Chin in the ribs. After the third kick there was a grunt and a glistening where the blankness of Big Chin's eyelids had been.

"Get up," De Spain said. "I ain't goin' to hurt you no more."

Big Chin got up. It took him a whole minute to get up. His mouth—what was left of it—was strained wide open. It made me think of another man's mouth and I stopped having pity for him. He pawed the air with his hands, looking for something to lean against.

De Spain said: "My pal here says you're soft without a gun in your hand. I wouldn't want a strong guy like you to be soft. Help yourself to my gat." He kicked the holster lightly so that it slid off the coat and close to Big Chin's foot. Big Chin bowed his shoulders to look down at it. He couldn't bend his neck any more.

"I'll talk," he grunted.

"Nobody asked you to talk. I asked you to get that gun in your hand. Don't make me cave you in again to make you do it. See—the gun in your hand."

Big Chin staggered down to his knees and his hand folded slowly over the butt of the gun. De Spain watched without moving a muscle.

"Attaboy. Now you got a gun. Now you're tough again. Now you can bump off some more women. Pull it outa the clip."

Very slowly, with what seemed to be enormous effort, Big Chin drew the gun out of the holster and knelt there with it dangling down between his legs.

"What, ain't you going to bump anybody off?" De Spain taunted him.

Big Chin dropped the gun out of his hand and sobbed.

"Hey, you!" De Spain barked. "Put that gun back where you got it, I want that gun clean, like I always keep it myself."

Big Chin's hand fumbled for the gun and got hold of it and slowly pushed it home in the leather sheath. The effort took all his remaining strength. He fell flat on his face over the holster.

De Spain lifted him by an arm and rolled him over on

his back and picked the holster up off the ground. He rubbed the butt of the gun with his hand and strapped the holster around his chest. Then he picked up his coat and put that on.

"Now we'll let him spill his guts," he said. "I don't believe in makin' a guy talk when he don't want to talk. Got a cigarette?"

I reached a pack out of my pocket with my left hand and shook a cigarette loose and held the pack out. I clicked the big flash on and held it on the projecting cigarette and on his big fingers as they came forward to take it.

"I don't need that," he said. He fumbled for a match and struck it and drew smoke slowly into his lungs. I doused the flash again. De Spain looked down the hill towards the sea and the curve of the shore and the lighted piers. "Kind of nice up here," he added.

"Cold," I said. "Even in summer. I could use a drink."

"Me too," De Spain said. "Only I can't work on the stuff."

VIII   Needle-Pusher

De Spain stopped the car in front of the Physicians and Surgeons Building and looked up at a lighted window on the sixth floor. The building was designed in a series of radiating wings so that all the offices had an outside exposure.

"Good grief," De Spain said. "He's up there right now. That guy don't never sleep at all, I guess. Take a look at that heap down the line."

I got up and walked down in front of the dark drugstore that flanked the lobby entrance of the building on one side. There was a long black sedan parked diagonally and correctly in one of the ruled spaces, as though it had been high noon instead of almost three in the morning. The sedan had a doctor's emblem beside the front license plate, the staff of Hippocrates and the serpents twisted around it. I put my flash into the car and read part of the name on the license holder and snapped the light off again. I went back to De Spain.

"Check," I said. "How did you know that was his window and what would he be doing here at this time of night?"

"Loading up his little needles," he said. "I've watched the guy some is how I know."

"Watched him why?"

He looked at me and said nothing. Then he looked back over his shoulder into the back part of the car. "How you doin', pal?"

A thick sound that might be trying to be a voice came from under a rug on the floor of the car. "He likes riding," De Spain said. "All these hard guys like riding around in cars. Okay. I'll tuck the heap in the alley and we'll go up."

He slid around the corner of the building without lights and the car sound died in the moonlit darkness. Across the street a row of enormous eucalyptus trees fringed a set of public tennis courts. The smell of kelp came up along the boulevard from the ocean.

De Spain came back around the corner of the building and we went up to the locked lobby door and knocked on the heavy plate glass. Far back there was light from an open elevator beyond a big bronze mailbox. An old man came out of the elevator and along the corridor to the door and stood looking out at us with keys in his hand. De Spain held up his police shield. The old man squinted at it and unlocked the door and locked it after us without saying a word. He went back along the hall to the elevator and rearranged the homemade cushion on the stool and moved his false teeth around with his tongue and said: "What you want?"

He had a long gray face that grumbled even when it didn't say anything. His trousers were frayed at the cuffs and one of his heelworn black shoes contained an obvious bunion. His blue uniform coat fitted him the way a stall fits a horse.

De Spain said: "Doc Austrian is upstairs, ain't he?"

"I wouldn't be surprised."

"I ain't trying to surprise you," De Spain said. "I'd have worn my pink tights."

"Yeah, he's up there," the old man said sourly.

"What time you last see Greb, the laboratory man on Four?"

"Didn't see him."

"What time you come on, Pop?"

"Seven."

"Okay. Take us up to Six."

The old man whooshed the doors shut and rode us up slowly and gingerly and whooshed the doors open again and sat like a piece of gray driftwood carved to look like a man.

De Spain reached up and lifted down the passkey that hung over the old man's head.

"Hey, you can't do that," the old man said.

"Who says I can't?"

The old man shook his head angrily, said nothing.

"How old are you, Pop?" De Spain said.

"Goin' on sixty."

"Goin' on sixty hell. You're a good juicy seventy. How come you got an elevator licence?"

The old man didn't say anything. He clicked his false teeth.

"That's better," De Spain said. "Just keep the old trap buttoned that way and everything will be wicky-wacky. Take her down, Pop."

We got out of the elevator and it dropped quietly in the enclosed shaft and De Spain stood looking down the hallway, jiggling the loose passkey on the ring. "Now listen," he said. "His suite is at the end, four rooms. There's a reception room made out of an office cut in half to make two reception rooms for adjoining suites. Out of that there's a narrow hall inside the wall of this hall, a couple small rooms and the doc's room. Got that?"

"Yeah," I said. "What did you plan to do—burgle it?"

"I kept an eye on the guy for a while, after his wife died."

"Too bad you didn't keep an eye on the redheaded office nurse," I said. "The one that got bumped off tonight."

He looked at me slowly, out of his deep black eyes, out of his dead-pan face.

"Maybe I did," he said. "As much as I had a chance."

"Hell, you didn't even know her name," I said, and stared at him. "I had to tell you."

He thought that over. "Well, seeing her in a white office uniform and seeing her naked and dead on a bed is kind of different, I guess."

"Sure," I said, and kept on looking at him.

"Okay. Now—you knock at the doc's office, which is the third door from the end, and when he opens up I'll sneak in at the reception room and come along inside and get an earful of whatever he says."

"It sounds all right," I said. "But I don't feel lucky."

We went down the corridor. The doors were solid wood and well fitted and no light showed behind any of them. I put my ear against the one De Spain indicated and heard faint movement inside. I nodded to De Spain down at the end of the hall. He fitted the passkey slowly into the lock and I rapped hard on the door and saw him go in out of the tail of my eye. The door shut behind him almost at once. I rapped on my door again.

It opened almost suddenly then, and a tall man was standing about a foot away from me with the ceiling light glinting on his pale sand-colored hair. He was in his shirt-sleeves and he held a flat leather case in his hand. He was rail-thin, with dun eyebrows and unhappy eyes. He had beautiful hands, long and slim, with square but not blunt fingertips. The nails were highly polished and cut very close.

I said: "Dr. Austrian?"

He nodded. His Adam's apple moved vaguely in his lean throat.

"This is a funny hour for me to come calling," I said, "but you're a hard man to catch up with. I'm a private detective from Los Angeles. I have a client named Harry Matson."

He was either not startled or so used to hiding his feelings that it didn't make any difference. His Adam's apple moved around again and his hand moved the leather case he was holding, and he looked at it in a puzzled sort of way and then stepped back.

"I have no time to talk to you now," he said. "Come back tomorrow."

"That's what Greb told me," I said.

He got a jolt out of that. He didn't scream or fall down

in a fit but I could see it jarred him. "Come in," he said thickly.

I went in and he shut the door. There was a desk that seemed to be made of black glass. The chairs were chromium tubing with rough wool upholstery. The door to the next room was half open and the room was dark. I could see the stretched white sheet on an examination table and the stirruplike things at the foot of it. I didn't hear any sound from that direction.

On top of the black glass desk a clean towel was laid out and on the towel a dozen or so hypodermic syringes lay with needles separate. There was an electric sterilizing cabinet on the wall and inside there must have been another dozen needles and syringes. The juice was turned on. I went over and looked at the thing while the tall, rail-thin man walked around behind his desk and sat down.

"That's a lot of needles working," I said, and pulled one of the chairs near the desk.

"What's your business with me?" His voice was still thick.

"Maybe I could do you some good about your wife's death," I said.

"That's very kind of you," he said calmly. "What kind of good?"

"I might be able to tell you who murdered her," I said.

His teeth glinted in a queer, unnatural half-smile. Then he shrugged and when he spoke his voice was no more dramatic than if we had been discussing the weather. "That *would* be kind of you. I had thought she committed suicide. The coroner and the police seemed to agree with me. But of course a private detective—"

"Greb didn't think so," I said, without any particular attempt at the truth. "The lab man who switched a sample of your wife's blood for a sample from a real monoxide case."

He stared at me levelly, out of deep, sad, remote eyes under the dun-colored eyebrows. "You haven't seen Greb," he said, almost with an inner amusement. "I happen to know he went East this noon. His father died in Ohio." He got up and went to the electric sterilizer and looked at his strap watch and then switched the juice off. He came back to the desk then and opened a flat box of cigarettes and put one in his mouth and pushed the box across the desk. I reached and took one. I half glanced at the dark examination room, but I saw nothing that I hadn't seen the last time I looked at it.

"That's funny," I said. "His wife didn't know that. Big Chin didn't know it. He was sitting there with her all tied up on the bed tonight, waiting for Greb to come back home, so he could bump him off."

Dr. Austrian looked at me vaguely now. He pawed around on his desk for a match and then opened a side drawer and took out a small white-handled automatic, and held it on the flat of his hand. Then he tossed a packet of matches at me with his other hand.

"You won't need the gun," I said. "This is a business talk which I'm going to show you it will pay to keep a business talk."

He took the cigarette out of his mouth and dropped it on the desk. "I don't smoke," he said. "That was just what one might call the necessary gesture. I'm glad to hear I won't need the gun. But I'd rather be holding it and not need it than be needing it and not hold it. Now, who is Big Chin, and what else important have you to say before I call the police?"

"Let me tell you," I said. "That's what I'm here for. Your wife played a lot of roulette at Vance Conried's club and lost the money you made with your little needles almost as fast as you made it. There's some talk she was going around with Conried in an intimate way also. You maybe didn't care about that, being out all night and too busy to bother being much of a husband to her. But you probably did care about the money, because you were risking a lot to get it. I'll come to that later.

"On the night your wife died she got hysterical over at Conried's and you were sent for and went over and needled her in the arm to quiet her. Conried took her home. You phoned your office nurse, Helen Matson—Matson's ex-wife —to go into your house and see if she was all right. Then later on Matson found her dead under the car in the garage and got hold of you, and you got hold of the chief of police, and there was a hush put on it that would have made a Southern senator sound like a deaf mute asking for a second plate of mush. But Matson, the first guy on the scene, had something. He didn't have any luck trying to peddle it to you, because you in your quiet way have a lot of guts. And perhaps your friend, Chief Anders, told you it wasn't evidence. So Matson tried to put the bite on Conried, figuring that if the case got opened up before the tough grand jury that's sitting now it would all bounce back on Conried's gambling joint, and he would be closed up tighter than a frozen piston, and the people behind him might get sore at him and take his polo ponies away from him.

"So Conried didn't like that idea and he told a mug named Moss Lorenz, the mayor's chauffeur now but formerly a strong-arm for Conried—he's the fellow I called Big Chin —to take care of Matson. And Matson lost his licence and was run out of Bay City. But he had his own brand of guts too, and he holed up in an apartment house in L.A. and kept on trying. The apartment house manager got wise to him somehow—I don't know how but the L.A. police will find out—and put him on the spot, and tonight Big Chin went up to town and bumped Matson off."

I stopped talking and looked at the thin, tall man. Nothing had changed in his face. His eyes flicked a couple of times and he turned the gun over on his hand. The office was very silent. I listened for breathing from the next room but I didn't hear anything.

"Matson is dead?" Dr. Austrian said very slowly. "I hope you don't think I had anything to do with that." His face glistened a little.

"Well, I don't know," I said. "Greb was the weak link in your setup and somebody got him to leave town today— fast—before Matson was killed, if it was at noon. And probably somebody gave him money, because I saw where he lived and it didn't look like the home of a fellow who was taking in any dough."

Dr. Austrian said very swiftly. "Conried, damn him! He called me up early this morning and told me to get Greb out of town. I gave him the money to go, but—" he stopped talking and looked mad at himself and then looked down at the gun again.

"But you didn't know what was up. I believe you, Doc. I really do. Put that gun down, won't you, just for a little while?"

"Go on," he said tensely. "Go on with your story."

"Okay," I said. "There's plenty more. First off the L.A. police have found Matson's body but they won't be down here before tomorrow; first, because it's too late, and second, because when they put the story together they won't want to bust the case. The Club Conried is within the L.A. city limits and the grand jury I was telling you about would just love that. They'll get Moss Lorenz and Moss will cop a plea and take a few years up in Quentin. That's the way those things are handled when the law wants to handle them. Next point is how I know what Big Chin did. He told us. A pal and I went around to see Greb and Big Chin was squatting there in the dark with Mrs. Greb all taped up on the bed and we took him. We took him up in the hills and gave him the boot and he talked. I felt kind of sorry for the poor guy. Two murders and he didn't even get paid."

"Two murders?" Dr. Austrian said queerly.

"I'll get to that after a while. Now you see where you stand. In a little while you are going to tell me who murdered your wife. And the funny thing is I am not going to believe you."

"My God!" he whispered. "My God!" He pointed the gun at me and immediately dropped it again, before I had time to start dodging.

"I'm a miracle man," I said. "I'm the great American detective—unpaid. I never talked to Matson, although he was trying to hire me. Now I'm going to tell you what he had on you, and how your wife was murdered, and why you didn't do it. All from a pinch of dust, just like the Vienna police."

He was not amused. He sighed between still lips and his face was old and gray and drawn under the pale sand-colored hair that painted his bony skull.

"Matson had a green velvet slipper on you," I said. "It was made for your wife by Verschoyle of Hollywood—custom-made, with her last number on it. It was brand-new and had never been worn. They made her two pairs exactly the same. She had it on one of her feet when Matson found her. And you know where he found her—on the floor of a garage to get to which she had to go along a concrete path from a side door of the house. So she couldn't have walked in that slipper. So she was carried. So she was murdered. Whoever put the slippers on her got one that had been worn and one that had not. And Matson spotted it and swiped the slipper. And when you sent him into the house to phone the chief you sneaked up and got the other worn slipper and put it on her bare foot. You knew Matson must have swiped that slipper. I don't know whether you told anybody or not. Okay?"

He moved his head half an inch downward. He shivered slightly, but the hand holding the bone-handled automatic didn't shiver.

"This is how she was murdered. Greb was dangerous to somebody, which proves she did *not* die of monoxide poisoning. She was dead when she was put under the car. She died of morphine. That's guessing. I admit, but it's a swell guess, because that would be the only way to kill her which would force you to cover up for the killer. And it was easy, to somebody who had the morphine and got a chance to use it. All they had to do was give her a second fatal dose in the same spot where you had shot her earlier in the evening. Then you came home and found her dead. And you had to cover up because you knew how she had died and you couldn't have that come out. You're in the morphine business."

He smiled now. The smile hung at the corners of his mouth like cobwebs in the corners of an old ceiling. He didn't even know it was there. "You interest me," he said. "I am going to kill you, I think, but you interest me."

I pointed to the electric sterilizer. "There are a couple dozen medicos like you around Hollywood—needle-pushers. They run around at night with leather cases full of loaded hypodermics. They keep dopes and drunks from going screwy—for a while. Once in a while one of them becomes an addict and then there's trouble. Maybe most of the people you fix up would land in the hoosegow or the psycho ward, if you didn't take care of them. It's a cinch they would lose their jobs, if they have jobs. And some of them have pretty big jobs. But it's dangerous because any sorehead can stick the Feds onto you and once they start checking your patients they'll find one that will talk. You try to protect yourself part of the way by not getting all of your dope through legitimate channels. I'd say Conried got some of it for you, and that was why you had to let him take your wife and your money."

Dr. Austrian said almost politely: "You don't hold very much back, do you?"

"Why should I? This is just a man-to-man talk. I can't prove any of it. That slipper Matson stole is good for a buildup, but it wouldn't be worth a nickel in court. And any defense attorney would make a monkey out of a little squirt like this Greb, even if they ever brought him back to testify. But it might cost you a lot of money to keep your medical licence."

"So it would be better for me to give you part of it now. Is that it?" he asked softly.

"No. Keep your money to buy life insurance. I have one more point to make. Will you admit, just man to man, that you killed your wife?"

"Yes," he said. He said it simply and directly, as though I had asked him if he had a cigarette.

"I thought you would," I said. "But you don't have to. You see the party that did kill your wife, because your wife was wasting money somebody else could have fun spending, also knew what Matson knew and was trying to shake Conried down herself. So she got bumped off—last night, on Brayton Avenue, and you don't have to cover up for her any more. I saw your photo on her mantel—*With all my love—Leland*—and I hid it. But you don't have to cover up for her any more. Helen Matson is dead."

I went sideways out of the chair as the gun went off. I had kidded myself by this time that he wouldn't try to shoot me, but there must have been part of me that wasn't sold on the idea. The chair tipped over and I was on my hands and knees on the floor, and then another much louder gun went off from the dark room with the examination table in it.

De Spain stepped through the door with the smoking police gun in his big right hand. "Boy, was that a shot," he said, and stood there grinning.

I came up on my feet and looked across the desk. Dr. Austrian sat there perfectly still, holding his right hand with his left, shaking it gently. There was no gun in his hand. I looked along the floor and saw it at the corner of the desk.

"Geez, I didn't even hit him," De Spain said. "All I hit was the gun."

"That's perfectly lovely," I said. "Suppose all he had hit was my head?"

De Spain looked at me levelly and the grin left his face. "You put him through it, I will say that for you," he growled. "But what was the idea of holding out on me on that green-slipper angle?"

"I got tired of being your stooge," I said. "I wanted a little play out of my own hand."

"How much of it was true?"

"Matson had the slipper. It must have meant something. Now that I've made it up I think it's all true."

Dr. Austrian got up slowly out of his chair and De Spain swung the gun on him. The thin, haggard man shook his head slowly and walked over to the wall and leaned against it.

"I killed her," he said in a dead voice to nobody at all. "Not Helen. I killed her. Call the police."

De Spain's face twisted and he stooped down and picked up the gun with the bone handle and dropped it into his pocket. He put his police gun back under his arm and sat down at the desk and pulled the phone towards him.

"Watch me get Chief of Homicide out of this," he drawled.

IX   A Guy with Guts

THE little chief of police came in springily, with his hat on the back of his head and his hands in the pockets of a thin dark overcoat. There was something in the right-hand overcoat pocket that he was holding on to, something large and heavy. There were two plainclothes men behind him and one of them was Weems, the chunky fat-faced man who had followed me over to Altair Street. Shorty, the uniformed cop we had ditched on Arguello Boulevard, brought up the rear.

Chief Anders stopped a little way inside the door and smiled at me unpleasantly. "So you've had a lot of fun in our town, I hear. Put the cuffs on him, Weems."

The fat-faced man stepped around him and pulled hand-cuffs out of his left hip pocket. "Nice to meet you again—with your pants down," he told me in an oily voice.

De Spain leaned against the wall beyond the door of the examination room. He rolled a match across his lips and stared silently. Dr. Austrian was in his desk chair again, hold-ing his head in his hands, staring at the polished black top of the desk and the towel of hypodermic needles and the small black perpetual calendar and the pen set and the hero doodads that were on the desk. His face was stone pale and he sat without moving, without even seeming to breathe.

De Spain said: "Don't be in too much of a hurry, Chief. This lad has friends in L.A. who are working on the Matson kill right now. And that kid reporter has a brother-in-law who is a cop. You didn't know that."

The chief made a vague motion with his chin. "Wait a minute, Weems." He turned to De Spain. "You mean they know in town that Helen Matson has been murdered?"

Dr. Austrian's face jerked up, haggard and drawn. Then he dropped it into his hands and covered his whole face with his long fingers.

De Spain said: "I meant Harry Matson, Chief. He was bumped off in L.A. tonight—last night—now—by Moss Lorenz."

The chief seemed to pull his thin lips back into his mouth, almost out of sight. He spoke with them like that. "How do you know that?"

"The shamus and me picked off Moss. He was hiding out in the house of a man named Greb, the lab man who did a job on the Austrian death. He was hiding there because it looked like somebody was going to open up the Austrian case wide enough for the mayor to think it was a new boule-vard and come out with a bunch of flowers and make a speech. That is, if Greb and the Matsons didn't get took care of. It seems the Matsons were workin' together, in spite of being divorced, shaking Conried down, and Conried put the pencil on them."

The chief turned his head and snarled at his stooges. "Get out in the hall and wait."

The plainclothes man I didn't know opened the door and went out, and after a slight hesitation Weems followed him. Shorty had his hand on the door when De Spain said: "I want Shorty to stay. Shorty's a decent cop—not like them two vice squad grafters you been sleepin' with lately."

Shorty let go of the door and went and leaned against the wall and smiled behind his hand. The chief's face colored. "Who detailed you to the Brayton Avenue death?" he barked.

"I detailed myself, Chief. I was in the dicks' room a minute or so after the call come in and I went over with Reed. He picked Shorty up too. Shorty and me was both off duty."

De Spain grinned, a hard, lazy grin that was neither amused nor triumphant. It was just a grin.

The chief jerked a gun out of his overcoat pocket. It was a foot long, a regular hogleg, but he seemed to know how to hold it. He said tightly: "Where's Lorenz?"

"He's hid. We got him all ready for you. I had to bruise him a little, but he talked. That right, shamus?"

I said: "He says something that might be yes or no, but he makes the sounds in the right places."

"That's the way I like to hear a guy talk," De Spain said. "You oughtn't to be wasting your strength on that homicide stuff, Chief. And them toy dicks you run around with don't know nothing about police work except to go through apartment houses and shake down all the women that live alone. Now, you give me back my job and eight men and I'll show you some homicide work."

The chief looked down at his big gun and then he looked at Dr. Austrian's bowed head. "So he killed his wife," he said softly. "I knew there was a chance of it, but I didn't believe it."

"Don't believe it now," I said. "Helen Matson killed her. Dr. Austrian knows that. He covered up for her, and you covered up for him, and he's still willing to cover up for her. Love is like that with some people. And this is some town, Chief, where a gal can commit a murder, get her friends and the police to cover it, and then start out to blackmail the very people that kept her out of trouble."

The chief bit his lip. His eyes were nasty, but he was thinking—thinking hard. "No wonder she got rubbed out," he said quietly. "Lorenz—"

I said: "Take a minute to think. Lorenz didn't kill Helen Matson. He said he did, but De Spain beat him up to the point where he would have confessed shooting McKinley."

De Spain straightened from the wall. He had both hands lazily in the pockets of his suit coat. He kept them there. He stood straight on wide-planted feet, a wick of black hair showing under the side of his hat.

"Huh?" he said almost gently. "What was that?"

I said: "Lorenz didn't kill Helen Matson for several reasons. It was too fussy a job for his type of mind. He'd have knocked her off and let her lay. Second, he didn't know Greb was leaving town, tipped off by Dr. Austrian who was tipped off, in turn, by Vance Conried, who is now up north providing himself with all the necessary alibis. And if Lorenz didn't know that much, he didn't know anything about Helen Matson. Especially as Helen Matson had never really got to Conried at all. She had just tried to. She told me that and she was drunk enough to be telling the truth. So Conried wouldn't have taken the silly risk of having her knocked off in her own apartment by the sort of man anybody would remember seeing if they saw him anywhere near that apartment. Knocking off Matson up in L.A. was something else again. That was way off the home grounds."

The chief said tightly: "The Club Conried is in L.A."

"Legally," I admitted. "But by position and clientele it's just outside Bay City. It's part of Bay City—and it helps to run Bay City."

Shorty said: "That ain't no way to talk to the chief."

"Let him alone," the chief said. "It's so long since I heard a guy think I didn't know they did it any more."

I said: "Ask De Spain who killed Helen Matson."

De Spain laughed harshly. He said: "Sure. I killed her."

Dr. Austrian lifted his face off his hands and turned his head slowly and looked at De Spain. His face was as dead, as expressionless as the big dead-pan copper's. Then he reached over and opened the right-hand drawer of his desk. Shorty flipped his gun out and said: "Hold it, Doc."

Dr. Austrian shrugged and quietly took a wide-mouthed bottle with a glass stopper out of the drawer. He loosened the stopper and held the bottle close to his nose. "Just smelling salts," he said dully.

Shorty relaxed and dropped the gun to his side. The chief stared at me and chewed his lip. De Spain stared at nothing, at nobody. He grinned loosely, kept on grinning.

I said: "He thinks I'm kidding. You think I'm kidding. I'm not kidding. He knew Helen—well enough to give her a gilt cigarette case with his photo on it. I saw it. It was a small hand-tinted photo and not very good and I had only seen him once. She told me it was an old sweet that wore out. Afterwards it came back to me who that photo was. But he concealed the fact that he knew her and he didn't act very much like a copper tonight, in a lot of ways. He didn't get me out of a jam and run around with me in order to be nice. He did it to find out what I knew before I was put under the lamps down at headquarters. He didn't beat Lorenz half to death just in order to make Lorenz tell the truth. He did it to make Lorenz tell anything De Spain wanted him to tell, including confessing to the murder of the Matson girl whom Lorenz probably didn't even know.

"Who called up headquarters and tipped the boys about the murder? De Spain. Who walked in there immediately afterwards and horned in on the investigation? De Spain. Who scratched the girl's body up in a fit of jealous rage because she had ditched him for a better prospect? De Spain. Who still has blood and cuticle under the nails of his right hand which a good police chemist can do a lot with? De Spain. Take a look. I took several."

The chief turned his head very slowly, as if it were on a pivot. He whistled and the door opened and the other men came back into the room. De Spain didn't move. The grin stayed on his face, carved there, a meaningless hollow grin that meant and looked as if it would never go away again.

He said quietly: "And you the guy I thought was my pal. Well, you have some wild ideas, shamus. I will say that for you."

The chief said sharply: "It doesn't make sense. If De

Spain did kill her, then he was the one who tried to put you in a frame and the one that got you out of it. How come?"

I said: "Listen. You can find out if De Spain knew the girl and how well. You can find out how much of his time tonight is not accounted for and make him account for it. You can find out if there is blood and cuticle under his nails and, within limits, whether it is or could be the girl's blood and the girl's skin. And whether it was there before De Spain hit Moss Lorenz, before he hit anybody. And he didn't scratch Lorenz. That's all you need and all you can use—except a confession. And I don't think you'll get that.

"As to the frame, I would say De Spain followed the girl over to the Club Conried, or knew she had gone there and went over himself. He saw her come out with me and he saw me put her in my car. That made him mad. He sapped me and the girl was too scared not to help him get me to her apartment and up into it. I don't remember any of that. It would be nice if I did, but I don't. They got me up there somehow, and they had a fight, and De Spain knocked her out and then he deliberately murdered her. He had some clumsy idea of making it look like a rape murder and making me the fall guy. Then he beat it, turned in an alarm, horned in on the investigation, and I got out of the apartment before I was caught there.

"He realized by this time that he had done a foolish thing. He knew I was a private dick from L.A., that I had talked to Dolly Kincaid, and from the girl he probably knew that I had gone to see Conried. And he may easily have known I was interested in the Austrian case. Okay. He turned a foolish play into a smart one by stringing along with me on the investigation I was trying to make, helping me on it, getting my story, and then finding himself another and much better fall guy for the murder of the Matson girl."

De Spain said tonelessly: "I'm goin' to start climbing on this guy in a minute, Chief. Okay?"

The chief said: "Just a minute. What made you suspect De Spain at all?"

"The blood and skin under his nails, and the brutal way he handled Lorenz, and the fact that the girl told me he had been her sweet and he pretended not to know who she was. What the hell more would I want?"

De Spain said: "This."

He shot from his pocket with the white-handled gun he had taken from Dr. Austrian. Shooting from the pocket takes a lot of practice of a kind cops don't get. The slug went a foot over my head and I sat down on the floor and Dr. Austrian stood up very quickly and swung his right hand into De Spain's face, the hand that held the wide-mouthed brown bottle. A colorless liquid splashed into his eyes and smoked down his face. Any other man would have screamed. De Spain pawed the air with his left hand and the gun in his pocket banged three times more and Dr. Austrian fell sideways across the end of the desk and then collapsed to the floor, out of range. The gun went on banging.

The other men in the room had all dropped to their knees. The chief jerked his hogleg up and shot De Spain twice in the body. Once would have been enough with that gun. De Spain's body twisted in the air and hit the floor like a safe. The chief went over and knelt beside him and looked at him silently. He stood up and came back around the desk, then went back and stooped over Dr. Austrian.

"This one's alive," he snapped. "Get on the phone, Weems."

The chunky, fat-faced man went around the far side of the desk and scooped the telephone towards him and started to dial. There was a sharp smell of acid and scorched flesh in the air, a nasty smell. We were standing up again now, and the little police chief was looking at me bleakly.

"He oughtn't to have shot at you," he said. "You couldn't have proved a thing. We wouldn't have let you."

I didn't say anything. Weems put the phone down and looked at Dr. Austrian again.

"I think he's croaked," he said, from behind the desk.

The chief kept on looking at me. "You take some awful chances, Mr. Dalmas. I don't know what your game is, but I hope you like your chips."

"I'm satisfied," I said. "I'd like to have had a chance to talk to my client before he was bumped off, but I guess I've done all I could for him. The hell of it is I liked De Spain. He had all the guts they ever made."

The chief said: "If you want to know about guts, try being a small-town chief of police some day."

I said: "Yeah. Tell somebody to tie a handkerchief around

De Spain's right hand, Chief. You kind of need the evidence yourself now."

A siren wailed distantly on Arguello Boulevard. The sound came faintly through the closed windows, like a coyote howling in the hills.

THE LADY IN THE LAKE

I   Not for Missing Persons

I WAS breaking a new pair of shoes in on my desk that
morning when Violets M'Gee called me up. It was a dull,
hot, damp August day and you couldn't keep your neck
dry with a bath towel.

"How's the boy?" Violets began, as usual. "No business
in a week, huh? There's a guy named Howard Melton over
in the Avenant Building lost track of his wife. He's district
manager for the Doreme Cosmetic Company. He don't want
to give it to Missing Persons for some reason. The boss
knows him a little. Better get over there, and take your
shoes off before you go in. It's a pretty snooty outfit."

Violets M'Gee is a homicide dick in the sheriff's office,
and if it wasn't for all the charity jobs he gives me, I might
be able to make a living. This looked a little different, so
I put my feet on the floor and swabbed the back of my
neck again and went over there.

The Avenant Building is on Olive near Sixth and has a
black-and-white rubber sidewalk out in front. The elevator
girls wear gray silk Russian blouses and the kind of flop-
over berets artists used to wear to keep the paint out of
their hair. The Doreme Cosmetic Company was on the seventh floor and had a good piece of it. There was a big glass-
walled reception room with flowers and Persian rugs and
bits of nutty sculpture in glazed ware. A neat little blonde
sat in a built-in switchboard at a big desk with flowers on
it and a tilted sign reading: MISS VAN DE GRAAF. She wore

Harold Lloyd cheaters and her hair was dragged back to where her forehead looked high enough to have snow on it.

She said Mr. Howard Melton was in conference, but she would take my card in to him when she had an opportunity, and what was my business, please? I said I didn't have a card, but the name was John Dalmas, from Mr. West.

"Who is Mr. West?" she inquired coldly. "Does Mr. Melton know him?"

"That's past me, sister. Not knowing Mr. Melton I would not know his friends."

"What is the nature of your business?"

"Personal."

"I see." She initialed three papers on her desk quickly, to keep from throwing her pen set at me. I went and sat in a blue leather chair with chromium arms. It felt, looked and smelled very much like a barber's chair.

In about half an hour a door opened beyond a bronze railing and two men came out backwards laughing. A third man held the door and echoed their laughter. They shook hands and the two men went away and the third man wiped the grin off his face in nothing flat and looked at Miss Van De Graaf. "Any calls?" he asked in a bossy voice.

She fluttered papers and said: "No, sir. A Mr.—Dalmas to see you—from a Mr.—West. His business is personal."

"Don't know him," the man barked. "I've got more insurance than I can pay for." He gave me a swift, hard look and went into his room and slammed the door. Miss Van De Graaf smiled at me with delicate regret. I lit a cigarette and crossed my legs the other way. In another five minutes the door beyond the railing opened again and he came out with his hat on and sneered that he was going out for half an hour.

He came through a gate in the railing and started for the entrance and then did a nice cutback and came striding over to me. He stood looking down at me—a big man, two inches over six feet and built to proportion. He had a well-massaged face that didn't hide the lines of dissipation. His eyes were black, hard, and tricky.

"You want to see me?"

I stood up, got out my billfold and gave him a card. He stared at the card and palmed it. His eyes became thoughtful.

"Who's Mr. West?"

"Search me."

He gave me a hard, direct, interested look. "You have the right idea," he said. "Let's go into my office."

The receptionist was so mad she was trying to initial three papers at once when we went past her through the railing.

The office beyond was long, dim and quiet, but not cool. There was a large photo on the wall of a tough-looking old bird who had held lots of noses to lots of grindstones in his time. The big man went behind about eight hundred dollars' worth of desk and tilted himself back in a padded high-backed director's chair. He pushed a cigar humidor at me. I lit a cigar and he watched me light it with cool, steady eyes.

"This is very confidential," he said.

"Uh-huh."

He read my card again and put it away in a gold-plated wallet. "Who sent you?"

"A friend in the sheriff's office."

"I'd have to know a little more about you than that."

I gave him a couple of names and numbers. He reached for his phone, asked for a line and dialed them himself. He got both the parties I had mentioned and talked. In four minutes he had hung up and tilted his chair again. We both wiped the backs of our necks.

"So far, so good," he said. "Now show me you're the man you say you are."

I got my billfold out and showed him a small photostat of my licence. He seemed pleased. "How much do you charge?"

"Twenty-five bucks a day and expenses."

"That's too much. What is the nature of the expenses?"

"Gas and oil, maybe a bribe or two, meals and whisky. Mostly whisky."

"Don't you eat when you're not working?"

"Yeah—but not so well."

He grinned. His grin like his eyes had a stony cast to it. "I think maybe we'll get along," he said.

He opened a drawer and brought out a Scotch bottle. We had a drink. He put the bottle on the floor, wiped his lips, lit a monogrammed cigarette and inhaled comfortably.

"Better make it fifteen a day," he said. "In times like these. And go easy on the liquor."

"I was just kidding you," I said. "A man you can't kid is a man you can't trust."

He grinned again. "It's a deal. First off though, your promise that in no circumstances you have anything to do with any cop friends you may happen to have."

"As long as you haven't murdered anybody, it suits me."

He laughed. "Not yet. But I'm a pretty tough guy still. I want you to trace my wife and find out where she is and what she's doing, and without her knowing it.

"She disappeared eleven days ago—August twelfth—from a cabin we have at Little Fawn Lake. That's a small lake owned by myself and two other men. It's three miles from Puma Point. Of course you know where that is."

"In the San Bernardino Mountains, about forty miles from San Bernardino."

"Yes." He flicked ash from his cigarette on the desk top and leaned over to blow it off. "Little Fawn Lake is only about three-eighths of a mile long. It has a small dam we built for real estate development—just at the wrong time. There are four cabins up there. Mine, two belonging to my friends, neither of them occupied this summer, and a fourth on the near side of the lake as you come in. That one is occupied by a man named William Haines and his wife. He's a disabled veteran with a pension. He lives there rent free and looks after the place. My wife has been spending the summer up there and was to leave on the twelfth to come in to town for some social activity over the weekend. She never came."

I nodded. He opened a locked drawer and took out an envelope. He took a photo and a telegram from the envelope, and passed the telegram across the desk. It had been sent from El Paso, Texas, on August 15th at 9:18 A.M. It was addressed to Howard Melton, 715 Avenant Building, Los Angeles. It read: *Am crossing to get Mexican divorce. Will marry Lance. Good luck and goodbye. Julia.*

I put the yellow form down on the desk. "Julia is my wife's name," Melton said.

"Who's Lance?"

"Lancelot Goodwin. He used to be my confidential secretary up to a year ago. Then he came into some money and quit. I have known for a long time that Julia and he were a bit soft on each other, if I may put it that way."

"It's all right with me," I said.

He pushed the photo across the desk. It was a snapshot on glazed paper showing a slim, small blonde and a tall, lean, dark, handsome guy, about thirty-five, a shade too handsome. The blonde could have been anything from eighteen to forty. She was that type. She had a figure and didn't act stingy with it. She wore a swimsuit which didn't strain the imagination and the man wore trunks. They sat against a striped beach umbrella on the sand. I put the snapshot down on top of the telegram.

"That's all the exhibits," Melton said, "but not all the facts. Another drink?" He poured it and we drank it. He put the bottle down on the floor again and his telephone rang. He talked a moment, then juggled the hood and told the operator to hold his calls for a while.

"So far there would be nothing much to it," he said. "But I met Lance Goodwin on the street last Friday. He said he hadn't seen Julia in months. I believed him, because Lance is a fellow without many inhibitions, and he doesn't scare. He'd be apt to tell me the truth about a thing like that. And I think he'll keep his mouth shut."

"Were there other fellows you thought of?"

"No. If there are any, I don't know them. My hunch is, Julia has been arrested and is in jail somewhere and has managed, by bribery or otherwise, to hide her identity."

"In jail for what?"

He hesitated a moment and then said very quietly: "Julia is a kleptomaniac. Not bad, and not all the time. Mostly when she is drinking too much. She has spells of that, too. Most of her tricks have been here in Los Angeles in the big stores where we have accounts. She's been caught a few times and been able to bluff out and have the stuff put on the bill. No scandal so far that I couldn't take care of. But in a strange town—" He stopped and frowned hard. "I have my job with the Doreme people to worry about," he said.

"She ever been printed?"

"How?"

"Had her fingerprints taken and filed?"

"Not that I know of." He looked worried at that.

"This Goodwin know about the sideline she worked?"

"I couldn't say. I hope not. He's never mentioned it, of course."

"I'd like his address."

"He's in the book. Has a bungalow over in the Chevy Chase district, near Glendale. Very secluded place. I've a hunch Lance is quite a chaser."

It looked like a very nice setup, but I didn't say so out loud. I could see a little honest money coming my way for a change. "You've been up to this Little Fawn Lake since your wife disappeared, of course."

He looked surprised. "Well, no. I've had no reason to. Until I met Lance in front of the Athletic Club I supposed he and Julia were together somewhere—perhaps even married already. Mexican divorces are quick."

"How about money? She have much with her?"

"I don't know. She has quite a lot of money of her own, inherited from her father. I guess she can get plenty of money."

"I see. How was she dressed—or would you know?"

He shook his head. "I hadn't seen her in two weeks. She wore rather dark clothes as a rule. Haines might be able to tell you. I suppose he'll have to know she disappeared. I think he can be trusted to keep his mouth shut." Melton smiled wryly. "She had a small octagonal platinum wrist watch with a chain of large links. A birthday present. It had her name inside. She had a diamond and emerald ring and a platinum wedding ring engraved inside: *Howard and Julia Melton. July 27th, 1926.*"

"But you don't suspect foul play, do you?"

"No." His large cheekbones reddened a little. "I told you what I suspected."

"If she's in somebody's jailhouse, what do I do? Just report back and wait?"

"Of course. If she's not, keep her in sight until I can get there, wherever it is. I think I can handle the situation."

"Uh-huh. You look big enough. You said she left Little Fawn Lake on August twelfth. But you haven't been up there. You mean she did—or she was just supposed to—or you guess it from the date of the telegram?"

"Right. There's one more thing I forgot. She did leave on the twelfth. She never drove at night, so she drove down the mountain in the afternoon and stopped at the Olympia

Hotel until train time. I know that because they called me up a week later and said her car was in their garage and did I want to call for it. I said I'd be over and get it when I had time."

"Okay, Mr. Melton. I think I'll run around and check over this Lancelot Goodwin a little first. He might happen not to have told you the truth."

He handed me the Other Cities phone book and I looked it up. Lancelot Goodwin lived at 3416 Chester Lane. I didn't know where that was, but I had a map in the car.

I said: "I'm going out there and snoop around. I'd better have a little money on account. Say a hundred bucks."

"Fifty should do to start," he said. He took out his gold-plated wallet and gave me two twenties and a ten. "I'll get you to sign a receipt—just as a matter of form."

He had a receipt book in his desk and wrote out what he wanted and I signed it. I put the two exhibits in my pocket and stood up. We shook hands.

I left him with the feeling that he was a guy who would not make many small mistakes, especially about money. As I went out the receptionist gave me the nasty eye. I worried about it almost as far as the elevator.

II   The Silent House

MY car was in a lot across the street, so I took it north to Fifth and west to Flower and from there down to Glendale Boulevard and so on into Glendale. That made it about lunch time, so I stopped and ate a sandwich.

Chevy Chase is a deep canyon in the foothills that separate Glendale from Pasadena. It is heavily wooded, and the streets branching off the main drag are apt to be pretty shut-in and dark. Chester Lane was one of them, and was dark enough to be in the middle of a redwood forest. Goodwin's house was at the deep end, a small English bungalow with a peaked roof and leaded windowpanes that wouldn't have let much light in, even if there had been any to let in. The house was set back in a fold of the hills, with a big oak tree practically on the front porch. It was a nice little place to have fun.

The garage at the side was shut up. I walked along a twisted path made of steppingstones and pushed the bell. I could hear it ring somewhere in the rear with that sound bells seem to have in an empty house. I rang it twice more. Nobody came to the door. A mockingbird flew down on the small, neat front lawn and poked a worm out of the sod and went away with it. Somebody started a car out of sight down the curve of the street. There was a brand-new house across the street with a *For Sale* sign stuck into the manure and grass seed in front of it. No other house was in sight.

I tried the bell one more time and did a snappy tattoo with the knocker, which was a ring held in the mouth of a lion. Then I left the front door and put an eye to the crack between the garage doors. There was a car in there, shining dimly in the faint light. I prowled around to the back yard and saw two more oak trees and a rubbish burner and three chairs around a green garden table under one of the trees. It looked so shady and cool and pleasant back there, I would have liked to stay. I went to the back door, which was half glass but had a spring lock. I tried turning the knob, which was silly. It opened and I took a deep breath and walked in.

This Lancelot Goodwin ought to be willing to listen to a little reason, if he caught me. If he didn't, I wanted to glance around his effects. There was something about him— maybe just his first name—that worried me.

The back door opened on a porch with high, narrow screens. From that another unlocked door, also with a spring lock, opened into a kitchen with gaudy tiles and an enclosed gas stove. There were a lot of empty bottles on the sink. There were two swing doors. I pushed the one towards the front of the house. It gave on an alcove dining room with a buffet on which there were more liquor bottles but not empty.

The living room was to my right under an arch. It was dark even in the middle of the day. It was nicely furnished, with built-in bookshelves and books that hadn't been bought in sets. There was a highboy radio in the corner, with a half-empty glass of amber fluid on top of it. And there was ice in the amber fluid. The radio made a faint humming sound and light glowed behind the dial. It was on, but the volume was down to nothing.

That was funny. I turned around and looked at the back corner of the room and saw something funnier.

A man was sitting in a deep brocade chair with slippered feet on a footstool that matched the chair. He wore an open-neck polo shirt and ice-cream pants and a white belt. His left hand rested easily on the wide arm of the chair and his right hand drooped languidly outside the other arm to the carpet, which was a solid dull rose. He was a lean, dark, handsome guy, rangily built. One of those lads who move fast and are much stronger than they look. His mouth was slightly open showing the edges of his teeth. His head was a little sideways, as though he had dozed off as he sat there, having himself a few drinks and listening to the radio.

There was a gun on the floor beside his right hand and there was a scorched red hole in the middle of his forehead.

Blood dripped very quietly from the end of his chin and fell on his white polo shirt.

For all of a minute—which in a spot like that can be as long as a chiropractor's thumb—I didn't move a muscle. If I drew a full breath, it was a secret. I just hung there, empty as a busted flush, and watched Mr. Lancelot Goodwin's blood form small pear-shaped globules on the end of his chin and then very slowly and casually drop and add themselves to the large patch of crimson that changed the whiteness of his polo shirt. It seemed to me that even in that time the blood dripped slower. I lifted a foot at last, dragged it out of the cement it was stuck in, took a step, and then hauled the other foot after it like a ball and chain. I moved across the dark and silent room.

His eyes glittered as I got close. I bent over to stare into them, to try and meet their look. It couldn't be done. It never can, with dead eyes. They are always pointed a little to one side or up or down. I touched his face. It was warm and slightly moist. That would be from his drink. He hadn't been dead more than twenty minutes.

I swung around hard, as if somebody were trying to sneak

up behind me with a blackjack, but nobody was. The silence held. The room was full of it, brimming over with it. A bird chirped outdoors in a tree, but that only made the silence thicker. You could have cut slices of it and buttered them.

I started looking at other things in the room. There was a silver-framed photo lying on the floor, back up, in front of the plaster mantel. I went over and lifted it with a handkerchief and turned it. The glass was cracked neatly from corner to corner. The photo showed a slim, light-haired lady with a dangerous smile. I took out the snapshot Howard Melton had given me and held it beside the photo. I was sure it was the same face, but the expression was different, and it was a very common type of face.

I took the photograph carefully into a nicely furnished bedroom and opened a drawer in a long-legged chest. I removed the photo from the frame, polished the frame off nicely with my handkerchief and tucked it under some shirts. Not very clever, but as clever as I felt.

Nothing seemed very pressing now. If the shot had been heard, and recognized as a shot, radio cops would have been there long ago. I took my photo into the bathroom and trimmed it close with my pocketknife and flushed the scraps down the toilet. I added the photo to what I had in my breast pocket, and went back to the living room.

There was an empty glass on the low table beside the dead man's left hand. It would have his prints. On the other hand somebody else might have taken a sip out of it and left other prints. A woman, of course. She would have been sitting on the arm of the chair, with a soft, sweet smile on her face, and the gun down behind her back. It had to be a woman. A man couldn't have shot him in just that perfectly relaxed position. I gave a guess what woman it was—but I didn't like her leaving her photo on the floor. That was bad publicity.

I couldn't risk the glass. I wiped it off and did something I didn't enjoy. I made his hand hold it again, then put it back on the table. I did the same thing with the gun. When I let his hand fall—the trailing hand this time—it swung and swung, like a pendulum on a grandfather's clock. I went to the glass on the radio and wiped it off. That would make them think she was pretty wise, a different kind of woman altogether—if there are different kinds. I collected four cigarette stubs with lipstick about the shade called "Carmen," a blond shade. I took them to the bathroom and gave them to the city. I wiped off a few shiny fixtures with a towel, did the same for the front doorknob, and called it a day. I couldn't wipe over the whole damn house.

I stood and looked at Lancelot Goodwin a moment longer. The blood had stopped flowing. The last drop on his chin wasn't going to fall. It was going to hang there and get dark and shiny and as permanent as a wart.

I went back through the kitchen and porch, wiping a couple more doorknobs as I went, strolled around the side of the house and took a quick gander up and down the street. Nobody being in sight, I tied the job up with ribbon by ringing the front doorbell again and smearing the button and knob well while I did it. I went to my car, got in and drove away. This had all taken less than half an hour. I felt as if I had fought all the way through the Civil War.

Two-thirds of the way back to town I stopped at the foot of Alesandro Street and tucked myself into a drugstore phone booth. I dialed Howard Melton's office number.

A chirpy voice said: "Doreme Cosmetic Company. Good afternoowun."

"Mr. Melton."

"I'll connect you with his secretary," sang the voice of the little blonde who had been off in the corner, out of harm's way.

"Miss Van De Graaf speaking." It was a nice drawl that could get charming or snooty with the change of a quarter-tone. "Who is calling Mr. Melton, please?"

"John Dalmas."

"Ah—does Mr. Melton know you, Mr.—ah—Dalmas?"

"Don't start that again," I said. "Ask him, girlie. I can get all the ritzing I need at the stamp window."

Her intaken breath almost hurt my eardrum.

There was a wait, a click, and Melton's burly businesslike voice said: "Yes? Melton talking. Yes?"

"I have to see you quick."

"What's that?" he barked.

"I said what you heard. There have been what the boys call developments. You know who you're talking to, don't you?"

"Oh—yes. Yes. Well, let me see. Let me look at my desk calendar."

"To hell with your desk calendar," I said. "This is serious. I have enough sense not to break in on your day, if it wasn't."

"Athletic Club—ten minutes," he said crisply. "Have me paged in the reading room."

"I'll be a little longer than that." I hung up before he could argue.

I was twenty minutes as a matter of fact.

The hop in the lobby of the Athletic Club scooted neatly into one of the old open-cage elevators they have there and was back in no time at all with a nod. He took me up to the fourth floor and showed me the reading room.

"Around to the left, sir."

The reading room was not built principally for reading. There were papers and magazines on a long mahogany table and leather bindings behind glass on the walls and a portrait of the club's founder in oil, with a hooded light over it. But mostly the place was little nooks and corners with enormous sloping high-backed leather chairs, and old boys snoozing in them peacefully, their faces violet with old age and high blood pressure.

I sneaked quietly around to the left. Melton sat there, in a private nook between shelves, with his back to the room, and the chair, high as it was, not high enough to hide his big dark head. He had another chair drawn up beside him. I slipped into it and gave him the eye.

"Keep your voice down," he said. "This place is for after-luncheon naps. Now, what is it? When I employed you, it was to save me bother, not to add bother to what I already have."

"Yeah," I said, and put my face close to his. He smelled of highballs, but nicely. "She shot him."

His stiff eyebrows went up a little. His eyes got the stony look. His teeth clamped. He breathed softly and twisted one large hand on his knee and looked down at it.

"Go on," he said, in a voice the size of a marble.

I craned back over the top of the chair. The nearest old geezer was snoozling lightly and blowing the fuzz in his nostrils back and forth with each breath.

"I went out there to Goodwin's place. No answer. Tried

the back door. Open. Walked in. Radio turned on, but muted. Two glasses with drinks. Smashed photo on floor below mantel. Goodwin in chair shot dead at close range. Contact wound. Gun on floor by his right hand. Twenty-five automatic—a woman's gun. He sat there as if he had never known it. I wiped glasses, gun, doorknobs, put his prints where they should be, left."

Melton opened and shut his mouth. His teeth made a grating noise. He made fists of both hands. Then he looked steadily at me with hard black eyes.

"Photo," he said thickly.

I reached it out of my pocket and showed it to him, but I held on to it.

"Julia," he said. His breath made a queer, sharp keening sound and his hand went limp. I slipped the photo back into my pocket. "What then?" he whispered.

"All. I may have been seen, but not going in or coming out. Trees in back. The place is well shaded. She have a gun like that?"

His head drooped and he held it in his hands. He held still for a while, then pushed it up and spread his fingers on his face and spoke through them at the wall we were facing.

"Yes. But I never knew her to carry it. I suppose he ditched her, the dirty rat." He said it quietly without heat.

"You're quite a guy," he said. "It's a suicide now, eh?"

"Can't tell. Without a suspect they're apt to handle it that way. They'll test his hand with paraffin to see if he fired the gun. That's routine now. But it sometimes doesn't work, and without a suspect they may let it ride anyway. I don't get the photo angle."

"I don't either," he whispered, still talking between his fingers. "She must have got panicked up very suddenly."

"Uh-huh. You realize I've put my head in a bag, don't you? It's my licence if I'm caught. Of course there's a bare chance it was suicide. But he doesn't seem the type. You've got to play ball, Melton."

He laughed grimly. Then he turned his head enough to look at me, but still kept his hands on his face. The gleam of his eyes shot through his fingers.

"Why did you fix it up?" he asked quietly.

"Damned if I know. I guess I took a dislike to him—

from that photo. He didn't look worth what they'd do to her—and to you."

"Five hundred, as a bonus," he said.

I leaned back and gave him a stony stare. "I'm not trying to pressure you. I'm a fairly tough guy—but not in spots like this. Did you give me everything you had?"

He said nothing for a long minute. He stood up and looked along the room, put his hands in his pockets, jingled something, and sat down again.

"That's the wrong approach—both ways," he said. "I wasn't thinking of blackmail—or offering to pay it. It isn't enough money. These are hard times. You take an extra risk, I offer you an extra compensation. Suppose Julia had nothing to do with it. That might explain the photo being left. There were plenty of other women in Goodwin's life. But if the story comes out and I'm connected with it at all, the home offices will bounce me. I'm in a sensitive business, and it hasn't been doing too well. They might be glad of the excuse."

"That's different," I said. "I asked you, did you give me everything you had."

He looked at the floor. "No. I suppressed something. It didn't seem important then. And it hurts the position badly now. A few days ago, just after I met Goodwin downtown, the bank called me and said a Mr. Lancelot Goodwin was there to cash a check for one thousand dollars made out to cash by Julia Melton. I told them Mrs. Melton was out of town, but that I knew Mr. Goodwin very well and I saw no objection to cashing the check, if it was in order and he was properly identified. I couldn't say anything else— in the circumstances. I suppose they cashed it. I don't know."

"I thought Goodwin had dough."

Melton shrugged stiffly.

"A blackmailer of women, huh? And a sappy one at that, to be taking checks. I think I'll play with you on it, Melton. I hate like hell to see these newspaper ghouls go to town on a yarn like that. But if they get to you, I'm out— if I can get out."

He smiled for the first time. "I'll give you the five hundred right now," he said.

"Nothing doing. I'm hired to find her. If I find her I get five hundred flat—all other bets off."

"You'll find me a good man to trust," he said.

"I want a note to this Haines up at your place at Little Fawn Lake. I want into your cabin. My only way to go at it is as if I'd never been to Chevy Chase."

He nodded and stood up. He went over to a desk and came back with a note on the club stationery.

Mr. William Haines,
Little Fawn Lake.

Dear Bill—

Please allow bearer, Mr. John Dalmas, to view my cabin and assist him in all ways to look over the property.

Sincerely,
HOWARD MELTON

I folded the note and put it away with my other gatherings from the day. Melton put a hand on my shoulder. "I'll never forget this," he said. "Are you going up there now?"

"I think so."

"What do you expect to find?"

"Nothing. But I'd be a sap not to start where the trail starts."

"Of course. Haines is a good fellow, but a little surly. He has a pretty blond wife that rides him a lot. Good luck."

We shook hands. His hand felt clammy as a pickled fish.

III   The Man With the Peg Leg

I MADE San Bernardino in less than two hours and for once in its life it was almost as cool as Los Angeles, and not nearly as sticky. I took on a cup of coffee and bought a pint of rye and gassed up and started up the grade. It was overcast all the way to Bubbling Springs. Then it suddenly got dry and bright and cool air blew down the gorges, and I finally came to the big dam and looked along the level blue reaches of Puma Lake. Canoes paddled on it, and rowboats with outboard motors and speedboats churned up the water and made a lot of fuss over nothing. Jounced around in their wake, people who had paid two dollars for a fishing licence wasted their time trying to catch a dime's worth of fish.

The road turned two ways from the dam. My way was the south shore. It skimmed along high among piled-up masses of granite. Hundred-foot yellow pines probed at the clear blue sky. In the open spaces grew bright green manzanita and what was left of the wild irises and white and purple lupine and bugle flowers and desert paintbrush. The road dropped to the lake level and I began to pass flocks of camps and flocks of girls in shorts on bicycles, on motor scooters, walking all over the highway, or just sitting under trees showing off their legs. I saw enough beef on the hoof to stock a cattle ranch.

Howard Melton had said to turn away from the lake at the old Redlands road, a mile short of Puma Point. It was a frayed asphalt ribbon that climbed into the surrounding mountains. Cabins were perched here and there on the slopes. The asphalt gave out and after a while a small, narrow dirt road sneaked off to my right. A sign at its entrance said: *Private Road to Little Fawn Lake. No Trespassing.* I took it and crawled around big bare stones and past a little waterfall and through yellow pines and black oaks and silence. A squirrel sat on a branch and tore a fresh pine cone to pieces and sent the pieces fluttering down like confetti. He scolded at me and beat one paw angrily on the cone.

The narrow road swerved sharply around a big tree trunk and then there was a five-barred gate across it with another sign. This one said: *Private—No Admittance.*

I got out and opened the gate and drove through and closed it again. I wound through trees for another couple of hundred yards. Suddenly below me was a small oval lake that lay deep in trees and rocks and wild grass, like a drop of dew caught in a furled leaf. At the near end there was a yellow concrete dam with a rope handrail across the top and an old mill wheel at the side. Near that stood a small cabin of native wood covered with rough bark. It had two sheet-metal chimneys and smoke lisped from one of them. Somewhere an axe thudded.

Across the lake, a long way by the road and the short way over the dam, there was a large cabin close to the water and two others not so large, spaced at wide intervals. At the far end, opposite the dam, was what looked like a small pier and band pavilion. A warped wooden sign on it read: *Camp Kilkare.* I couldn't see any sense in that, so I walked down a path to the bark-covered cabin and pounded on the door.

The sound of the axe stopped. A man's voice yelled from somewhere behind. I sat down on a big stone and rolled an unlit cigarette around in my fingers. The owner of the cabin came around its side with an axe in his hands. He was a thick-bodied man, not very tall, with a dark, rough, unshaven chin, steady brown eyes and grizzled hair that curled. He wore blue denim pants and a blue shirt open on a muscular brown neck. When he walked he seemed to give his right foot a little kick outwards with each step. It swung out from his body in a shallow arc. He walked slowly and came up to me, a cigarette dangling from his thick lips. He had a city voice.

"Yeah?"

"Mr. Haines?"

"That's me."

"I have a note for you." I took it out and gave it to him. He threw the axe to one side and looked squintingly at the note, then turned and went into the cabin. He came out wearing glasses, reading the note as he came.

"Oh, yeah," he said. "From the boss." He studied the note again. "Mr. John Dalmas, huh? I'm Bill Haines. Glad to know you." We shook hands. He had a hand like a steel trap.

"You want to look around and see Melton's cabin, huh? What's the matter? He ain't selling, for God's sake?"

I lit my cigarette and flipped the match into the lake. "He has more than he needs here," I said.

"Land sure. But it says the cabin—"

"He wanted me to look it over. It's a pretty nice cabin, he says."

He pointed. "That one over there, the big one. Milled redwood walls, celarex lined and then knotty pine inside. Composition shingle roof, stone foundations and porches, bathroom, shower and toilet. He's got a spring-filled reservoir back in the hill behind. I'll say it's a nice cabin."

I looked at the cabin, but I looked at Bill Haines more. His eyes had a glitter and there were pouches under his eyes, for all his weathered look.

"You wanta go over now? I'll get the keys."

"I'm kind of tired after that long drive up. I sure could use a drink, Haines."

He looked interested, but shook his head. "I'm sorry, Mr. Dalmas, I just finished up a quart." He licked his broad lips and smiled at me.

"What's the mill wheel for?"

"Movie stuff. They make a picture up here once in a while. That's another set down at the end. They made *Love Among the Pines* with that. The rest of the sets are tore down. I heard the picture flopped."

"Is that so? Would you join me in a drink?" I brought out my pint of rye.

"Never been heard to say no. Wait'll I get some glasses."

"Mrs. Haines away?"

He stared at me with sudden coldness. "Yeah," he said very slowly. "Why?"

"On account of the liquor."

He relaxed, but kept an eye on me for a moment longer. Then he turned and walked his stiff-legged walk back into the cabin. He came out with a couple of the little glasses they pack fancy cheese in. I opened my bottle and poured a couple of stiff ones and we sat holding them, Haines with his right leg almost straight out in front of him, the foot twisted a little outwards.

"I copped that in France," he said, and drank. "Old Peg-leg Haines. Well, it got me a pension and it ain't hurt me with the ladies. Here's to crime." He finished his drink.

We set our glasses down and watched a bluejay go up a big pine, hopping from branch to branch without pausing to balance, like a man running upstairs.

"Cold and nice here, but lonely," Haines said. "Too damn lonely." He watched me with the corners of his eyes. He had something on his mind.

"Some people like that." I reached for the glasses and did my duty with them.

"Gets me. I been drinkin' too much account of it gets me. It gets me at night."

I didn't say anything. He put his second drink down in a swift, hard gulp. I passed the bottle to him silently. He sipped his third drink, cocked his head on one side, and licked at his lip.

"Kind of funny what you said there—about Mrs. Haines bein' away."

"I just thought maybe we ought to take our bottle out of sight of the cabin."

"Uh-huh. You a friend of Melton's?"

"I know him. Not intimately."

Haines looked across at the big cabin.

"That damn floozie!" he snarled suddenly, his face twisted.

I stared at him. "Lost me Beryl, the damn tart," he said bitterly. "Had to have even one-legged guys like me. Had to get me drunk and make me forget I had as cute a little wife as ever a guy had."

I waited, nerves taut.

"The hell with him, too! Leavin' that tramp up here all alone. I don't have to live in his goddam cabin. I can live anywheres I like. I got a pension. War pension."

"It's a nice place to live," I said. "Have a drink."

He did that, turned angry eyes on me. "It's a lousy place to live," he snarled. "When a guy's wife moves out on him and he don't know where she's at—maybe with some other guy." He clenched an iron left fist.

After a moment he unclenched it slowly and poured his glass half full. The bottle was looking pretty peaked by this time. He put his big drink down in a lump.

"I don't know you from a mule's hind leg," he growled, "but what the hell! I'm sick of bein' alone. I been a sucker— but I ain't just human. She has looks—like Beryl. Same size, same hair, same walk as Beryl. Hell, they coulda been sisters. Only just enough different—if you get what I mean." He leered at me, a little drunk now.

I looked sympathetic.

"I'm over there to burn trash," he scowled, waving an arm. "She comes out on the back porch in pajamas like they was made of cellophane. With two drinks in her hands. Smiling at me, with them bedroom eyes. 'Have a drink, Bill.' Yeah. I had a drink. I had nineteen drinks. I guess you know what happened."

"It's happened to a lot of good men."

"Leaves her alone up here, the —— —— ——! While he plays around in L.A. And Beryl walks out on me—two weeks come Friday."

I stiffened. I stiffened so hard that I could feel my muscles strain all over my body. Two weeks come Friday would be a week ago last Friday. That would be August twelfth— the day Mrs. Julia Melton was supposed to have left for El Paso, the day she had stopped over at the Olympia Hotel down at the foot of the mountains.

Haines put his empty glass down and reached into his buttoned shirt pocket. He passed me a dog-eared piece of paper. I unfolded it carefully. It was written in pencil.

I'd rather be dead than live with you any longer, you lousy cheater—Beryl. That was what it said.

"Wasn't the first time," Haines said, with a rough chuckle. "Just the first time I got caught." He laughed. Then he scowled again. I gave him back his note and he buttoned it up in the pocket. "What the hell am I tellin' you for?" he growled at me.

A bluejay scolded at a big speckled woodpecker and the woodpecker said "Cr-racker!" just like a parrot.

"You're lonely," I said. "You need to get it off your chest. Have another drink. I've had my share. You were away that afternoon—when she left you?"

He nodded moodily and sat holding the bottle between

his legs. "We had a spat and I drove on over to the north shore to a guy I know. I felt meaner than flea dirt. I had to get good and soused. I done that. I got home maybe two A.M.—plenty stinko. But I drive slow account of this trick pin. She's gone. Just the note left."

"That was a week ago last Friday, huh? And you haven't heard from her since?"

I was being a little too exact. He gave me a hard questioning glance, but it went away. He lifted the bottle and drank moodily and held it against the sun. "Boy, this is damn near a dead soldier," he said. "*She* scrammed too." He jerked a thumb towards the other side of the lake.

"Maybe they had a fight."

"Maybe they went together."

He laughed raucously. "Mister, you don't know my little Beryl. She's a hell cat when she starts."

"Sounds as if they both are. Did Mrs. Haines have a car? I mean, you drove yours that day, didn't you?"

"We got two Fords. Mine has to have the foot throttle and brake pedal over on the left, under the good leg. She took her own."

I stood up and walked to the water and threw my cigarette stub into it. The water was dark blue and looked deep. The level was high from the spring flood and in a couple of places the water licked across the top of the dam.

I went back to Haines. He was draining the last of my whisky down his throat. "Gotta get some more hooch," he said thickly. "Owe you a pint. You ain't drunk nothing."

"Plenty more where it came from," I said. "When you feel like it I'll go over and look at that cabin."

"Sure. We'll walk around the lake. You don't mind me soundin' off that way at you—about Beryl?"

"A guy sometimes has to talk his troubles to somebody," I said. "We could go across the dam. You wouldn't have to walk so far."

"Hell, no. I walk good, even if it don't look good. I ain't been around the lake in a month." He stood up and went into the cabin and came out with some keys. "Let's go."

We started towards the little wooden pier and pavilion at the far end of the lake. There was a path close to the water, winding in and out among big rough granite boulders. The dirt road was farther back and higher up. Haines walked slowly, kicking his right foot. He was moody, just drunk enough to be living in his own world. He hardly spoke. We reached the little pier and I walked out on it. Haines followed me, his foot thumping heavily on the planks. We reached the end, beyond the little open band pavilion, and leaned against a weathered dark green railing.

"Any fish in here?" I asked.

"Sure. Rainbow trout, black bass. I ain't no fish-eater myself. I guess there's too many of them."

I leaned out and looked down into the deep still water. There was swirl down there and a greenish form moved under the pier. Haines leaned beside me. His eyes stared down into the depths of the water. The pier was solidly built and had an underwater flooring—wider than the pier itself—as if the lake had once been at a much lower level, and this underwater flooring had been a boat landing. A flat-bottomed boat dangled in the water on a frayed rope.

Haines took hold of my arm. I almost yelled. His fingers bit into my muscles like iron claws. I looked at him. He was bent over, staring like a loon, his face suddenly white and glistening. I looked down into the water.

Languidly, at the edge of the underwater flooring, something that looked vaguely like a human arm and hand in a dark sleeve waved out from under the submerged boarding, hesitated, waved back out of sight.

Haines straightened his body slowly and his eyes were suddenly sober and frightful. He turned from me without a word and walked back along the pier. He went to a pile of rocks and bent down and heaved. His panting breath came to me. He got a rock loose and his thick back straightened. He lifted the rock breast high. It must have weighed a hundred pounds. He walked steadily back out on the pier with it, game leg and all, reached the end railing and lifted the rock high above his head. He stood there a moment holding it, his neck muscles bulging above his blue shirt. His mouth made some vague distressful sound. Then his whole body gave a hard lurch and the big stone smashed down into the water.

It made a huge splash that went over both of us. It fell straight and true through the water and crashed on the edge of the submerged planking. The ripples widened swiftly and the water boiled. There was a dim sound of boards breaking underwater. Waves rippled off into the distance and the water down there under our eyes began to clear. An old rotten plank suddenly popped up above the surface and sank back with a flat slap and floated off.

The depths cleared still more. In them something moved. It rose slowly, a long, dark, twisted something that rolled as it came up. It broke surface. I saw wool, sodden black now —a sweater, a pair of slacks. I saw shoes, and something that bulged shapeless and swollen over the edges of the shoes. I saw a wave of blond hair straighten out in the water and lie still for an instant.

The thing rolled then and an arm flapped in the water and the hand at the end of the arm was no decent human hand. The face came rolling up. A swollen, pulpy, gray-white mass of bloated flesh, without features, without eyes, without mouth. A thing that had once been a face. Haines looked down at it. Green stones showed below the neck that belonged to the face. Haines' right hand took hold of the railing and his knuckles went as white as snow under the hard brown skin.

"Beryl!" His voice seemed to come to me from a long way off, over a hill, through a thick growth of trees.

IV The Lady in the Lake

A LARGE white card in the window, printed in heavy block capitals, said: KEEP TINCHFIELD CONSTABLE. Behind the window was a narrow counter with piles of dusty folders on it. The door was glass and lettered in black paint: *Chief of Police. Fire Chief. Town Constable. Chamber of Commerce. Enter.*

I entered and was in what was nothing but a small one-room pineboard shack with a potbellied stove in the corner, a littered rolltop desk, two hard chairs, and the counter. On the wall hung a large blueprint map of the district, a calendar, a thermometer. Beside the desk telephone numbers had been written laboriously on the wood in large deeply bitten figures.

A man sat tilted back at the desk in an antique swivel chair, with a flat-brimmed Stetson on the back of his head and a huge spittoon beside his right foot. His large hairless hands were clasped comfortably on his stomach. He wore a pair of brown pants held by suspenders, a faded and much washed tan shirt buttoned tight to his fat neck, no tie. What I could see of his hair was mousy-brown except the temples, which were snow-white. On his left breast there was a star. He sat more on his left hip than his right, because he wore a leather hip holster with a big black gun in it down inside his hip pocket.

I leaned on the counter and looked at him. He had large ears and friendly gray eyes and he looked as if a child could pick his pocket.

"Are you Mr. Tinchfield?"

"Yep. What law we got to have, I'm it—come election anyways. There's a couple good boys running against me and they might up and whip me." He sighed.

"Does your jurisdiction extend to Little Fawn Lake?"

"What was that, son?"

"Little Fawn Lake, back in the mountains. You cover that?"

"Yep. Guess I do. I'm deppity sheriff. Wasn't no more room on the door." He eyed the door, without displeasure. "I'm all them things there. Melton's place, eh? Something botherin' there, son?"

"There's a dead woman in the lake."

"Well, I swan." He unclasped his hands and scratched his ear and stood up heavily. Standing up he was a big, powerful man. His fat was just cheerfulness. "Dead, you said? Who is it?"

"Bill Haines' wife, Beryl. Looks like suicide. She's been in the water a long time, Sheriff. Not nice to look at. She left him ten days ago, he said. I guess that's when she did it."

Tinchfield bent over the spittoon and discharged a tangled mass of brown fiber into it. It fell with a soft plop. He worked his lips and wiped them with the back of his hand.

"Who are you, son?"

"My name is John Dalmas. I came up from Los Angeles with a note to Haines from Mr. Melton—to look at the property. Haines and I were walking around the lake and we went out on the little pier the movie people built there once. We saw something down in the water underneath. Haines threw a large rock in and the body came up. It's not nice to look at, Sheriff."

"Haines up there?"

"Yeah. I came down because he's pretty badly shaken."

"Ain't surprised at that, son." Tinchfield opened a drawer in his desk and took out a full pint of whisky. He slipped it inside his shirt and buttoned the shirt again. "We'll get Doc Menzies," he said. "And Paul Loomis." He moved calmly around the end of the counter. The situation seemed to bother him slightly less than a fly.

We went out. Before going out he adjusted a clock card hanging inside the glass to read—*Back at 6 p.m.* He locked the door and got into a car that had a siren on it, two red spotlights, two amber foglights, a red-and-white fire plate, and various legends on the side which I didn't bother to read.

"You wait here, son. I'll be back in a frog squawk."

He swirled the car around in the street and went off down the road towards the lake and pulled up at a frame building opposite the stage depot. He went into this and came out with a tall, thin man. The car came slowly swirling back and I fell in behind it. We went through the village, dodging girls in shorts and men in trunks, shorts and pants, most of them naked and brown from the waist up. Tinchfield stood on his horn, but didn't use his siren. That would have started a mob of cars after him. We went up a dusty hill and stopped at a cabin. Tinchfield honked his horn and yelled. A man in blue overalls opened the door.

"Get in, Paul."

The man in overalls nodded and ducked back into the cabin and came out with a dirty lion hunter's hat on his head. We went back to the highway and along to the branch road and so over to the gate on the private road. The man in overalls got out and opened it and closed it after our cars had gone through.

When we came to the lake, smoke was no longer rising from the small cabin. We got out.

Doc Menzies was an angular yellow-faced man with bug eyes and nicotine-stained fingers. The man in blue overalls and the lion hunter's hat was about thirty, dark, swarthy, lithe, and looked underfed.

We went to the edge of the lake and looked towards the pier. Bill Haines was sitting on the floor of the pier, stark naked, with his head in his hands. There was something beside him on the pier.

"We can ride a ways more," Tinchfield said. We got back into the cars and went on, stopped again, and all trooped down to the pier.

The thing that had been a woman lay on its face on the pier with a rope under the arms. Haines' clothes lay to one side. His artificial leg, gleaming with leather and metal, lay beside them. Without a word spoken Tinchfield slipped the bottle of whisky out of his shirt and uncorked it and handed it to Haines.

"Drink hearty, Bill," he said casually. There was a sickening, horrible smell on the air. Haines didn't seem to notice it, nor Tinchfield and Menzies. Loomis got a blanket from the car and threw it over the body, then he and I backed away from it.

Haines drank from the bottle and looked up with dead eyes. He held the bottle down between his bare knee and his stump and began to talk. He spoke in a dead voice, without looking at anybody or anything. He spoke slowly and told everything he had told me. He said that after I went he had got the rope and stripped and gone into the water and got the thing out. When he had finished he stared at the wooden planks and became as motionless as a statue.

Tinchfield put a cut of tobacco in his mouth and chewed on it for a moment. Then he shut his teeth tight and leaned down and turned the body over carefully, as if he was afraid it would come apart in his hands. The late sun shone on the loose necklace of green stones I had noticed in the water. They were roughly carved and lustreless, like soapstone. A gilt chain joined them. Tinchfield straightened his broad back and blew his nose hard on a tan handkerchief.

"What you say, Doc?"

Menzies spoke in a tight, high, irritable voice. "What the hell do you want me to say?"

"Cause and time of death," Tinchfield said mildly.

"Don't be a damn fool, Jim," the doctor said nastily.

"Can't tell nothing, eh?"

"By looking at that? Good God!"

Tinchfield sighed and turned to me. "Where was it when you first seen it?"

I told him. He listened with his mouth motionless and his eyes blank. Then he began to chew again. "Funny place to be. No current here. If there was any, 'twould be towards the dam."

Bill Haines got to his foot, hopped over to his clothes and strapped his leg on. He dressed slowly, awkwardly, dragging his shirt over his wet skin. He spoke again without looking at anybody.

"She done it herself. Had to. Swum under the boards there and breathed water in. Maybe got stuck. Had to. No other way."

"One other way, Bill," Tinchfield said mildly, looking at the sky.

Haines rummaged in his shirt and got out his dog-eared note. He gave it to Tinchfield. By mutual consent everybody moved some distance away from the body. Then Tinchfield went back to get his bottle of whisky and put it away under his shirt. He joined us and read the note over and over.

"It don't have a date. You say this was a couple of weeks ago?"

"Two weeks come Friday."

"She left you once before, didn't she?"

"Yeah," Haines didn't look at him. "Two years ago. I got drunk and stayed with a chippy." He laughed wildly.

The sheriff calmly read the note once more. "Note left that time?" he inquired.

"I get it," Haines snarled. "I get it. You don't have to draw me pictures."

"Note looks middlin' old," Tinchfield said gently.

"I had it in my shirt ten days," Haines yelled. He laughed wildly again.

"What's amusing you, Bill?"

"You ever try to drag a person six feet under water?"

"Never did, Bill."

"I swim pretty good—for a guy with one leg. I don't swim that good."

Tinchfield sighed. "Now that don't mean anything, Bill.

Could have been a rope used. She could have been weighted down with a stone, maybe two stones, head and foot. Then after she's under them boards the rope could be cut loose. Could be done, son."

"Sure. I done it," Haines said and roared laughing. "Me— I done it to Beryl. Take me in, you —— s ——s!"

"I aim to," Tinchfield said mildly. "For investigation. No charges yet, Bill. You could have done it. Don't tell me different. I ain't saying you did, though. I'm just sayin' you could."

Haines sobered as quickly as he had gone to pieces.

"Any insurance?" Tinchfield asked, looking at the sky.

Haines started. "Five thousand. That does it. That hangs me. Okay. Let's go."

Tinchfield turned slowly to Loomis. "Go back there in the cabin, Paul, and get a couple of blankets. Then we better all get some whisky inside our nose."

Loomis turned and walked back along the path that skirted the lake towards the Haines' cabin. The rest of us just stood. Haines looked down at his hard brown hands and clenched them. Without a word he swept his right fist up and hit himself a terrible blow in the face.

"You —— ——!" he said in a harsh whisper.

His nose began to bleed. He stood lax. The blood ran down his lip, down the side of his mouth to the point of his chin. It began to drip off his chin.

That reminded me of something I had almost forgotten.

V   The Golden Anklet

I TELEPHONED Howard Melton at his Beverly Hills home an hour after dark. I called from the telephone company's little log-cabin office half a block from the main street of Puma Point, almost out of hearing of the .22's at the shooting gallery, the rattle of the ski balls, the tooting of fancy auto horns, and the whine of hillbilly music from the dining room of the Indian Head Hotel.

When the operator got him she told me to take the call in the manager's office. I went in and shut the door and sat down at a small desk and answered the phone.

"Find anything up there?" Melton's voice asked. It had a thickish edge to it, a three-highball edge.

"Nothing I expected. But something has happened up here you won't like. Want it straight—or wrapped in Christmas paper?"

I could hear him cough. I didn't hear any other sounds from the room in which he was talking. "I'll take it straight," he said steadily.

"Bill Haines claims your wife made passes at him—and they scored. They got drunk together the very morning of the day she went away. Haines had a row with his wife about it afterwards, and then he went over to the north shore of Puma Lake to get drunk some more. He was gone until two a.m. I'm just telling you what he says, you understand."

I waited. Melton's voice said finally: "I heard you. Go on, Dalmas." It was a toneless voice, as flat as a piece of slate.

"When he got home both the women had gone. His wife Beryl had left a note saying she'd rather be dead than live with a lousy cheater any more. He hasn't seen her since—until today."

Melton coughed again. The sound made a sharp noise in my ear. There were buzzes and crackles on the wire. An operator broke in and I asked her to go brush her hair. After the interruption Melton said: "Haines told all this to you, a complete stranger?"

"I brought some liquor with me. He likes to drink and he was aching to talk to somebody. The liquor broke down the barriers. There's more. I said he didn't see his wife again until today. Today she came up out of your little lake. I'll let you guess what she looked like."

"Good God!" Melton cried.

"She was stuck down under the underwater boarding below the pier the movie people built. The constable here, Jim Tinchfield, didn't like it too well. He's taken Haines in. I think they've gone down to see the D.A. in San Bernardino and have an autopsy and so on."

"Tinchfield thinks Haines killed her?"

"He thinks it could have happened that way. He's not saying everything he thinks. Haines put on a swell broken-hearted act, but this Tinchfield is no fool. He may know a lot of things about Haines that I don't know."

"Did they search Haines' cabin?"

"Not while I was around. Maybe later."

"I see." He sounded tired now, spent.

"It's a nice dish for a county prosecutor close to election time," I said. "But it's not a nice dish for us. If I have to appear at an inquest, I'll have to state my business, on oath. That means telling what I was doing up there, to some extent, at least. And that means pulling you in."

"It seems," Melton's voice said flatly, "that I'm pulled in already. If my wife—" He broke off and swore. He didn't speak again for a long time. Wire noises came to me and a sharper crackling, thunder somewhere in the mountains along the lines.

I said at last: "Beryl Haines had a Ford of her own. Not Bill's. His was fixed up for his left leg to do the heavy work. The car is gone. And that note didn't sound like a suicide note to me."

"What do you plan to do now?"

"It looks as though I'm always being sidetracked on this job. I may come down tonight. Can I call you at your home?"

"Any time," he said. "I'll be home all evening and all night. Call me any time. I didn't think Haines was that sort of a guy at all."

"But you knew your wife had drinking spells and you left her up here alone."

"My God," he said, as if he hadn't heard me. "A man with a wooden—"

"Oh let's skip that part of it," I growled. "It's dirty enough without. Goodbye."

I hung up and went back to the outer office and paid the girl for the call. Then I walked back to the main street and got into my car parked in front of the drugstore. The street was full of gaudy neon signs and noise and glitter. On the dry mountain air every sound seemed to carry a mile.

I could hear people talking a block away. I got out of my car again and bought another pint at the drugstore and drove away from there.

When I got to the place back along the highway where the road turned off to Little Fawn Lake, I pulled over to the side and thought. Then I started up the road into the mountains towards Melton's place.

The gate across the private road was shut and padlocked now. I tucked my car off to the side in some bushes and climbed over the gate and pussyfooted along the side of the road until the starlit glimmer of the lake suddenly bloomed at my feet. Haines' cabin was dark. The cabins on the other side of the lake were vague shadows against the slope. The old mill wheel beside the dam looked funny as hell up there all alone. I listened—didn't hear a sound. There are no night birds in the mountains.

I padded along to Haines' cabin and tried the door—locked. I went around to the back and found another locked door. I prowled around the cabin walking like a cat on a wet floor. I pushed on the one screenless window. That was locked also. I stopped and listened some more. The window was not very tight. Wood dries out in that air and shrinks. I tried my knife between the two sashes, which opened inward, like small cottage windows. No dice. I leaned against the wall and looked at the hard shimmer of the lake and took a drink from my pint. That made me tough. I put the bottle away and picked up a big stone and smacked the window frame in without breaking the glass. I heaved up on the sill and climbed into the cabin.

A flash hit me in the face.

A calm voice said: "I'd rest right there, son. You must be all tired out."

The flash pinned me against the wall for a moment and then a light switch clicked and a lamp went on. The flash died. Tinchfield sat there peacefully in a leather Morris chair beside a table over the edge of which a brown-fringed shawl dangled foolishly. Tinchfield wore the same clothes as he had worn that afternoon, and the addition of a brown wool windbreaker over his shirt. His jaws moved quietly.

"That movie outfit strung two miles of wire up here," he said reflectively. "Kind of nice for the folks. Well, what's on your mind, son—besides breakin' and enterin'?"

I picked out a chair and sat down and looked around the cabin. The room was a small square room with a double bed and a rag rug and a few modest pieces of furniture. An open door at the back showed the corner of a cookstove.

"I had an idea," I said. "From where I sit now it looks lousy."

Tinchfield nodded and his eyes studied me without rancor. "I heard your car," he said. "I knew you was on the private road and comin' this way. You walk right nice, though. I didn't hear you walk worth a darn. I've been mighty curious about you, son."

"Why?"

"Ain't you kind of heavy under the left arm, son?"

I grinned at him. "Maybe I better talk," I said.

"Well, you don't have to bother a lot about pushin' in that winder. I'm a tolerant man. I figure you got a proper right to carry that six-gun, eh?"

I reached into my pocket and laid my open billfold on his thick knee. He lifted it and held it carefully to the lamplight, looking at the photostat licence behind the celluloid window. He handed the billfold back to me.

"I kind of figured you was interested in Bill Haines," he said. "A private dective, eh? Well, you got a good hard build on you and your face don't tell a lot of stories. I'm kind of worried about Bill myself. You aim to search the cabin?"

"I did have the idea."

"It's all right by me, but there ain't really no necessity. I already pawed around considerable. Who hired you?"

"Howard Melton."

He chewed a moment in silence. "Might I ask to do what?"

"To find his wife. She skipped out on him a couple of weeks back."

Tinchfield took his flat-crowned Stetson off and rumpled his mousy hair. He stood up and unlocked and opened the door. He sat down again and looked at me in silence.

"He's very anxious to avoid publicity," I said. "On account of a certain failing his wife has which might lose him his job." Tinchfield eyed me unblinkingly. The yellow lamplight made bronze out of one side of his face. "I don't mean liquor or Bill Haines," I added.

"None of that don't hardly explain your wantin' to search Bill's cabin," he said mildly.

"I'm just a great guy to poke around."

He didn't budge for a long minute, during which he was probably deciding whether or not I was kidding him, and if I was, whether he cared.

He said at length: "Would this interest you at all, son?" He took a folded piece of newspaper from the slanting pocket of his windbreaker and opened it up on the table under the lamp. I went over and looked. On the newspaper lay a thin gold chain with a tiny lock. The chain had been snipped through neatly by a pair of cutting pliers. The lock was not unlocked. The chain was short, not more than four or five inches long and the lock was tiny and hardly any larger around than the chain itself. There was a little white powder on both chain and newspaper.

"Where would you guess I found that?" Tinchfield asked.

I moistened a finger and touched the white powder and tasted it. "In a sack of flour. That is, in the kitchen here. It's an anklet. Some women wear them and never take them off. Whoever took this one off didn't have the key."

Tinchfield looked at me benignly. He leaned back and patted one knee with a large hand and smiled remotely at the pineboard ceiling. I rolled a cigarette around in my fingers and sat down again.

Tinchfield refolded the piece of newspaper and put it back in his pocket. "Well, I guess that's all—unless you care to make a search in my presence."

"No," I said.

"It looks like me and you are goin' to do our thinkin' separate."

"Mrs. Haines had a car, Bill said. A Ford."

"Yep. A blue coupé. It's down the road a piece, hid in some rocks."

"That doesn't sound much like a planned murder."

"I don't figure anything was planned, son. Just come over him sudden. Maybe choked her, and he has awful powerful hands. There he is—stuck with a body to dispose of. He done it the best way he could think of and for a pegleg he done pretty damn well."

"The car sounds more like a suicide," I said. "A planned suicide. People have been known to commit suicide in such a way as to make a murder case stick against somebody they were mad at. She wouldn't take the car far away, because she had to walk back."

Tinchfield said: "Bill wouldn't neither. That car would be mighty awkward for him to drive, him being used to use his left foot."

"He showed me that note from Beryl before we found the body," I said. "And I was the one that walked out on the pier first."

"You and me could get along, son. Well, we'll see. Bill's a good feller at heart—except these veterans give themselves too many privileges in my opinion. Some of 'em did three weeks in a camp and act like they was wounded nine times. Bill must have been mighty sentimental about this piece of chain I found."

He got up and went to the open door. He spat his chaw out into the dark. "I'm a man sixty-two years of age," he said over his shoulder. "I've known folks to do all manner of funny things. I would say offhand that jumpin' into a cold lake with all your clothes on, and swimmin' hard to get down under that board, and then just dyin' there was a funny thing to do. On the other hand, since I'm tellin' you all my secrets and you ain't tellin' me nothing, I've had to speak to Bill a number of times for slapping his wife around when he was drunk. That ain't goin' to sound good to a jury. And if this here little chain come off Beryl Haines' leg, it's just about enough to set him in that nice new gas chamber they got up north. And you and me might as well mosey on home, son."

I stood up.

"And don't go smokin' that cigarette on the highway," he added. "It's contrary to the law up here."

I put the unlit cigarette back in my pocket and stepped out into the night. Tinchfield switched the lamp off and locked up the cabin and put the key in his pocket. "Where at are you stayin', son?"

"I'm going down to the Olympia in San Bernardino."

"It's a nice place, but they don't have the climate we have up here. Too hot."

"I like it hot," I said.

We walked back to the road and Tinchfield turned to the right. "My car's up a piece towards the end of the lake. I'll say good night to you, son."

"Good night, Sheriff. I don't think he murdered her."

He was already walking off. He didn't turn. "Well, we'll see," he said quietly.

I went back to the gate and climbed it and found my car and started back down the narrow road past the waterfall. At the highway I turned west towards the dam and the grade to the valley.

On the way I decided that if the citizens around Puma Lake didn't keep Tinchfield constable, they would be making a very bad mistake.

VI   Melton Ups the Ante

IT was past ten-thirty when I got to the bottom of the grade and parked in one of the diagonal slots in front of the Hotel Olympia in San Bernardino. I pulled an overnight bag out of the back of my car and had taken about four steps with it when a bellhop in braided pants and a white shirt and black bow tie had it out of my hand.

The clerk on duty was an egg-headed man with no interest in me. I signed the register.

The hop and I rode a four-by-four elevator to the second floor and walked a couple of blocks around corners. As we walked it got hotter and hotter. The hop unlocked a door into a boy's-size room with one window on an airshaft.

The hop, who was tall, thin, yellow, and as cool as a slice of chicken in aspic, moved his gum around in his face, put my bag on a chair, opened the window and stood looking at me. He had eyes the color of a drink of water.

"Bring us up some ginger ale and glasses and ice," I said. "Us?"

"That is, if you happen to be a drinking man."

"After eleven I reckon I might take a chance."

"It's now ten thirty-nine," I said. "If I give you a dime, will you say 'I sho'ly do thank you'?"

He grinned and snapped his gum.

He went out, leaving the door open. I took off my coat and unstrapped my holster. It was wearing grooves in my hide. I removed my tie, shirt, undershirt and walked around the room in the draft from the open door. The draft smelled of hot iron. I went into the bathroom sideways—it was that kind of bathroom—doused myself with cold water and was breathing more freely, when the tall, languid hop returned with a tray. He shut the door and I brought out my bottle. He mixed a couple of drinks and we drank. The perspiration started from the back of my neck down my spine, but I felt better all the same. I sat on the bed holding my glass and looking at the hop.

"How long can you stay?"

"Doing what?"

"Remembering."

"I ain't a damn bit of use at it."

"I have money to spend," I said, "in my own peculiar way." I took my wallet from my coat and spread bills along the bed.

"I beg yore pardon," the hop said. "You're a copper?"

"Private."

"I'm interested. This likker makes my mind work."

I gave him a dollar bill. "Try that on your mind. Can I call you Tex?"

"You done guessed it," he drawled, tucking the bill neatly into the watch pocket of his pants.

"Where were you on Friday the twelfth of August, in the late afternoon?"

He sipped his drink and thought, shaking the ice very gently and drinking past his gum. "Here. Four-to-twelve shift," he answered finally.

"A lady named Mrs. George Atkins, a small, slim, pretty blonde, checked in and stayed until time for the night train east. She put her car in the hotel garage and I believe it is still there. I want the lad that checked her in. That wins another dollar." I separated it from my stake and laid it by itself on the bed.

"I sho'ly do thank you," the hop said, grinning. He finished his drink and left the room, closing the door quietly. I finished my drink and made another. Time passed. Finally the wall telephone rang. I wedged myself into a small space between the bathroom door and the bed and answered it.

"That was Sonny. Off at eight tonight. He can be reached, I reckon."

"How soon?"

"You want him over?"

"Yeah."

"Half an hour, if he's home. Another boy checked her out. A fellow we call Les. He's here."

"Okay. Shoot him up."

I finished my second drink and thought well enough of it to mix a third before the ice melted. I was stirring it when the knock came, and I opened to a small, wiry, carrot-headed, green-eyed rat with a tight little girlish mouth.

"Drink?"

"Sure," he said. He poured himself a large one and added a whisper of mixer. He put the mixture down in one swallow, tucked a cigarette between his lips and snapped a match alight while it was still coming up from his pocket. He blew smoke, fanned it with his hand, and stared at me coldly. I noticed, stitched over his pocket instead of a number, the word *Captain*.

"Thanks," I said. "That will be all."

"Huh?" His mouth twisted unpleasantly.

"Beat it."

"I thought you wanted to see me," he snarled.

"You're the night bell captain?"

"Check."

"I wanted to buy you a drink. I wanted to give you a buck. Here. Thanks for coming up."

He took the dollar and hung there, smoke trailing from his nose, his eyes beady and mean. He turned then with a swift, tight shrug and slipped out of the room soundlessly.

Ten minutes passed, then another knock, very light. When I opened the lanky lad stood there grinning. I walked away from him and he slipped inside and came over beside the bed. He was still grinning.

"You didn't take to Les, huh?"

"No. Is he satisfied?"

"I reckon so. You know what captains are. Have to have their cut. Maybe you better call me Les, Mr. Dalmas."

"So you checked her out."

"Not if Mrs. George Atkins was her name, I didn't."

I took the photo of Julia from my pocket and showed it to him. He looked at it carefully, for a long time. "She looked like that," he said. "She gave me four bits, and in this little town that gets you remembered. Mrs. Howard Melton was the name. There's been talk about her car. I guess we just don't have much to talk about here."

"Uh-huh. Where did she go from here."

"She took a hack to the depot. You use nice likker, Mr. Dalmas."

"Excuse me. Help yourself." When he had I said: "Remember anything about her? She have any visitors?"

"No, sir. But I do recall something. She was addressed by a gentleman in the lobby. A tall, good-lookin' jasper. She didn't seem pleased to see him."

"Ah." I took the other photo out of my pocket and showed it to him. He studied that carefully also.

"This don't look quite so much like her. But I'm sure it's the gentleman I spoke of."

"Ah."

He picked up both photos again and held them side by side. He looked a little puzzled. "Yes, sir. That's him all right," he said.

"You're an accommodating guy," I said. "You'd remember almost anything, wouldn't you?"

"I don't get you, sir."

"Take another drink. I owe you four bucks. That's five in all. It's not worth it. You hops are always trying to pull some gag."

He took a very small one and balanced it in his hand, his yellow face puckered. "I do the best I can," he said stiffly. He drank his drink, put the glass down silently and moved to the door. "You can keep your goddam money," he said. He took the dollar out of his watch pocket and threw it on the floor. "To hell with you, you ——" he said softly.

He went out.

I picked up the two photos and held them side by side and scowled at them. After a long moment an icy finger touched my spine. It had touched it once before, very briefly, but I had shaken off the feeling. It came back now to stay.

I went to the tiny desk and got an envelope and put a five-dollar bill in it and sealed it and wrote "Les" on it. I put my clothes on and my bottle on my hip and picked up my overnight bag and left the room.

Down in the lobby the redhead jumped at me. Les stayed back by a pillar, his arms folded, silent. I went to the desk and asked for my bill.

"Anything wrong, sir?" The clerk looked troubled.

I paid the bill and walked out to my car and then turned and went back to the desk. I gave the clerk the envelope with the five in it. "Give this to the Texas boy, Les. He's mad at me, but he'll get over it."

I made Glendale before 2 a.m. and looked around for a place where I could phone. I found an all-night garage.

I got out dimes and nickels and dialed the operator and got Melton's number in Beverly Hills. His voice, when it finally came over the wire, didn't sound very sleepy.

"Sorry to call at this hour," I said, "but you told me to. I traced Mrs. Melton to San Bernardino and to the depot there."

"We knew that already," he said crossly.

"Well, it pays to be sure. Haines' cabin has been searched. Nothing much was found. If you thought he knew where Mrs. Melton—"

"I don't know what I thought," he broke in sharply. "After what you told me I thought the place ought to be searched. Is that all you have to report?"

"No." I hesitated a little. "I've had a bad dream. I dreamed there was a woman's bag in a chair in that Chester Lane house this morning. It was pretty dark in there from the trees and I forgot to remove it."

"What color bag?" His voice was as stiff as a clam shell.

"Dark blue—maybe black. The light was bad."

"You'd better go back and get it," he snapped.

"Why?"

"That's what I'm paying you five hundred dollars for—among other things."

"There's a limit to what I have to do for five hundred bucks—even if I had them."

He swore. "Listen, fella. I owe you a lot, but this is up to you and you can't let me down."

"Well, there might be a flock of cops on the front step.

And then again the place might be as quiet as a pet flea. Either way I don't like it. I've had enough of that house."

There was a deep silence from Melton's end. I took a long breath and gave him some more: "What's more, I think you know where your wife is, Melton. Goodwin ran into her in the hotel in San Bernardino. He had a check of hers a few days ago. You met Goodwin on the street. You helped him get the check cashed, indirectly. I think you know. I think you just hired me to backtrack over her trail and see that it was properly covered."

There was more heavy silence from him. When he spoke again it was in a small, chastened voice. "You win, Dalmas. Yeah—it was blackmail all right, on that check business. But I don't know where she is. That's straight. And that bag has to be got. How would seven hundred and fifty sound to you?"

"Better. When do I get it?"

"Tonight, if you'll take a check. I can't make better than eighty dollars in cash before tomorrow."

I hesitated again. I knew by the feel of my face that I was grinning. "Okay," I said at last. "It's a deal. I'll get the bag unless there's a flock of johns there."

"Where are you now?" He almost whistled with relief.

"Azusa. It'll take me about an hour to get there," I lied.

"Step on it," he said. "You'll find me a good guy to play ball with. You're in this pretty deep yourself, fella."

"I'm used to jams," I said, and hung up.

VII   A Pair of Fall Guys

I DROVE back to Chevy Chase Boulevard and along it to the foot of Chester Lane where I dimmed my lights and turned in. I drove quickly up around the curve to the new house across from Goodwin's place. There was no sign of life around it, no cars in front, no sign of a stakeout that

I could spot. That was a chance I had to take, like another and worse one I was taking.

I drove into the driveway of the house and got out and lifted up the unlocked swing-up garage door. I put my car inside, lowered the door and snaked back across the street as if Indians were after me. I used all the cover of Goodwin's trees to the back yard and put myself behind the biggest of them there. I sat down on the ground and allowed myself a sip from my pint of rye.

Time passed, with a deadly slowness. I expected company, but I didn't know how soon. It came sooner than I expected.

In about fifteen minutes a car came up Chester Lane and I caught a faint glisten of it between the trees, along the side of the house. It was running without lights. I liked that. It stopped somewhere near and a door closed softly. A shadow moved without sound at the corner of the house. It was a small shadow, a foot shorter than Melton's would have been. He couldn't have driven from Beverly Hills in that time anyway.

Then the shadow was at the back door, the back door opened, and the shadow vanished through it into deeper darkness. The door closed silently. I got up on my feet and sneaked across the soft, moist grass. I stepped silently into Mr. Goodwin's porch and from there into his kitchen. I stood still, listening hard. There was no sound, no light beyond me. I took the gun out from under my arm and squeezed the butt down at my side. I breathed shallowly, from the top of my lungs. Then a funny thing happened. A crack of light appeared suddenly under the swing door to the dining room. The shadow had turned the lights up. Careless shadow! I walked across the kitchen and pushed the swing door open and left it that way. The light poured into the alcove dining room from beyond the living-room arch. I went that way, carelessly—much too carelessly. I stepped past the arch.

A voice at my elbow said: "Drop it—and keep on walking."

I looked at her. She was small, pretty after a fashion, and her gun pointed at my side very steadily.

"You're not clever," she said. "Are you?"

I opened my hand and let the gun fall. I walked four steps beyond it and turned.

"No," I said.

The woman said nothing more. She moved away, circling a little, leaving the gun on the floor. She circled until she faced me. I looked past her at the corner chair with the footstool. White buck shoes still rested on the footstool. Mr. Lance Goodwin still sat negligently in the chair, with his left hand on the wide brocaded arm and his right trailing to the small gun on the floor. The last blood drop had frozen on his chin. It looked black and hard and permanent. His face had a waxy look now.

I looked at the woman again. She wore well-pressed blue slacks and a double-breasted jacket and a small tilted hat. Her hair was long and curled in at the ends and it was a dark red color with glints of blue in the shadows—dyed. Red spots of hastily applied rouge burned on her cheeks too high up. She pointed her gun and smiled at me. It wasn't the nicest smile I had ever seen.

I said: "Good evening, Mrs. Melton. What a lot of guns you must own."

"Sit down in the chair behind you and clasp your hands behind your neck and keep them there. That's important. Don't get careless about it." She showed me her teeth to her gums.

I did as she suggested. The smile dropped from her face—a hard little face, even though pretty in a conventional sort of way. "Just wait," she said. "That's important, too. Maybe you could guess how important that is."

"This room smells of death," I said. "I suppose that's important, too."

"Just wait, smart boy."

"They don't hang women any more in this state," I said. "But two cost more than one. A lot more. About fifteen years more. Think it over."

She said nothing. She stood firmly, pointing the gun. This was a heavier gun, but it didn't seem to bother her. Her ears were busy with the distance. She hardly heard me. The time passed, as it does, in spite of everything. My arms began to ache.

At last he came. Another car drifted quietly up the street outside and stopped and its door closed quietly. Silence for a moment, then the house door at the back opened. His steps were heavy. He came through the open swing door and into the lighted room. He stood silent, looking around it, a hard frown on his big face. He looked at the dead man in the chair, at the woman with her gun, last of all at me. He stopped and picked up my gun and dropped it into his side pocket. He came to me quietly, almost without recognition in his eyes, stepped behind me and felt my pockets. He took out the two photos and the telegram. He stepped away from me, near the woman. I put my arms down and rubbed them. They both stared at me quietly.

At last he said softly: "A gag, eh? First off I checked your call and found out it came from Glendale—not from Azusa. I don't know just why I did that, but I did. Then I made another call. The second call told me there wasn't any bag left in this room. Well?'

"What do you want me to say?"

"Why the trick-work? What's it all about?" His voice was heavy, cold, but more thoughtful than menacing. The woman stood beside him, motionless, holding her gun.

"I took a chance," I said. "You took one too—coming here. I hardly thought it would work. The idea, such as it was, that you would call her quickly about the bag. She would know there wasn't one. You would both know then that I was trying to pull something. You'd be very anxious to know what it was. You'd be pretty sure I wasn't working with any law, because I knew where you were and you could have been jumped there without any trouble at all. I wanted to bring the lady out of hiding—that's all. I took a long chance. If it didn't work, I had to think up a better way."

The woman made a contemptuous sound and said: "I'd like to know why you hired this snooper in the first place, Howie."

He ignored her. He looked at me steadily out of stony black eyes. I turned my head and gave him a quick, hard wink. His mouth got rigid at once. The woman didn't see it. She was too far to the side.

"You need a fall guy, Melton," I said. "Bad."

He turned his body a little so that his back was partly to the woman. His eyes ate my face. He lifted his eyebrows a little and half nodded. He still thought I was for sale.

He did it nicely. He put a smile on his face and turned towards her and said, "How about getting out of here and talking it over in a safer place?" and while she was listening and her mind was on the question his big hand struck down sharply at her wrist. She yelped and the gun dropped. She reeled back and clenched both her fists and spat at him.

"Aw, go sit down and get wise to yourself," he said dryly.

He stooped and picked up her gun and dropped it into his other pocket. He smiled then, a large confident smile. He had forgotten something completely. I almost laughed— in spite of the spot I was in. The woman sat down in a chair behind him and leaned her head in her hands broodingly.

"You can tell me about it now," Melton said cheerfully. "Why I need a fall guy, as you say."

"I lied to you over the phone a little. About Haines' cabin. There's a wise old country cop up there who went through it with a sifter. He found a gold anklet in the flour bag, cut through with pliers."

The woman let out a queer yelp. Melton didn't even bother to look at her. She was staring at me with all her eyes now.

"He might figure it out," I said, "and he might not. He doesn't know Mrs. Melton stayed over at the Hotel Olympia, for one thing, and that she met Goodwin there. If he knew that, he'd be wise in a second. That is, if he had photos to show the bellhops, the way I had. The hop who checked Mrs. Melton out and remembered her on account of her leaving her car there without any instructions remembered Goodwin, remembered him speaking to her. He said she was startled. He wasn't so sure about Mrs. Melton from the photos. He knew Mrs. Melton."

Melton opened his mouth a little in a queer grimace and grated the edges of his teeth together. The woman stood up noiselessly behind him and drifted back, inch by inch, into the dark back part of the room. I didn't look at her. Melton didn't seem to hear her move.

I said: "Goodwin trailed her into town. She must have come by bus or in a rent car, because she left the other in San Bernardino. He trailed her to her hideout without her knowing it, which was pretty smart, since she must

have been on her guard, and then he jumped her. She
stalled him for a while—I don't know with what story—
and he must have had her watched every minute, because
she didn't slip away from him. Then she couldn't stall
him any longer and she gave him that check. That was just
a retainer. He came back for more and she fixed him up
permanently—over there in the chair. You didn't know
that, or you would never have let me come out here this
morning."

Melton smiled grimly. "Right, I didn't know that," he
said. "Is that what I need a fall guy for?"

I shook my head. "You don't seem to want to understand me," I said. "I told you Goodwin knew Mrs. Melton
personally. That's not news, is it? What would Goodwin
have on Mrs. Melton to blackmail her for? Nothing. He
wasn't blackmailing Mrs. Melton. Mrs. Melton is dead. She
has been dead for eleven days. She came up out of Little
Fawn Lake today—in Beryl Haines' clothes. That's what
you need a fall guy for—and you have one, two of them,
made to order."

The woman in the shadows of the room stooped and
picked something up and rushed. She panted as she rushed.
Melton turned hard and his hands jerked at his pockets,
but he hesitated just too long, looking at the gun she had
snatched up from the floor beside Goodwin's dead hand,
the gun that was the thing he had forgotten about.

"You —— ——!" she said.

He still wasn't very scared. He made placating movements with his empty hands. "Okay, honey, we'll play it
your way," he said softly. He had a long arm. He could
reach her now. He had done it already when she held a
gun. He tried it once more. He leaned towards her quickly
and swept his hand. I put my feet under me and dived for
his legs. It was a long dive—too long.

"I'd make a swell fall guy, wouldn't I?" she said raspingly,
and stepped back. The gun banged three times.

He jumped at her with the slugs in him, and fell hard
against her and carried her to the floor. She ought to have
thought of that too. They crashed together, his big body
pinning her down. She wailed and an arm waved up towards
me holding the gun. I smacked it out of her hand. I grabbed
at his pockets and got my gun out and jumped away from

them. I sat down. The back of my neck felt like a piece of ice. I sat down and held the gun on my knee and waited.

His big hand reached out and took hold of the claw-shaped leg of a davenport and whitened on the wood. His body arched and rolled and the woman wailed again. His body rolled back and sagged and the hand let go of the davenport leg. The fingers uncurled quietly and lay limp on the nap of the carpet. There was a choking rattle—and silence.

She fought her way out from under him and got to her feet panting, glaring like an animal. She turned without a sound and ran. I didn't move. I just let her go.

I went over and bent down above the big, sprawled man and held a finger hard against the side of his neck. I stood there silently, leaning down, feeling for a pulse, and listening. I straightened up slowly and listened some more. No sirens, no car, no noise. Just the dead stillness of the room. I put my gun back under my arm and put the light out and opened the front door and walked down the path to the sidewalk. Nothing moved on the street. A big car stood at the curb, beside the fireplug, up at the dead-end beyond Goodwin's place. I crossed the street to the new house and got my car out of its garage and shut the garage up again and started for Puma Lake again.

VIII   Keep Tinchfield Constable

THE cabin stood in a hollow, in front of a growth of jack-pines. A big barnlike garage with cordwood piled on one side was open to the morning sun and Tinchfield's car glistened inside it. There was a cleated walk down to the front door and smoke lisped from the chimney.

Tinchfield opened the door himself. He wore an old gray roll-collar sweater and his khaki pants. He was fresh-shaved and as smooth as a baby.

"Well, step in, son," he said peacefully. "I see you go to work bright and early. So you didn't go down the hill last night, eh?"

I went past him into the cabin and sat in an old Boston rocker with a crocheted antimacassar over its back. I rocked in it and it gave out a homey squeak.

"Coffee's just about ready to pour," Tinchfield said genially. "Emma'll lay a plate for you. You got a kind of tuckered-out look, son."

"I went back down the hill," I said. "I just came back up. That wasn't Beryl Haines in the lake yesterday."

Tinchfield said: "Well, I swan."

"You don't seem a hell of a lot surprised," I growled.

"I don't surprise right easy, son. Particularly before breakfast."

"It was Julia Melton," I said. "She was murdered—by Howard Melton and Beryl Haines. She was dressed in Beryl's clothes and put down under those boards, six feet under water, so that she would stay long enough not to look like Julia Melton. Both the women were blondes, of the same size and general appearance. Bill said they were enough alike to be sisters. Not twin sisters, probably."

"They were some alike," Tinchfield said, staring at me gravely. He raised his voice. "Emma!"

A stout woman in a print dress opened the inner door of the cabin. An enormous white apron was tied around what had once been her waist. A smell of coffee and frying bacon rushed out.

"Emma, this is Detective Dalmas from Los Angeles. Lay another plate and I'll pull the table out from the wall a ways. He's a mite tired and hungry."

The stout woman ducked her head and smiled and put silver on the table.

We sat down and ate bacon and eggs and hot cakes and drank coffee by the quart. Tinchfield ate like four men and his wife ate like a bird and kept hopping up and down like a bird to get more food.

We finished at last and Mrs. Tinchfield gathered up the dishes and shut herself in the kitchen. Tinchfield cut a large slice of plug and tucked it carefully into his face and I sat down in the Boston rocker again.

"Well, son," he said, "I guess I'm ready for the word.

I was a mite anxious about that there piece of gold chain
bein' hid where it was, what with the lake so handy. But
I'm a slow thinker. What makes you think Melton murdered his wife?"

"Because Beryl Haines is still alive, with her hair dyed
red."

I told him my story, all of it, fact by fact, concealing
nothing. He said nothing until I had finished.

"Well, son," he said then, "you done a mighty smart piece
of detectin' work there—what with a little luck in a couple
of places, like we all have to have. But you didn't have
no business to be doin' it at all, did you?"

"No. But Melton took me for a ride and played me for
a sucker. I'm a stubborn sort of guy."

"What for do you reckon Melton hired you?"

"He had to. It was a necessary part of his plan to have
the body correctly identified in the end, perhaps not for some
time, perhaps not until after it had been buried and the
case closed. But he had to have it identified in the end in
order to get his wife's money. That or wait for years to
have the courts declare her legally dead. When it was correctly identified, he would have to show that he had made
an effort to find her. If his wife was a kleptomaniac, as
he said, he had a good excuse for hiring a private dick instead of going to the police. But he had to do something.
Also there was the menace of Goodwin. He might have
planned to kill Goodwin and frame me for it. He certainly
didn't know Beryl had beat him to it, or he wouldn't have
let me go to Goodwin's house.

"After that—and I was foolish enough to come up here
before I had reported Goodwin's death to the Glendale
police—he probably thought I could be handled with money.
The murder itself was fairly simple, and there was an angle
to it that Beryl didn't know or think about. She was probably in love with him. An underprivileged woman like that,
with a drunken husband, would be apt to go for a guy
like Melton.

"Melton couldn't have known the body would be found
yesterday, because that was pure accident, but he would have
kept me on the job and kept hinting around until it was
found. He knew Haines would be suspected of murdering
his wife and the note she left was worded to sound a bit

unlike a real suicide note. Melton knew his wife and Haines were getting tight together up here and playing games.

"He and Beryl just waited for the right time, when Haines had gone off to the north shore on a big drunk. Beryl must have telephoned him from somewhere. You'll be able to check that. He could make it up here in three hours' hard driving. Julia was probably still drinking. Melton knocked her out, dressed her in Beryl's clothes and put her down in the lake. He was a big man and could do it alone, without much trouble. Beryl would be acting as lookout down the only road into the property. That gave him a chance to plant the anklet in the Haines cabin. Then he rushed back to town and Beryl put on Julia's clothes and took Julia's car and luggage and went to the hotel in San Bernardino.

"There she was unlucky enough to be seen and spoken to by Goodwin, who must have known something was wrong, by her clothes or her bags or perhaps hearing her spoken to as Mrs. Melton. So he followed her into town and you know the rest. The fact that Melton had her lay this trail shows two things, as I see it. One, that he intended to wait some time before having the body properly identified. It would be almost certain to be accepted as the body of Beryl Haines on Bill's say-so, especially as that put Bill in a very bad spot.

"The other thing is that when the body was identified as Julia Melton, then the false trail laid by Beryl would make it look as though she and Bill had committed the murder to collect her insurance. I think Melton made a bad mistake by planting that anklet where he did. He should have dropped it into the lake, tied to a bolt or something, and later on, accidentally on purpose, fished it out. Putting it in Haines' cabin and then asking me if Haines' cabin had been searched was a little too sloppy. But planned murders are always like that."

Tinchfield switched his chaw to the other side of his face and went to the door to spit. He stood in the open door with his big hands clasped behind him.

"He couldn't have pinned nothing on Beryl," he said over his shoulder. "Not without her talkin' a great deal, son. Did you think of that?"

"Sure. Once the police were looking for her and the case

broke wide open in the papers—I mean the real case—he would have had to bump Beryl off and make it look like a suicide. I think it might have worked."

"You hadn't ought to have let that there murderin' woman get away, son. There's other things you hadn't ought to have done, but that one was bad."

"Whose case is this?" I growled. "Yours—or the Glendale police's? Beryl will be caught all right. She's killed two men and she'll flop on the next trick she tries to pull. They always do. And there's collateral evidence to be dug up. That's police work—not mine. I thought you were running for re-election, against a couple of younger men. I didn't come back up here just for the mountain air."

He turned and looked at me slyly. "I kind of figured you thought old man Tinchfield might be soft enough to keep you out of jail, son." Then he laughed and slapped his leg. "Keep Tinchfield Constable," he boomed at the big outdoors. "You're darn right they will. They'd be dum fools not to—after this. Let's mosey on over to the office and call the 'cutor down in Berdoo." He sighed. "Just too dum smart that Melton was," he said. "I like simple folks."

"Me too," I said. "That's why I'm here."

They caught Beryl Haines on the California-Oregon line, doubling back south to Yreka in a rent car. The highway patrol stopped her for a routine border fruit inspection, but she didn't know that. She pulled another gun. She still had Julia Melton's luggage and Julia Melton's clothes and Julia Melton's checkbook, with nine blank checks in it traced from one of Julia Melton's genuine signatures. The check cashed by Goodwin proved to be another forgery.

Tinchfield and the county prosecutor went to bat for me with the Glendale police, but I got hell from them just the same. From Violets M'Gee I got the large and succulent razzberry, and from the late Howard Melton I got what was left of the fifty dollars he had advanced me. They kept Tinchfield constable, by a landslide.

NO CRIME
IN THE MOUNTAINS

I

THE letter came just before noon, special delivery, a dime-store envelope with the return address F. S. Lacey, Puma Point, California. Inside was a check for a hundred dollars, made out to cash and signed Frederick S. Lacey, and a sheet of plain white bond paper typed with a number of strikeovers. It said:

Mr. John Evans.
Dear Sir:

I have your name from Len Esterwald. My business is urgent and extremely confidential. I enclose a retainer. Please come to Puma Point Thursday afternoon or evening, if at all possible, register at the Indian Head Hotel, and call me at 2306.

Yours,

FRED LACEY

There hadn't been any business in a week, but this made it a nice day. The bank on which the check was drawn was about six blocks away. I went over and cashed it, ate lunch, and got the car out and started off.

It was hot in the valley, hotter still in San Bernardino, and it was still hot at five thousand feet, fifteen miles up the high-gear road to Puma Lake. I had done forty of the fifty miles of curving, twisting highway before it started to

cool off, but it didn't get really cool until I reached the
dam and started along the south shore of the lake past the
piled-up granite boulders and the sprawled camps in the
flats beyond. It was early evening when I reached Puma
Point and I was as empty as a gutted fish.

The Indian Head Hotel was a brown building on a
corner, opposite a dance hall. I registered, carried my suitcase upstairs and dropped it in a bleak, hard-looking room
with an oval rug on the floor, a double bed in the corner,
and nothing on the bare pine wall but a hardware-store
calendar all curled up from the dry mountain summer. I
washed my face and hands and went downstairs to eat.

The dining-drinking parlor that adjoined the lobby was
full to overflowing with males in sports clothes and liquor
breaths and females in slacks and shorts with blood-red
fingernails and dirty knuckles. A fellow with eyebrows like
John L. Lewis was prowling around with a cigar screwed
into his face. A lean, pale-eyed cashier in shirt-sleeves was
fighting to get the race results from Hollywood Park on
a small radio that was as full of static as the mashed potato
was full of water. In the deep, black corner of the room
a hillbilly symphony of five defeatists in white coats and
purple shirts was trying to make itself heard above the
brawl at the bar.

I gobbled what they called the regular dinner, drank a
brandy to sit on it, and went out on to the main stem. It
was still broad daylight, but the neon lights were turned on
and the evening was full of the noise of auto horns, shrill
voices, the rattle of bowls, the snap of .22's at the shooting
gallery, jukebox music, and behind all this the hoarse, hard
mutter of speedboats on the lake. At a corner opposite the
postoffice a blue-and-white arrow said *Telephone*. I went
down a dusty side road that suddenly became quiet and
cool and piny. A tame doe deer with a leather collar on its
neck wandered across the road in front of me. The phone
office was a log cabin, and there was a booth in the corner
with a coin-in-the-slot telephone. I shut myself inside and
dropped my nickel and dialed 2306. A woman's voice answered.

I said: "Is Mr. Fred Lacey there?"

"Who is calling, please?"

"Evans is the name."

"Mr. Lacey is not here right now, Mr. Evans. Is he expecting you?"

That gave her two questions to my one. I didn't like it. I said: "Are you Mrs. Lacey?"

"Yes. I am Mrs. Lacey." I thought her voice was taut and overstrung, but some voices are like that all the time.

"It's a business matter," I said. "When will he be back?"

"I don't know exactly. Some time this evening, I suppose. What did you—"

"Where is your cabin, Mrs. Lacey?"

"It's . . . it's on Ball Sage Point, about two miles west of the village. Are you calling from the village? Did you—"

"I'll call back in an hour, Mrs. Lacey," I said, and hung up. I stepped out of the booth. In the other corner of the room a dark girl in slacks was writing in some kind of account book at a little desk. She looked up and smiled and said: "How do you like the mountains?"

I said: "Fine."

"It's very quiet up here," she said. "Very restful."

"Yeah. Do you know anybody named Fred Lacey?"

"Lacey? Oh, yes, they just had a phone put in. They bought the Baldwin cabin. It was vacant for two years, and they just bought it. It's out at the end of Ball Sage Point, a big cabin on high ground, looking out over the lake. It has a marvelous view. Do you know Mr. Lacey?"

"No," I said, and went out of there.

The tame doe was in the gap of the fence at the end of the walk. I tried to push her out of the way. She wouldn't move, so I stepped over the fence and walked back to the Indian Head and got into my car.

There was a gas station at the east end of the village. I pulled up for some gas and asked the leathery man who poured it where Ball Sage Point was.

"Well," he said. "That's easy. That ain't hard at all. You won't have no trouble finding Ball Sage Point. You go down here about a mile and a half past the Catholic church and Kincaid's Camp, and at the bakery you turn right and then you keep on the road to Willerton Boys' Camp, and it's the first road to the left after you pass on by. It's a dirt road, kind of rough. They don't sweep the snow off in winter, but it ain't winter now. You know somebody out there?"

"No." I gave him money. He went for the change and came back.

"It's quiet out there," he said. "Restful. What was the name?"

"Murphy," I said.

"Glad to know you, Mr. Murphy," he said, and reached for my hand. "Drop in any time. Glad to have the pleasure of serving you. Now, for Ball Sage Point you just keep straight on down this road—"

"Yeah," I said, and left his mouth flapping.

I figured I knew how to find Ball Sage Point now, so I turned around and drove the other way. It was just possible Fred Lacey would not want me to go to his cabin.

Half a block beyond the hotel the paved road turned down towards a boat landing, then east again along the shore of the lake. The water was low. Cattle were grazing in the sour-looking grass that had been under water in the spring. A few patient visitors were fishing for bass or bluegill from boats with outboard motors. About a mile or so beyond the meadows a dirt road wound out towards a long point covered with junipers. Close inshore there was a lighted dance pavilion. The music was going already, although it still looked like late afternoon at that altitude. The band sounded as if it was in my pocket. I could hear a girl with a throaty voice singing "The Woodpecker's Song." I drove on past and the music faded and the road got rough and stony. A cabin on the shore slid past me, and there was nothing beyond it but pines and junipers and the shine of the water. I stopped the car out near the tip of the point and walked over to a huge tree fallen with its roots twelve feet in the air. I sat down against it on the bone-dry ground and lit a pipe. It was peaceful and quiet and far from everything. On the far side of the lake a couple of speedboats played tag, but on my side there was nothing but silent water, very slowly getting dark in the mountain dusk. I wondered who the hell Fred Lacey was and what he wanted and why he didn't stay home or leave a message if his business was so urgent. I didn't wonder about it very long. The evening was too peaceful. I smoked and looked at the lake and the sky, and at a robin waiting on the bare spike at the top of a tall pine for it to get dark enough so he could sing his good-night song.

At the end of half an hour I got up and dug a hole in the soft ground with my heel and knocked my pipe out and stamped down the dirt over the ashes. For no reason at all, I walked a few steps towards the lake, and that brought me to the end of the tree. So I saw the foot.

It was in a white duck shoe, about size nine. I walked around the roots of the tree.

There was another foot in another white duck shoe. There were pinstriped white pants with legs in them, and there was a torso in a pale-green sport shirt of the kind that hangs outside and has pockets like a sweater. It had a buttonless V-neck and chest hair showed through the V. The man was middle-aged, half bald, had a good coat of tan and a line mustache shaved up from the lip. His lips were thick, and his mouth, a little open as they usually are, showed big strong teeth. He had the kind of face that goes with plenty of food and not too much worry. His eyes were looking at the sky. I couldn't seem to meet them.

The left side of the green sport shirt was sodden with blood in a patch as big as a dinner plate. In the middle of the patch there might have been a scorched hole. I couldn't be sure. The light was getting a little tricky.

I bent down and felt matches and cigarettes in the pockets of the shirt, a couple of rough lumps like keys and silver in his pants pockets at the sides. I rolled him a little to get at his hip. He was still limp and only a little cooled off. A wallet of rough leather made a tight fit in his right hip pocket. I dragged it out, bracing my knee against his back.

There was twelve dollars in the wallet and some cards, but what interested me was the name on his photostat driver's licence. I lit a match to make sure I read it right in the fading daylight.

The name on the licence was Frederick Shield Lacey.

II

I PUT the wallet back and stood up and made a full circle, staring hard. Nobody was in sight, on land or on the water. In that light, nobody could have seen what I was doing unless he was close.

I walked a few steps and looked down to see if I was making tracks. No. The ground was half pine needles of many years past, and the other half pulverized rotten wood.

The gun was about four feet away, almost under the fallen tree. I didn't touch it. I bent down and looked at it. It was a .22 automatic, a Colt with a bone grip. It was half buried in a small pile of the powdery, brown, rotted wood. There were large black ants on the pile, and one of them was crawling along the barrel of the gun.

I straightened up and took another quick look around. A boat idled offshore out of sight around the point. I could hear an uneven stutter from the throttled-down motor, but I couldn't see it. I started back toward the car. I was almost up to it. A small figure rose silently behind a heavy manzanita bush. The light winked on glasses and on something else, lower down in a hand.

A voice said hissingly: "Placing the hands up, please."

It was a nice spot for a very fast draw. I didn't think mine would be fast enough. I placed the hands up.

The small figure came around the manzanita bush. The shining thing below the glasses was a gun. The gun was large enough. It came towards me.

A gold tooth winked out of a small mouth below a black mustache.

"Turning around, please," the nice little voice said soothingly. "You seeing man lie on ground?"

"Look," I said, "I'm a stranger here. I—"

"Turning around very soon," the man said coldly.

I turned around.

The end of the gun made a nest against my spine. A light, deft hand prodded me here and there, rested on the gun under my arm. The voice cooed. The hand went to my hip. The pressure of my wallet went away. A very neat pickpocket. I could hardly feel him touch me.

"I look at wallet now. You very still," the voice said. The gun went away.

A good man had a chance now. He would fall quickly to the ground, do a back flip from a kneeling position, and come up with his gun blazing in his hand. It would happen very fast. The good man would take the little man with glasses the way a dowager takes her teeth out, in one smooth motion. I somehow didn't think I was that good.

The wallet went back on my hip, the gun barrel back into my back.

"So," the voice said softly. "You coming here you making mistake."

"Brother, you said it," I told him.

"Not matter," the voice said. "Go away now, go home. Five hundred dollars. Nothing being said five hundred dollars arriving one week from today."

"Fine," I said. "You having my address?"

"Very funny," the voice cooed. "Ha, ha."

Something hit the back of my right knee, and the leg folded suddenly the way it will when hit at that point. My head began to ache from where it was going to get a crack from the gun, but he fooled me. It was the old rabbit punch, and it was a honey of its type. Done with the heel of a very hard little hand. My head came off and went halfway across the lake and did a boomerang turn and came back and slammed on top of my spine with a sickening jar. Somehow on the way it got a mouthful of pine needles.

There was an interval of midnight in a small room with the windows shut and no air. My chest labored against the ground. They put a ton of coal on my back. One of the hard lumps pressed into the middle of my back. I made some noises, but they must have been unimportant. Nobody bothered about them. I heard the sound of a boat motor get louder, and a soft thud of feet walking on the pine needles, making a dry, slithering sound. Then a couple of heavy grunts and steps going away. Then steps coming back and a burry voice, with a sort of accent.

"What did you get there, Charlie?"

"Oh nothing," Charlie said cooingly. "Smoking pipe, not doing anything. Summer visitor, ha, ha."

"Did he see the stiff?"

"Not seeing," Charlie said. I wondered why.

"Okay, let's go."

"Ah, too bad," Charlie said. "Too bad." The weight got off my back and the lumps of hard coal went away from my spine. "Too bad," Charlie said again. "But must do."

He didn't fool this time. He hit me with the gun. Come around and I'll let you feel the lump under my scalp. I've got several of them.

Time passed and I was up on my knees, whining. I put a foot on the ground and hoisted myself on it and wiped my face off with the back of my hand and put the other foot on the ground and climbed out of the hole it felt like I was in.

The shine of water, dark now from the sun but silvered by the moon, was directly in front of me. To the right was the big fallen tree. That brought it back. I moved cautiously towards it, rubbing my head with careful fingertips. It was swollen and soft, but not bleeding. I stopped and looked back for my hat, and then remembered I had left it in the car.

I went around the tree. The moon was bright as it can only be in the mountains or on the desert. You could almost have read the paper by its light. It was very easy to see that there was no body on the ground now and no gun lying against the tree with ants crawling on it. The ground had a sort of smoothed-out, raked look.

I stood there and listened, and all I heard was the blood pounding in my head, and all I felt was my head aching. Then my hand jumped for the gun and the gun was there. And the hand jumped again for my wallet and the wallet was there. I hauled it out and looked at my money. That seemed to be there, too.

I turned around and plowed back to the car. I wanted to go back to the hotel and get a couple of drinks and lie down. I wanted to meet Charlie after a while, but not right away. First I wanted to lie down for a while. I was a growing boy and I needed rest.

I got into the car and started it and tooled it around on

the soft ground and back on to the dirt road and back along that to the highway. I didn't meet any cars. The music was still going well in the dancing pavilion off to the side, and the throaty-voiced singer was giving out "I'll Never Smile Again."

When I reached the highway I put the lights on and drove back to the village. The local law hung out in a one-room pine-board shack halfway up the block from the boat landing, across the street from the firehouse. There was a naked light burning inside, behind a glass-paneled door.

I stopped the car on the other side of the street and sat there for a minute looking into the shack. There was a man inside, sitting bareheaded in a swivel chair at an old roll-top desk. I opened the car door and moved to get out, then stopped and shut the door again and started the motor and drove on.

I had a hundred dollars to earn, after all.

III

I DROVE two miles past the village and came to the bakery and turned on a newly oiled road towards the lake. I passed a couple of camps and then saw the brownish tents of the boys' camp with lights strung between them and a clatter coming from a big tent where they were washing dishes. A little beyond that the road curved around an inlet and a dirt road branched off. It was deeply rutted and full of stones half embedded in the dirt, and the trees barely gave it room to pass. I went by a couple of lighted cabins, old ones built of pine with the bark left on. Then the road climbed and the place got emptier, and after a while a big cabin hung over the edge of the bluff looking down on the lake at its feet. The cabin had two chimneys and a rustic fence, and a double garage outside the fence. There was a long porch on the lake side, and steps going down to the water. Light came from the windows. My headlights tilted up enough to catch the name Baldwin painted on a wooden board nailed to a tree. This was the cabin, all right.

The garage was open and a sedan was parked in it. I stopped a little beyond and went far enough into the garage to feel the exhaust pipe of the car. It was cold. I went through a rustic gate up a path outlined in stones to the porch. The door opened as I got there. A tall woman stood there, framed against the light. A little silky dog rushed out past her, tumbled down the steps and hit me in the stomach with two front paws, then dropped to the ground and ran in circles making noises of approval.

"Down, Shiny!" the woman called. "Down! Isn't she a funny little dog? Funny itty doggie. She's half coyote."

The dog ran back into the house. I said: "Are you Mrs. Lacey? I'm Evans. I called you up about an hour ago."

"Yes, I'm Mrs. Lacey," she said. "My husband hasn't come in yet. I—well, come in, won't you?" Her voice had a remote sound, like a voice in the mist.

She closed the door behind me after I went in and stood there looking at me, then shrugged a little and sat down in a wicker chair. I sat down in another just like it. The dog appeared from nowhere, jumped in my lap, wiped a neat tongue across the end of my nose and jumped down again. It was a small grayish dog with a sharp nose and a long, feathery tail.

It was a long room with a lot of windows and not very fresh curtains at them. There was a big fireplace, Indian rugs, two davenports with faded cretonne slips over them, more wicker furniture, not too comfortable. There were some antlers on the wall, one pair with six points.

"Fred isn't home yet," Mrs. Lacey said again. "I don't know what's keeping him."

I nodded. She had a pale face, rather taut, dark hair that was a little wild. She was wearing a double-breasted scarlet coat with brass buttons, gray flannel slacks, pigskin clog sandals, and no stockings. There was a necklace of cloudy amber around her throat and a bandeau of old-rose material in her hair. She was in her middle thirties, so it was too late for her to learn how to dress herself.

"You wanted to see my husband on business?"

"Yes. He wrote me to come up and stay at the Indian Head and phone him."

"Oh—at the Indian Head," she said, as if that meant something. She crossed her legs, didn't like them that way, and uncrossed them again. She leaned forward and cupped a long chin in her hand. "What kind of business are you in, Mr. Evans?"

"I'm a private detective."

"It's . . . it's about the money?" she asked quickly.

I nodded. That seemed safe. It was usually about money. It was about a hundred dollars that I had in my pocket, anyhow.

"Of course," she said. "Naturally. Would you care for a drink?"

"Very much."

She went over to a little wooden bar and came back with two glasses. We drank. We looked at each other over the rims of our glasses.

"The Indian Head," she said. "We stayed there two nights when we came up. While the cabin was being cleaned up. It had been empty for two years before we bought it. They get so dirty."

"I guess so," I said.

"You say my husband wrote to you?" She was looking down into her glass now. "I suppose he told you the story."

I offered her a cigarette. She started to reach, then shook her head and put her hand on her kneecap and twisted it. She gave me the careful up-from-under look.

"He was a little vague," I said. "In spots."

She looked at me steadily and I looked at her steadily. I breathed gently into my glass until it misted.

"Well, I don't think we need be mysterious about it," she said. "Although as a matter of fact I know more about it than Fred thinks I do. He doesn't know, for example, that I saw that letter."

"The letter he sent me?"

"No. The letter he got from Los Angeles with the report on the ten-dollar bill."

"How did you get to see it?" I asked.

She laughed without much amusement. "Fred's too secretive. It's a mistake to be too secretive with a woman. I sneaked a look at it while he was in the bathroom. I got it out of his pocket."

I nodded and drank some more of my drink. I said: "Uh-huh." That didn't commit me very far, which was a good idea as long as I didn't know what we were talking about. "But how did you know it was in his pocket?" I asked.

"He'd just got it at the post office. I was with him." She laughed, with a little more amusement this time. "I saw that there was a bill in it and that it came from Los Angeles. I knew he had sent one of the bills to a friend there who is an expert on such things. So of course I knew this letter was a report. It was."

"Seems like Fred doesn't cover up very well," I said. "What did the letter say?"

She flushed slightly. "I don't know that I should tell you. I don't really know that you are a detective or that your name is Evans."

"Well, that's something that can be settled without violence," I said. I got up and showed her enough to prove it. When I sat down again the little dog came over and sniffed at the cuffs on my trousers. I bent down to pat her head and got a handful of spit.

"It said that the bill was beautiful work. The paper, in particular, was just about perfect. But under a comparison microscope there were very small differences of registration. What does that mean?"

"It means that the bill he sent hadn't been made from a government plate. Anything else wrong?"

"Yes. Under black light—whatever that is—there appeared to be slight differences in the composition of the inks. But the letter added that to the naked eye the counterfeit was practically perfect. It would fool any bank teller."

I nodded. This was something I hadn't expected. "Who wrote the letter, Mrs. Lacey?"

"He signed himself Bill. It was on a plain sheet of paper. I don't know who wrote it. Oh, there was something else. Bill said that Fred ought to turn it in to the Federal people right away, because the money was good enough to make a lot of trouble if much of it got into circulation. But, of course, Fred wouldn't want to do that if he could help it. That would be why he sent for you."

"Well, no, of course not," I said. This was a shot in the

dark, but it wasn't likely to hit anything. Not with the amount of dark I had to shoot into.

She nodded, as if I had said something.

"What is Fred doing now, mostly?" I asked.

"Bridge and poker, like he's done for years. He plays bridge almost every afternoon at the athletic club and poker at night a good deal. You can see that he couldn't afford to be connected with counterfeit money, even in the most innocent way. There would always be someone who wouldn't believe it *was* innocent. He plays the races, too, but that's just fun. That's how he got the five hundred dollars he put in my shoe for a present for me. At the Indian Head."

I wanted to go out in the yard and do a little yelling and breast beating, just to let off steam. But all I could do was sit there and look wise and guzzle my drink. I guzzled it empty and made a lonely noise with the ice cubes and she went and got me another one. I took a slug of that and breathed deeply and said: "If the bill was so good, how did he know it was bad, if you get what I mean?"

Her eyes widened a little. "Oh—I see. He didn't, of course. Not that one. But there were fifty of them, all ten-dollar bills, all new. And the money hadn't been that way when he put it in the shoe."

I wondered if tearing my hair would do me any good. I didn't think—my head was too sore. Charlie. Good old Charlie! Okay, Charlie, after a while I'll be around with my gang.

"Look," I said. "Look, Mrs. Lacey. He didn't tell me about the shoe. Does he always keep his money in a shoe, or was this something special on account of he won it at the races and horses wear shoes?"

"I told you it was a surprise present for me. When I put the shoe on I would find it, of course."

"Oh." I gnawed about half an inch off my upper lip. "But you didn't find it?"

"How could I when I sent the maid to take the shoes to the shoemaker in the village to have lifts put on them? I didn't look inside. I didn't know Fred had put anything in the shoe."

A little light was coming. It was very far off and coming very slowly. It was a very little light, about half a firefly's worth.

I said: "And Fred didn't know that. And this maid took the shoes to the shoemaker. What then?"

"Well, Gertrude—that's the maid's name—said she hadn't noticed the money, either. So when Fred found out about it and had asked her, he went over to the shoemaker's place, and he hadn't worked on the shoes and the roll of money was still stuffed down into the toe of the shoe. So Fred laughed and took the money out and put it in his pocket and gave the shoemaker five dollars because he was lucky."

I finished my second drink and leaned back. "I get it now. Then Fred took the roll out and looked it over and he saw it wasn't the same money. It was all new ten-dollar bills, and before it had probably been various sizes of bills and not new or not all new."

She looked surprised that I had to reason it out. I wondered how long a letter she thought Fred had written me. I said: "Then Fred would have to assume that there was some reason for changing the money. He thought of one and sent a bill to a friend of his to be tested. And the report came back that it was very good counterfeit, but still counterfeit. Who did he ask about it at the hotel?"

"Nobody except Gertrude, I guess. He didn't want to start anything. I guess he just sent for you."

I snubbed my cigarette out and looked out of the open front windows at the moonlit lake. A speedboat with a hard white headlight slid muttering along in the water, far off over the water, and disappeared behind a wooded point.

I looked back at Mrs. Lacey. She was still sitting with her chin propped in a thin hand. Her eyes seemed far away.

"I wish Fred would come home," she said.

"Where is he?"

"I don't know. He went out with a man named Frank Luders, who is staying at the Woodland Club, down at the far end of the lake. Fred said he owned an interest in it. But I called Mr. Luders up a while ago and he said Fred had just ridden uptown with him and got off at the post office. I've been expecting Fred to phone and ask me to pick him up somewhere. He left hours ago."

"They probably have some card games down at the Woodland Club. Maybe he went there."

She nodded. "He usually calls me, though."

I stared at the floor for a while and tried not to feel

like a heel. Then I stood up. "I guess I'll go on back to the
hotel. I'll be there if you want to phone me. I think I've
met Mr. Lacey somewhere. Isn't he a thickset man about
forty-five, going a little bald, with a small mustache?"

She went to the door with me. "Yes," she said. "That's
Fred, all right."

She had shut the dog in the house and was standing outside herself as I turned the car and drove away. God, she
looked lonely.

IV

I was lying on my back on the bed, wobbling a cigarette
around and trying to make up my mind just why I had
to play cute with this affair, when the knock came at the
door. I called out. A girl in a working uniform came in
with some towels. She had dark, reddish hair and a pert,
nicely made-up face and long legs. She excused herself and
hung some towels on the rack and started back to the door
and gave me a sidelong look with a good deal of fluttering
eyelash in it.

I said, "Hello, Gertrude," just for the hell of it.

She stopped, and the dark-red head came around and the
mouth was ready to smile.

"How'd you know my name?"

"I didn't. But one of the maids is Gertrude. I wanted to
talk to her."

She leaned against the door frame, towels over her arm.
Her eyes were lazy. "Yeah?"

"Live up here, or just up here for the summer?" I asked.

Her lip curled. "I should say I don't live up here. With
these mountain screwballs? I should say not."

"You doing all right?"

She nodded. "And I don't need any company, mister."
She sounded as if she could be talked out of that.

I looked at her for a minute and said: "Tell about that money somebody hid in a shoe."

"Who are you?" she asked coolly.

"The name is Evans. I'm a Los Angeles detective." I grinned at her, very wise.

Her face stiffened a little. The hand holding the towels clutched and her nails made a scratching around on the cloth. She moved back from the door and sat down in a straight chair against the wall. Trouble dwelt in her eyes.

"A dick," she breathed. "What goes on?"

"Don't you know?"

"All I heard was Mrs. Lacey left some money in a shoe she wanted a lift put on the heel, and I took it over to the shoemaker and he didn't steal the money. And I didn't, either. She got the money back, didn't she?"

"Don't like cops, do you? Seems to me I know your face," I said.

The face hardened. "Look, copper, I got a job and I work at it. I don't need any help from any copper. I don't owe anybody a nickel."

"Sure," I said. "When you took those shoes from the room did you go right over to the shoemaker with them?"

She nodded shortly.

"Didn't stop on the way at all?"

"Why would I?"

"I wasn't around then. I wouldn't know."

"Well, I didn't. Except to tell Weber I was going out for a guest."

"Who's Mr. Weber?"

"He's the assistant manager. He's down in the dining room a lot."

"Tall, pale guy that writes down all the race results?"

She nodded. "That would be him."

"I see," I said. I struck a match and lit my cigarette. I stared at her through smoke. "Thanks very much much," I said.

She stood up and opened the door. "I don't think I remember you," she said, looking back at me.

"There must be a few of us you didn't meet," I said.

She flushed and stood there glaring at me.

"They always change the towels this late in your hotel?" I asked her, just to be saying something.

"Smart guy, ain't you?"

"Well, I try to give that impression," I said with a modest smirk.

"You don't put it over," she said, with a sudden trace of thick accent.

"Anybody handle those shoes except you—after you took them?"

"No. I told you I just stopped to tell Mr. Weber—" She stopped dead and thought a minute. "I went to get him a cup of coffee," she said. "I left them on his desk by the cash register. How the hell would I know anybody handled them? And what difference does it make if they got their dough back all right?"

"Well, I see you're anxious to make me feel good about it. Tell me about this guy, Weber. He been here long?"

"Too long," she said nastily. "A girl don't want to walk too close to him if you get what I mean. What am I talking about?"

"About Mr. Weber."

"Well, to hell with Mr. Weber—if you get what I mean."

"You been having any trouble getting it across?"

She flushed again "And strictly off the record," she said, "to hell with you."

"If I get what you mean," I said.

She opened the door and gave me a quick, half-angry smile and went out.

Her steps made a tapping sound going along the hall. I didn't hear her stop at any other doors. I looked at my watch. It was after half past nine.

Somebody came along the hall with heavy feet, went into the room next to me and banged the door. The man started hawking and throwing shoes around. A weight flopped on the bed springs and started bounding around. Five minutes of this and he got up again. Two big, unshod feet thudded on the floor, a bottle tinkled against a glass. The man had himself a drink, lay down on the bed again, and began to snore almost at once.

Except for that and the confused racket from downstairs in the dining room and the bar there was the nearest thing you get to silence in a mountain resort. Speedboats stuttered out on the lake, dance music murmured here and there, cars went by blowing horns, the .22's snapped in the shooting gallery, and kids yelled at each other across the main drag.

It was so quiet that I didn't hear my door open. It was half open before I noticed it. A man came in quietly, half closed the door, moved a couple of steps farther into the room and stood looking at me. He was tall, thin, pale, quiet, and his eyes had a flat look of menace.

"Okay, sport," he said. "Let's see it."

I rolled around and sat up. I yawned. "See what?"

"The buzzer."

"What buzzer?"

"Shake it up, half-smart. Let's see the buzzer that gives you the right to ask questions of the help."

"Oh, that," I said, smiling weakly. "I don't have any buzzer, Mr. Weber."

"Well, that is very lovely," Mr. Weber said. He came across the room, his long arms swinging. When he was about three feet from me he leaned forward a little and made a very sudden movement. An open palm slapped the side of my face hard. It rocked my head and made the back of it shoot pain in all directions.

"Just for that," I said, "you don't go to the movies to-night."

He twisted his face into a sneer and cocked his right fist. He telegraphed his punch well ahead. I would almost have had time to run out and buy a catcher's mask. I came up under the fist and stuck a gun in his stomach. He grunted unpleasantly. I said: "Putting the hands up, please."

He grunted again and his eyes went out of focus, but he didn't move his hands. I went around him and backed towards the far side of the room. He turned slowly, eying me. I said: "Just a moment until I close the door. Then we will go into the case of the money in the shoe, other-wise known as the Clue of the Substituted Lettuce."

"Go to hell," he said.

"A right snappy comeback," I said. "And full of origi-nality."

I reached back for the knob of the door, keeping my eyes on him. A board creaked behind me. I swung around, adding a little power to the large, heavy, hard and business-like hunk of concrete which landed on the side of my jaw. I spun off into the distance, trailing flashes of lightning, and did a nose dive out into space. A couple of thousand years passed. Then I stopped a planet with my back, opened my eyes fuzzily and looked at a pair of feet.

They were sprawled out at a loose angle, and legs came towards me from them. The legs were splayed out on the floor of the room. A hand hung down limp, and a gun lay just out of its reach. I moved one of the feet and was surprised to find it belonged to me. The lax hand twitched and reached automatically for the gun, missed it, reached again and grabbed the smooth grip. I lifted it. Somebody had tied a fifty-pound weight to it, but I lifted it anyway. There was nothing in the room but silence. I looked across and was staring straight at the closed door. I shifted a little and ached all over. My head ached. My jaw ached. I lifted the gun some more and then put it down again The hell with it. I should be lifting guns around for what. The room was empty. All visitors departed. The droplight from the ceiling burned with an empty glare. I rolled a little and ached some more and got a leg bent and a knee under me. I came up grunting hard, grabbed the gun again and climbed the rest of the way. There was a taste of ashes in my mouth.

"Ah, too bad," I said out loud. "Too bad. Must do. Okay, Charlie. I'll be seeing you."

I swayed a little, still groggy as a three-day drunk, swiveled slowly and prowled the room with my eyes.

A man was kneeling in prayer against the side of the bed. He wore a gray suit and his hair was a dusty blond color. His legs were spread out, and his body was bent forward on the bed and his arms were flung out. His head rested sideways on his left arm.

He looked quite comfortable. The rough deer-horn grip of the hunting knife under his left shoulder-blade didn't seem to bother him at all.

I went over to bend down and look at his face. It was the face of Mr. Weber. Poor Mr. Weber! From under the handle of the hunting knife, down the back of his jacket, a dark streak extended.

It was not mercurochrome.

I found my hat somewhere and put it on carefully, and put the gun under my arm and waded over to the door. I reversed the key, switched the light off, went out and locked the door after me and dropped the key into my pocket.

I went along the silent hallway and down the stairs to the office. An old wasted-looking night clerk was reading the paper behind the desk. He didn't even look at me. I glanced through the archway into the dining room. The same noisy crowd was brawling at the bar. The same hillbilly symphony was fighting for life in the corner. The guy with the cigar and the John L. Lewis eyebrows was minding the cash register. Business seemed good. A couple of summer visitors were dancing in the middle of the floor, holding glasses over each other's shoulders.

V

I WENT out of the lobby door and turned left along the street to where my car was parked, but I didn't go very far before I stopped and turned back into the lobby of the hotel. I leaned on the counter and asked the clerk: "May I speak to the maid called Gertrude?"

He blinked at me thoughtfully over his glasses.

"She's off at nine-thirty. She's gone home."

"Where does she live?"

He stared at me without blinking this time.

"I think maybe you've got the wrong idea," he said.

"If I have, it's not the idea you have."

He rubbed the end of his chin and washed my face with his stare. "Something wrong?"

"I'm a detective from L.A. I work very quietly when people let me work quietly."

"You'd better see Mr. Holmes," he said. "The manager."

"Look, pardner, this is a very small place. I wouldn't have to do more than wander down the row and ask in the bars and eating places for Gertrude. I could think up a reason. I could find out. You would save me a little time and maybe save somebody from getting hurt. Very badly hurt."

He shrugged. "Let me see your credentials, Mr.—"

"Evans." I showed him my credentials. He stared at them a long time after he had read them, then handed the wallet back and stared at the ends of his fingertips.

"I believe she's stopping at the Whitewater Cabins," he said.

"What's her last name?"

"Smith," he said, and smiled a faint, old, and very weary smile, the smile of a man who has seen too much of one world. "Or possibly Schmidt."

I thanked him and went back out on the sidewalk. I walked half a block, then turned into a noisy little bar for a drink. A three-piece orchestra was swinging it on a tiny stage at the back. In front of the stage there was a small dance floor, and a few fuzzy-eyed couples were shagging around flat-footed with their mouths open and their faces full of nothing.

I drank a jigger of rye and asked the barman where the Whitewater Cabins were. He said at the east end of the town, half a block back, on a road that started at the gas station.

I went back for my car and drove through the village and found the road. A pale blue neon sign with an arrow on it pointed the way. The Whitewater Cabins were a cluster of shacks on the side of the hill with an office down front. I stopped in front of the office. People were sitting out on their tiny front porches with portable radios. The night seemed peaceful and homey. There was a bell in the office.

I rang it and a girl in slacks came in and told me Miss Smith and Miss Hoffman had a cabin kind of off by itself because the girls slept late and wanted quiet. Of course, it was always kind of busy in the season, but the cabin where they were—it was called Tuck-Me-Inn—was quiet and it was at the back, way off to the left, and I wouldn't have any trouble finding it. Was I a friend of theirs?

I said I was Miss Smith's grandfather, thanked her and went out and up the slope between the clustered cabins to the edge of the pines at the back. There was a long woodpile at the back, and at each end of the cleared space there was a small cabin. In front of the one to the left there was a coupé standing with its lights dim. A tall blond girl was putting a suitcase into the boot. Her hair was tied in a blue handkerchief, and she wore a blue sweater and blue pants. Or dark enough to be blue, anyhow. The cabin behind her was lighted, and the little sign hanging from the roof said *Tuck-Me-Inn*.

The blond girl went back into the cabin, leaving the boot of the car open. Dim light oozed out through the open door. I went very softly up on the steps and walked inside.

Gertrude was snapping down the top of a suitcase on a bed. The blond girl was out of sight, but I could hear her out in the kitchen of the little white cabin.

I couldn't have made very much noise. Gertrude snapped down the lid of the suitcase, hefted it and started to carry it out. It was only then that she saw me. Her face went very white, and she stopped dead, holding the suitcase at her side. Her mouth opened, and she spoke quickly back over her shoulder: "Anna—*achtung!*"

The noise stopped in the kitchen. Gertrude and I stared at each other.

"Leaving?" I asked.

She moistened her lips. "Going to stop me, copper?"

"I don't guess. What you leaving for?"

"I don't like it up here. The altitude is bad for my nerves."

"Made up your mind rather suddenly, didn't you?"

"Any law against it?"

"I don't guess. You're not afraid of Weber, are you?"

She didn't answer me. She looked past my shoulder. It was an old gag, and I didn't pay any attention to it. Behind me, the cabin door closed. I turned, then. The blond girl was behind me. She had a gun in her hand. She looked at me thoughtfully, without any expression much. She was a big girl, and looked very strong.

"What is it?" she asked, speaking a little heavily, in a voice almost like a man's voice.

"A Los Angeles dick," replied Gertrude.

"So," Anna said. "What does he want?"

"I don't know," Gertrude said. "I don't think he's a real dick. He don't seem to throw his weight enough."

"So," Anna said. She moved to the side and away from

the door. She kept the gun pointed at me. She held it as if guns didn't make her nervous—not the least bit nervous. "What do you want?" she asked throatily.

"Practically everything," I said. "Why are you taking a powder?"

"That has been explained," the blond girl said calmly. "It is the altitude. It is making Gertrude sick."

"You both work at the Indian Head?"

The blond girl said: "Of no consequence."

"What the hell," Gertrude said. "Yeah, we both worked at the hotel until tonight. Now we're leaving. Any objection?"

"We waste time," the blond girl said. "See if he has a gun."

Gertrude put her suitcase down and felt me over. She found the gun and I let her take it, big-hearted. She stood there looking at it with a pale, worried expression. The blond girl said: "Put the gun down outside and put the suitcase in the car. Start the engine of the car and wait for me."

Gertrude picked her suitcase up again and started around me to the door.

"That won't get you anywhere," I said. "They'll telephone ahead and block you on the road. There are only two roads out of here, both easy to block."

The blond girl raised her fine, tawny eyebrows a little. "Why should anyone wish to stop us?"

"Yeah, why are you holding that gun?"

"I did not know who you were," the blond girl said. "I do not know even now. Go on, Gertrude."

Gertrude opened the door, then looked back at me and moved her lips one over the other. "Take a tip, shamus, and beat it out of this place while you're able," she said quietly.

"Which of you saw the hunting knife?"

They glanced at each other quickly, then back at me. Gertrude had a fixed stare, but it didn't look like a guilty kind of stare. "I pass," she said. "You're over my head."

"Okay," I said. "I know you didn't put it where it was. One more question: How long were you getting that cup of coffee for Mr. Weber the morning you took the shoes out?"

"You are wasting time, Gertrude," the blond girl said impatiently, or as impatiently as she would ever say anything. She didn't seem an impatient type.

Gertrude didn't pay any attention to her. Her eyes held a tight speculation. "Long enough to get him a cup of coffee."

"They have that right in the dining room."

"It was stale in the dining room. I went out to the kitchen for it. I got him some toast, also."

"Five minutes?"

She nodded. "About that."

"Who else was in the dining room besides Weber?"

She stared at me very steadily. "At that time I don't think anybody. I'm not sure. Maybe someone was having a late breakfast."

"Thanks very much," I said. "Put the gun down carefully on the porch and don't drop it. You can empty it if you like. I don't plan to shoot anyone."

She smiled a very small smile and opened the door with the hand holding the gun and went out. I heard her go down the steps and then heard the boot of the car slammed shut. I heard the starter, then the motor caught and purred quietly.

The blond girl moved around to the door and took the key from the inside and put it on the outside. "I would not care to shoot anybody," she said. "But I could do it if I had to. Please do not make me."

She shut the door and the key turned in the lock. Her steps went down off the porch. The car door slammed and the motor took hold. The tires made a soft whisper going down between the cabins. Then the noise of the portable radios swallowed that sound.

I stood there looking around the cabin, then walked through it. There was nothing in it that didn't belong there. There was some garbage in a can, coffee cups not washed, a saucepan full of grounds. There were no papers, and nobody had left the story of his life written on a paper match.

The back door was locked, too. This was on the side away from the camp, against the dark wilderness of the trees. I shook the door and bent down to look at the lock. A straight bolt lock. I opened a window. A screen was nailed over it against the wall outside. I went back to the door and gave it the shoulder. It held without any trouble at all. It also started my head blazing again. I felt in my pockets and was disgusted. I didn't even have a five-cent skeleton key.

I got the can opener out of the kitchen drawer and worked a corner of the screen loose and bent it back. Then I got up on the sink and reached down to the outside knob of the door and groped around. The key was in the lock. I turned it and drew my hand in again and went out of the door. Then I went back and put the lights out. My gun was lying on the front porch behind a post of the little railing. I tucked it under my arm and walked downhill to the place where I had left my car.

VI

THERE was a wooden counter leading back from beside the door and a potbellied stove in the corner, and a large blueprint map of the district and some curled-up calendars on the wall. On the counter were piles of dusty-looking folders, a rusty pen, a bottle of ink, and somebody's sweat-darkened Stetson.

Behind the counter there was an old golden-oak roll-top desk, and at the desk sat a man, with a tall corroded brass spittoon leaning against his leg. He was a heavy, calm man, and he sat tilted back in his chair with large, hairless hands clasped on his stomach. He wore scuffed brown army shoes, white socks, brown wash pants held up by faded suspenders, a khaki shirt buttoned to the neck. His hair was mousy-brown except at the temples, where it was the color of dirty snow. On his left breast there was a star. He sat a little more on his left hip than on his right, because there was a brown leather hip holster inside his right hip pocket, and about a foot of .45 gun in the holster.

He had large ears, and friendly eyes, and he looked about

as dangerous as a squirrel, but much less nervous. I leaned on the counter and looked at him, and he nodded at me and loosed a half-pint of brown juice into the spittoon. I lit a cigarette and looked around for some place to throw the match.

"Try the floor," he said. "What can I do for you, son?"

I dropped the match on the floor and pointed with my chin at the map on the wall. "I was looking for a map of the district. Sometimes chambers of commerce have them to give away. But I guess you wouldn't be the chamber of commerce."

"We ain't got no maps," the man said. "We had a mess of them a couple of years back, but we run out. I was hearing that Sid Young had some down at the camera store by the post office. He's the justice of the peace here, besides running the camera store, and he gives them out to show them whereat they can smoke and where not. We got a bad fire hazard up here. Got a good map of the district up there on the wall. Be glad to direct you any place you'd care to go. We aim to make the summer visitors to home."

He took a slow breath and dropped another load of juice.

"What was the name?" he asked.

"Evans. Are you the law around here?"

"Yep. I'm Puma Point constable and San Berdoo deppity sheriff. What law we gotta have, me and Sid Young is it. Barron is the name. I come from L.A. Eighteen years in the fire department. I come up here quite a while back. Nice and quiet up here. You up on business?"

I didn't think he could do it again so soon, but he did. That spittoon took an awful beating.

"Business?" I asked.

The big man took one hand off his stomach and hooked a finger inside his collar and tried to loosen it. "Business," he said calmly. "Meaning, you got a permit for that gun, I guess?"

"Hell, does it stick out that much?"

"Depends what a man's lookin' for," he said, and put his feet on the floor. "Maybe you 'n' me better get straightened out."

He got to his feet and came over to the counter and I put my wallet on it, opened out so that he could see the photostat of the licence behind the celluloid window. I drew out the L.A. sheriff's gun permit and laid it beside the licence.

He looked them over. "I better kind of check the number," he said.

I pulled the gun out and laid it on the counter beside his hand. He picked it up and compared the numbers. "I see you got three of them. Don't wear them all to onst, I hope. Nice gun, son. Can't shoot like mine, though." He pulled his cannon off his hip and laid it on the counter. A Frontier Colt that would weigh as much as a suitcase. He balanced it, tossed it into the air and caught it spinning, then put it back on his hip. He pushed my .38 back across the counter.

"Up here on business, Mr. Evans?"

"I'm not sure. I got a call, but I haven't made a contact yet. A confidential matter."

He nodded. His eyes were thoughtful. They were deeper, colder, darker than they had been.

"I'm stopping at the Indian Head," I said.

"I don't aim to pry into your affairs, son," he said. "We don't have no crime here. Onst in a while a fight or a drunk driver in summertime. Or maybe a couple hard-boiled kids on a motorcycle will break into a cabin just to sleep and steal food. No real crime, though. Mighty little inducement to crime in the mountains. Mountain folks are mighty peaceable."

"Yeah," I said. "And again, no."

He leaned forward a little and looked into my eyes.

"Right now," I said, "you've got a murder."

Nothing much changed in his face. He looked me over feature by feature. He reached for his hat and put it on the back of his head.

"What was that, son?" he asked calmly.

"On the point east of the village out past the dancing pavilion. A man shot, lying behind a big fallen tree. Shot through the heart. I was down there smoking for half an hour before I noticed him."

"Is that so?" he drawled. "Out Speaker Point, eh? Past Speaker's Tavern. That the place?"

"That's right," I said.

"You taken a longish while to get around to telling me, didn't you?" The eyes were not friendly.

"I got a shock," I said. "It took me a while to get myself straightened out."

He nodded. "You and me will now drive out that way. In your car."

"That won't do any good," I said. "The body has been moved. After I found the body I was going back to my car and a Japanese gunman popped up from behind a bush and knocked me down. A couple of men carried the body away and they went off in a boat. There's no sign of it there at all now."

The sheriff went over and spat in his gobboon. Then he made a small spit on the stove and waited as if for it to sizzle, but it was summer and the stove was out. He turned around and cleared his throat and said: "You'd kind of better go on home and lie down a little while, maybe." He clenched a fist at his side. "We aim for the summer visitors to enjoy theirselves up here." He clenched both his hands, then pushed them hard down into the shallow pockets in the front of his pants.

"Okay," I said.

"We don't have no Japanese gunmen up here," the sheriff said thickly. "We are plumb out of Japanese gunmen."

"I can see you don't like that one," I said. "How about this one? A man named Weber was knifed in the back at the Indian Head a while back. In my room. Somebody I didn't see knocked me out with a brick, and while I was out this Weber was knifed. He and I had been talking together. Weber worked at the hotel. As cashier."

"You said this happened in your room?"

"Yeah."

"Seems like," Barron said thoughtfully, "you could turn out to be a bad influence in this town."

"You don't like that one, either?"

He shook his head. "Nope. Don't like this one, neither. Unless, of course, you got a body to go with it."

"I don't have it with me," I said, "but I can run over and get it for you."

He reached and took hold of my arm with some of the hardest fingers I ever felt. "I'd hate for you to be in your right mind, son," he said. "But I'll kind of go over with you. It's a nice night."

"Sure," I said, not moving. "The man I came up here to

work for is called Fred Lacey. He just bought a cabin out on Ball Sage Point. The Baldwin cabin. The man I found dead on Speaker Point was named Frederick Lacey, according to the driver's licence in his pocket. There's a lot more to it, but you wouldn't want to be bothered with the details, would you?"

"You and me," the sheriff said, "will now run over to the hotel. You got a car?"

I said I had.

"That's fine," the sheriff said. "We won't use it, but give me the keys."

VII

THE man with the heavy, furled eyebrows and the screwed-in cigar leaned against the closed door of the room and didn't say anything or look as if he wanted to say anything. Sheriff Barron sat straddling a straight chair and watching the doctor, whose name was Menzies, examine the body. I stood in the corner where I belonged. The doctor was an angular, bug-eyed man with a yellow face relieved by bright red patches on his cheeks. His fingers were brown with nicotine stains, and he didn't look very clean.

He puffed cigarette smoke into the dead man's hair and rolled him around on the bed and felt him here and there. He looked as if he was trying to act as if he knew what he was doing. The knife had been pulled out of Weber's back. It lay on the bed beside him. It was a short, wide-bladed knife of the kind that is worn in a leather scabbard attached to the belt. It had a heavy guard which would seal the wound as the blow was struck and keep blood from getting back on the handle. There was plenty of blood on the blade.

"Sears Sawbuck Hunter's Special No. 2438," the sheriff said, looking at it. "There's a thousand of them around the lake. They ain't bad and they ain't good. What do you say, Doc?"

The doctor straightened up and took a handkerchief out. He coughed hackingly into the handkerchief, looked at it, shook his head sadly and lit another cigarette.

"About what?" he asked.

"Cause and time of death."

"Dead very recently," the doctor said. "Not more than two hours. There's no beginning of rigor yet."

"Would you say the knife killed him?"

"Don't be a damn fool, Jim Barron."

"There's been cases," the sheriff said, "where a man would be poisoned or something and they would stick a knife into him to make it look different."

"That would be very clever," the doctor said nastily. "You had many like that up here?"

"Only murder I had up here," the sheriff said peacefully, "was old Dad Meacham over to the other side. Had a shack in Sheedy Canyon. Folks didn't see him around for a while, but it was kinda cold weather and they figured he was in there with his oil stove resting up. Then when he didn't show up they knocked and found the cabin was locked up, so they figured he had gone down for the winter. Then come a heavy snow and the roof caved in. We was over there a-trying to prop her up so he wouldn't lose all his stuff, and, by gum, there was Dad in bed with an axe in the back of his head. Had a little gold he'd panned in summer—I guess that was what he was killed for. We never did find out who done it."

"You want to send him down in my ambulance?" the doctor asked, pointing at the bed with his cigarette.

The sheriff shook his head. "Nope. This is a poor county, Doc. I figure he could ride cheaper than that."

The doctor put his hat on and went to the door. The man with the eyebrows moved out of the way. The doctor opened the door. "Let me know if you want me to pay for the funeral," he said, and went out.

"That ain't no way to talk," the sheriff said.

The man with the eyebrows said: "Let's get this over with and get him out of here so I can go back to work. I got a movie outfit coming up Monday and I'll be busy. I got to find me a new cashier, too, and that ain't so easy."

"Where you find Weber?" the sheriff asked. "Did he have any enemies?"

"I'd say he had at least one," the man with the eyebrows said. "I got him through Frank Luders over at the Woodland Club. All I know about him is he knew his job and he was able to make a ten-thousand-dollar bond without no trouble. That's all I needed to know."

"Frank Luders," the sheriff said. "That would be the man that's bought in over there. I don't think I met him. What does he do?"

"Ha, ha," the man with the eyebrows said.

The sheriff looked at him peacefully. "Well, that ain't the only place where they run a nice poker game, Mr. Holmes."

Mr. Holmes looked blank. "Well, I got to go back to work," he said. "You need any help to move him?"

"Nope. Ain't going to move him right now. Move him before daylight. But not right now. That will be all for now, Mr. Holmes."

The man with the eyebrows looked at him thoughtfully for a moment, then reached for the doorknob.

I said: "You have a couple of German girls working here, Mr. Holmes. Who hired them?"

The man with the eyebrows dragged his cigar out of his mouth, looked at it, put it back and screwed it firmly in place. He said: "Would that be your business?"

"Their names are Anna Hoffman and Gertrude Smith, or maybe Schmidt," I said. "They had a cabin together over at the Whitewater Cabins. They packed up and went down the hill tonight. Gertrude is the girl that took Mrs. Lacey's shoes to the shoemaker."

The man with the eyebrows looked at me very steadily.

I said: "When Gertrude was taking the shoes, she left them on Weber's desk for a short time. There was five hundred dollars in one of the shoes. Mr. Lacey had put it in there for a joke, so his wife would find it."

"First I heard of it," the man with the eyebrows said. The sheriff didn't say anything at all.

"The money wasn't stolen," I said. "The Laceys found it still in the shoe over at the shoemaker's place."

The man with the eyebrows said: "I'm certainly glad that got straightened out all right." He pulled the door open and went out and shut it behind him. The sheriff didn't say anything to stop him.

He went over into the corner of the room and spat in the wastebasket. Then he got a large khaki-colored handkerchief out and wrapped the bloodstained knife in it and slipped it down inside his belt, at the side. He went over and stood looking down at the dead man on the bed. He straightened his hat and started towards the door. He opened the door and looked back at me. "This is a little tricky," he said. "But it probably ain't as tricky as you would like for it to be. Let's go over to Lacey's place."

I went out and he locked the door and put the key in his pocket. We went downstairs and out through the lobby and crossed the street to where a small, dusty, tan-colored sedan was parked against the fireplug. A leathery young man was at the wheel. He looked underfed and a little dirty, like most of the natives. The sheriff and I got in the back of the car. The sheriff said: "You know the Baldwin place out to the end of Ball Sage, Andy?"

"Yup."

"We'll go out there," the sheriff said. "Stop a little to this side." He looked up at the sky. "Full moon all night, tonight," he said. "And it's sure a dandy."

VIII

THE cabin on the point looked the same as when I had seen it last. The same windows were lighted, the same car stood in the open double garage, and the same wild, screaming bark burst on the night.

"What in heck's that?" the sheriff asked as the car slowed. "Sounds like a coyote."

"It's half a coyote," I said.

The leathery lad in front said over his shoulder, "You want to stop in front, Jim?"

"Drive her down a piece. Under them old pines."

The car stopped softly in black shadow at the roadside. The sheriff and I got out. "You stay here, Andy, and don't let nobody see you," the sheriff said. "I got my reasons."

We went back along the road and through the rustic gate. The barking started again. The front door opened. The sheriff went up on the steps and took his hat off.

"Mrs. Lacey? I'm Jim Barron, constable at Puma Point. This here is Mr. Evans, from Los Angeles. I guess you know him. Could we come in a minute?"

The woman looked at him with a face so completely shadowed that no expression showed on it. She turned her head a little and looked at me. She said, "Yes, come in," in a lifeless voice.

We went in. The woman shut the door behind us. A big gray-haired man sitting in an easy chair let go of the dog he was holding on the floor and straightened up. The dog tore across the room, did a flying tackle on the sheriff's stomach, turned in the air and was already running in circles when she hit the floor.

"Well, that's a right nice little dog," the sheriff said, tucking his shirt in.

The gray-haired man was smiling pleasantly. He said: "Good evening." His white, strong teeth gleamed with friendliness.

Mrs. Lacey was still wearing the scarlet double-breasted coat and the gray slacks. Her face looked older and more drawn. She looked at the floor and said: "This is Mr. Frank Luders from the Woodland Club. Mr. Bannon and"—she stopped and raised her eyes to look at a point over my left shoulder—"I didn't catch the other gentleman's name," she said.

"Evans," the sheriff said, and didn't look at me at all. "And mine is Barron, not Bannon." He nodded at Luders. I nodded at Luders. Luders smiled at both of us. He was big, meaty, powerful-looking, well kept and cheerful. He didn't have a care in the world. Big, breezy Frank Luders, everybody's pal.

He said: "I've known Fred Lacey for a long time. I just dropped by to say hello. He's not home, so I am waiting a little while until a friend comes by in a car to pick me up."

"Pleased to know you, Mr. Luders," the sheriff said. "I

heard you had bought in at the club. Didn't have the pleasure of meeting you yet."

The woman sat down very slowly on the edge of a chair.
I sat down. The little dog, Shiny, jumped in my lap, washed
my right ear for me, squirmed down again and went under
my chair. She lay there breathing out loud and thumping the
floor with her feathery tail.

The room was still for a moment. Outside the windows
on the lake side there was a very faint throbbing sound. The
sheriff heard it. He cocked his head slightly, but nothing
changed in his face.

He said: "Mr. Evans here come to me and told me a
queer story. I guess it ain't no harm to mention it here,
seeing Mr. Luders is a friend of the family."

He looked at Mrs. Lacey and waited. She lifted her eyes
slowly, but not enough to meet his. She swallowed a couple
of times and nodded her head. One of her hands began to
slide slowly up and down the arm of her chair, back and
forth, back and forth. Luders smiled.

"I'da liked to have Mr. Lacey here," the sheriff said.
"You think he'll be in pretty soon?"

The woman nodded again. "I suppose so," she said in a
drained voice. "He's been gone since midafternoon. I don't
know where he is. I hardly think he would go down the hill
without telling me, but he has had time to do that. Something might have come up."

"Seems like something did," the sheriff said. "Seems like
Mr. Lacey wrote a letter to Mr. Evans, asking him to come
up here quickly. Mr. Evans is a detective from L.A."

The woman moved restlessly. "A detective?" she breathed.

Luders said brightly: "Now why in the world would Fred
do that?"

"On account of some money that was hid in a shoe," the
sheriff said.

Luders raised his eyebrows and looked at Mrs. Lacey. Mrs.
Lacey moved her lips together and then said very shortly:
"But we got that back, Mr. Bannon. Fred was having a
joke. He won a little money at the races and hid it in one of
my shoes. He meant it for a surprise. I sent the shoe out
to be repaired with the money still in it, but the money
was still in it when we went over to the shoemaker's place."

"Barron is the name, not Bannon," the sheriff said. "So you got your money back all intact, Mrs. Lacey?"

"Why—of course. Of course, we thought at first, it being a hotel and one of the maids having taken the shoe—well, I don't know just what we thought, but it was a silly place to hide money—but we got it back, every cent of it."

"And it was the same money?" I said, beginning to get the idea and not liking it.

She didn't quite look at me. "Why, of course. Why not?"

"That ain't the way I heard it from Mr. Evans," the sheriff said peacefully, and folded his hands across his stomach. "There was a slight difference, seems like, in the way you told it to Evans."

Luders leaned forward suddenly in his chair, but his smile stayed put. I didn't even get tight. The woman made a vague gesture and her hand kept moving on the chair arm. "I . . . told it . . told what to Mr Evans?"

The sheriff turned his head very slowly and gave me a straight, hard stare. He turned his head back. One hand patted the other on his stomach.

"I understand Mr. Evans was over here earlier in the evening and you told him about it, Mrs. Lacey. About the money being changed?"

"Changed?" Her voice had a curiously hollow sound. "Mr. Evans told you he was here earlier in the evening? I . . . I never saw Mr. Evans before in my life."

I didn't even bother to look at her. Luders was my man. I looked at Luders. It got me what the nickel gets you from the slot machine. He chuckled and put a fresh match to his cigar.

The sheriff closed his eyes. His face had a sort of sad expression. The dog came out from under my chair and stood in the middle of the room looking at Luders. Then she went over in the corner and slid under the fringe of a daybed cover. A snuffling sound came from her a moment, then silence.

"Hum, hum, dummy," the sheriff said, talking to himself. "I ain't really equipped to handle this sort of a deal. I don't have the experience. We don't have no fast work like that up here. No crime at all in the mountains. Hardly." He made a wry face.

He opened his eyes. "How much money was that in the shoe, Mrs. Lacey?"

"Five hundred dollars." Her voice was hushed.

"Where at is this money, Mrs. Lacey?"

"I suppose Fred has it."

"I thought he was goin' to give it to you, Mrs. Lacey."

"He was," she said sharply. "He is. But I don't need it at the moment. Not up here. He'll probably give me a check later on."

"Would he have it in his pocket or would it be in the cabin here, Mrs. Lacey?"

She shook her head. "In his pocket, probably. I don't know. Do you want to search the cabin?"

The sheriff shrugged his fat shoulders. "Why, no, I guess not, Mrs. Lacey. It wouldn't do me no good if I found it. Especially if it wasn't changed."

Luders said: "Just how do you mean changed, Mr. Barron?"

"Changed for counterfeit money," the sheriff said.

Luders laughed quietly. "That's really amusing, don't you think? Counterfeit money at Puma Point? There's no opportunity for that sort of thing up here, is there?"

The sheriff nodded at him sadly. "Don't sound reasonable, does it?"

Luders said: "And your only source of information on the point is Mr. Evans here—who claims to be a detective? A private detective, no doubt?"

"I thought of that," the sheriff said.

Luders leaned forward a little more. "Have you any knowledge other than Mr. Evans' statement that Fred Lacey sent for him?"

"He'd have to know something to come up here, wouldn't he?" the sheriff said in a worried voice. "And he knew about that money in Mrs. Lacey's slipper."

"I was just asking a question," Luders said softly.

The sheriff swung around on me. I was already wearing my frozen smile. Since the incident in the hotel I hadn't looked for Lacey's letter. I knew I wouldn't have to look, now.

"You got a letter from Lacey?" he asked me in a hard voice.

I lifted my hand towards my inside breast pocket. Barron threw his right hand down and up. When it came up it held the Frontier Colt. "I'll take that gun of yours first," he said between his teeth. He stood up.

I pulled my coat open and held it open. He leaned down over me and jerked the automatic from the holster. He looked at it sourly a moment and dropped it into his left hip pocket. He sat down again. "*Now* look," he said easily.

Luders watched me with bland interest. Mrs. Lacey put her hands together and squeezed them hard and stared at the floor between her shoes.

I took the stuff out of my breast pocket. A couple of letters, some plain cards for casual notes, a packet of pipe cleaners, a spare handkerchief. Neither of the letters was the one. I put the stuff back and got a cigarette out and put it between my lips. I struck the match and held the flame to the tobacco. Nonchalant.

"You win," I said, smiling. "Both of you."

There was a slow flush on Barron's face and his eyes glittered. His lips twitched as he turned away from me.

"Why not," Luders asked gently, "see also if he really is a detective?"

Barron barely glanced at him. "The small things don't bother me," he said. "Right now I'm investigatin' a murder."

He didn't seem to be looking at either Luders or Mrs. Lacey. He seemed to be looking at a corner of the ceiling. Mrs. Lacey shook, and her hands tightened so that the knuckles gleamed hard and shiny and white in the lamplight. Her mouth opened very slowly, and her eyes turned up in her head. A dry sob half died in her throat.

Luders took the cigar out of his mouth and laid it carefully in the brass dip on the smoking stand beside him. He stopped smiling. His mouth was grim. He said nothing.

It was beautifully timed. Barron gave them all they needed for the reaction and not a second for a comeback. He said, in the same almost indifferent voice: "A man named Weber, cashier in the Indian Head Hotel. He was knifed in Evans' room. Evans was there, but he was knocked out before it happened, so he is one of them boys we hear so much about and don't often meet—the boys that get there first."

"Not me," I said. "They bring their murders and drop them right at my feet."

The woman's head jerked. Then she looked up, and for

the first time she looked straight at me. There was a queer light in her eyes, shining far back, remote and miserable.

Barron stood up slowly. "I don't get it," he said. "I don't get it at all. But I guess I ain't making any mistake in takin' this feller in." He turned to me. "Don't run too fast, not at first, bud. I always give a man forty yards."

I didn't say anything. Nobody said anything.

Barron said slowly: "I'll have to ask you to wait here till I come back, Mr. Luders. If your friend comes for you, you could let him go on. I'd be glad to drive you back to the club later."

Luders nodded. Barron looked at a clock on the mantel. It was a quarter to twelve. "Kinda late for a old fuddy-duddy like me. You think Mr. Lacey will be home pretty soon, ma'am?"

"I . . . I hope so," she said, and made a gesture that meant nothing unless it meant hopelessness.

Barron moved over to open the door. He jerked his chin at me. I went out on the porch. The little dog came halfway out from under the couch and made a whining sound. Barron looked down at her.

"That sure is a nice little dog," he said. "I heard she was half coyote. What did you say the other half was?"

"We don't know," Mrs. Lacey murmured.

"Kind of like this case I'm working on," Barron said, and came out on to the porch after me.

IX

We walked down the road without speaking and came to the car. Andy was leaning back in the corner, a dead half cigarette between his lips.

We got into the car. "Drive down a piece, about two hundred yards," Barron said. "Make plenty of noise."

Andy started the car, raced the motor, clashed the gears, and the car slid down through the moonlight and around a curve of the road and up a moonlit hill sparred with the shadows of tree trunks.

"Turn her at the top and coast back, but not close," Barron said. "Stay out of sight of that cabin. Turn your lights off before you turn."

"Yup," Andy said.

He turned the car just short of the top, going around a tree to do it. He cut the lights off and started back down the little hill, then killed the motor. Just beyond the bottom of the slope there was a heavy clump of manzanita, almost as tall as ironwood. The car stopped there. Andy pulled the brake back very slowly to smooth out the noise of the ratchet.

Barron leaned forward over the back seat. "We're goin' across the road and get near the water," he said. "I don't want no noise and nobody walkin' in no moonlight."

Andy said: "Yup."

We got out. We walked carefully on the dirt of the road, then on the pine needles. We filtered through the trees, behind fallen logs, until the water was down below where we stood. Barron sat down on the ground and then lay down. Andy and I did the same. Barron put his face close to Andy.

"Hear anything?"

Andy said: "Eight cylinders, kinda rough."

I listened. I could tell myself I heard it, but I couldn't be sure. Barron nodded in the dark. "Watch the lights in the cabin," he whispered.

We watched. Five minutes passed, or enough time to seem like five minutes. The lights in the cabin didn't change. Then there was a remote, half-imagined sound of a door closing. There were shoes on wooden steps.

"Smart. They left the light on," Barron said in Andy's ear.

We waited another short minute. The idling motor burst into a roar of throbbing sound, a stuttering, confused racket, with a sort of hop, skip and jump in it. The sound sank to a heavy purring roar and then quickly began to fade. A dark shape slid out on the moonlit water, curved with a beautiful line of froth and swept past the point out of sight.

Barron got a plug of tobacco out and bit. He chewed

comfortably and spat four feet beyond his feet. Then he got up on his feet and dusted off the pine needles. Andy and I got up.

"Man ain't got good sense chewin' tobacco these days," he said. "Things ain't fixed for him. I near went to sleep back there in the cabin." He lifted the Colt he was still holding in his left hand, changed hands and packed the gun away on his hip.

"Well?" he said, looking at Andy.

"Ted Rooney's boat," Andy said. "She's got two sticky valves and a big crack in the muffler. You hear it best when you throttle her up, like they did just before they started."

It was a lot of words for Andy, but the sheriff liked them.

"Couldn't be wrong, Andy? Lots of boats get sticky valves."

Andy said: "What the hell you ask me for?" in a nasty voice.

"Okay, Andy, don't get sore."

Andy grunted. We crossed the road and got into the car again. Andy started it up, backed and turned and said: "Lights?"

Barron nodded. Andy put the lights on. "Where to now?"

"Ted Rooney's place," Barron said peacefully. "And make it fast. We got ten miles to there."

"Can't make it in less'n twenty minutes," Andy said sourly. "Got to go through the Point."

The car hit the paved lake road and started back past the dark boys' camp and the other camps, and turned left on the highway. Barron didn't speak until we were beyond the village and the road out to Speaker Point. The dance band was still going strong in the pavilion.

"I fool you any?" he asked me then.

"Enough."

"Did I do something wrong?"

"The job was perfect," I said, "but I don't suppose you fooled Luders."

"That lady was mighty uncomfortable," Barron said. "That Luders is a good man. Hard, quiet, full of eyesight. But I fooled him some. He made mistakes."

"I can think of a couple," I said. "One was being there at all. Another was telling us a friend was coming to pick him up, to explain why he had no car. It didn't need explaining. There was a car in the garage, but you didn't know whose car it was. Another was keeping that boat idling."

"That wasn't no mistake," Andy said from the front seat. "Not if you ever tried to start her up cold."

Barron said: "You don't leave your car in the garage when you come callin' up here. Ain't no moisture to hurt it. The boat could have been anybody's boat. A couple of young folks could have been in it getting acquainted. I ain't got anything on him, anyways, so far as he knows. He just worked too hard tryin' to head me off."

He spat out of the car. I heard it smack the rear fender like a wet rag. The car swept through the moonlit night, around curves, up and down hills, through fairly thick pines and along open flats where cattle lay.

I said: "He knew I didn't have the letter Lacey wrote me. Because he took it away from me himself, up in my room at the hotel. It was Luders that knocked me out and knifed Weber. Luders knows that Lacey is dead, even if he didn't kill him. That's what he's got on Mrs. Lacey. She thinks her husband is alive and that Luders has him."

"You make this Luders out a pretty bad guy," Barron said calmly. "Why would Luders knife Weber?"

"Because Weber started all the trouble. This is an organization. Its object is to unload some very good counterfeit ten-dollar bills, a great many of them. You don't advance the cause by unloading them in five-hundred-dollar lots, all brand-new, in circumstances that would make anybody suspicious, would make a much less careful man than Fred Lacey suspicious."

"You're doing some nice guessin', son," the sheriff said, grabbing the door handle as we took a fast turn, "but the neighbors ain't watchin' you. I got to be more careful. I'm in my own back yard. Puma Lake don't strike me as a very good place to go into the counterfeit money business."

"Okay," I said.

"On the other hand, if Luders is the man I want, he might be kind of hard to catch. There's three roads out of the valley, and there's half a dozen planes down to the east end of the Woodland Club golf course. Always is in summer."

"You don't seem to be doing very much worrying about it," I said.

"A mountain sheriff don't have to worry a lot," Barron said calmly. "Nobody expects him to have any brains. Especially guys like Mr. Luders don't."

X

THE boat lay in the water at the end of a short painter, moving as boats move even in the stillest water. A canvas tarpaulin covered most of it and was tied down here and there, but not everywhere it should have been tied. Behind the short rickety pier a road twisted back through juniper trees to the highway. There was a camp off to one side, with a miniature white lighthouse for its trademark. A sound of dance music came from one of the cabins, but most of the camp had gone to bed.

We came down there walking, leaving the car on the shoulder of the highway. Barron had a big flash in his hand and kept throwing it this way and that, snapping it on and off. When we came to the edge of the water and the end of the road to the pier, he put his flashlight on the road and studied it carefully. There were fresh-looking tire tracks.

"What do you think?" he asked me.

"Looks like tire tracks," I said.

"What do you think, Andy?" Barron said. "This man is cute, but he don't give me no ideas."

Andy bent over and studied the tracks. "New tires and big ones," he said, and walked towards the pier. He stooped down again and pointed. The sheriff threw the light where he pointed. "Yup, turned around here," Andy said. "So what? The place is full of new cars right now. Come October and they'd mean something. Folks that live up here buy one tire at a time, and cheap ones, at that. These here are heavy-duty all-weather treads."

"Might see about the boat," the sheriff said.

"What about it?"

"Might see if it was used recent," Barron said.

"Hell," Andy said, "we know it was used recent, don't we?"

"Always supposin' you guessed right," Barron said mildly.

Andy looked at him in silence for a moment. Then he spat on the ground and started back to where we had left the car. When he had gone a dozen feet he said over his shoulder: "I wasn't guessin'." He turned his head again and went on, plowing through the trees.

"Kind of touchy," Barron said. "But a good man." He went down on the boat landing and bent over it, passing his hand along the forward part of the side, below the tarpaulin. He came back slowly and nodded. "Andy's right. Always is, durn him. What kind of tires would you say those marks were, Mr. Evans? They tell you anything?"

"Cadillac V-12," I said. "A club coupé with red leather seats and two suitcases in the back. The clock on the dash is twelve and one-half minutes slow."

He stood there, thinking about it. Then he nodded his big head. He sighed. "Well, I hope it makes money for you," he said, and turned away.

We went back to the car. Andy was in the front seat behind the wheel again. He had a cigarette going. He looked straight ahead of him through the dusty windshield.

"Where's Rooney live now?" Barron asked.

"Where he always lived," Andy said.

"Why, that's just a piece up the Bascomb road."

"I ain't said different," Andy growled.

"Let's go there," the sheriff said, getting in. I got in beside him.

Andy turned the car and went back half a mile and then started to turn. The sheriff snapped to him: "Hold it a minute."

He got out and used his flash on the road surface. He got back into the car. "I think we got something. Them tracks down by the pier don't mean a lot. But the same tracks up here might turn out to mean more. If they go on in to Bascomb, they're goin' to mean plenty. Them old gold camps over there is made to order for monkey business."

The car went into the side road and climbed slowly into

a gap. Big boulders crowded the road, and the hillside was studded with them. They glistened pure white in the moonlight. The car growled on for half a mile and then Andy stopped again.

"Okay, Hawkshaw, this is the cabin," he said. Barron got out again and walked around with his flash. There was no light in the cabin. He came back to the car.

"They come by here," he said. "Bringing Ted home. When they left they turned towards Bascomb. You figure Ted Rooney would be mixed up in something crooked, Andy?"

"Not unless they paid him for it," Andy said.

I got out of the car and Barron and I went up towards the cabin. It was small, rough, covered with native pine. It had a wooden porch, a tin chimney guyed with wires, and a sagging privy behind the cabin at the edge of the trees. It was dark. We walked up on the porch and Barron hammered on the door. Nothing happened. He tried the knob. The door was locked. We went down off the porch and around the back, looking at the windows. They were all shut. Barron tried the back door, which was level with the ground. That was locked, too. He pounded. The echoes of the sound wandered off through the trees and echoed high up on the rise among the boulders.

"He's gone with them," Barron said. "I guess they wouldn't dast leave him now. Prob'ly stopped here just to let him get his stuff—some of it. Yep."

I said: "I don't think so. All they wanted of Rooney was his boat. That boat picked up Fred Lacey's body out at the end of Speaker Point early this evening. The body was probably weighted and dropped out in the lake. They waited for dark to do that. Rooney was in on it, and he got paid. Tonight they wanted the boat again. But they got to thinking they didn't need Rooney along. And if they're over in Bascomb Valley in some quiet little place, making or storing counterfeit money, they wouldn't at all want Rooney to go over there with them."

"You're guessing again, son," the sheriff said kindly. "Anyways, I don't have no search warrant. But I can look over Rooney's dollhouse a minute. Wait for me."

He walked away towards the privy. I took six feet and hit the door of the cabin. It shivered and split diagonally across the upper panel. Behind me, the sheriff called out, "Hey," weakly, as if he didn't mean it.

I took another six feet and hit the door again. I went in with it and landed on my hands and knees on a piece of linoleum that smelled like a fish skillet. I got up to my feet and reached up and turned the key switch of a hanging bulb. Barron was right behind me, making clucking noises of disapproval.

There was a kitchen with a wood stove, some dirty wooden shelves with dishes on them. The stove gave out a faint warmth. Unwashed pots sat on top of it and smelled. I went across the kitchen and into the front room. I turned on another hanging bulb. There was a narrow bed to one side, made up roughly, with a slimy quilt on it. There was a wooden table, some wooden chairs, an old cabinet radio, hooks on the wall, an ashtray with four burned pipes in it, a pile of pulp magazines in the corner on the floor.

The ceiling was low to keep the heat in. In the corner there was a trap to get up to the attic. The trap was open and a stepladder stood under the opening. An old water-stained canvas suitcase lay open on a wooden box, and there were odds and ends of clothing in it.

Barron went over and looked at the suitcase. "Looks like Rooney was getting ready to move out or go for a trip. Then these boys come along and picked him up. He ain't finished his packing, but he got his suit in. A man like Rooney don't have but one suit and don't wear that 'less he goes down the hill."

"He's not here," I said. "He ate dinner here, though. The stove is still warm."

The sheriff cast a speculative eye at the stepladder. He went over and climbed up it and pushed the trap up with his head. He raised his torch and shone it around overhead. He let the trap close and came down the stepladder again.

"Likely he kept the suitcase up there," he said. "I see there's a old steamer trunk up there, too. You ready to leave?"

"I didn't see a car around," I said. "He must have had a car."

"Yep. Had a old Plymouth. Douse the light."

He walked back into the kitchen and looked around that and then we put both the lights out and went out of the house. I shut what was left of the back door. Barron was examining tire tracks in the soft decomposed granite, trailing them back over to a space under a big oak tree where a couple of large darkened areas showed where a car had stood many times and dripped oil.

He came back swinging his flash, then looked towards the privy and said: "You could go on back to Andy. I still gotta look over that dollhouse."

I didn't say anything. I watched him go along the path to the privy and unlatch the door, and open it. I saw his flash go inside and the light leaked out of a dozen cracks and from the ramshackle roof. I walked back along the side of the cabin and got into the car. The sheriff was gone a long time. He came back slowly, stopped beside the car and bit off another chew from his plug. He rolled it around in his mouth and then got to work on it.

"Rooney," he said, "is in the privy. Shot twice in the head." He got into the car. "Shot with a big gun, and shot very dead. Judgin' from the circumstances I would say somebody was in a hell of a hurry."

XI

THE road climbed steeply for a while following the meanderings of a dried mountain stream the bed of which was full of boulders. Then it leveled off about a thousand or fifteen hundred feet above the level of the lake. We crossed a cattle stop of spaced narrow rails that clanked under the car wheels. The road began to go down. A wide undulating flat appeared with a few browsing cattle in it. A lightless farmhouse showed up against the moonlit sky. We reached a wider road that ran at right angles. Andy stopped the car and Barron got out with his big flashlight again and ran the spot slowly over the road surface.

"Turned left," he said, straightening. "Thanks be there

ain't been another car past since them tracks were made."
He got back into the car.

"Left don't go to no old mines," Andy said. "Left goes
to Worden's place and then back down to the lake at the
dam."

Barron sat silent a moment and then got out of the car
and used his flash again. He made a surprised sound over
to the right of the T intersection. He came back again,
snapping the light off.

"Goes right, too," he said. "But goes left first. They
doubled back, but they been somewhere off west of here
before they done it. We go like they went."

Andy said: "You sure they went left first and not last?
Left would be a way out to the highway."

"Yep. Right marks overlays left marks," Barron said.

We turned left. The knolls that dotted the valley were
covered with ironwood trees, some of them half dead. Ironwood grows to about eighteen or twenty feet high and then
dies. When it dies the limbs strip themselves and get a gray-
white color and shine in the moonlight.

We went about a mile and then a narrow road shot off
towards the north, a mere track. Andy stopped. Barron got
out again and used his flash. He jerked his thumb and Andy
swung the car. The sheriff got in.

"Them boys ain't too careful," he said. "Nope. I'd say
they ain't careful at all. But they never figured Andy could
tell where that boat come from, just by listenin' to it."

The road went into a fold of the mountains and the
growth got so close to it that the car barely passed without
scratching. Then it doubled back at a sharp angle and rose
again and went around a spur of hill and a small cabin
showed up, pressed back against a slope with trees on all
sides of it.

And suddenly, from the house or very close to it, came
a long, shrieking yell which ended in a snapping bark. The
bark was choked off suddenly.

Barron started to say: "Kill them—" but Andy had already cut the lights and pulled off the road. "Too late, I
guess," he said dryly. "Must've seen us, if anybody's watchin'."

Barron got out of the car. "That sounded mighty like a
coyote, Andy."

"Yup."

"Awful close to the house for a coyote, don't you think, Andy?"

"Nope," Andy said. "Light's out, a coyote would come right up to the cabin lookin' for buried garbage."

"And then again it could be that little dog," Barron said.

"Or a hen laying a square egg," I said. "What are we waiting for? And how about giving me back my gun? And are we trying to catch up with anybody, or do we just like to get things all figured out as we go along?"

The sheriff took my gun off his left hip and handed it to me. "I ain't in no hurry," he said. "Because Luders ain't in no hurry. He coulda been long gone, if he was. They was in a hurry to get Rooney, because Rooney knew something about them. But Rooney don't know nothing about them now because he's dead and his house locked up and his car driven away. If you hadn't bust in his back door, he could be there in his privy a couple of weeks before anybody would get curious. Them tire tracks looks kind of obvious, but that's only because we know where they started. They don't have any reason to think we could find that out. So where would we start? No, I ain't in any hurry."

Andy stooped over and came up with a deer rifle. He opened the left-hand door and got out of the car.

"The little dog's in there," Barron said peacefully. "That means Mrs. Lacey is in there, too. And there would be somebody to watch her. Yep, I guess we better go up and look, Andy."

"I hope you're scared," Andy said. "I am."

We started through the trees. It was about two hundred yards to the cabin. The night was very still. Even at that distance I heard a window open. We walked about fifty feet apart. Andy stayed back long enough to lock the car. Then he started to make a wide circle, far out to the right.

Nothing moved in the cabin as we got close to it, no light showed. The coyote or Shiny, the dog, whichever it was, didn't bark again.

We got very close to the house, not more than twenty yards. Barron and I were about the same distance apart. It was a small rough cabin, built like Rooney's place, but larger. There was an open garage at the back, but it was empty. The cabin had a small porch of fieldstone.

Then there was the sound of a short, sharp struggle in the cabin and the beginning of a bark, suddenly choked off. Barron fell down flat on the ground. I did the same. Nothing happened.

Barron stood up slowly and began to move forward a step at a time and a pause between each step. I stayed out. Barron reached the cleared space in front of the house and started to go up the steps to the porch. He stood there, bulky, clearly outlined in the moonlight, the Colt hanging at his side. It looked like a swell way to commit suicide.

Nothing happened. Barron reached the top of the steps, moved over tight against the wall. There was a window to his left, the door to his right. He changed his gun in his hand and reached out to bang on the door with the butt, then swiftly reversed it again, and flattened to the wall.

The dog screamed inside the house. A hand holding a gun came out at the bottom of the opened window and turned.

It was a tough shot at the range. I had to make it. I shot. The bark of the automatic was drowned in the duller boom of a rifle. The hand drooped and the gun dropped to the porch. The hand came out a little farther and the fingers twitched, then began to scratch at the sill. Then they went back in through the window and the dog howled. Barron was at the door, jerking at it. And Andy and I were running hard for the cabin, from different angles.

Barron got the door open and light framed him suddenly as someone inside lit a lamp and turned it up.

I made the porch as Barron went in, Andy close behind me. We went into the living room of the cabin.

Mrs. Fred Lacey stood in the middle of the floor beside a table with a lamp on it, holding the little dog in her arms. A thickset, blondish man lay on his side under the window, breathing heavily, his hand groping around aimlessly for the gun that had fallen outside the window.

Mrs. Lacey opened her arms and let the dog down. It leaped and hit the sheriff in the stomach with its small, sharp nose and pushed inside his coat at his shirt. Then it dropped to the floor again and ran around in circles, silently, weaving its hind end with delight.

Mrs. Lacey stood frozen, her face as empty as death. The man on the floor groaned a little in the middle of his heavy breathing. His eyes opened and shut rapidly. His lips moved and bubbled pink froth.

"That sure is a nice little dog, Mrs. Lacey," Barron said, tucking his shirt in. "But it don't seem a right handy time to have him around—not for some people."

He looked at the blond man on the floor. The blond man's eyes opened and became fixed on nothing.

"I lied to you," Mrs. Lacey said quickly. "I had to. My husband's life depended on it. Luders has him. He has him somewhere over here. I don't know where, but it isn't far off, he said. He went to bring him back to me, but he left this man to guard me. I couldn't do anything about it, sheriff. I'm—I'm sorry."

"I knew you lied, Mrs. Lacey," Barron said quietly. He looked down at his Colt and put it back on his hip. "I knew why. But your husband is dead, Mrs. Lacey. He was dead long ago. Mr. Evans here saw him. It's hard to take, ma'am, but you better know it now."

She didn't move or seem to breathe. Then she went very slowly to a chair and sat down and leaned her face in her hands. She sat there without motion, without sound. The little dog whined and crept under her chair.

The man on the floor started to raise the upper part of his body. He raised it very slowly, stiffly. His eyes were blank. Barron moved over to him and bent down.

"You hit bad, son?"

The man pressed his left hand against his chest. Blood oozed between his fingers. He lifted his right hand slowly, until the arm was rigid and pointing to the corner of the ceiling. His lips quivered, stiffened, spoke.

"Heil Hitler!" he said thickly.

He fell back and lay motionless. His throat rattled a little and then that, too, was still, and everything in the room was still, even the dog.

"This man must be one of them Nazis," the sheriff said. "You hear what he said?"

"Yeah," I said.

I turned and walked out of the house, down the steps and down through the trees again to the car. I sat on the running board and lit a cigarette, and sat there smoking and thinking hard.

After a little while they all came down through the trees. Barron was carrying the dog. Andy was carrying his rifle in his left hand. His leathery young face looked shocked.

Mrs. Lacey got into the car and Barron handed the dog in to her. He looked at me and said: "It's against the law to smoke out here, son, more than fifty feet from a cabin."

I dropped the cigarette and ground it hard into the powdery gray soil. I got into the car, in front beside Andy.

The car started again and we went back to what they probably called the main road over there. Nobody said anything for a long time, then Mrs. Lacey said in a low voice: "Luders mentioned a name that sounded like Sloat. He said it to the man you shot. They called him Kurt. They spoke German. I understand a little German, but they talked too fast. Sloat didn't sound like German. Does it mean anything to you?"

"It's the name of an old gold mine not far from here," Barron said. "Sloat's Mine. You know where it is, don't you, Andy?"

"Yup. I guess I killed that feller, didn't I?"

"I guess you did, Andy."

"I never killed nobody before," Andy said.

"Maybe I got him," I said. "I fired at him."

"Nope," Andy said. "You wasn't high enough to get him in the chest. I was."

Barron said: "How many brought you to that cabin, Mrs. Lacey? I hate to be asking you questions at a time like this, ma'am, but I just got to."

The dead voice said: "Two. Luders and the man you killed. He ran the boat."

"Did they stop anywhere—on this side of the lake, ma'am?"

"Yes. They stopped at a small cabin near the lake. Luders was driving. The other man, Kurt, got out, and we drove on. After a while Luders stopped and Kurt came up with us in an old car. He drove the car into a gully behind some willows and then came on with us."

"That's all we need," Barron said. "If we get Luders, the job's all done. Except I can't figure what it's all about."

I didn't say anything. We drove on to where the T inter-

Then he put his hands up. We turned slowly. Frank Luders stood about four feet away from us, with a tommy gun held waist-high. Its muzzle looked as big as the Second Street tunnel in L.A.

Luders said quietly: "I prefer that you face the other way. When Charlie comes back from the car, he will light the lamps inside. Then we shall all go in."

We faced the long, low car again. Luders whistled sharply. The small man came back around the corner of the car, stopped a moment, then went towards the door. Luders called out: "Light the lamps, Charlie. We have visitors."

The small man went quietly into the car and a match scratched and there was light inside.

"Now, gentlemen, you may walk," Luders said. "Observing, of course, that death walks close behind you and conducting yourselves accordingly."

We walked.

XIII

"Take their guns and see if they have any more of them, Charlie."

We stood backed against a wall near a long wooden table. There were wooden benches on either side of the table. On it was a tray with a bottle of whisky and a couple of glasses, a hurricane lamp and an old-fashioned farmhouse oil lamp of thick glass, both lit, a saucer full of matches and another full of ashes and stubs. In the end of the cabin, away from the table, there was a small stove and two cots, one tumbled, one made up as neat as a pin.

The little Japanese came towards us with the light shining on his glasses.

"Oh having guns," he purred. "Oh too bad."

He took the guns and pushed them backwards across the table to Luders. His small hands felt us over deftly.

Barron winced and his face reddened, but he said nothing. Charlie said: "No more guns. Pleased to see, gentlemen. Very nice night, I think so. You having picnic in moonlight?"

Barron made an angry sound in his throat. Luders said: "Sit down, please, gentlemen, and tell me what I can do for you."

We sat down. Luders sat down opposite. The two guns were on the table in front of him and the tommy gun rested on it, his left hand holding it steady, his eyes quiet and hard. His was no longer a pleasant face, but it was still an intelligent face. Intelligent as they ever are.

Barron said: "Guess I'll chew. I think better that way." He got his plug out and bit into it and put it away. He chewed silently and then spat on the floor.

"Guess I might mess up your floor some," he said. "Hope you don't mind."

The Jap was sitting on the end of the neat bed, his shoes not touching the floor. "Not liking much," he said hissingly, "very bad smell."

Barron didn't look at him. He said quietly: "You aim to shoot us and make your getaway, Mr. Luders?"

Luders shrugged and took his hand off the machine gun and leaned back against the wall.

Barron said: "You left a pretty broad trail here except for one thing. How we would know where to pick it up. You didn't figure that out because you wouldn't have acted the way you did. But you was all staked out for us when we got here. I don't follow that."

Luders said: "That is because we Germans are fatalists. When things go very easily, as they did tonight—except for that fool, Weber—we become suspicious. I said to myself, 'I have left no trail, no way they could follow me across the lake quickly enough. They had no boat, and no boat followed me. It would be impossible for them to find me. Quite impossible.' So I said, 'They will find me just because to me it appears impossible. Therefore, I shall be waiting for them.' "

"While Charlie toted the suitcases full of money out to the car," I said.

"What money?" Luders asked, and didn't seem to look at either of us. He seemed to be looking inward, searching.

I said: "Those very fine new ten-dollar bills you have been bringing in from Mexico by plane."

Luders looked at me then, but indifferently. "My dear friend, you could not possibly be serious?" he suggested.

"Phooey. Easiest thing in the world. The border patrol has no planes now. They had a few coast-guard planes a while back, but nothing came over, so they were taken off. A plane flying high over the border from Mexico lands on the field down by the Woodland Club golf course. It's Mr. Luders' plane and Mr. Luders owns an interest in the club and lives there. Why should anybody get curious about that? But Mr. Luders doesn't want half a million dollars' worth of queer money in his cabin at the club, so he finds himself an old mine over here and keeps the money in this refrigerator car. It's almost as strong as a safe and it doesn't look like a safe."

"You interest me," Luders said calmly. "Continue."

I said: "The money is very good stuff. We've had a report on it. That means organization—to get the inks and the right paper and the plates. It means an organization much more complete than any gang of crooks could manage. A government organization. The organization of the Nazi government."

The little Jap jumped up off the bed and hissed, but Luders didn't change expression. "I'm still interested," he said laconically.

"I ain't," Barron said. "Sounds to me like you're tryin' to talk yourself into a vestful of lead."

I went on: "A few years ago the Russians tried the same stunt. Planting a lot of queer money over here to raise funds for espionage work and, incidentally, they hoped, to damage our currency. The Nazis are too smart to gamble on that angle. All they want is good American dollars to work with in Central and South America. Nice mixed-up money that's been used. You can't go into a bank and deposit a hundred thousand dollars in brand-new ten-dollar bills. What's bothering the sheriff is why you picked this particular place, a mountain resort full of rather poor people."

"But that does not bother you with your superior brain, does it?" Luders sneered.

"It don't bother me a whole lot either," Barron said.

"What bothers me is folks getting killed in my territory. I ain't used to it."

I said: "You picked the place primarily because it's a swell place to bring the money into. It's probably one of hundreds all over the country, places where there is very little law enforcement to dodge but places where in the summertime a lot of strange people come and go all the time. And places where planes set down and nobody checks them in or out. But that isn't the only reason. It's also a swell place to unload some of the money, quite a lot of it, if you're lucky. But you weren't lucky. Your man Weber pulled a dumb trick and made you unlucky. Should I tell you just why it's a good place to spread queer money if you have enough people working for you?"

"Please do," Luders said, and patted the side of the machine gun.

"Because for three months in the year this district has a floating population of anywhere from twenty to fifty thousand people, depending on the holidays and weekends. That means a lot of money brought in and a lot of business done. And there's no bank here. The result of that is that the hotels and bars and merchants have to cash checks all the time. The result of that is that the deposits they send out during the season are almost all checks and the money stays in circulation. Until the end of the season, of course."

"I think that is very interesting," Luders said. "But if this operation were under my control, I would not think of passing very much money up here. I would pass a little here and there, but not much. I would test the money out, to see how well it was accepted. And for a reason that you have thought of. Because most of it would change hands rapidly and, if it was discovered to be queer money, as you say, it would be very difficult to trace the source of it."

"Yeah," I said. "That would be smarter. You're nice and frank about it."

"To you," Luders said, "it naturally does not matter how frank I am."

Barron leaned forward suddenly. "Look here, Luders, killin' us ain't going to help you any. If you come right down to it, we don't have a thing on you. Likely you killed this man Weber, but the way things are up here, it's going to be mighty hard to prove it. If you been spreading bad money, they'll get you for it, sure, but that ain't a hangin' matter. Now I've got a couple pair handcuffs in my belt, so happens, and my proposition is you walk out of here with them on, you and your Japanese pal."

Charlie the Jap said: "Ha, ha. Very funny man. Some boob I guess yes."

Luders smiled faintly. "You put all the stuff in the car, Charlie?"

"One more suitcase coming right up," Charlie said.

"Better take it on out, and start the engine, Charlie."

"Listen, it won't work, Luders," Barron said urgently. "I got a man back in the woods with a deer rifle. It's bright moonlight. You got a fair weapon there, but you got no more chance against a deer rifle than Evans and me got against you. You'll never get out of here unless we go with you. He seen us come in here and how we come. He'll give us twenty minutes. Then he'll send for some boys to dynamite you out. Them were my orders."

Luders said quietly: "This work is very difficult. Even we Germans find it difficult. I am tired. I made a bad mistake. I used a man who was a fool, who did a foolish thing, and then he killed a man because he had done it and the man knew he had done it. But it was my mistake also. I shall not be forgiven. My life is no longer of great importance. Take the suitcase to the car, Charlie."

Charlie moved swiftly towards him. "Not liking, no," he said sharply. "That damn heavy suitcase. Man with rifle shooting. To hell."

Luders smiled slowly. "That's all a lot of nonsense, Charlie. If they had men with them, they would have been here long ago. That is why I let these men talk. To see if they were alone. They are alone. Go, Charlie."

Charlie said hissingly: "I going, but I still not liking."

He went over to the corner and hefted the suitcase that stood there. He could hardly carry it. He moved slowly to the door and put the suitcase down and sighed. He opened the door a crack and looked out. "Not see anybody," he said. "Maybe all lies, too."

Luders said musingly: "I should have killed the dog and the woman too. I was weak. The man Kurt, what of him?"

"Never heard of him," I said. "Where was he?"

Luders stared at me. "Get up on your feet, both of you."

I got up. An icicle was crawling around on my back. Barron got up. His face was gray. The whitening hair at the side of his head glistened with sweat. There was sweat all over his face, but his jaws went on chewing.

He said softly: "How much you get for this job, son?"

I said thickly: "A hundred bucks but I spent some of it."

Barron said in the same soft tone: "I been married forty years. They pay me eighty dollars a month, house and firewood. It ain't enough. By gum, I ought to get a hundred." He grinned wryly and spat and looked at Luders. "To hell with you, you Nazi bastard," he said.

Luders lifted the machine gun slowly and his lips drew back over his teeth. His breath made a hissing noise. Then very slowly he laid the gun down and reached inside his coat. He took out a Luger and moved the safety catch with his thumb. He shifted the gun to his left hand and stood looking at us quietly. Very slowly his face drained of all expression and became a dead gray mask. He lifted the gun, and at the same time he lifted his right arm stiffly above shoulder height. The arm was as rigid as a rod.

"Heil Hitler!" he said sharply.

He turned the gun quickly, put the muzzle in his mouth and fired.

XIV

The Jap screamed and streaked out of the door. Barron and I lunged hard across the table. We got our guns. Blood fell on the back of my hand and then Luders crumpled slowly against the wall.

Barron was already out of the door. When I got out behind him, I saw that the little Jap was running hard down the hill towards a clump of brush.

Barron steadied himself, brought the Colt up, then lowered it again.

"He ain't far enough," he said. "I always give a man forty yards."

He raised the big Colt again and turned his body a little and, as the gun reached firing position, it moved very slowly and Barron's head went down a little until his arm and shoulder and right eye were all in a line.

He stayed like that, perfectly rigid for a long moment, then the gun roared and jumped back in his hand and a lean thread of smoke showed faint in the moonlight and disappeared.

The Jap kept on running. Barron lowered his Colt and watched him plunge into a clump of brush.

"Hell," he said. "I missed him." He looked at me quickly and looked away again. "But he won't get nowhere. Ain't got nothing to get with. Them little legs of his ain't hardly long enough to jump him over a pine cone."

"He had a gun," I said. "Under his left arm."

Barron shook his head. "Nope. I noticed the holster was empty. I figure Luders got it away from him. I figure Luders meant to shoot him before he left."

Car lights showed in the distance, coming dustily along the road.

"What made Luders go soft?"

"I figure his pride was hurt," Barron said thoughtfully. "A big organizer like him gettin' hisself all balled to hell by a couple of little fellows like us."

We went around the end of the refrigerator car. A big new coupé was parked there. Barron marched over to it and opened the door. The car on the road was near now. It turned off and its headlights raked the big coupé. Barron stared into the car for a moment, then slammed the door viciously and spat on the ground.

"Caddy V-12," he said. "Red leather cushions and suitcases in the back." He reached in again and snapped on the dashlight. "What time is it?"

"Twelve minutes to two," I said.

"This clock ain't no twelve and a half minutes slow," Barron said angrily. "You slipped on that." He turned and faced me, pushing his hat back on his head. "Hell, you seen it parked in front of the Indian Head," he said.

"Right."

"I thought you was just a smart guy."

"Right," I said.

"Son, next time I got to get almost shot, could you plan to be around?"

The car that was coming stopped a few yards away and a dog whined. Andy called out: "Anybody hurt?"

Barron and I walked over to the car. The door opened and the little silky dog jumped out and rushed at Barron. She took off about four feet away and sailed through the air and planted her front paws hard against Barron's stomach, then dropped back to the ground and ran in circles.

Barron said: "Luders shot hisself inside there. There's a little Jap down in the bushes we got to round up. And there's three, four suitcases full of counterfeit money we got to take care of."

He looked off into the distance, a solid, heavy man like a rock. "A night like this," he said, "and it's got to be full of death."

About the Author

RAYMOND CHANDLER was born in Chicago, Illinois, on July 23, 1888, but spent most of his boyhood and youth in England, where he attended Dulwich College and later worked as a free-lance journalist for *The Westminster Gazette* and *The Spectator*. During World War I, he served in France with the First Division of the Canadian Expeditionary Force, transferring later to the Royal Flying Corps (R.A.F.). In 1919 he returned to the United States, settling in California, where he eventually became director of a number of independent oil companies. The Depression put an end to his business career, and in 1933, at the age of forty-five, he turned to writing, publishing his first stories in *Black Mask*. His first novel, *The Big Sleep,* was published in 1939. Never a prolific writer, he published only one collection of stories and seven novels in his lifetime. In the last year of his life he was elected president of the Mystery Writers of America. He died in La Jolla, California, on March 26, 1959.

KEEP YOURSELF IN SUSPENSE...

from BALLANTINE BOOKS